In Their Absence

J.J.Roberts

Contents

Chapter 1   5

Chapter 2   17

Chapter 3   27

Chapter 4   36

Chapter 5   39

Chapter 6   45

Chapter 7   51

Chapter 8   59

Chapter 9   64

Chapter 10   69

Chapter 11   73

Chapter 12   79

Chapter 13   86

Chapter 14   94

Chapter 15   100

Chapter 16   112

Chapter 17   121

Chapter 18   131

Chapter 19	135
Chapter 20	142
Chapter 21	150
Chapter 22	167
Chapter 23	177
Chapter 24	183
Chapter 25	191
Chapter 26	193
Chapter 27	200
Chapter 28	205
Chapter 29	212
Chapter 30	215
Chapter 31	218
Chapter 32	223
Chapter 33	234
Chapter 34	242
Chapter 35	254
Chapter 36	260
Chapter 37	269
Chapter 38	277
Chapter 39	288
Chapter 40	301
Chapter 41	312

Chapter 42	323
Chapter 43	330
Chapter 44	340
Chapter 45	355
Chapter 46	367
Chapter 47	378
Chapter 48	394
Chapter 49	413
Chapter 50	426
Chapter 51	439
Chapter 52	453
Chapter 53	470
Chapter 54	484
Chapter 55	506
Chapter 56	522
Chapter 57	534

Chapter 1

Claire ~ Monday ~ day 1

By her second prison visit Claire had learnt that skirts and high-heels were not sensible attire. The hard floors echoed noisily under foot drawing raised eyebrows and leers in her direction. At first she was convinced the prison guards deliberately sat Will in the furthest corner so they and the other prisoners could ogle her sashaying across the room like Marilyn Monroe.

'Next time, dress in something...less feminine,' Will kindly suggested. 'The pat and rummage might be less groping too.'

On her third visit, Claire downgraded to jeans, trainers and a fleece.

'Jesus,' Will muttered, looking her up and down. 'You look like a benefit scrounger.'

Nevertheless, Claire adopts this new uniform for subsequent visits. No one gives her a second glance and on the plus side, Will is being seated much closer to the entrance.

Today the cold November weather with its blustery wind and lashing rain forces Claire to don her lined boots and thick coat. But once she enters the warm visitors' hall, the coat is yanked off; draped over her arm it weighs like a winter duvet.

Seated at a nearby table, Will grins excitedly, his fists are clenched with joy like a baby waiting for its first mouthful of mushed food. It reminds Claire how much he looks forward to her visits. For several months she has been the only person Will sends visiting orders to, and though she understands he can't be doing with all the tears and pleas for explanations, it's becoming a strain to keep both of their spirits afloat, but she tries with gossip on lots of different subjects and nothing about prisons.

'Good morning, Claire,' he says brightly. 'They've run out of gin again, so I've got you a tea.'

Wrapping her coat around the back of the plastic chair, she glances at the weak milky tea. The sides of the plastic cup are distorted, melting from the scalding liquid. 'Yeah, thanks for that; looks lovely,' she replies sarcastically.

He smiles. 'How was your journey?'

She sits opposite. 'It wasn't too bad. At least the train was on time; I found myself a nice seat by the window and read my paper.'

Will frowns. 'How come you came on the train? Isn't your car fixed yet?'

Shit, she thinks, trying to keep her expression blank. What did I tell him was wrong with it? Cam belt or was it the clutch?

'I can't afford it till payday so meanwhile I've become very acquainted with bus and train timetables. Now I'm sitting at the top of my pay band, there's no rise; the weather's so cold I've had to put the heating on for longer and Christmas is around the corner. I could do without that.'

'I don't think I'll bother with Christmas this year either,' he jokes though his face is deadpan.

Claire laughs and inspects the yellowy grey tea. Her throat is dry from the journey and she wishes she'd bought another bottle of water from the station vending machine. The tea looks disgusting; she moves it to the side, out of the way. 'How are things with you?'

'Consistent. Every day is like the day before. At least I can expect no surprises,' Will replies, sipping his tea. He pulls a face of disgust but swallows it. 'Tell me your news,' and eagerly rests his arms on the table for Claire to begin.

*

'And tonight,' Claire announces with a major lack of enthusiasm, 'I've got to go to Mum's because it's her birthday. I've tried everything to get out of it but my excuses are rubbish; if you weren't in here, you could have been my Get out of Jail free card...so to speak.'

'Nice pun. It can't be that bad. Who wouldn't enjoy your mum's flamboyant vol-au-vents? Do you remember those disgusting crab and cranberry ones she did for your 22nd? I was picking shell out of my molars all night. And your dad? Looking down his nose at anyone who doesn't know the difference between Sauvignon Blanc and Chardonnay. You could learn a lot from that guy.' He wags a finger at her.

'I don't want to learn about wine; I only want to drink it,' Claire jokes seriously. 'Bottles of it.'

'Ooh, don't let Drew hear you say that,' he scolds. 'You must swirl wine first by the stem! Inhale its petrol and gooseberry scents...'

'And hold it against a white tablecloth to assess its colour!'

They both erupt into loud laughter.

A prison officer strolling past with his arms behind his back, keys jangling in his fist, raises an amused eyebrow.

'Are the Evil Sisters coming along to this soiree?' Will asks, removing his black-rimmed glasses to polish the lens on the green bib he has to wear over his red sweatshirt.

'Of course. Olivia wouldn't pass up the chance of leaving without an armful of doggy bags. You know how she likes to scrounge food. Her loser boyfriend will get bladdered on the free booze!'

'And what does Sally come for?'

'To play the dutiful daughter and fawn over Mum and Dad.'

'Well, somebody has to; they can't rely on you. What's with calling him Dad?' asks Will, intrigued. 'You've done that a few times today. Last time you visited, it was Andrew-my-mother's-husband.'

Claire shrugs. 'Depends on my mood and whether he's pissing me off, which at the moment he isn't.'

Will nods and changes the subject, asking if Claire has recently heard from Ryan, their other best friend.

'Oh, yes, I had an e-mail. He's left Bangkok where he spent the last six months and gone to Ibiza; he's met a señorita.'

'Ibiza's a bit tame for him, isn't it?'

'That's what I thought but he could never resist the lure of a pretty face and shapely legs. Actually I got a present from him last week: a carved wooden elephant…'

'Does it contain drugs?' Will lowers his voice appropriately.

'I bloody hope not!' Claire says, horrified. 'I read in a magazine that elephants bring good luck if they face outside so I positioned it looking out of the window in the hope that I might meet a nice man rather than an over-keen moron. But after my recent luck… you know the car trouble, my pay being frozen and the men! I turned the damn thing into the room. He's on watch to make sure any good luck *stays* in the flat.'

'And how is the over-keen moron? Or have you given him the elbow and moved on?'

She shakes her head. 'Charlton's still around.' And she ignores the curl of Will's upper lip. He can't understand why she insists on labelling her lovers with nicknames; although she did explain that given his job he could easily look up these men if he knew their real names.

'It was supposed to be a bit of fun,' Claire explains. 'Someone to go out for a drink with, a meal, the cinema, some no strings...' She pauses, thinks of another word for sex; after all Will is her friend, some topics are best left unspoken. 'Well, you know.'

'Well, I haven't had it for a while,' he jokes, 'but I was engaged so my fiancée and I must have...you know at some point.'

Claire laughs. This is what she loves and misses about Will: his sense of humour, his ability to laugh at himself; he always makes her feel better, brightens up the situations she finds herself in.

'Charlton's too serious. All he talks about are weekends away and staying over. If I'm not careful a pair of men's slippers will appear next to mine and he'll start redecorating. I like my space and my orange living room. And I don't want my weekends taken up with romantic hand holding on long leafy walks.'

Will listens, nodding thoughtfully while twisting the curled lock of hair around his first finger.

Claire smiles remembering how much money he's spent over the years on designer glasses and haircuts. His hair has been the most important thing to him ever since their college days. The day she saw him delicately styling his dark hair in the mirror the way a pianist caresses piano keys, she realised who Will looked like. On the hi-fi a song was playing. It gave her the clue she needed: the dark quiff, the sideburns and the black-rimmed spectacles

'You look like Morrissey!' she pronounced. And it stuck. They staggered to and from pubs singing his songs. Even now a decade and a half later, Will's hair hasn't changed and every time Claire hears a Morrissey song it makes her smile.

'That's understandable considering you can't stand the outdoors,' Will is saying. 'Leafy walks can be pleasant with someone you love, not with someone who's out-stayed their welcome. Charlton sounds about as much fun as a wet weekend in a leaky tent, Claire.'

'It isn't fun; it's boring.'

'Then bin him. Put your foot down with a firm hand,' and Claire notices the look on Will's face as if someone has flicked a switch inside him onto pause. It's the sort of thing Will's dad would have said. But not now, she thinks.

Claire shares his sadness but she hasn't come all this way to put Will on a downer so continues talking.

'I'll arrange a mid-week surprise for him. He won't like it but that's tough.'

Will glances up at the clock on the wall and Claire follows his gaze. Five minutes left. These visits go so quick. Why don't the days go as quickly she wonders.

'Have you thought anymore about the anti-depressants?'

'There's no point; I'm not ready to come off them, Will. I can't do it until you're home.'

'It's a long time to wait for me,' he reminds gently.

'It's only one hundred and twenty eight days,' she insists. 'I don't have any other friends to talk to, Will, only you. I don't need anyone else.'

Will smiles and lays his arm across the tabletop, opening his palm for her to take his hand. His skin feels rough and chapped.

Suddenly a loud noise rings throughout the hall. It sounds like a school bell and has a similar response to one too. Heads look up and around to locate the bell, to see if it's just a fire drill; clocks and watches are sought to check that visiting time really is at an end. Prisoners sigh and groan; goodbye hugs and farewell kisses are exchanged.

Claire squeezes his hand and forces the appearance of a smile despite sadness weighing heavy inside. She hates that bell, hates walking out the door and leaving her best friend in this shit hole.

'You will stay safe,' she pleads.

He grins. 'You know me – head down, eyes front, speak when spoken to, and back against the wall. Especially in the showers.'

Claire grimaces.

'That's it ladies and gentlemen,' announces a prison officer holding his hands up for attention. 'Please make your way to the exits.'

The dawdlers groan loudly, some mutter swear words; chairs are shoved back, their feet scrape noisily on the shiny floor; coats and bags are put back on their persons.

They look at each other: Will smiles that reassuring smile that fills her equally with joy that he's okay and will soon be out, and also with despair that he isn't walking out of here with her.

She tightens her grip on his hand. He flinches and looks down at their entwined fingers.

'Sorry,' she says apologetically, releasing her hold.

'It's alright.' He flexes his fingers and leans further across the table.

They have seconds left; most of the visitors are on their feet, moving towards the exit.

'Claire.'

She looks up, blinks away the tears.

'Find us a holiday for when I get out of here. We need something to look forward to.'

It's just what she needs: a quest, a date to plan for, a trip away from everything and everyone. 'I'll get onto it straightaway,' she promises, unwrapping her coat from the chair.

'See you in a couple of weeks.'

At the doorway, she turns and watches him rise and disappear through the barred door to continue his two year prison sentence.

*

It's late afternoon when the train pulls into Kelsall station; the shops have a couple of hours of opening left so Claire heads straight for them needing retail therapy. She needs to take her mind off all the thoughts swirling inside her head. She will never understand why when Will was about to make the biggest commitment of his life he threw it all away so thoughtlessly. He gave his reasons in court, which were admirable, but he put his brother before the one person who should always take precedence. In a way Claire is selfishly glad he did. Despite Will reassuring her that they'd still be close, she knew once he said 'I do', he belonged to another and the tie between them would be loosened.

Claire strides up the puddle strewn pavement purposefully. When she reaches the brightly lit jewellers she doesn't waste time looking in the window; she knows what she's after. The bright lights and mirrors of the display cabinets are dazzling.

She peers through the glass. Wow, it's beautiful.

The little gold and silver charm owl with the turquoise eyes sits on its cream plush cushion. She's had her eye on it for a while, but was always waiting for pay day or just a damn good reason to buy it. Today she needs it. The owl will cheer her up.

'Hi Claire! My God, I haven't seen you for ages. How are you?'

The enthusiastic voice startles Claire and she jumps almost smacking her forehead on the warm polished glass. A hand places itself on her shoulder to steady her.

Nisha's dazzling white smile greets Claire and the two automatically embrace and hold each other at arms' length for a good look-over.

'How are you?' Claire asks. 'You look great but then it's no surprise; your life is way more interesting than mine.'

Nisha laughs. 'Maybe, it's certainly far seedier. Business is booming. We're inundated with suspicious wives and husbands! I've had to take on two more operatives.'

'Bet they're not as good as me!'

'No way,' Nisha replies without any hesitation. 'You'll always be the best. I loved working with you. We had such a laugh.'

'Well, if you ever need a gorgeous charming blonde operative you know who to call!'

Nisha's dark eyes widen. 'Do you mean that, Claire? Would you come back?'

Claire considers the proposal. 'I could do with the extra money. I've got a few bills to pay and Christmas is coming.'

Nisha squeezes Claire's forearm with enthusiasm. 'Please say yes. We sprung some of our best traps together and it won't be a problem putting you back on the books. I never took you off them.'

Claire laughs. 'In that case, how can I say no? I've missed the flirting...and the dressing up!'

'We wore some great dresses. Get them laundered and I'll give you a call very soon. Is that the time?

I'd better go.' Nisha kisses Claire's cheek before leaving.

Claire smiles. If she can get a few jobs working with Nisha again not only will it inject some fun into her dull life but the cash will go towards her repayment. The last thing she wants is to give Leo an excuse to come around and dish out a warning.

'Good afternoon,' says the shop assistant with a big smile. At her ears and on her wrists are various bits of jewellery the shop sells. 'Can I help you with anything?'

'Yes, please, can I have a look at the owl?' Claire points to it.

A few minutes later, she leaves the shop swinging the little jewellery bag by her side and heads for Thornton's to buy a box of chocolates for her mum. The charm was a frivolous buy, an expensive way to cheer herself up but compared to what she owes Leo, the owl is nothing, and if Andrew stumps up later, none of this will matter. The important thing, she thinks, is to always to make yourself feel good.

Chapter 2

Sally ~ Monday ~ day 1

From her seat at the large farmhouse table, Sally watches her mum Marion clear away the birthday party debris. She wraps a large piece of tinfoil over the birthday cake and gathers up used serviettes. Sally knows she should help. She's only one of a few guests still here. Everyone else has gone, citing work and children to get up for the next morning.

Marion pauses to survey her family slobbing around the table and smiles lovingly. Sally knows how much her mum loves it when they're all together, blissfully but ignorantly assuming her three daughters love seeing each other. Sally marvels at the pretence they perform to convince her of this. Claire and Olivia have a bristly relationship. There's always an undercurrent between them, lying still like water in a stagnant pond, but every so often there's a ripple and a wave breaks the surface. Claire calls Liv a jealous cow. Sally puts it down to Liv being the middle child and that they don't share the same Dad with Claire. Claire's parents divorced when she was 7. Marion remarried Andrew the following year and they had Olivia and Sally. Liv has spent a lifetime being jealous of her dad being a dad to someone unrelated.

Marion whisks the cake away; Sally was hoping to take a piece home for Fergus. She wishes her boyfriend was here tonight; they could have left earlier, but Fergus has a wall to finish building.

Sally considers helping again, then maybe she can leave. She looks at the available help.

Claire is typically busy with her phone, but it isn't a game she's playing. She's been receiving messages all evening. The text message alert which sounds like a doorbell makes Claire scowl; the email alert which sounds like an owl hoot makes her smile coyly.

Olivia is lazily spooning red pepper hummus into her mouth with a finger. She finished the last of the celery and carrot sticks and can't be bothered to get a spoon. Liv's boyfriend Dan is in the conservatory with his mobile and three bottles of continental lager.

Andrew sits at the head of the table, swirling brandy; the gold ring on his little finger chinks against the glass. Sally can smell the warming liquor. He sips from the bulbed glass and holds it up against the light to see the legs of the liquid running down the inside of the glass. He runs a wine import and distribution business, and employs Liv and Sally.

Bottles galore – green, white and brown stand clustered together in little groups amongst the half-finished dishes of dips, salads and nibbles. Olivia moves on to the bowl of black olives. Claire's mobile hoots. Marion takes the tray of dips and breadsticks back through to the kitchen. Liv stares at Sally; she wants Sally to ask Claire what she's been doing all night on her mobile.

Instead, Sally says to Claire: 'How's the running?'

Claire looks up sharply, surprised by the sudden interest. 'Yeah, fine, thanks.'

Liv glares but Sally deliberately continues the conversation even though she can see Claire wants to return to her messages. 'When's your run again? January?' Claire nods. 'I promised to sponsor you, didn't I? Where's your form?'

Claire removes a dog-eared form from the side pocket of her designer handbag and slides it across the table avoiding the blob of coleslaw that dropped off Liv's cracker. Out of interest Sally scans the donors' names for any that she may recognise. Must be hospital staff, she concludes. I wonder if she's deliberately not asking family for sponsorship.

'Liv?' she says, waving it at her sister whose face is positively thunderous.

'What? On my wage? You're joking,' Liv retorts. 'Not unless a certain someone gives me a rise.' And she nods at her father.

Andrew snorts into his glass as if to say 'no chance.'

'What's the route you're running?' Sally knows she's being cruel, continuing this conversation when it's making all three of them uncomfortable but she likes the little buzz it gives her in winding up Liv who must be dying to know the answers to the questions she'd really like Sally to ask.

'It's on the form,' Claire replies. 'I'm running the route of the race. It makes it easier on the day.'

'Good thinking,' Sally says but her voice lacks sincerity. Nevertheless she studies the route concluding that Claire must be mad to want to run three miles for a charity she has no affiliation to. She passes the form back saying, 'Good luck,' but it sounds weak.

Marion returns from the kitchen and starts clearing the table, noisily dropping plates and dishes into each other so she can get the dishwasher started. The sisters all sigh with relief, grateful for the distraction.

'I'll do that, Mum,' Claire offers getting to her feet, sliding her phone into her handbag. 'You sit down.' She takes the stack of plates.

'It won't take a minute, love,' Marion insists.

'Marion!' her husband says as he swirls the brandy. 'Sit down. Do as you're told.'

'Yeah, let *her* do it, Mum,' Olivia puts in. 'She didn't help put the food out so she can clear up.'

'I was late leaving work,' Claire defends. 'One of the pathologists gave me—'

'Yeah, whatever.' Olivia raises a hand to cut Claire off.

Sally shakes her head with disgust. If Olivia had said that to her, she'd have leant over the table and pushed her face into the olives. She pushes her chair back suddenly, grabbing the stack of dishes.

'You can help too, Liv,' she barks. 'Before you eat so much that you can't move.'

'What did you say?' Liv demands, stomping after Sally.

Inside the kitchen, Sally places the dishes on the sideboard for Claire to stack in the dishwasher; she turns on the tap at the sink to wash the wine glasses and watches Olivia with amusement.

Olivia is replacing the lids on the dips, putting mostly full pots back into the fridge, the rest she leaves to the side. This is the trick Liv regularly performs at family parties. She'll slyly ask Marion if she can take the half empty ones home.

'I don't know why Mum always has to go overboard with the food,' Liv complains. 'There's enough here to feed the whole of the Third World!'

'She likes to put on a spread,' Sally replies squeezing washing-up liquid into the stream of hot water. The smell of lemon fills the kitchen refreshing her a little.

'That's rich coming from you, Liv,' Claire snaps. 'You swipe most of it home with you.'

Olivia pauses from stuffing crackers back into their foil packet to raise a confrontational eyebrow at Claire. 'Why not when all Mum's going to do is chuck it in the bin. It'll do for my lunch tomorrow.'

'Yeah, whatever,' Claire replies.

As the water fills the bowl, Sally watches Claire carefully dropping the cutlery into the dishwasher's cutlery basket. As her hand places the breadknife into the pull-out top shelf, her charm bracelet catches on a fork prong. She pauses to untangle it but Liv has grasped her next round of ammunition.

'Ooh, nice bracelet, Claire,' she cries. 'Let's have a look.' She grabs Claire's narrow wrist and holds it up to the light. Claire struggles but Liv's grip is strong.

Sally freezes with dread as if the music has stopped in a game of Musical Statues. Olivia is obsessed with Claire's jewellery, shoes, handbags, and where she gets the money from to afford them. 'We're trying to tidy up, Liv. We've got work tomorrow.'

Liv ignores her. 'I'm looking for something that Dan can get me for Christmas? Do you think it'll be out of his price range, Claire?'

Claire snatches her wrist away and hides it behind her back. 'Probably, Olivia, yes.'

'Are you sure? You've got one and you're only a medical secretary, but then you have nice things, designer clothes and shoes...' Olivia pretends to be confused. 'And then there's your flat...'

'My flat?' Claire looks at her.

'It's lovely, in a nice area with your own parking space...'

'I work and save...' Claire explains leaning forward into battle. 'You should try it.'

'I work!' Liv protests and Sally winces.

'Are you jealous that I've got my own flat? But I suppose you must be because you're not going to have that with Dan the dealer, are you?'

'What did you call him?' Liv shouts.

'Claire!' Sally exclaims but she's realising that she may as well not be here. Nobody is taking any notice of her.

'Don't be so naïve, Olivia,' Claire is preaching, 'You don't need to be Columbo to see he's a dealer. He looks like one! If you want your own place in a nicer area then he'll have to pedal more drugs at the school gates, won't he?'

Sally has often wondered herself what Dan does. She asked him last time they were all together and he replied, 'A bit of DJing.' The month before he claimed to be a nightclub promoter.

'How dare you accuse Dan of being a drug dealer? You're just jealous that I have a bloke and you don't!' Liv screams childishly.

Claire shakes her head. 'I'd rather be a lonely old spinster than have him. Take consolation, Olivia, that you will have something one day that I won't. When you're both sixty-something and Dad pops his clogs all this,' and she sweeps her arms wide, 'will be yours and Sally's, not mine. You can waste it how you like. You'll finally be able to buy your own home, maybe buy a charm bracelet too.'

The kitchen door flings opens and Marion appears, hands on hips, a stern frown creasing her forehead. 'Girls! That's enough, before someone says something they'll regret.'

'I think we've gone beyond that point, Mum,' Claire says, 'but at least we've all said how we honestly feel.'

'Claire started it,' Liv points out childishly. 'She accused Dan of being a drug dealer.'

'Claire,' Marion snaps. 'Where on heaven did you get something ridiculous like that from?'

'From Will,' Liv announces and everyone looks at her. 'If anyone knew, he would.'

Claire shakes her head. 'If I did get it from Will then there's a good chance it's true, isn't it?'

'You can't believe anything he tells you. Look what he did!' Liv shouts.

'Shut up, Olivia. You don't know what you're talking about, as usual,' Claire says.

'You're no better than me. If I'm living with a dealer and you're friends with...'

'I haven't seen Will since he was sentenced. Not that it's any of your business. Thanks for dinner, Mum. Sorry about the row. But what do you expect when she's here?' She kisses her mum on the cheek and opens the other kitchen door, the one that leads to the front door.

'Claire, before you go your dad wants a quick word. He's in the study.'

Claire's shoulders sink. 'Oh, great.'

Sally wonders why Claire assumes it's bad news. It's not like he's going to offer a wad of cash to make things better. He's as stingy as they come.

Chapter 3

Fiona ~ Tuesday ~ day 2

Fiona waddles into the stuffy warm office laden down with bags, her long woollen scarf tightly wound around her neck. The radio is on loud, tuned to the usual commercial station; an annoying jingle is playing advertising cheap booze for Christmas parties.

Fucking Christmas, Fiona thinks, scowling at the radio. Just what I need.

She manoeuvres around the enormous printer which juts into the centre of the room and dumps her bags on her swivel chair which spins around propelling her plastic lunchbox out and onto the floor. The brown bread sandwich falls apart and grated cheese sticks to the inside of the lid. She stares at the box and mutters, 'Bastard.'

It's not the collapsed sandwich she wants to kick across the floor but Nigel, her ex-husband-to-be. Well, his head. The corner of the envelope pokes out of her bag where she thrust it in earlier because she was in a rush after Stan pushed her too far towards the edge again.

Despite Claire's empty chair at the neighbouring desk, Fiona knows she's in. Her red cardigan is wrapped around the back of the chair and a cup of coffee, its steam swirling upwards, sits on the coaster.

Fiona smiles with relief. I missed her yesterday, she thinks. She was vague about what she was doing on her day off. I really need to talk to her at lunchtime, show her this awful letter. She won't believe his latest stunt.

'Morning Fi,' says Tara pleasantly. Tara is the head secretary and Fiona can't abide her. All she talks about is how wonderful her two children are, the funny things they do and say, and the baby she's 7 weeks from giving birth to. The other secretary is Anne who's in her early fifties with two grand-children so the pair of them love to bore everyone with kid chat. Claire usually smiles politely and goes along with it, but Fiona struggles especially since it's looking like motherhood has been taken away from her.

'Morning Tara,' Fiona replies, hiding the mess on her chair from view.

'Can you type these PM reports up for Dr Sullivan as soon as possible? You know what he's like.' Tara cradles her swollen abdomen with her hand, her wedding ring glinting under the office lights. Fiona averts her eyes; she can't stand it when Tara touches herself like this.

Fiona smiles and politely replies that she'll get on with it straightaway. Please would be nice, she thinks.

'Cheers, Fi,' Tara says, slapping the file on the corner of the desk.

She's so false, Fiona thinks switching her computer on. That vacant smile gets on my wick. I wish she wouldn't say Fi like that, managing to make it rhyme with ugly failure.

Fiona logs onto the system and whilst the slow PC whirrs and clunks into action, her mind drifts back to Nigel and the last time he was at their house. He was carrying a box of his belongings to his van as if he couldn't wait to get away. It took all her strength and pride not to wrap her arms around his legs and pull him back towards the open front door.

'If you don't love me anymore,' she cried, 'then why were we trying for a baby? Tell me that.'

He looked at her, the top of his football trophy sticking out of the flaps of the box. He didn't need to think of a more considerate answer. He told her the truth.

'I thought it would make me love you.'

Fiona shakes her head. She knows she shouldn't keep going over this and punishing herself but she can't help but prod and poke it.

Bet he loves that slut more than me. Let's have a look. Fiona logs onto the hospital patient database, looking around but none of her colleagues are watching and Claire still isn't back.

She knows his slut's details off by heart. She silently sings the six digit patient number. 'Four six one, eight nine one.'

The information loads and Fiona clicks through the tabs quickly. There's a maternity tab for every female regardless whether they've ever had a pregnancy. Fiona clicks on it expecting it to be blank.

But it isn't.

Two weeks ago the slut had an appointment with the midwife and that can only mean one thing.

The slut and Fiona's husband are having a baby.

Fiona's stomach plummets as if someone has dropped a brick into it.

They're pregnant, she wants to scream. How dare they. How fucking dare they!

She breathes deeply, trying to calm down; the data may have been entered incorrectly. She clears the patient form and re-enters the data but receives the same answer.

It can't be true. He couldn't get me pregnant and we tried for months and months. I did everything right.

'Morning Fiona.'

Fiona jumps, sees Claire smiling at her and hastily minimises the screen leaving just her e-mail open.

'Hi Claire. How was your day off? Do anything exciting?' Fiona desperately tries to slow down her talking. She's gabbling nervously. She wants to point accusingly at the screen and show Claire what Nigel's done.

'It was okay. Met a friend, went to my mum's birthday party, caught up with some housework. It was just nice to have a lie-in.'

'Yeah, yeah, it is.' Her eyes wander back to the screen.

'You okay? You look kind of spooked...'

Fiona lowers her voice and confides her discovery. 'Nigel's slut's pregnant.'

Claire's eyes widen. 'No way! How did you find out?'

Fiona stops herself before revealing her source. She could get into a lot of trouble if found to be looking up information on a patient she has absolutely no need to. Though Claire is trusted with personal stuff like the breakdown of her marriage and Stan, Fiona's not sure she should admit this.

'My Mum saw them in *Mothercare*.'

Claire's eyes glance at the screen but she can't possibly see from there.

'And to top it off, I've had a letter too,' and Fiona bends underneath her desk to yank the envelope out, crumpling it even more.

Claire interrupts her. 'Do you mind if I look at it later, Fi? Sorry but I've got something I need to get on with. I don't want Tara on my back.'

'Yeah, no problem. We'll look at it at lunchtime; we'll have more time.'

Claire looks regretful. 'I can't do lunch today. I've got to go out. Tell you what though - Tara's leaving early today; she has an appointment with the midwife. We'll look at it when she's buggered off.'

Fiona nods with disappointment. There won't be any time: Claire has forgotten that Fiona has to leave early today herself. She has to take Stan to the doctors for a blood pressure check.

Claire gets on with her work and Fiona stares angrily at her computer. What's so bloody important that Claire has to go out at lunchtime? She never goes out. I hope it's not something that's going to be a regular occurrence.

Fiona maximises the screen for one last look as if in that short time the slut will have had an abortion or better still a miscarriage. That'd hurt more, Fiona thinks cruelly.

About an hour later when Fiona's struggling to read whether Dr Sullivan has written haemoptysis or haematemesis, the door opens and Isla the trainee mortuary technician waltzes in, her long black plait lying over her shoulder like a rope and her pale blue scrubs hanging off her slender frame like baggy pyjamas.

'Morning all,' she calls and gets an enthusiastic response from everyone except Fiona who has no time for her. It annoys Fiona that Isla has been here less than 6 months and is hugely popular amongst the lab staff and the pathologists and for what she often wonders. For being younger and empty-headed.

Isla has picked up the little teddy bear that sits on Claire's monitor and makes him peep out at her from over the top.

'Stop it!' Claire scolds, laughing.

'How was the party? Was the evil twin there?'

Claire laughs. 'Sally and Olivia aren't twins.'

'They look like twins and there's always one that's evil.'

Fiona wonders when Isla met Claire's sisters. She hasn't even seen a photo of them.

'We had a huge row. Sisterly jealousy. You know what it's like.'

'I do. I have three,' Isla agrees. 'All those weddings my dad will have to fork out for. Bet he's wishing a couple of us were spinsters.'

'My step-father has decided to punish me.'

'How, with a cane across the bottom? '

'There's a thought I don't want in my head. He'll probably cut me out of the will. Here it is.' Claire pulls the file from under a pile of stuff and hands it to Isla.

'Thanks, chick,' Isla says. 'Better go. We've got a messy one to do.'

'Ooh, anything interesting?' Anne asks leaning back till the spine of the chair creaks and threatens to snap in two.

'A juicy one covered in maggots!'

'Ugh!' the women cry in horror. Fiona rolls her eyes.

'Hope none of you have got rice for tea,' Isla shouts.

'Derek's doing us a curry tonight.' Anne pulls a face. 'Don't fancy it now.'

'Have chips with it instead,' laughs Isla. 'Bye bye ladies!' and she's gone leaving the air spinning in her wake as if a tornado has done a turn in the office.

'I love that girl,' Anne says. 'She's dead funny.'

Fiona glances at Claire to see if she agrees but she's smiling at her mobile. She relies on Claire, treats her as her confidante. Without her, who else has Fiona got to talk to? She wonders if Claire is meeting Isla at lunchtime, which is why she's cancelled her. Why couldn't she have been invited too? Mind, Fiona thinks confidently, do I really want to spend my lunch-hour with Isla? No, thank you.

Chapter 4

Claire ~ Tuesday ~ day 2

Claire gently shakes her head as she reads Ralph/Charlton's reply. He's totally missed the tone of her text. I've got to end it, she thinks, finishing her coffee. Will's right. It's no fun anymore. Why aren't there any suitable men around? Apart from Mr Weeks. Things are good with him; he knows where we both stand. But he goes home every Friday, and weekends are long and lonely without someone.

The mobile silently vibrates again and Claire's heart jumps with excitement. Please be a message from someone interesting. A text appears on the screen. Her heart sinks and her anger levels peak.

It's Ralph telling her he has a present for her tomorrow night.

She rolls her eyes. It'll be a bottle of cheap wine, warm most likely, or a box of chocolates when he knows I'm training for my run.

She doesn't reply but slaps the mobile down on the desk. I wonder if I should change the photo on my dating profile. It's a month out of date and I'm sure I could conjure up some other enticing pastimes other than shopping, reading and running!

'Excuse me, Claire,' says a well spoken male voice.

It's Dr Heathcote, or Dr H as he likes to be called. He's one of the friendlier pathologists who doesn't mind a laugh and a joke in the mortuary and lab as long as people don't overstep the mark.

'Those PM reports I gave you earlier,' he begins.

'Yes, I have them here. Somewhere,' she says looking at the papers strewn untidily across her desk.

'I need to replace number 712 with this one.' He waves a post-mortem report at her. 'I don't know what I was thinking. The coroner will think I've gone mad!'

'Sure, no problem,' and Claire takes the papers from him.

'Have you got the original?'

'Again... somewhere here.'

'Can you make sure you shred it? Don't want it falling into the wrong hands.'

'Yeah, Dr H, will do.'

'Thanks, Claire,' he says with a smile before turning and leaving the office.

Claire slides the offending PM report into her desk drawer to destroy later. Her mobile vibrates again and she sighs. Bloody Ralph but as she picks the mobile up an e-mail appears and it's just the good news she's been hoping for.

'Hello C. Love the picture. I'm 36, married but extremely bored. See attached pic and if you like the look maybe you'd fancy having a chat on messenger later. John x'

Claire grins and her eyes light up. Suddenly she feels as if her luck has changed. Once she's fucked Ralph off and sorted out that other worry, she can relax.

She clicks on the attachment, holds her breath hoping John's a bit of a looker. His face appears and as Claire studies it, she begins to nod with satisfaction. Fair hair, nice brown eyes, straight teeth and nicely proportioned features. Yes, she thinks, he's worthy of a chat later. She starts typing a reply wondering if that's his real name and if she can squeeze a short chat in before Mr Weeks arrives.

Chapter 5

Olivia ~ Tuesday ~ day 2

Olivia feels guilty. It's not just that she had to ring her mother this morning to tell her she'd been up all night vomiting, but she feels bad for upsetting her. Does Mum know that Dad's giving money to Claire? That's how she can afford a nice flat in a nice area and it pisses me off that I live in a tiny flat opposite a kebab shop which doesn't shut till after midnight in a street where grown men shout obscenities and threats at each other, a dog is forever barking, and cars with noisy booming exhausts race up and down at all hours. If he's helping Claire then why isn't helping me, his real daughter? Get me out of this dump and away from...

A loud phlegmy snort from the living room causes Olivia to jump and pull a face of disgust. Pig, she thinks. She reaches for her green tea. It's just the right temperature now.

For the last 12 months Dan's been nurturing the seeds of jealously already planted in her head about her family. He frequently bad mouths her parents, calling her mum pretentious for serving fancy expensive food, he calls Andrew a pompous wanker with his boring talk of wine and he brags that he wouldn't mind giving Sally one, and that Claire must be fleecing her parents and how come she's getting away with that when she isn't even Andrew's daughter?

Liv tries to object, tell Dan he's wrong, ask him not to lust after her sister and defend her parents. After all, her Dad gave her a job when she dropped out of uni. That must have been hugely humiliating for them, sending her off to university to study history like she'd always wanted and after failing her first year exams, she comes crawling back and into a job in her Dad's office filing, typing and making the tea. Four years later, Olivia has progressed to assisting the marketing manager. And who's the manager of accounts? Sally is. Olivia shakes her head. She's successfully managed to keep Sally's job title from Dan. He'd certainly have something to say about that.

'Babe!' he calls from the living room. Olivia can't hear the rest so she gets up and wanders into the lounge where Dan is seated on the floor, his back against the threadbare ribbed settee. His black holey socks lie curled up like dog turds at his feet where he's hooked them off with his toes. The game he's been playing all morning is paused on the telly. Blood drips down the inside of the screen like iced droplets of cranberry juice in a glass. A big gun almost like a cannon points at a zombie which is caught mid-flight rushing towards them, its wide black mouth open.

'What, Dan?' she asks.

'What you doing for dinner? I'm fucking starving.'

'I'm not hungry. I still feel...'

'Yeah, but I am. This is hungry work. Can you get me a chippy? Bit of fresh air will do you good.'

Olivia sighs silently, nods, turns and pads down the hall to put on some shoes. Don't suppose you've any money, she wants to ask. I bought the last one and probably every chippy, Chinese and Indian since we met.

Olivia takes her mobile off the hall shelf where it's charging. No texts. She calls out a bye, gets no reply so opens the front door. The smell of fried food hits her nose and her stomach complains with a painful cramp.

I'll be sick before I get there, she thinks, picturing herself heaving outside in a bin or worse, the pavement.

The chip shop is abundant with school kids, overweight women in slippers and ill-fitting leggings, and workmen with dirty hands and overalls.

I should eat something, she thinks, it'll at least give me something to bring up rather than green bile.

'Yes, love?' says the woman behind the counter. Her face is dripping with melted foundation. Her skin looks like warm caramel.

'Fish, chips and curry sauce, please.'

The woman gets to work quickly and skilfully, hoisting a golden battered fish onto a tray and heaping pile after pile of chips on top.

'Salt an' vinegar, love?'

'Please,' Olivia says, a thought suddenly distracts her: Claire's summoning to Dad's study last night and the conversation Olivia overheard.

Olivia had crept to the closed study door and leant her head against the wood, her heart thundering in her chest and ears. She was terrified her Mum was going to catch her, or her Dad would suddenly open the door and catch her.

'Because of that! That's utterly ridiculous!' Claire was shouting.

A quieter calmer response from Dad that Liv strained to hear.

'Please, don't!' Claire begged. 'Do you have any idea of-'

'Lower your voice,' he ordered.

'Do you know what will happen if I don't-'

'This is your own doing. I won't give you any more money.'

'Liv!' Sally hissed as she appeared at the top of the stairs. 'What are you doing?'

Liv dragged Sally into the spare bedroom and explained what she'd heard: that Dad was giving money to Claire but it sounded like tonight it was going to stop.

Sally stared. 'You actually heard him say he's not giving her any more money?'

'Yes! Claire's well pissed off. Bang goes those shoes she's had her eyes on.'

'You might have misunderstood,' Sally suggested but Olivia was adamant. 'Why does he do it? He's never offered as much as fifty quid to me and Fergus. Nor you and Dan. Why give to Claire? What's so special about her?'

'Search me. But I told you she was getting money from someone,' Liv whispered proudly.

They cautiously opened the door, keen to hear more titbits, but they found the study door wide open and heard the thump of Claire's feet as she stomped downstairs and out of the house. They were too late.

*

Olivia presses the warm food parcel to her tummy as she walks back to the flat and it begins to have a soothing effect. A group of lads are loitering a few feet from her front door. One is sitting on a bike far too small for his size. His long legs straddle the seat; his huge white trainers rest on their heels either side of the front wheel. He looks up as Olivia approaches and smiles lecherously.

'Hey, good stuff that. Thanks very much!'

Olivia nods, smiling weakly. Her step quickens to the front door and she finds Dan right where she left him, shooting zombies.

He pauses the game and jumps to his feet, grabs the parcel and drops back onto the carpet, ripping apart the paper and stabbing a chip with a fork. 'Fancy an Indian later?' he asks, cheerfully. 'On me? I've come into a bit of money.'

Chapter 6

Stewart ~ Tuesday ~ day 2

'Hello, Stewart Murray speaking,' says Stewart, squeezing the mobile between the top of his shoulder and his jaw so he can continue writing out his team's positions. He's glad now he listened to his wife and moved with the times, changing his mobile to this faster Smartphone that enables him to keep up-to-date with sports news. He doesn't know how he ever lived without it.

'Hi, Stewart,' says a cheery but hesitant voice. 'It's Claire Millward.'

'Claire! Hello, fancy hearing from you. How are you? I don't think I've still got your number, must have lost it when I switched phone.'

'You've changed your phone? Wow! I bet you've got all the sports' apps, haven't you?' She chuckles.

'You know me too well.' He puts the pen down and holds the phone more comfortably to his ear. He anticipates this being a long chat. If Claire just wants to say hi, how are you, she would have text. But then, would she? He hasn't heard from her for six months, just after last season finished. End of season, end of the affair, but they parted on good terms, as friends.

'Every Saturday teatime I put the radio on to find out the score. Third in the league! Fancy your chances for promotion or is it too early to tell?'

Stewart laughs. Claire pretended to understand football terminology and tried her best to remember fixtures and player positions; she consoled him after defeats and loved celebrating a win; it was endearing and the one thing he needed whilst trying to juggle his job, the team and his wife's illness. Claire made everything so much easier because there were never any strings, no bullshit and no demands.

'It's too early to tell but we're doing well. New signings have settled in and finally I feel that we've got a team that can make it. Unlike the shower I had last season,' he mutters. 'But I'm sure you don't want to hear about how I need to find a replacement goalkeeper and how my star striker has a groin injury.'

'Oh, I don't know,' giggles Claire, 'the groin injury sounds interesting. How did he do that?'

'Reaching for a ball.'

'Whose?'

'Shut up, you smutty girl. You're incorrigible.'

Claire laughs.

'Tell me how you are. Things okay?' Stewart reaches for his tea, pushing his notebook away. He'll come back to that later. He needed a break anyway. Formations were writhing on the paper like a nest of snakes.

'Work's busy. Lots of people are intent on dying before Christmas so they can get out of buying presents. My fingertips are worn down from the mountain of typing and I can't see over my desk. But it makes the days go quickly.'

'I loved listening to all your gossip about the doctors and the lab staff, especially over a bottle of wine. How's your friend, the one whose husband left her? Has he gone back?'

'No. And there's no chance now that he's got his girlfriend pregnant. I promised to listen to her woes later. It's ironic really. Me helping her with the kind of relationships I prefer. It's a good job she doesn't know me well.'

'She always sounded like a nutcase to me. Who the hell would offer to look after an elderly uncle…'

'Great uncle. And he's moved in now,' Claire tells him. 'He seriously cramps her style but she thinks she's doing a good thing. It's a good job no one else at work knows about this; they'd crucify her.'

Stewart could never understand how a woman in her late thirties would want to live with an incontinent old man with memory problems and heart disease.

It's good to chat, he thinks. It's lovely to hear her cheerful voice and playful laugh. He remembers how they met: a charity dinner at the football ground where Stewart had recently taken the team into the top four of the league. Claire's friends were sponsors of the club and had a spare ticket so she went. Stewart's wife couldn't make it; she was recovering from her operation. He felt lost without her, and Claire felt like a spare part. They were introduced and hit it off. Stewart had caught sight of them together in a reflection laughing and chatting, and he thought what a lovely couple they made. The sort of pairing you'd see on the cover of a Mills & Boon novel. Him tall, dark and average looking; Claire blonde, pretty, slender. Stewart had never cheated before but he felt a connection with Claire that took him by surprise. They swapped phone numbers; Stewart putting the number in under the pseudonym of Clive. They met three weeks later after an away match. It lasted longer than Stewart thought it would.

When their affair ended, Stewart mourned it like a bereavement. Several times he almost crumbled and picked up the phone. Something was missing, it felt wrong, he felt sad, he didn't want his wife, but they'd made the decision together. Claire and he talked about it. It was the right thing to do. Even if they got back together, where could it go? Claire wanted affairs. She didn't want the comfortable stasis of a proper relationship. She wanted the thrill, the secrecy, and the quickies. They wouldn't have that if they were a public couple. Stewart deliberately deleted her number, wiping out the temptation. And eventually as he settled down, his flagging marriage was rejuvenated and he and his wife started injecting fun into things: date nights and pretending they were strangers and copping off like teenagers. She had never guessed where this spark had come from.

Stewart wants to ask if Claire's seeing anyone, if the relationship she substituted for theirs worked out in the end, but he can't. He feels that sense of jealousy already creeping out from the centre of his chest. It's sure to affect his voice and then she'll know how bothered he is.

'Stew, I need to ask you something, a favour,' she's saying and he thinks with sadness that it wasn't to say hello after all, or can we be friends who actually meet up; there's a reason for this call. Something she can't come right out and ask, something she has to introduce with pleasant chat and quaint memories, something she needs to butter him up for.

'Please don't think too badly of me but I didn't know who else to ask,' Claire continues so apologetically that it makes Stewart sit up straight, attention focused.

'Whatever's the matter, Claire? You don't usually sound so serious. You can ask me anything, you know that and if I can help, I will.'

He hears her sigh heavily down the phone as she gathers her courage to start.

'I've got myself in a bit of a sticky situation with money...'

Chapter 7

Ralph ~ Wednesday ~ day 3

Ralph squeezes his van next to Claire's neighbour's hatchback, cursing how much room she's taken up. Her offside wheels straddle the white line.

'Selfish bitch,' he mutters.

He's never spoken to the woman, but knows her name is Bev and that she's a nosy cow. Every time he comes here, her net curtains start twitching or she finds an excuse to open her front door: put out empty milk bottles or sweep the dried leaves from her doorstep. She's overweight and walks funny; he thinks she must need a new hip judging by the crippled way she walks. She never speaks or waves. Ralph hates coming to Claire's flat but there isn't anywhere else for them to meet. His place is way out of bounds and he can't afford hotel rooms.

He grabs the Asda carrier bag off the passenger seat and marches up to the communal glass door. It irritates him that Claire hasn't left her front door ajar since she knows he's coming. He knocks hard and drums his fingertips on the doorjamb. She keeps him waiting, increasing his irritation. On the fourth knock, the door opens.

'Why didn't you unlock the door?' he demands. 'You knew I was coming. In fact why don't you give me a key? I wouldn't have to stand on ceremony here like a paying guest.'

'A what?' Claire asks, frowning.

'Forget it.' Ralph pushes past her and enters the lounge-cum-dining room, looking around for the surprise he hopes she's got for him. After all, he's bought her a present, but there's nothing. Not even a can of beer or a cup of tea. He turns to her and recognises an expression he's seen on previous girlfriends. Claire isn't happy; he's done something or forgotten to do something. His mind races over past events and recent conversations, seeking out a clue and a suitable excuse.

Claire sits on the armchair, not on the settee, which suggests that she doesn't want him near her. But he hasn't got all night. He has to be home by 8 because Antonia's out tonight and he's on babysitting duty. He hopes he isn't going to end up playing some sort of weird cryptic game where Claire gives him clues as to the cause of her mood and Ralph has to guess. We're wasting time, he thinks, glancing down the hall at the closed bedroom room. There's a different kind of game we could be playing.

'Here, I bought you this,' he says, holding up the carrier bag.

'What is it?' she asks, bored.

'If you open it, you'll find out.' He swings it toward her and her fingertips touch the hard glass base but she doesn't catch it.

'Come on, you retard,' he mocks, 'catch it.'

Claire folds her arms across her chest, offended at the insult; her breast bulges across her arm and Ralph sees bare skin.

'I'll open it, shall I?' And he rummages inside and pulls out a bottle of Bailey's. 'Ta da! Your favourite. They're on offer in Asda. That'll get you pissed like nothing else and even though I can't have none tonight, I am free Saturday evening. She's got her friends coming around. You having a small one now? Or a large one? And what about a drink?' He laughs dirtily, slamming the Bailey's down and taking a brandy glass from the cupboard.

'Not for me, thanks,' Claire replies, unimpressed.

'S'up to you,' he says all offended, putting the glass back down.

'Ralph, we need to talk.'

He sighs. 'What have I done?' He takes the settee, pushing aside the caramel-coloured teddy bear that's always sitting there watching with its glassy brown eyes. He puts a cushion on its face.

'Our affair has run its course...'

The day he has dreaded is here. The day Claire calls time on him.

He feels sick, his stomach is somewhere in his chest, clogging up his throat, tightening its grip so much that he feels he can't breathe or swallow.

'It was fun, Ralph, but it's not what I want anymore.'

He swallows the hard lump of sickly dread and finds his voice. 'What do you mean it's not what you want anymore? What *do* you want then, other men, a proper relationship? I can give you that, Claire,' he offers, throwing open his arms desperately. 'I'll leave her if you want. Fuck knows things aren't getting better. I'll tell her tonight that the marriage is over.'

'I don't want you to leave your wife, Ralph. You have children...besides a full-time relationship with you or another man is not what I want either. I don't do relationships and you're starting to believe that this is one...'

'I'll back off then and give you a break; see other men if you want. I don't want you to but please don't finish it, Claire,' he pleads, putting his hands together as if in prayer and sitting forward in his seat.

'It's finished.'

'Is it boring? Then we'll go away for the odd weekend, inject some fun into things, spend more time together...'

Claire shakes her head again and his hopes plummet. 'No, Ralph. It's over.'

'You can't just dump me without an explanation.'

Her tone changes, becomes accusing and harsh. 'Okay then. You're too serious. You're strangling me and you're not even my boyfriend! You bring cheap alcohol, supermarket flowers and a smell of workman into my flat. You have your jump and you go. It leaves me unfulfilled and bored.'

'Bored! Thanks a lot, love. You're not so great yourself,' but he knows that he's lying. Sex with Claire is the best he's ever had, the best he's ever likely to get. Their affair came when he needed it the most, when he discovered the trick his wife had played on him.

'Don't make this difficult, Ralph. I want you to go.' Claire stands up, arms still folded.

'Well, I'm not going to.' He can see she's worried and that empowers him. He might be able to wear her down into giving him another chance. And if he frightens her a bit then that's not a bad thing.

'Yes, you are. I have to go out and I'm not leaving you here.'

'You'll have to because I'm not going.'

'Until when? When your wife rings asking where you are, when you're coming home? Tell you what, let's not waste any time and give her a call now.' Claire snatches her mobile off the table and thrusts it at him. She shakes it at him. 'Go on, ring her. Or shall I do it?'

'Don't be stupid. Put the phone down.' He knows Claire doesn't have her number.

Claire replaces it but steps toward the corner of the work surface where Ralph has left his phone along with his wallet. She picks it up and starts pressing buttons.

'What are you doing?' He leaps to his feet and reaches for the phone but Claire twists her torso around, holding her arms away from him, out of his reach. 'Give me the phone. Claire!' He grabs her wrists in one of his hands like his fingers are one half of a pair of handcuffs. Claire struggles, starts shouting to let her go. With his free hand, he tugs the phone out of her grasp and shoves it in his back pocket.

'Get out of my house or I will tell your wife!' Claire threatens, rubbing her sore wrists. 'I am not bluffing.'

'You're fucking mental,' he spits. 'I feel sorry for you. You're gonna die a lonely miserable woman. No one will ever want you.'

'Good. I don't want to be wanted.'

He glares at her, his nostrils flaring angrily. He shoves the bottle of Bailey's awkwardly back into the carrier bag and stomps to the front door. He doesn't call out a final goodbye but slams the door shut and marches back to the van, roaring away like a teenager in a souped up Corsa.

*

Ralph unwinds the window and spits out the chewing gum. The little white ball lands on the ground and rolls back towards his tyre to get stuck on its tread when he drives off. He groans.

How much longer, he wonders, when's this bloke gonna show or when she's gonna go out? Just my luck that it's neither. She's most likely curled up on the sofa with a microwaveable lasagne and the soaps and there is no bloke. I mean I don't have any proof, but if she's sleeping with me then it stands to reason there'll be others.

Ralph has never given much thought to the possibility that when he gets out of Claire's bed, that vacant warm spot is taken by someone else. He pulls a face. What's the point of having an affair unless it betters your life? I wasn't in it for the short-term. I want out of my marriage. Away from *her* and less of *them*. Bloody kids draining my money, my energy and my happiness. And *her* wallowing in kids' parties, kids' after-school activities and gossiping with the other sexless mums. They only want you for one thing and then you're back to being relegated to the side-lines, only lending a hand when they want a night-out.

The pale blue Jaguar moves slowly towards him, gliding effortlessly like a shark through water. Nice car, he thinks as his gaze follows it in the side mirror. Thoughtfully, the driver indicates his intention to turn left into the space just vacated by Ralph.

Is this him?

Ralph watches as the driver's door opens and a dark-haired man in a smart suit gets out. He opens the boot and removes a huge bouquet composed of pink and lilac flowers.

'Bet they aren't supermarket bought,' he grumbles.

Ralph leans out of the window and watches as the man approaches the communal door; the security light above the frame snaps on illuminating him as he steps inside the hall; his arm rises like a barrier and pushes open Claire's front door.

For him, Claire has left it ajar.

Chapter 8

Sally ~ Thursday ~ day 4

'If this is a continuation of Tuesday's text messages then you can bugger off,' Olivia warns without looking up from the computer screen.

Sally rolls her eyes. 'You've been off sick for two days; I just want to know if you're feeling better. It sounds like you've got morning sickness,' she laughs.

'Would that be a bad thing?' Olivia asks all affronted.

'No, of course not,' Sally replies somewhat hesitantly. It will be lovely to be an aunt, as long as the father isn't Dan, she thinks. He's very definitely not father material. Sally moves the stapler aside so she can perch on the corner of the desk. 'If I arranged a drink after work, would you come?'

'Yes. And if *she* shows I'm off. You can talk to her.'

'Oh, come on, Liv. Don't be ridic-'

Olivia spins around in her chair, her toes skimming sharply across Sally's shins. Sally jumps back. 'I'm not being ridiculous. You heard the same as me the other night. Claire is fleecing Dad!'

'Shh,' Sally says, looking around the empty office in case a colleague has returned. They certainly don't need to be privy to private family business. 'There might be a very good reason behind it.'

'Like what? I don't get anything and he's my Dad! What makes her so special? He treats her like a mistress, buying her jewellery and a new clutch.'

'She told me it was a cam belt,' Sally says. thoughtfully.

'Whatever it was,' Liv says dismissively, 'it's not important.'

'It is though. She lied about it.'

'She's lying about loads, like where her money comes from. No way is she earning the sort of wages that would buy a bracelet like that. Look at her handbags and shoes. They cost a fortune!' Olivia turns miserably back to the screen and Sally sees just how hurt she is by their Dad's favouritism. Sally ought to feel as angry but doesn't want to waste energy on getting wound up when it won't provide honest answers. The best thing to do is to speak to Claire. If Andrew has loaned Claire money then it must be for a very good reason, one she and Olivia are not aware of.

'We need to ask Dad what's going on,' Liv says, her hand absentmindedly swirling the mouse arrow around the screen like it's been let loose. Sally averts her eyes as the mesmerising movement starts to make her feel dizzy.

'Are you brave enough to do that?' Sally was on the receiving end of her Dad's temper last week. It can be phenomenal and he often sulks for days.

'Not really,' Liv admits. 'But Claire certainly isn't going to tell us. You know how defensive and argumentative she is.'

'If we all went for a drink, we can ask her about the money instead of speculating. I'm sure if we approached this in an adult manner, we'd find out what's going on; we can repair our relationship with her too.'

'She's not going to tell us anything. And I don't give a toss about our relationship. When Mum has another family do, Dan and me are not going if Claire's there. And you won't persuade me otherwise, so forget it.'

'Liv, she's our sister.'

'She's a half sister. All yours,' Liv childishly snaps.

Sally sighs heavily. 'Why are you so difficult?'

'Why are you so determined to iron this out so diplomatically? And don't say it's because she's a sister.'

'We're a family. There shouldn't be rifts. We were all close once. I loved growing up with two sisters. Didn't you?'

Liv frowns. 'Sisters grow up, they get friends and boyfriends, they don't need each other anymore. It happens. And it's happened to us. Accept it.'

But Sally knows she could never accept it. Having a much older sister like Claire meant having someone who was on her side. When Sally grew up, Claire became a friend she could get advice from, recent advice not out-of-date advice like from her mum or her peers who hadn't experienced anything yet themselves. Sally read something about sisters that always stuck in her mind, something about sisters being friends for all your life, sharing memories, and they love unconditionally. Sally glances at the top of Liv's head. Her long dark hair is parted at the front and tied back with a band with a red material daisy attached. She wonders if Liv remembers that Claire bought her that. They were shopping in the January sales a couple of years ago. Liv saw it in an accessory shop but had no money left. Unbeknown to Liv, Claire had sneaked up to the till, paid for it and presented it to Liv on the bus home. Liv had been overjoyed and regularly worn it since.

How soon she forgets.

'I'm going to arrange a drink. I'd really like you to come even if you just want to hear what she has to say about the money.'

'You know who we could talk to?' Liv says. 'Mum.'

Sally shrugs. 'Maybe.' She wanders back to her desk, her mind already searching for words and phrases and tones of voice that could possibly help them get the information they need. She feels worn out with worry and upset, but there's a tiny sliver of hope that they might find out what's been going on.

Chapter 9

Claire ~ Thursday ~ day 4

Tara leaves the office, closing the door behind her. A collective sigh of relief sweeps around the room and the secretaries smile at each other. Anne picks up her phone to ring her sister and see how her back is today. Fiona wheels herself over to Claire and hands her the letter.

Claire reads slowly, digesting everything. Nigel wants a slice of the proceeds from the flat Fiona rents out. Originally he said he didn't want anything, not one item of furniture they'd purchased together; he wanted off the mortgage. Fiona didn't think Nigel would ever mention the flat since it was a property she had years before they met, which he only lived in for 6 months anyway.

Claire looks up; she's absolutely disgusted. 'The nerve of him.'

'It's her,' Fiona replies. 'It's all the slut's doing. Now she's up the duff, she wants things: three-wheeled pushchairs, designer baby wear, and she expects me to pay for it! Why should I? I mean, Nigel contributed nothing towards the mortgage on my flat. Occasionally he'd buy food, give me something towards the bills, but not the mortgage.' Fiona's voice is rising and Claire glances over at Anne, but she's gabbling away.

'You're right, Fi. Why should you give him anything? He walked out on you. You were willing to work at the marriage. He didn't even try.'

'Exactly!'

'Have you spoken to your solicitor?'

'Well, that's another thing. He's been told he can *only* contact me through my solicitor but still he sends me disgusting demanding letters like this. I rang her the day I got it, even faxed it over to her office. She's very good. She's got a response for him.' Fiona beams and Claire is intrigued.

'What is it?'

Fiona leans forward and Claire can smell cheese and onion on her breath. Claire props her head up on her elbow, her fingers lightly covering her nose. Now she can smell lime scented hand-cream.

'Nigel had three thousand pounds worth of debt and my parents paid it off.'

Claire wishes she had a mum like Fiona's.

'It was on the understanding that Nigel paid her back, but he never has and so my solicitor has very kindly reminded him of that. Let's see if he carries on with this latest stunt after that.'

'Brilliant, Fi, brilliant.'

Fiona slides the letter back into its envelope. 'Yesterday was a shit day. I'd hit rock bottom with it all. I couldn't sleep, eat; I didn't want to come to work or stay at home and now the sun has come out. I just want the divorce to come through. I've removed all his stuff from the house and still he finds a way in. Through the letter box usually.'

Claire smiles. 'How do you feel about the pregnancy now?'

'How do you think? It makes me angry because we were trying for a baby. When he left he said there was no-one else. I believed him because I stupidly thought who else would want him, where could he meet someone else. But there was someone and she was right under my nose. It's all her fault. She knew he was married, knew he was mine. She couldn't find someone herself so she had to have my husband.'

'If he'd have loved you, he would have pushed her away...'

But Fiona is shaking her head in disagreement. 'He's a man,' she replies as if this explains everything. 'He loved me, but he was flattered by her attention. Plus they're the same age. They have more in common.'

'There's only a couple of years between you.' Claire watches her tone of voice but is annoyed that the 'other woman' is getting the blame when as far as she's concerned it's the husband who cheats. Unless the mistress is in a relationship too.

'It's his fault, Fi,' Claire continues. 'He should have spoken to you if he was unhappy, not turned to the first pretty face that came along.'

'She isn't pretty!' Fiona snaps. Startled, Anne looks across. Claire's eyes widen at how forceful and angry Fiona gets over this. 'Her nose is too big and she's really skinny. She looks anorexic.'

'She'll be the size of a house soon,' Claire jokes.

'Yeah, carrying the child I should have had!'

It's as if the sender knows Claire needs a life-line. Her mobile vibrates with the arrival of a text. She glances quickly at it. It's from Mr Weeks rearranging their next meeting. Claire hides her grin and quickly changes the subject.

'How did Stan get on at the doctor's?'

'He's been referred to a cardiologist because he needs a pacemaker. That's more time off I'll have to take to bring him to his appointment,' Fiona complains.

Claire smiles sympathetically. No one else in the office or in the whole department knows about Stan living with Fiona. No one would understand how Fiona could give a home to an elderly great uncle, related only by marriage. But then no one knows about Claire and her life. Something she and Fiona have in common.

'Hope it gets sorted soon. Must be awful for him feeling light headed and lethargic all the time.'

'It's awful for me too. He's driving me round the bend,' Fiona whines. 'I have to do everything. I'm worn out fetching and carrying for him.'

Claire glances at the clock. Tara will be returning soon. Anne has returned to her typing and Claire mutters that they'd better do the same. Fiona pulls a face but wheels herself back to her desk.

Claire slyly rereads the text from Mr Weeks. As usual he's added a row of kisses which he'll cash in later. Such a nice man. She thinks about her chat on messenger with John earlier. Things got quite heated to the point where she had to call time on it and cool herself down by putting the kettle on. He's keen to meet up in the next couple of weeks when he's in town on business. Claire hasn't felt this good in ages! And after Ralph left last night, she swept clean the drawer in her bedroom. Time to fill it with new goodies and scents!

Chapter 10

Hock ~ Thursday ~ day 4

Hock stares into the middle distance, his ears still tuned into the activities around him: the excited chatter of his children as they eat breakfast, Lois's attempts to spoon mush into their youngest son's mouth whilst he tries to shove a toy car in, and the whirr of the washing machine as it spins its second load of kids' clothes that morning. He hasn't been with it for two days; soon Lois will tire of his vagueness and remind him that he has to get back to reality.

Hock's anger bubbles like the rattling lid on a boiling pan; this *fucking news* is a joke. And he told her, that pompous Coroner's Officer bitch, that it was a joke, that the pathologist must be a fucking imbecile if he expected him to believe it wasn't neglect. 'It stinks of a fucking cover-up,' he told her and she'd asked him not to swear.

'You were offered an independent post mortem,' she reminded him condescendingly.

He sneered. An independent post mortem had been briefly mentioned but not encouraged given the circumstances. He called her corrupt, threatened to get his own autopsy done, no matter what the cost, until Lois put a hand on his shoulder and quietly said, 'Don't you think your mother's had enough.'

He agreed and hung up, but now he feels lost, like he's on a badly made raft out at sea, not knowing which direction to start paddling in.

He thinks about how lovely his mother was but hot tears sting his tired eyes and he wipes them away with the cuff of his rugby shirt. No, he tells himself firmly, not here, not in front of the kids, and as if someone has clicked their fingers in his face, Hock snaps out of his trance and looks around the table at his family.

Lois is hastily trying to stack the dishwasher before the kids leave for school. Hock tears a sheet of kitchen roll off to clean Archie's face.

'Dad? When we go to Nana's funeral, can I wear my orange dress? I know it's a summer dress and it's cold out but Nana liked orange,' asks Caitlin, his ten year old.

Hock smiles. 'What a good idea, Cat. Nana would love that.'

'Dad, can I wear my-' begins Jamie, the eight year old.

'Course you can wear your onesie, Jay.'

'Dad!' Jamie screeches. 'Onesies are for babies. It's for Archie and Grace.'

Hock laughs out loud. He loves to wind his children up. And they love to be wound up. This is just the tonic he needs.

'And my name is Jamie!'

'That's what I said, Jay.'

'Mum! Tell Dad!'

'Get your coats, please. It's time to go.' Lois ushers the children away from the table like she's herding erratic chickens out of a pen and out into the hall, where her twin teenagers are examining their hairstyles in the mirror. 'What have you both done to your hair?'

Hock lifts Archie from his high-chair and unhooks the bib from around his neck. There's dried food on his chubby thighs and on the inside of his feet.

'You're gonna need another bath, son,' Hock tells him.

'Oh, thanks, babe. Don't forget his bubbles,' Lois says, grabbing her car keys off the sideboard and winking. 'Back in a bit. Right you lot, out!'

Once the front door has closed, Hock puts Archie back and hands him his toy, which he shoves into his toothless mouth. Hock reaches for his mobile and dials a number.

It's promptly answered.

'It's me.'

'I know. Your picture came up,' laughs Hock's associate.

'You still in contact with that mate of yours, the ex-porter?'

'Yeah. Got his number somewhere...'

'Find it and let me have it.'

'I'll text it straightaway.'

'Don't let me down, Dan. This is more important than you can possibly imagine.'

Chapter 11

Claire – Friday ~ day 5

She glances at her sports watch but struggles to read the jiggling numbers in the fading light. 4.89 km, 31.25 minutes. I can do it, Claire thinks brightly, I'm going to do it. And with that burst of confidence, she literally puts her feet down and concentrates on reaching the lamp-post outside her flat before the time reaches 32 minutes. Her feet pound the battered tarmac, her lungs feel like they're bleeding but she ignores the pain and sprints for her makeshift finishing line.

Almost, almost, she tells herself, you can do it, you're doing great!

Ahead of her, stepping out of her front door and turning to lock it, is her neighbour Bev, who's just off to babysit her grandchildren like she does every Friday. She hears the stamping and no doubt Claire's heavy breathing and turns to watch, leaning heavily on her crutch.

'Come on, girl! The gold medal is in sight!'

Claire tries not to laugh; she needs all her breath but does grin at the encouragement.

Bev's fist is raised and Claire thinks she could do with Bev in January when she does this run for real. She hasn't arranged for anyone to cheer her on.

She crosses the finishing line and her finger jabs the stop button. 31.57m.

'Yes!' Claire cries, breathlessly. 'A new personal best.' Bev hobbles over, smiling broadly. 'I beat 32 minutes. I'm so pleased. I had a feeling I would tonight.'

'Well done you.'

'I know it's only three seconds but I've been trying to break 32 minutes for weeks and weeks.'

'I admire your dedication, love. I've seen you out here all weathers pounding the pavements. I wish I could still run,' Bev says, her voice tinged with sadness.

'Did you used to run?'

'Yes, before all this of course.' And she taps her swollen knee. 'Still, you never know. Once Mr Ameer gives me my new knee, I may join you on a swift ten miler.'

Claire remembers her stretches and grabs hold of the lamp-post for support as she grabs her foot with the other hand and stretches her thigh muscles.

'I take it you've got a race coming up? You've certainly put in some practice. When is it?'

'It's the end of January. It's quite a big run, at least ten thousand people. But you can run for any charity, whatever you want so I'm doing it for the

Alzheimer's Society. My friend's dad was diagnosed with it and I wanted to do something. My aim is to run it without stopping.'

'And I'm sure you will. They'll be very proud of you.'

Claire smiles, pondering whether to continue to keep the run a secret from Will or confess what she's up to. She swaps legs and feels the muscle in her thigh stretch.

'Do you run by the park? You need to be careful around there, what with them youths hanging around.'

'I avoid that area like the plague. I've been running the route of the race; it goes through the woods. At this time of night, half six, there's plenty of dog walkers and other runners too. I wouldn't run it if it was too secluded.'

Bev's smile widens. 'Let me give you a tip, Claire, for looking after your muscles. Before you get out the shower, turn the water to cold and aim it at your legs. The cold reduces soreness.'

'Thanks, Bev. The back of my thighs ache something rotten after a run.'

'That should help then.' Bev points her key fob at her car and presses a button. The car beeps and flashes its indicator lights twice. She hobbles over, opening the boot to drop in her shopping bag and handbag. 'When did you want to borrow my car again?'

'Oh, it's next Saturday.'

'Make sure you remind me. Mind like a sieve.'

Claire reaches around to the small of her back and unzips the secret pocket in her running tights and removes her front door key.

The warm flat welcomes her and the sweat which felt cool on her skin outside feels sticky now so she peels off her top. The phone base in the hall is flashing red and the red numbers say 02. Messages, she thinks. She undoes her trainers and kicks them under the hall table.

It'll be Sally again. Wasting her breath and my time.

Claire pours herself a cold glass of water and presses the play button. She resumes her stretches whilst the voices speak.

'Hi Claire. It's me.'

Sally. No surprise there.

'I've spoken to Liv and she's really sorry about what happened. She'd love to meet up...'

Yeah, right, Claire thinks sarcastically.

'She knows she was in the wrong...'

That's a first.

'Give me a ring and we'll sort out an evening to meet. I know Mum will be pleased if we can sort it out.'

Emotional blackmail, so unlike you Sally, thinks Claire as she places the empty glass on the draining board. The message ends and the next one starts with a little cough, a male cough, and Claire thinks: Stewart.

'Hi, Claire. It's me, Stewart. I need to talk to you about our phone call earlier this week...give me a ring on my mobile. I'm in all evening. Speak to you later.'

That doesn't sound good, Claire thinks. He sounds nervous. She shakes her head, feeling a little despondent. He has the means to help, how can he say no? No, she tells herself; don't jump to conclusions just because he sounds jumpy; he doesn't want his wife knowing about this. But if he needs a little persuasion...

Claire takes the pen off the top of the fridge and turns to the calendar. She re-reads her time and distance, and neatly writes both numbers under today's date. God, end of the month soon and then it'll be the home run to Christmas, she thinks. More money to spend on other people and oh, shit, Christmas dinner! How the hell am I going to get out of that one?

She wishes her parents would go on another Caribbean cruise like they did a couple of years ago and the sisters just spent the holidays with their other halves or on their own in Claire's case. Best damn Christmas I ever had, Claire thinks. Didn't get up till after noon, stayed in my pyjamas all day and ate chocolate and watched lots of films. And Boxing Day went to Will and Justine's for dinner and then to the pub. Great days and they're all gone now. I've got one more Christmas to suffer before Will's out and then maybe *we'll* go on cruise. Yes, Claire thinks positively, I like the sound of that.

Draping her lime green bath sheet over the heated towel rail to warm up for after her shower, Claire takes off her sweaty running kit and drops it all in the washing basket. She turns on the shower, reminding herself to turn it to cold afterwards. That's gonna hurt, she thinks, but no one ever said running was injury free.

Chapter 12

Stewart ~ Friday ~ day 5

It's almost an hour since he left his message on Claire's answer phone, and Stewart is restless. He can't sit, he's up and down, in and out of the kitchen, picking up the newspaper, swapping it for the remote control, only to put that down again and all this is accompanied with sighs and huffs. Across the room, his wife is noticing but saying very little now. She's berated him already this evening for being up and down like a yo-yo, it was making her sick and she was sure he'd ring back soon. Who, Stewart had asked. The man you rang, she replied. Yes, yes, he'll ring, Stewart said confidently, but when?

Stewart goes into the dining room to pour himself another whisky. The neck of the bottle rests on the tumbler. 'No,' he tells himself firmly and rests the bottle upright. Must remain sober, I can't weaken.

'Stewart!' his wife calls from the lounge. 'Your phone!'

He grabs it off the arm of the chair and swipes his finger across the screen, almost shouting, 'Stewart Murray.'

'Hi, it's Claire.'

'Hello, thank you for getting back to me,' he says in a business-like voice, stepping into the study and closing the door.

'You're welcome,' Claire replies in an amused tone.

'I'm in the study now. My wife was listening.'

'Are you alright? You sound nervous, reminds me of our first date. In fact, you sound worse because you were happy then.'

'I'm alright,' he lies, but he isn't. Stewart hates stress, hates loose ends; he likes things to be sorted quickly and when they aren't, he becomes restless and jumpy.

'I do appreciate this, Stewart,' Claire says with feeling. 'I know how it looks, that I've only contacted you for one reason but it wasn't easy. I'm in an awful mess; I've got to come up with some money quickly.'

Stewart is barely listening, instead he is kicking himself at his hesitancy, at not adhering to his script which is to leap in and firmly tell her he can't help, he has no money, but now his resolve is weakening as her sob story begins to dig in under his skin and threaten the foundations of his replies. Anything he says now will sound pathetic and cowardly.

'Please say you can help me,' she begs and he can picture her, her hands clutching the phone to her ear, her breath held as she waits on the edge of despair for his positive answer.

'Claire, I would love to help but,' and he adds the but quickly so she knows there is one, 'I don't think I can.'

Silence and then 'Oh, right, okay,' and he hears her sigh deeply. 'Are you sure?'

'I don't have that sort of money...'

'You used to,' Claire reminds him.

'I know, but not anymore...'

'Have you still got the Jag? And the Audi?'

'Are you suggesting I sell my cars?' he laughs. His wife would certainly have something to say about that.

'No! Of course not. I'm just saying that you have expensive cars and they cost money to run.'

'I had to sell the Jag anyway. We needed the money for my wife's hospital treatment,' Stewart explains. It is a kind of a half-truth. He sold the Jag, used some of the money to fund his wife's stay on the private ward and used the rest to pay for a holiday, but Claire doesn't need to know that.

'Do you remember when you gave me all those bundles of notes to make that bet for you? How much was it? Yes! Twenty thousand! Wow! I had never seen that much money before.'

Stewart stops. He holds his breath as he realises just where this is going, like a path that suddenly appears in dense woodland, it meanders around a corner to a place he can't escape from. He stands quickly, catching his hip on the corner of the desk. He softly yelps and sits heavily. Oh, fuck, no. How has she realised? She knows fuck all about football and regulations, that's why he asked her to do it so there'd never be any comeback, and now she's all clued up and using it to her advantage.

'It was just a bet.'

'I can still remember your strict instructions: Desai's betting shop on the Parade and put twenty thousand on them to lose. And I did it. I was terrified I was going to get mugged, and when they lost on the Saturday, I couldn't believe it. You didn't seem surprised though. You must have had a lucky tip.'

It's the way she says 'lucky tip' that sends Stewart's head into a spin. His mouth is suddenly dry like a hangover mouth and he looks around for something to drink. A vase of lilies stands on the windowsill in the bay window and he considers sipping the water. She *knows*. She fucking *knows*. There was no lucky tip. She's leading up to something.

Don't give her anything. She may be bluffing. She doesn't know anything about football, showing no real interest when you were together. Like a typical woman she was only interested in the men's legs!

'How much did you win? Forty thousand, wasn't it? I wish I had the fifteen hundred you gave me as a thank you now. That'd help my situation. I shouldn't have spent it. I can't even remember what I bought with it. I spend money like it's water. Bit like you and cars.'

'Yes,' he mutters.

'I take it you haven't got any of that money left then?' she asks hopefully and as he opens his mouth to lie no, she says, 'And you won't be making any more colossal bets either?'

'No...as I said I've spent a lot of money on my wife's care. Things have been tight...'

'I understand, Stewart. And thank you for being frank. Look, I'd better go and reassess my options. Good luck with the games ahead and I'll...well, you know...if I'm ever at a match, I'll wave hello.' She hangs up.

'Shit,' he hisses and throws the mobile onto the desk. It bounces into the framed photo of the team winning the FA Trophy two years ago. He could lose that, his integrity would be destroyed forever; he'd be unemployable, no more than that – banned. Banned from going anywhere near a football for the rest of his life.

Did she actually make a threat? Claire is sharp. Her life is based around dishonesty, her relationships are clandestine. What does she intend to do?

'I should have just given her some money.'

If he drew a few hundred out, would his wife notice, would it be enough to seal Claire's mouth? What if she wanted more at a later date? What if this is a game she's playing for the long-term? Perhaps this is what she's been working for all along: the long ball. Have an affair, break up, stay silent for a couple of years then get back into contact with some begging story. So I pay up like a mug, but she keeps dipping her hand into my wallet until someone else comes along or maybe she's got a few of us on the go. The bitch.

Stewart deletes her call from his history and slides the mobile into his pocket, as if it's in danger of running its mouth off. How can I find out about her intentions, without actually asking her? If I mention it, I could end up putting the idea into her head. She must realise the devastation she could cause, what then? How do I shut her up?

A soft tentative tapping interrupts his fantastical murderous thoughts and he opens the door. It's his wife.

'Your programme's just starting.'

He settles down to watch his favourite documentary show. It's about football but he can't remember what the topic is – the rise of new hooliganism probably, racism.

The narrator's voice begins: 'Tonight – corruption in our beautiful game.'

Stewart automatically changes the channel. He senses his wife's confused frown.

'I'll watch it another time. You have your soaps on, love.'

She smiles with glee.

Chapter 13

Leo ~ Friday ~ day 5

For all the money he was fortunate enough to win on the lottery, Leo won't spend it on clothes. As far as he's concerned, soap is soap, cheap shampoo is good enough, and as long as it fits and it isn't twenty years out of date, he'll wear it. His money is for making more money and spending on things that matter like game consoles, the latest mobile phone, TV box sets and huge televisions to watch them on. However, today he has a meeting with someone he needs to impress and for only the third time in his life, Leo wishes he was a bit more clued up about fashion.

He examines his jeans. There's a dried spot of toothpaste on the thigh and they're a bit worn at the knees. He pulls a face. He's not going to buy a new pair of trousers just for one meeting. He's showered and shaved, and is wearing an ironed shirt, that'll do. He's sure Hock will be concerned with more important matters. He locks the house up and smiles when he sees his ice-white Range Rover sitting on his block paved drive with its personalised plate.

'Hello Beautiful.' He climbs inside and sets off for the meeting place.

Leo passes Ryder Drive, remembering there's a young couple who live there that owe him...how much? Six hundred and counting. The first loan was to buy Christmas presents and the second was for their kids' first summer holiday abroad. The debt continues to mount up and the season of goodwill is coming around again. Leo makes a mental note to call in on them on the way back. That'll be a nice surprise over their Friday night dinner.

The Spread Eagle is a family pub. The unmistakable noise of rowdy children and chattering parents comes from inside. He pushes open the door, the warm smell of chips and beer enveloping him instantly. He waits at the sticky bar with its wet circular glass marks and dog-eared menus. A small boy runs up to a man standing a few feet away from Leo, screaming and pulling at the back pocket of his jeans that he needs a 'Wee wee.'

Leo hates children. Hates the noise they make and the way they dominate everywhere now. You can't be an adult anywhere, they run amok and God help you if you complain – you get it in the neck from the parents! Leo does concede that kids have kept him in business. If it wasn't for the little shits demanding every new toy or video game and the parents forking out for them then Leo would have to find another business venture.

'Diet coke, please,' Leo says to the barman, a young lad with acne around his mouth.

'Ice?'

'No, ta.' Ice hurts his teeth.

'Three fifty.'

Leo's eyes narrow at the cost. Should have asked for a glass of tap water; at least it's fucking free. He puts his hand into his pocket feeling for the collection of the coins when a deep commanding voice says, 'Pint of Foster's too. I'll get these, Leo.'

Leo turns to Hock. It's been a while since he's seen him, but he's never forgotten the sheer strength of the man. Although only half a foot taller than Leo, Hock has twice the chest and collar size. He camouflages his size well under heavy coats and rugby shirts but those that know him, know that he could crush a windpipe with one hand and break a skull with one foot.

His hair's thinning, Leo thinks. He didn't have that receding hairline the last time I saw him.

'We'll sit in the conservatory; it's quieter,' Hock suggests. They pick up their glasses and weave their way around tables, chairs and kids having tantrums.

Why the fuck did we have to meet here? But Leo remembers something important: Hock adores kids. He has two families' worth of the brats.

Hock chooses a table in the furthest corner of the conservatory and takes the chair facing into the room. Leo fishes the lemon slice from his coke and deposits it on a beer mat.

He doesn't know why he's been summoned, what Hock could possibly want. All Dan said on the phone was, 'I've passed your mobile number onto Mr Hock. He needs to talk to you.' It's enough to get Leo worried. Their businesses aren't headed in the same direction so Leo can't see how their paths could have crossed, but he's worried that they have somewhere. On the plus side, Hock seems friendly, he's bought Leo a drink, but Leo isn't stupid. He knows assassins visit with smiles on their faces. If Hock wants a 'quiet word', what better place than a public one.

'What contacts have you still got at the hospital, Leo?'

Leo pulls a face of immediate surprise. 'Mostly porters; mates, you know. We still meet up for a few beers now and again.'

'Doctors?' Hock throws the question at him like it's a Frisbee, his eyes fixed on Leo.

The look almost throws Leo back into his seat and he fumbles for an answer like he's grabbing for a bar of wet soap. 'A couple maybe. Some of the more friendly ones say hello or thanks if you do something for them.'

'Any of them surgeons?'

Leo laughs but it catches in his mouth when Hock's eyes narrow into slits. 'No! There aren't many surgeons who'd lower themselves to speak to a porter. They think they're God's gift to medicine, performing life saving operations. Arrogant gits. Medical doctors are more civil.' Hock frowns and Leo realises that he doesn't understand the difference between surgeons and medical. He doesn't bother explaining not unless he's asked to.

'What about pathologists?'

Leo shakes his head straightaway. 'Didn't have anything to do with them. Pathology is more or less a separate department in the hospital. The only time a porter would encounter pathology staff would be collecting specimens or dropping patients off at the mortuary. Even then we'd only see mortuary technicians.'

Hock looks disheartened. He stares at the lager, his hand tightly grasping the glass.

'Is there someone at the hospital you particularly want to find out about?'

Hock looks up, his eyes are sad. 'My mother died as I'm sure Dan told you. She was misdiagnosed, the surgeon ballsed up. She had a post-mortem but the pathologist has lied. It was a bullshit cause of death. The whole lot of them have lied from start to finish, covering their own backs. It's a disgusting travesty.'

Leo doesn't know what to say. The threads holding together Hock's temper and grief are almost visibly straining under it all. His other hand is clenched into a fist so tight it must be crushing his thumb which is tucked inside his curved fingers. Leo heard that under extreme pressure Hock self-harms.

'Who do you want to know about? The surgeon?'

'I want to know everything about him and the pathologist, but most of all I want to know how they covered up her death because I am not accepting this!' Hock unfurls his fingers to slam it on the table and Leo can see a spot of blood on Hock's palm where his thumbnail has pierced the skin.

'That's not going to be easy, Hock. Junior doctors won't grass up a surgeon; they won't put their careers in jeopardy.'

'I'll speak to the surgeon and the pathologist myself. I've tried ringing the hospital; even spoke to his secretary but the obstructive bitch wouldn't put me through...'

'Whose secretary?'

'The pathologist's. I told her he cut my Mum open and I had a right to question what he found...'

Leo's barely listening to Hock's rant as his mind flicks through his mental address book of clients. He knows a pathologist's secretary; he struggles to recall her name but knows the important stuff like how much she owes and that full payment is due soon.

'I might be able to help.'

Leo's words are like a weak sun parting dark storm clouds. Hock's thin mouth upturns into a smile albeit a devious one.

'A pathologist's secretary owes me money, I think...'

'You think?' Hock demands, leaning forward. The clouds are darkening the sky again. The smear of blood on the beer glass from Hock's hand concerns Leo.

It might be mine next, he thinks fearfully. 'I'm positive. She owes several grand and is struggling to pay up, keeps asking for more time. I've reminded her time is running out; I'm not running a charity.'

'So, she's a desperate girl?' Hock asks, his voice sing-song.

Leo nods. 'The sort that'd sell her Grandma to pay off a debt.'

Hock laughs loudly. 'That's what I wanted to hear, Leo. What I wanted to hear. I think you've just made my day. Whisky, is it?'

'A small one would be great. Cheers, Hock.'

Chapter 14

Nisha ~ Saturday ~ day 6

'I must tell you, Mrs Snell, that sometimes it's less painful if the truth remains unknown...' Mrs Hughes gently warns, leaning forward, hands clasped like a vicar's.

'Mrs Hughes,' begins Mrs Snell somewhat condescendingly, 'I appreciate this is a speech that you give all your clients, a kind of disclaimer, but I'm an adult. I'm capable of handling the truth. The unknown, however, is unbearable. I won't hold you or your company responsible for any misery caused.' Her broad smile relaxes Mrs Hughes and her partner, Nisha, who sits beside her.

'Okay. The next step is to find a suitable woman. Now, you said your husband likes white women, what age would you say?'

'Not too young. He prefers a woman not a girl. Early thirties is a good start.'

Nisha is secretly pleased because this rules her out straightaway. She dreads it when a client says, 'My husband likes Asian women. It's his secret desire. Yes, yes, like her. She's perfect.' And a finger is jabbed in Nisha's direction.

Mrs Hughes slides the photograph album towards Mrs Snell, turning it to face her. Every operative employed by the agency has a current photo inside the album. 'Long hair or shorter?'

'Not short. Not like a tomboy.'

Mrs Hughes slides a pad of yellow post-it-notes towards Mrs Snell and says, 'Have a look through the album and when you spot someone suitable just pop a post-it-note on the page. Would you like another coffee?'

'That'd be lovely, thank you.' Mrs Snell slides her glasses off her head and onto her nose, and begins to study each page.

Nisha wonders about Mrs Snell like she does with all the clients. Some partners want to find out how faithful their partners are before they get married, move in together, have a baby, which is understandable if they've been hurt before. Some people have suspicions due to a change in their partner's behaviour: joining a gym, working late, surprise gifts. Occasionally clients tell of a sudden interest in sex from their partners. Mrs Snell hasn't said anything particular. Her husband has an important job which requires him to work away in the week, returning home at the weekends to her and their children, who are at university. He currently rents a comfortable house in the town, which she rarely visits. She says she hasn't found anything incriminating at the house. No unfamiliar items of women's clothing, no receipts for meals at expensive restaurants.

'Why do you think your husband may be having an affair?' Mrs Hughes had asked.

She took her time in answering. 'He claims the office requires him to work of a weekend now; it's hardly worth him bothering making the journey home. In the company of friends, he's very content, chatting easily. And yet, when it's just the two of us, it's as if a switch has been flicked. Conversations are very formal, often strained. He has virtually no interest in my life and that upsets me, and I wonder if he feels that his homecoming is a chore, that he has something better to be doing. My husband cannot be without someone. I thought that someone was me, but I'm not sure anymore and I need to know if our marriage is over.'

Nisha reckons the Snells have simply forgotten how to talk to each other, which is not surprising given their living arrangements. Has Mrs Snell spoken to him about her concerns or have things got so bad, she can't even do that? Maybe he has a history of cheating, maybe there's something else that she isn't saying because she's embarrassed. It can be difficult to speak of these things to strangers, especially ones you're employing to trap your husband! Nisha has seen clients in absolute bits over their suspicions, almost begging the agency not to find anything. Others are unemotional, almost businesslike; it's just another problem that needs sorting. Maybe Mrs Snell is just a practical woman, deft at keeping her feelings hidden.

Mrs Hughes returns with a tray laden with a pot of fresh coffee and places it on the desk.

'Have you spotted an ideal lady yet?' she asks.

Mrs Snell looks up over her glasses. 'A couple, yes.' She turns the book around for Mrs Hughes to see.

She starts at the first marked page and from where Nisha is standing she can see the problem with the choice straightaway. 'Ahh, this lady has just started maternity leave,' apologises Mrs Hughes and turns to the next choice. 'She's out of the country at the moment. Due back first week in December...'

'I can't wait till then,' Mrs Snell replies annoyed.

Onto the third choice and both Mrs Hughes and Nisha smile with confidence.

'She's an excellent choice,' enthuses Nisha. 'Nice, friendly girl, talkative, complimentary; she can be whatever you need her to be. I've worked with her loads of times and she always gets the right result.'

'Yes, but Nisha, is she what Mrs Snell requires. Her husband may not want talkative and nice. He may like shy and serious.'

'I'd never get a result if I thrusted a girl like that on him,' laughs Mrs Snell. 'He likes confident women. Can I choose a name? Is that acceptable?'

'Of course,' replies Nisha. They've been asked some odd requests in the past. Fake names aren't unusual.

'Rachel. It reminds him of his favourite actress and ex-girlfriend.'

'Rachel it is,' Mrs Hughes repeats, writing it down. 'What we need from you are possible dates and locations which your husband will be attending, such as a hotel or a bar that we can arrange the honey-trap for.'

'I'm meeting my husband after my appointment here so I can do some enquiring and let you know as soon as I can about possible dates. Certainly the sooner this goes ahead the better. I won't waste any time.'

'And I'll speak to our operative later today.'

Mrs Snell collects her bag from the floor and stands, smiling with contentment and something else that Nisha can't quite recognise. 'One final thing...'

'Yes?'

'The photo of his indiscretion...I will be able to keep it, won't I?'

'Yes, of course. It's yours to do with as you please.'

Mrs Snell's smile widens and Nisha wonders. As far as his wife is concerned there's no question of him falling into a trap, not if, but when. She is unequivocally sure it's going to snap tight around him.

Chapter 15

Sally ~ Saturday ~ day 6

Sally eyes up the selection of posh cookies. She shouldn't have another; she should leave a choice for Fergus, who is busy outside with her dad discussing where in the garden he wants the raised beds building.

Mum and Dad must be getting old if they want to start growing produce, Sally thinks. I can't even successfully look after a cactus. I should throw mine away. I only got it because there was a cute plastic squirrel attached.

Marion turns from the stove where she's warming milk for hot chocolate. 'Have another biccie if you want, love.'

'I shouldn't, Mum. I'm putting weight on all over the place,' Sally replies.

'Yeah, especially around your mouth.' Olivia laughs, crumbs peppering her bottom lip.

'Hark at you! You're hardly going to win Slimmer of the Year, are you?'

Liv shrugs. 'No, but I don't care.' And she reaches for another cherry and almond cookie. 'Anyway if I take up running like Claire then I can eat my own weight in biscuits and not put on an ounce.'

Sally glances at her mum but Marion is concentrating on the pan. They need to try harder if they want to steer the conversation onto Claire and her finances.

'You must be mad to take up exercise in this weather. It's too cold to do anything but eat and drink merrily!' Sally pushes away the plate of biscuits. 'Not that I can afford to do that.'

'Tell me about it,' Liv complains. 'It's why I scrounge from Mum. I can't afford to actually buy food.'

'Fergus is only managing to work a few days a week at the moment. He's considering returning to college to learn plastering or plumbing, but these courses cost money.' Sally sighs heavily. 'And Christmas is just a few weeks away. Liv, if you're lucky you might get a Satsuma in your stocking.'

'I'm going to tell people not to bother buying for me; it'll save me having to get them anything.'

'It is difficult to know what to get people,' Marion comments, carefully pouring hot milk into the mugs. 'So, if there is anything you two particularly want let us know as soon as possible.'

A cheque for ten grand will do nicely, Sally thinks.

'Claire's asked for money...'

Liv pounces like a cat on a baby bird. 'No surprise there then. What's it for this time: new boots, new clutch or is it a cam belt? I'd have thought Claire had enough money considering all the clothes, jewellery and handbags she's got. How many charms does a bracelet need?' She looks at Sally.

'It's only cheap costume jewellery,' Marion says.

'Mum,' Sally interrupts, 'Claire's bracelet is not costume jewellery! The charms are about forty pound each.'

'Oh.' Marion's neatly plucked eyebrows leap in surprise. 'Well, she works.'

'I don't see how she can afford all these expensive items on a medical secretary's wage. She still has a mortgage, doesn't she?' Liv asks.

'Well, yes.'

'Maybe she has a second job,' Sally suggests. 'She could be working behind a bar at the weekends.'

Sally can tell by her mum's pained expression this is an awkward subject and that if they want information they need to change their technique. They sound jealous and spiteful; criticising Claire won't get them anywhere. If her mum clams up they will blow any future opportunities.

'Sorry if I sound bitter, Mum, but I can't help feeling a little jealous of Claire,' Sally admits humbly. 'Things are such a struggle at the moment. It's very good of Dad to employ Fergus to build a wall but it's not consistent work and that's what we need. We really wanted to redecorate this year, fill that blasted mechanic's pit in, lay new carpets – the one in the hall is so threadbare it's slippery now. I nearly took a tumble yesterday.'

Marion smiles with sympathy. 'I'm sure your dad would lend you some money to get these things done. If the carpet's dangerous then you must get it replaced.'

'Thanks, Mum, but I can't afford to repay it. I doubt we ever could.'

Sally notices that her mum says 'lend' and not give. It wouldn't be a gift, so does that mean Claire owes him money and she can't pay it back?

'Can't Dad just give us some money?' enquires Liv half-serious. 'As an advance on our inheritance? That's if we're in the will and he isn't leaving it all to an elephant sanctuary!'

'You know what your dad's like with money,' Marion replies.

We certainly do, Sally thinks. She carefully contemplates her next question. They need to get a move on. It's cold outside and soon the men will come in for their drinks.

'Has Claire ever borrowed from Dad? Does he give fair interest rates?' she asks adding sugar to her hot chocolate and a smile to sweeten the question.

'I don't think she ever has,' Marion replies.

Doesn't mean she's never asked for a loan, Sally thinks, although a new cam belt or clutch are very good reasons.

'Are you sure Claire's never borrowed even a couple of quid from Dad? I'm sure I heard her say...' Liv casually remarks.

'Not to my knowledge, love. And your dad would say.'

Sally sips her drink, the hot liquid scalds her top lip and she winces. Judging by the conversation she overheard last week through the study door, Dad is not telling Mum about lending their money. Which is odd, because thousands is a large deficit to explain; can Claire even pay back such a sum quickly. Sally just can't see her dad keeping secrets. But it appears he was going to.

'He might not tell you,' Liv suggests, 'if it wasn't much money. I mean, what's a couple of hundred quid between father and daughter.'

Marion narrows her eyes at Liv. 'If Claire needed money, why wouldn't she ask me? Your dad's money is mine as well.'

Sally blows on her mug to cool the liquid down. She hasn't anticipated her mum being a hard nut to crack but maybe she's right that Claire hasn't borrowed money. Whatever they heard that night on the stairs, they got it wrong.

'Do you both think Claire is getting something you aren't?' Marion asks.

This time Sally and Liv are taken aback and they glance guiltily at each other.

'Claire isn't being favoured over either of you. You're all treated the same.'

'I'm sure we are,' Liv replies, her tone a little sarcastic.

Marion leans across the table. 'Do you? Because you're asking a lot of questions about Claire's finances. If you're curious as to where her money comes from and how she affords things, then you should ask Claire. We don't hold her purse strings. She may have another job, a rich boyfriend, a bonus from work, a small bequest...'

'From who? Her father?' scoffs Liv.

'He's not dead, but he may have leant her some money. He had a good job, he's an only child, bound to inherit from his father when he passes away.'

'He hasn't seen Claire for years, has he?' Sally asks, hoping to keep the momentum going.

Marion shrugs. 'How would I know? Claire's an adult. If she's seeing Philip, then I doubt she'd tell me.'

'Why? It's hardly going to upset you. Your divorce was over twenty years ago,' Liv points out bluntly.

Marion lowers her head and rubs her eyes. All Sally knows is that he committed adultery, their mum found out and there was no reconciliation. Of course it was painful at the time, but surely not now?

'If Claire was seeing her dad,' Marion says quietly, 'she'd feel...guilty, like she'd betrayed me, especially since...'

Sally remains quiet and stares at Liv to do the same. Their mum is explaining. Any prompting from them now might shut her up for good. Sally holds her breath, hoping the back door doesn't open now.

'...she found him in bed with his *woman*.'

Sally's eyes widen. Liv gasps; she's dying to speak.

Marion removes her hands and looks at Sally and Olivia who are both rapt with attention.

'Your Gran was ill,' she begins patiently. 'She was recovering from a chest infection. I spent a lot of time there looking after her. Philip was working nights. It was the school holidays, Claire was seven and her friend's mum was giving her lunch until Philip got up and I was home. Claire and her friend were playing outside but when it started to rain they decided to play indoors with their *Sindys*. Claire's favourite doll was at home, tucked up in her bed.'

Liv moves her cup into the centre of the table, knocking the teaspoon out of the sugar bowl. Sally flinches violently, fearing the noise may derail their mum.

'It's not the same playing with other children's toys, is it?' Marion asks and they shake their heads. 'So I never blamed her for wanting to fetch it. They went to the house and spotted the open kitchen window. They'd have made excellent house breakers.' She chuckles. 'They dragged the dustbin over and managed to lift the arm of the window. Claire climbed inside and onto the draining board. She assumed her dad was asleep, but knew she had to be quiet because if he heard a noise he'd think it was a burglar. When she got to the top of the stairs, there was a pair of high heels outside our bedroom door. She knew they weren't mine.' Marion pauses as Andrew's voice is heard by the back door, but dies away as he leads Fergus around to the front of the house. 'She heard noises: panting and lowered voices, so she crept towards the open door pushing it ever so slightly open.'

Bloody hell, Sally thinks. What a thing to discover.

'They were in our bed. Philip and this woman. They didn't see her. After Philip had gone to work, she told me what she'd seen. That was it: marriage over.' Marion reaches for her cup and takes a long drink.

How awful, Sally thinks. What kind of a man does that to his wife and child?

'Claire grassed him up then,' Liv concludes succinctly.

Marion awkwardly laughs. 'In a way, but she was a child; she didn't really know what she saw.'

'She knew she had to tell you.'

'Well, yes; she felt guilty about sneaking into the house...'

'She was aware if she told you about Philip frolicking in bed with his floozy, you'd ask what she was doing in the house and then she'd have to admit breaking and entering...'

'It was hardly that, Olivia.'

'She didn't care about getting in trouble for housebreaking as long as she grassed her dad up.'

'He'd been having an affair for three months! Your Gran's illness and my absence was a bloody gift to him. If Claire hadn't insisted on having the doll, I may have never known about the affair.'

'Surely you noticed something? Strange perfume in the bedroom, an earring among the bedclothes, a guilty expression on Philip's face...'

'Stop right there!' Marion demands, her voice rising angrily. 'Are you blaming me and your sister for his affair? Do you think I was stupid and blind for not seeing what was right under my nose?'

Liv opens her mouth but closes it when she doesn't know what to say.

'Maybe Claire got it wrong,' Sally dares to suggest and her mum turns to her, raising an eyebrow. 'She might have made a mistake.'

'What do you mean? She made it up?'

'Maybe,' Sally continues. 'She had a child's imagination. What if she got the idea off the telly? It's something juicy to tell your friend. A bit like I saw Mummy kissing Santa Klaus.'

Liv starts laughing. 'That's brilliant, Sal.'

'Claire did not make it up,' Marion defends angrily. 'I confronted Philip and he admitted it. He left and we got divorced. Honestly I don't know how you pair can sit there and suggest your sister is a liar! It's despicable. If it hadn't been for her, neither of you would have been born.'

'I'm wondering if Claire told Philip what she saw,' Olivia says and her tone of voice fills Sally with dread. 'She might have offered to keep quiet in return for a new *Sindy*.'

'Oh, don't be ridiculous, Olivia!' Marion exclaims but Liv is laughing.

'I'm joking, Mum.'

'That's enough,' Marion says, holding a hand up like a policeman stopping oncoming traffic. 'I won't discuss it anymore. I don't even know why I brought it up since it's nothing to do with either of you. And you'd better not discuss this with Claire either.'

'That's fine with me since I won't be seeing her again,' Liv answers haughtily.

'Why can't you grow up, Olivia, and make up with your sister...'

'Half sister.'

'If something happens,' Marion warns, 'you'll regret it.'

'Doubt it.'

'Darling!' Andrew calls from the hall. 'Fergus says he can start the wall on Monday.'

'What, love?' She gets up and goes into the hall, closing the door.

'You bloody idiot!' Sally leans over the table at Liv. 'What was all that about Claire grassing her dad up? She was seven years old! What planet are you on?'

'Don't tell me you weren't thinking the same thing with your 'are you sure she didn't see it on the telly'? You suggested Claire was a liar! That's worse than mine that she was a grass. Kids tell tales. Not all kids are filthy liars.'

'We aren't going to get anything more out of Mum now.'

'She knows fuck all anyway. If Dad's lending money to Claire, she doesn't know about it.'

'I don't care anymore. I'm not ruining my relationship with Mum over some snippet of hearsay that we might have misheard. And I'm not souring my relationship with Claire either. She's my sister and I care about her.'

'Good for you,' Liv says, sitting back and pouting. 'But don't bitch to me when you find out I was right all along.'

Chapter 16

Claire ~ Sunday ~ day 7

He doesn't offer Claire a drink but then Leo's a moneylender; he's not in the business of giving anybody anything for free. His interest rates aren't bad though and that's the main thing.

Claire sits opposite Leo at the circular table in the booth at the Grazing Lamb. She can't understand why he's picked a noisy family pub and on a Sunday lunchtime; they usually meet at a much quieter venue like a cafe and on a weekday. Somewhere they can avoid the squeal of children too.

Leo drinks his red J20, the ice cubes clinking merrily. Claire knows he can't abide ice so can't understand why he asked for them unless he didn't buy the drink. Maybe that's the fault of his companion who sits beside him. Claire hasn't seen him before but notices he's been allowed lager.

He looks like every other stocky, balding, aggressive idiot on the street, driving a white van, stewarding at non-league football matches or letting his kids run amok in pubs like these. She wonders why Leo is now employing a bodyguard.

'We weren't supposed to meet for a couple of weeks yet. Is there any particular reason you've bought it forward?' she asks, ignoring the silent companion.

Leo looks at the stranger and it occurs to her that his sole role was just to get her here; the stranger is the lead on this.

The stranger takes another slug of his Foster's before turning his small colourless eyes towards her.

'I have a proposition for you,' he says, his voice gruff.

Oh, Jesus, Claire thinks with horror. A proposition? What kind? What does he think I am?

'Leo says you owe him a fair bit of money and that you're having difficulty paying up.'

'Not really. I can get the money. But that's between me and Leo...' she tells him forcefully. 'It's nothing to do with you...whoever you are.'

'I'm Phillip Hock, and it is now.'

'Leo,' she hisses across the table. 'What's going on? What have you done? We had an arrangement. I can repay; it's not a problem. You didn't have to-'

Leo has reclined onto the beige leather seating, an irritating smirk on his rodent-like features.

Hock raises a huge hand; there's a silver ring on his wedding ring finger. 'Hear me out.'

'I don't think I want to. I'm a medical secretary; I'm not a call girl.'

'Please lower your voice.' Hock glances around but no one is paying them attention. 'It's precisely because you're a secretary that I know you can help. There'll be something in it for you too.'

'What, like a five grand reduction in my repayment?' she jokes seriously.

'Do you work for Dr Heathcote?'

'Amongst other pathologists, yes.'

'Is he good at his job? Methodical, experienced?'

Where's he going with this? Has he had dealings with him somehow?

'I guess so. He's had no complaints from anyone.' She doesn't mean it flippantly as if the dead can't complain. She's referring to the Coroner, colleagues.

'I have a complaint,' Hock tells her. 'He carved my mother open and then had the audacity to lie that she had a bad heart; she was strong, her blood pressure wasn't high. I don't buy it at all. Either him or the surgeon, or both together have cooked this up.'

Claire can't believe this man is accusing a pathologist of covering up a cause of death. For what purpose? She thinks. Often relatives are upset and they make wild accusations against ward doctors and nurses, claiming their loved one was "murdered" but often that's just down to their own guilt. What's this about a surgeon, which one? Is he suggesting a conspiracy?

'I don't understand. Why is a surgeon involved? Did your mother have an operation?' She doesn't really want to know, doesn't want to get dragged into this complaint, but she doubts she can walk away easily. At least not without hearing him out.

'My mother had cancer. Mr Erikson, her surgeon, shelved her biopsy results allowing the cancer to spread. When she died, this Dr Heathcote claimed it was her heart, that the cancer hadn't spread, but how could it not have? It was aggressive.'

Something it has in common with you then, she thinks.

'Were you not offered an independent post-mortem? It was your-' she asks but Hock slams an open palm down on the table making everyone and the glasses jump into the air.

Claire sits back, her eyes wide with fear.

'Oh, yes, if you can call it that,' he says with contempt. 'That stuck up bitch in the Coroner's office definitely didn't encourage me. Now, if I want one, I've got to fucking pay, and I don't see why I should. Besides, my mother's suffered enough. I want answers and I'll get them with your help.' And he smiles, a wolfish smile that wrenches Claire's guts.

'What do you expect me to do? I'm a typist.'

'I want you to get your spade out and start digging around. Unearth a copy of my mother's autopsy report, her hospital notes; I want information on the pathologist and the surgeon. Preferably where they live.'

'And how am I supposed to get their addresses?'

'Ask them if you have to, I don't care.'

Claire looks at Leo but he's eyeing up the list of desserts on the back page of the menu.

'No way. No way am I jeopardising my job by disclosing personal details about staff members. Find another slave.'

This time Leo speaks. 'Not even for a reduction in what you owe or an extension to the deadline? A bit of snooping isn't worth that?'

'How about we turn it the other way around?' Hock suggests, leaning towards her threateningly; his large frame casts a shadow over half the table. 'Let's add some interest: thirty quid a day and we'll bring the deadline forward by a week. How's that grab you?'

'Leo!' Claire implores desperately. 'Please don't. This isn't what we arranged.'

'Claire, think carefully before you refuse,' Leo says. 'A reduction and a time extension are a gift;

don't throw it away because of some moral shit. Do this bit of digging and help yourself.'

Any kind of reduction, however small, is a benefit to Claire; it means she won't need to borrow so much off Andrew. An extension to the deadline means it will give her more time to work on changing his mind because that may take some doing.

'Claire,' prompts Hock. 'Help yourself or things could get way out of your control.'

She can find the information he wants easily enough. Last year Dr Heathcote had his gall bladder removed. His details will be in the patient database. As for Mr Erikson, Claire knows one of the surgical secretaries. They attended Pilates together. With a good enough reason, she could get his address.

She looks at them in turn, feeling distinctly ganged up on. She nods in defeat.

'I'll do it. I can even speak to the mortuary technician who did the post-mortem, see if they remember anything.'

Hock smiles with glee.

She feels awful: guilty and treacherous. She can't believe Dr Heathcote would write the wrong cause of death, let alone forge one. There has never been anything untoward in the paperwork she has typed for him. The idea that he's corrupt is incomprehensible. He'd be risking his integrity and job if it was found to be true. What could he possibly have to benefit from covering up? Perhaps he was helping out an old medical friend who might have got themselves into a bit of a situation. And Claire knows what that feels like.

'I want some information by Monday evening,' Hock tells her and she looks up, her mouth open to protest about this deadline. It doesn't give her much time. 'My mother's name is Phyllis Hock.'

She nods again, defeated.

'Right, Leo, I've got to pick my kids up.' He stands, his frame moving the table towards Claire a couple of centimetres. 'I look forward to hearing positive news from you, Claire.'

She waits until Hock leaves the dining area and disappears around a corner before turning to Leo. She glares at him as he fishes the melting ice cubes out of his drink and deposits them into Hock's empty glass.

He's as weak as me, she concludes, accepting this pub as a meeting place and ice cubes in his drink. Two things he hates.

'How could you do this to me, Leo? He's a fucking thug.'

He looks up. 'You don't know anything about him.'

'I can see exactly what kind of person he is just from that one conversation.'

'He's not as bad as he seems; he's upset. He was close to his mum.'

'What, like Ronnie and Reggie close?'

Leo laughs. 'Yep.'

'Great,' she snaps, throwing her arms up. 'So, when I give him the bad news, because I doubt I'm going to find the tiniest shred of evidence of a conspiracy, he's going to get *really* upset and then what? He'll be just as angry with you for putting him onto me.'

Leo frowns and his jaw tightens that he hasn't spotted this flaw in his plan.

'Just do what he wants; it's never a clever move to turn down one of Hock's requests.'

'It's hardly a request,' she says, pushing the table into Leo as she stands. The move jerks him backwards but she hides the smirk from view and leaves him sitting there. Once outside, she digs her mobile out of her pocket, which has been on silence during the meeting. There's a missed call and a voicemail.

'Hi Claire, it's Nisha. I've got some great news! A job has come up which you're perfect for. Give me a ring and we'll go over the details. I'm really looking forward to working with you on this one. Speak to you soon. Bye!'

Claire smiles to herself. 'Thanks, Nisha, but will you pay me five grand for a night's work so I don't have to snoop on my colleagues? That would be even better news.'

Claire cuts across the car park towards home thinking about Andrew and how he reneged on his offer. She needs to make a move on that score, and if he needs reminding how important his lifestyle and marriage is then she has no choice but to resort to extortion.

Chapter 17

Claire ~ Monday ~ day 8

The pathology department is quiet. Although lights are on in a couple of the pathologists' offices, the secretaries' office is in darkness. Claire won't be disturbed for at least an hour. She presses in the four digit code and opens the door; her heart is thumping. A low humming noise comes from the small fridge in the corner that houses her colleagues' lunches and their communal milk. She turns the lights on. The fluorescent strip buzzes into action and casts a stark whiteness over the surfaces. Already, Claire is a bundle of nerves.

She goes to her desk and sighs at the piles of waiting paperwork. Hock's mother's post-mortem was last week so there's a good chance the report still requires typing up. Where to start? She curses herself for being so bloody untidy. The pile of reports on the keyboard relate to histological samples so she moves them aside. Under them are letters requiring typing so they go too.

A flash of yellow post-it-note catches her eye. Scribbled on it is a reminder she wrote to herself that these have to be typed up first thing Monday morning. She smiles. This is the pile. She sits down and begins sifting through them. Phyllis Hock is the last report.

Claire opens it to the last page to where the cause of death is written. Under 1a, Dr Heathcote has written coronary artery atherosclerosis and in 1b is ischaemic heart disease. Mrs Hock was an elderly lady; he would expect to find a dicky ticker and crunchy arteries in someone of her age. The cancer Hock claims really killed her has been placed under two, which means it has contributed towards her death but not directly caused it. Nothing wrong with that, Claire thinks, and reads on, turning back to the first page which lists the weight of each organ and any observations. Under the heading of *Heart*, Dr Heathcote has noted the weight as being 600 grams; large for an elderly woman but not if she has heart disease. The heart is a muscle; the more it works the bigger it grows.

Claire reads that the old lady had severe coronary artery atherosclerosis which means the arteries feeding the heart were extremely narrowed and crunchy. Again nothing unusual in that. She reads the rest of the document and is disheartened but relieved that there isn't anything odd to find. But Hock isn't going to be comforted by that.

Claire puts the document to one side to photocopy for him and sits back in the chair, contemplating her next move. She forages around in her desk drawer for the emergency KitKat.

'What's all this crap?' she says, lifting out a pile of paper: annual leave sheets, competencies record sheet, scrap paper and a crumpled post-mortem report.

She pulls it out, tearing the corner and reads the name across the top: Phyllis Hock.

This is the report Dr Heathcote asked her to shred.

Suddenly Claire's heart feels as if it's been woken with a jolt. It thumps with apprehension. Why are there two reports on one death? She reads this cause of death. '1a – metastatic carcinoma of the liver. 1b – carcinoma of the caecum. Under two are ischaemic heart disease, diabetes mellitus.' Basically the cancer in her bowel has spread to her liver. Heart disease now has contributed but not caused her death.

'Was Hock right?' Claire mutters.

But there could be a perfectly reasonable explanation for Dr H to write a second report containing a different cause of death. He was busy, he wrote down what he saw, went away to read the biopsy results and thought about it. His only error was rushing to write it. Claire continues reading the report. Everything is identical to the other report – the weight of the organs and the observations. However, as soon as she starts to read about the bowel she realises there are big differences. In the other report, he has written that the cancer was confined to the caecum, that it hadn't spread beyond; it effectively hadn't killed her. But in *this* report, the one he insisted she shred, he notes at length how there were large cancerous seedlings in the liver and lungs, basically advanced secondaries. Mrs Hock was riddled with it.

'Oh, God,' Claire breathes. 'Poor lady.' No wonder Hock's pissed off. If her biopsy results, essentially the results taken when she first exhibited with a problem, were shelved and forgotten about, this gave the cancer time to spread to other organs and ultimately render Mrs Hock with incurable cancer. Whoever ignored them is responsible for this lady's death. But why would Dr Heathcote risk his career and integrity for Mr Erikson, that's assuming that the surgeon asked him to?

There's no doubt the reports are just what Hock needs, providing all the evidence to avenge his mother's death. And it's right and fair that it comes out. But everyone will know it's me who's shopped the doctors, Claire reminds herself. It's all very well starting a crusade but where's that ultimately going to leave me? Dr Heathcote specifically asked me to type the second report and shred the first. He's unlikely to forget that. If I give this to Hock, will he protect me? Not on my life, Claire thinks. I can kiss my job goodbye. And any reduction off my loan isn't going to help me pay back the remainder when I'm jobless and very much unemployable.

Claire contemplates her next move. This is worth a lot to Hock. More than what he's offered. Maybe three or four grand. It'd be worth a lot to Dr Heathcote and Mr Erikson too, she laughs. And a thought enters her head. I wonder who'd bid the most amount of money for this.

'Morning!' a voice sings loudly.

Claire jumps violently, the reports slide off her lap and onto the floor below her desk.

Anne plonks her handbag onto her chair and begins removing her coat and gloves. 'It's freezing out. God knows what December's going to be like if November is this cold. Did you have a good weekend, Claire? Tea?' And she rattles the kettle at Claire.

'Yes, please.'

Anne leaves the room to fetch the water. Claire takes the opportunity to photocopy the original PM report and slide it safely into a side pocket of her handbag. She wonders if it's worth getting the notes as there may be something incriminating in them. And she can talk to Isla; she loves chatting about her job and may be able to recall something. It will back up Claire's findings.

Claire kicks her handbag back under her desk amongst all the tangled cables from the PC just as the door opens and Fiona comes in looking harassed and untidy as usual. Clutched in her fist is a letter and Claire hopes it isn't another one from Nigel. She's not in the mood to lend her shoulder today.

'Is anyone else here?' Fiona barks at her.

'Anne's gone to fill the kettle.'

'Good. She'll be gassing for hours. I need a couple of hours off this afternoon to take Stan to a hospital appointment. I don't know what to tell Tara though. I suppose I could say it's for my mum.'

Hi Claire, had a nice weekend? Claire thinks sarcastically. Fine, thanks for asking, Fi. How about you? Bet you didn't because all you do is moan and complain about your life.

'I'm sure whatever you tell Tara, will be fine with her,' Claire remarks, entering her login and password into the appropriate boxes on the monitor. Out of the corner of her eye, Fiona is staring, taken aback by her sharp tone.

'Just because you've had a shit weekend, don't take it out on me,' snaps Fiona.

Claire gasps at the nerve of her but says nothing. The harsh words and their accompanying tone thicken the atmosphere in the office, hanging between them like something waiting to be mixed and dissolved into the air and forgotten about by an apologetic smile or a verbal sorry.

Instead Claire stands and leaves the office without a word.

She heads off down the corridor to the exit, muttering, 'Stupid bitch.'

*

Claire taps the four digit code into the worn keypad and opens the door to the mortuary. The sweet smell of disinfectant invades her nostrils. The office to the left is empty and the one to the right is nicely channelling the sounds of the post-mortem room to her ears. She can hear the buzzing of the bone saw and laughter.

She doesn't want to poke her head around the door to the PM room in case Frank's around and he shows her something awful, such is the sense of humour of mortuary technicians, so she walks across to the doorbell by the office door and is about to press it when Isla appears behind her, wearing her usual baggy scrubs but with her hair jammed under a hairnet.

'Hey you! What brings you over here?' she says cheerfully.

'Apart from wanting to escape Fiona's bad mood, Dr H asked me to pop over for the notes on Phyllis Hock. Her family have got some questions.'

'I don't envy you putting up with her misery; she's such an old frump,' laughs Isla and Claire smiles with agreement. 'I think the notes are in here.' Isla leads Claire into the office/kitchen. A big desk stands in the middle of the room with chairs around the walls. Piles of patients' notes and mortuary paperwork are stacked on every surface. A grimy kettle and stained mugs stand on the draining board.

Isla starts with the notes on a nearby chair. 'How was your weekend? Do anything exciting?'

'No, but it was okay. How was yours?'

'It was a mate's birthday so we all drank and ate too much. I thought my hangover was going to spread into today too but a sausage bap saw me right!'

Claire laughs. 'I don't know how you can have an appetite with what you do.'

'What can I say? I'm very odd. Here they are. Careful! They're heavy.'

Claire takes them, her arms dropping under the weight. 'You're not joking, are you?' She balances the notes on her hip and asks Isla if she remembers Mrs Hock's PM.

'Is she the one with the bowel cancer?'

'Yeah, family are querying whether the cancer had spread.'

Isla's brow crinkles as she tries to recall the finer details. 'Oh, yes. I don't want to gross you out so soon after breakfast. Is that the time? I've got to put someone out for a viewing. Look, I'll see you at lunchtime. Oh, wait, can't today, I'm on some stupid course.'

'Tomorrow?'

'Yeah, tomorrow.'

When Claire returns to her desk, her arms numb from the weight of the notes, she finds a notification on her mobile. Mr Weeks is cancelling their date due to an after work function but is free on another night instead.

'You're a popular girl,' Tara says as she passes Claire's desk. 'Your mobile's been pinging every two minutes.'

'It's all the men she has on the go,' Fiona pipes up cattily.

'Oh!' says Tara with interest. 'You sound a tad jealous, Fi.'

Claire tries to hide her own embarrassment by going along with it. She grins proudly that yes, she does have a different man each night.

'I'm not,' Fiona denies hotly, making Anne and Tara snigger. 'I'm not bothering with men again. They're not worth it.'

'They are! You can't beat someone to snuggle up to on a cold winter's night. You must miss that.'

'No. All I need on a cold winter's night is a hot chocolate and my soaps.'

'Not me,' continues Tara dreamily. 'I wouldn't swap my husband and children for *Coronation Street* and hot chocolate. Do you agree, Claire?'

'Oh, yes. You can't beat a man to warm your cold feet against!'

Tara laughs and rolls her eyes at Claire at how sad and lonely Fiona's life must be.

Claire smiles conspiratorially. It feels good, liberating, to gang up on Fiona instead of defending her or ignoring her colleagues' criticisms of her. How ironic is it that I'm agreeing with Tara about how sad and pathetic Fiona is, Claire thinks, when I have to borrow other women's husbands for a cuddle. What does that make me?

Chapter 18

Stewart ~ Tuesday ~ day 9

Stewart walks the well-trodden carpet in front of his office windows, hands clasped behind his back, eyes fixed on the comings and goings of the football ground, one ear tuned to Paul, his assistant manager. Paul's belief is to rest their injured striker, but as the forthcoming game is against the team that tops the league Stewart wants to risk starting with the striker and substituting him when he shows signs of fatigue. Stewart admires himself for hearing Paul out even if he is talking bollocks.

Paul draws his speech to a close and sits back to anxiously await Stewart's response.

Stewart continues to stare out of the window, not even honouring Paul's opinion with eye to eye contact. My people-watching, he's silently saying, is far more important than your views on my team choice.

'Vaughan is our best chance, no, correction; our *only* chance of getting a couple of early goals against the Bucks,' Stewart states. 'I need someone who can put the ball in the back of the net! Who would you have me choose? And don't say Ingram, please. He has neither the skill nor the balls to perform at a big game.'

'I think he's ready; he just needs a ch-' insists Paul.

'This isn't the game for that. I need goals on the scoreboard.'

'He does have skill...'

Stewart turns from the window, shaking his head in disagreement and Paul quietens. 'He lacks confidence. When he wants to say something, up goes his hand like a timid schoolboy! Is he going to do that on the pitch?' And to emphasise his point Stewart puts on a childlike voice. 'Please Mr Centre-back, can I place this ball in the back of your net?'

Paul tries to keep his face straight.

'No, you can't,' continues Stewart in a deeper voice, pretending to be the centre-back. 'Now, fuck off and don't bother me again.'

'That's a bit of an exaggeration.'

'No. It isn't. Vaughan's happy to start. He'll bandage himself up, take every precaution to protect himself, and take every opportunity to put us into an early lead or we will lose this match, Paul.' Stewart sighs. 'I know what the fans are writing about me on their forums; the players read those forums, and I can't afford for them to lose faith in themselves or me.'

'I know.'

'Two weeks into the season and those flag waving bastards were calling for my sacking. And now they're calling for me to rest Vaughan. I won't be dictated to by fucking armchair managers!'

Paul nods in agreement. 'Everyone's entitled to their opinion.'

Stewart raises an eyebrow.

Paul coughs uncomfortably. 'But, yeah, you're right. We don't need to hear it.'

'No, we don't. Now I'll have a word with Ingram; he'll be disappointed, which is your doing, Paul.' Stewart wags a finger at him. 'Can't afford to raise the hopes of these kids. Honestly, at times you're like Santa handing out presents, and then I come along and before they've unwrapped it I whisk it away. Don't make me look bad, Paul.'

'Sorry, Stewart. I'll speak to Ingram; he came to me,' Paul insists, 'so I should...'

'Well, he should have come to me; I wouldn't have buoyed him up like you have.'

In the car park below the window, Stewart hears the clunk of an expensive car door shutting followed by raised voices. Intrigued, he turns back to the window and looks out. The chairman is shaking hands with a smartly suited Asian man across the bonnet of a white BMW M3.

Stewart frowns and peers closer at the stranger, taking care not to headbutt the glass. The stranger looks familiar: late thirties, dressed in a black suit with a snazzy patterned pink tie. He oozes money and clout. Stewart eyes the car, nodding appreciatively, but when the Chairman holds out a hand to usher the stranger towards his office, Stewart clocks the personalised number plate and icy horror runs through his gut.

DES41.

Mr Desai. The bookie. Stewart's bookie. The one he asked Claire to place a bet with.

What the hell is he doing here?

Chapter 19

Fiona ~ Tuesday ~ day 9

With cold fingers, Fiona fumbles to swipe the door card across the sensor; the tassels of her long scarf draping along the wet ground like she's a ball of wool unravelling. Safely out of the cold rain, she rearranges her belongings and turns to walk down the corridor, her expression changing when Frank steps out of an office doorway. She doesn't bother smoothing out her scowl of contempt. She cannot abide the chief mortuary technician and his laddish sense of humour.

'Good morning, Fiona! Beautiful day isn't it?' he sings loudly, walking towards her. He's dressed in pale blue scrubs and white mortuary slippers; his tattooed forearms show a mural featuring anchors and unreadable words; a mischievous grin adorns his unshaven face.

'Yes,' she replies icily sarcastic, 'if you like freezing rain.'

'Who notices the weather when you're in love? You should take a leaf out of Gene Kelly's book and get yourself out dancing in the rain.'

Fiona frowns with confusion.

'Be careful you don't fracture his hip though. Probably osteoporotic.' Frank winks before pressing the door release switch and pirouetting back into the rain singing a line from the said musical. Fiona watches as he sashays across the staff car park towards the mortuary. Once he reaches the other door, he turns and waves at her. She quickly disappears inside the building, embarrassed to have been seen watching him, his loud laugh ringing in her ears.

Idiot, she thinks, climbing the staircase. She hurries past the staffroom; two laboratory technicians look up and grin. Fiona shakes the look away and opens the office door.

Tara is standing in the middle of the floor in an odd stance: like a prisoner caught scaling a fence; her smile is like a doll's - false and painted. Isla is sitting on the corner of Anne's desk giggling, her fingers curled around her mouth like a child stuffing in a stolen biscuit. Anne smiles an awkward hello at Fiona. Claire isn't here, but the kettle is missing so she's probably gone to fill it.

Nobody says hello.

Fiona approaches her desk, but stops abruptly when she sees it. Sellotaped to the monitor is a large pornographic photograph which completely covers the screen. It's not good quality but it's clear to see what it is. An elderly naked man, with thinning grey hair, sagging muscles and scrawny legs, a strategically placed Zimmer frame obscures his nether regions.

'What's this?' Her question is squeezed out through a tightening throat.

She glances at her colleagues, but none are able to speak. Isla has buried her head amongst her thick ponytail; Anne and Tara are shaking their heads, their lips pressed together.

Fiona's hand shakes as it reaches out to tear the offending picture off the screen. Her handbag strap slides down her shoulder weighing her arm down; her sandwich box topples out of the unzipped bag and lands upside down on the chair. Fiona doesn't notice. Her fingers grasp the corner of the paper and tug it.

'Who did this?' she demands, the paper shakes in her grasp.

Still no reply so she whips around to face them, but they're unable to speak. The three women are shaking and shivering with barely controlled amusement.

'Did you do this?' Fiona shouts at Tara since she was nearest to her desk.

Suddenly, Isla breaks free and laughs wildly like a manic howler monkey; Tara is bent over the desk as if she's going into premature labour, her red lipsticked mouth is open with laughter; Anne's hand is clamped over her mouth, but her tittering is loud.

'Fiona, if you want to you can put your pin-up on the board,' Tara manages to say, her grin wide like a joker's. 'I've got my Robbie Williams' calendar up.'

'If he's not old enough for you, I can get a picture of a skeleton,' Isla offers.

'Who put this up? I want to know!' Fiona looks from face to face, searching for guilt.

Tara ignores her and turns to the other two women. 'The thing is we were only talking yesterday about how nice it is to have a man to cuddle up to on a cold winter's night. Fiona said she preferred hot chocolate and soap operas...' Her tone is mocking, but Fiona feels they've already discussed this but it's necessary to repeat it to build up to the punch line.

Isla rolls her eyes at this and Anne comments that she wouldn't swap her hubby for *Emmerdale*.

'Yes, well,' continues Tara, 'Fiona disagreed and then it turns out she has got a man!'

'No way!' Isla crows.

'Albeit a toothless octogenarian!'

Isla and Anne break into more raucous laughter and fall about on the furniture like clowns performing a slapstick routine.

Fiona's humiliation roots her to the spot, her face hot like burning coals. Does she mean Stan? How does she know about him? Fiona brought him to the hospital yesterday afternoon for his appointment. The cardiac clinic is as far away from pathology as you can get. How did anyone from here see her? What were they doing in that part of the vast sprawling hospital?

'Where did you meet?' Anne asks, giggling. 'A tea dance? A World War One exhibition?'

'Ugh, I couldn't shag someone old enough to be my granddad,' Isla says, shuddering. 'Disgusting.'

'What?' Fiona hisses suddenly. 'What did you say?' And she steps towards them threateningly, her eyes staring madly at Isla, her fingers still clutching the dirty picture.

'I just said...'

'You nasty obscene bitch. How dare you make suggestions that are untrue and none of your business!'

'I was just joking, Fiona,' Isla retorts, standing up to her. 'Jees.'

'Joking? Is that what you call it? It could have been my granddad or an uncle. You've assumed because you're thick and it's more fun that it has to be something dirty and wrong. You're pathetic. I'd rather leave you poor bitches to your dirty guessing and gossiping than tell you what's going on.' Fiona strides for the door, the picture turning damp in the corner where her sweaty fingers grip it.

'Fiona! Come on, it was a joke!' Tara calls after her.

Fiona turns. 'Fuck off, Tara.'

Tara steps backwards colliding with the opening door; Claire is returning with the kettle. She puts a hand out to stop being trodden on by Tara's heels.

'What's going on?' she asks, her eyes darting between Fiona whose face is dark and thunderous and the other three who are backed against the desk.

Then it becomes clear to Fiona: Claire is the only one who knows.

'You and your big mouth, Claire,' Fiona shouts. 'I thought we were friends. I didn't think for one second that you'd gossip behind my back.'

'What are you talking about, Fi?' Claire asks, incredulous.

Fiona pushes past them, this time knocking Claire into Tara who lands spread-eagled on the desk. She marches off down the corridor towards the Ladies.

Twenty minutes later Fiona returns to the office which is heavy with an atmosphere. She switches on her computer and refreshes herself with the work that needs doing. No one looks at her or speaks. Claire is busy typing and glancing at her mobile as usual. Tara isn't here. But shortly later she returns and goes over to Fiona.

'I've complained to Prof about your language, Fiona. He'll be speaking to you later.' Her voice is cold and businesslike.

Fiona looks up, proud smile on her face. She spent her time in the toilet working out her own game plan. 'Fine. I will look forward to speaking to him and showing him the picture you stuck up on my PC. So glad I didn't shred it.'

Chapter 20

Claire ~ Tuesday ~ day 9

'I remember Mrs Hock because her bowel was all stuck down,' Isla recalls, spearing a square of ham with her fork and dipping it into the blob of mayonnaise. She puts it in her mouth and stares at Claire. 'Oh, God, sorry, Claire. It's not what you want to hear when you're having your lunch, is it?'

'It's okay. I'm not squeamish,' Claire replies, glancing down at her cheese sandwich, glad she didn't bring ham too.

'The caecum was unrecognisable, all hard and white. Cancer smells, you know,' Isla tells her knowledgeably, 'of smoky bacon crisps. I never touch them now.'

'Had the cancer spread? Was it in her lungs, liver...'

Isla nods. 'Yeah, her liver was riddled with it, and once it's there you've had it.'

'Yes, I know. Did Dr Heathcote say anything?'

'What like?'

Something like the surgeon has a lot to answer for, Claire ponders.

They're sitting in a corner of the hospital restaurant at a table by a large fake plant. Claire has taken up two places at the table with her lunchbox and handbag; she doesn't want anyone joining them whilst she questions Isla who's proving to be a chatterbox on the subject. She loves to talk about her job even though she isn't supposed to especially not in a public place where people can overhear.

'Did he think the cancer had killed her? Did he suggest that more could have been done for her? If she'd been operated on, she might have had a few more years.'

Isla shakes her head. 'She was in her eighties. Probably wouldn't have survived the surgery. Her heart wasn't brilliant either.'

'No. The family felt that the surgeon didn't act on her biopsy results quick enough.'

Isla nods. 'Mr Erikson rang that day, demanding to speak to Dr Heathcote. Ignorant git.'

'Did you hear what was said?' Claire's hopes soar because the mortuary has a hands-free speaker phone in the PM room for safety and cleanliness reasons.

'No. We had to go back to using the old phone. We couldn't hear the person on the other end. It was stupid. I don't know why we had to have it in the first place. I don't like people hearing what I'm saying. Frank has ears like a bat.'

'Maybe Mr Erikson was asking Dr H to cover up the death?' Claire suggests dramatically.

Isla dark eyes widen. 'Yeah, maybe. Dr H told him he'd speak to him after the PM.'

Claire hides her interest by neatly clipping the lid back onto the lunchbox. She's amazed how the details are returning to Isla drip by drip. It's starting to sound more and more suspicious. Claire pictures Mr Erikson panicking at what's going to be found at PM, how his negligence will be evident so he rings Dr Heathcote who can't discuss it in a noisy PM room with staff around. Dr H wrote the cause of death as he saw it and gave it to Claire to type. So why are there two causes of death?

'Erikson rang back after the PM when we were making a cup of tea,' Isla says. 'He assumed Dr H was still with us but Frank had to transfer the call to Dr H's office. I remember because Frank called him Sony. As in...'

Claire smiles. 'I get it.'

So they did discuss it, Claire thinks triumphantly, and the result was Dr H agreeing to write a second cause of death exonerating Mr Erikson. That explains the two reports and Dr H insisting Claire shred the first. It's starting to look very much like a cover-up.

Isla reaches for her yogurt, but before she tears off the lid, she leans forward and whispers, 'Who's this bloke of Fiona's?'

Claire finds it odd that Isla lowers her voice to discuss a colleague, but is unable to when discussing patient confidentiality.

'I don't know and I'm not getting involved. I've already had it in the neck from her because she thinks I told you lot.'

'I can't believe you knew about him! Fancy keeping *that* to yourself. Kev saw her,' Isla reveals as she tears off the lid and a little spurt of raspberry yogurt spits out into the middle of the table. Kevin is the other mortuary technician. He's older than Claire and is the worst gossip in the department. 'He was returning some pacemakers to cardio respiratory and spotted her. He ran all the way back to tell us about it.'

Claire doesn't waste her breath trying to explain that Stan is Fiona's great uncle. She doubts she'd be believed. She glances at her watch. Almost time to go and Claire has had enough of Isla's ridiculousness. Plus she's got all the information she needs on Mrs Hock now. 'We'd better get going, Isla.' She gathers her things and stands up.

Isla shoves her lunch debris back in her carrier bag and gets to her feet. 'Are you coming to the Christmas party? It should be a right piss up. Sit with us! We'll have a great time.'

Claire smiles politely, glad she's opted out, citing her sister's birthday as an excuse. She can't think of anything worse than sitting with Frank, Kev and Isla listening to their malicious small-mindedness.

'I'm not going this year. It's my sister's birthday.'

'Which one? The evil one?' Isla asks as she meanders around the tables towards the exit.

'They're both evil,' Claire mutters.

Isla laughs. 'Perfect excuse for getting out of it. "No I haven't got you a card or a present and I'm not celebrating your birthday, sis, because you're a nasty bitch." Tell her something like that.'

Claire considers it. Sally hasn't been back in touch and there's been no mention of Olivia's birthday so it's possible that Claire can save money and time by forgetting about it. Her mobile beeps and she pulls it out of the side pocket of her handbag to read the text from Nisha reminding her what time she's picking her up tonight.

The honey trap, Claire thinks with a wicked smile. An evening of harmless flirting with a good looking man is just the tonic I need.

*

Claire pushes open the office door and walks into the smell of Tara's lunch. The pregnancy has blessed her with a craving for *Pot Noodles.* Claire's nose wrinkles with disgust and she contemplates opening the window, but fears Fiona would complain. The office is deathly silent; the radio which is normally on low is off. Tara and Anne are away from their desks, but Fiona is working busily at hers.

Claire wonders if she should speak to Fiona, apologise even though she isn't to blame, she could offer to make them both a cup of tea, but Fiona hasn't even looked up though she must have heard the door open.

Sod her, Claire thinks, switching the radio back on and up.

Almost immediately, Fiona says, 'Claire.'

Claire turns, a smile ready to greet her, but Fiona's face is unfriendly.

'There was a phone call for you earlier. I had to answer it because you weren't here.'

'I was at lunch,' Claire explains apologetically, feeling that she has to explain her whereabouts. She moves the pile of growing work out of the way, but the disturbance pushes her pen to the edge of the desk where it plummets to the floor.

'Whatever. It was a man called Ralph. He was adamant he wanted to speak to you.'

Claire bends down to retrieve the pen; her expression is hidden under the shadow of the desk. Shit, she thinks. What the bloody hell does he want?

'Did he say anything?' Claire asks, sitting upright in the chair and keeping her voice casual.

Fiona frowns. 'Like what?'

'When my car is likely to be ready? He's my mechanic. I was hoping to have my car back by this weekend.' The thought comes to Claire quickly and makes her smile.

'No. He didn't mention your car. He asked if you were there, I said no. He asked when you'd be back, I told him I didn't know. He asked if you could ring him. He sounded agitated and keen that you return his call.'

I bet he is. 'Thanks, Fi,' Claire says.

'My name is Fiona,' and she swivels back to her computer, nose in the air.

Claire rolls her eyes and twists the pen thoughtfully in her hand. What does he think he can achieve by pestering me? How many times do I have to tell him it's over? For fuck's sake! I thought he got the message, I thought threatening to tell his wife would have an effect. Why is he getting in contact now?

Claire clicks the end of the pen; the nib goes in and out but a sharp glance from Fiona halts her action.

What does he think he can say that'll change my mind? The best thing is to ignore his call and if he rings again, I'll threaten to get an injunction or something, tell him I've been to a solicitor because I feel harassed. That'll shut him up. He won't want to explain a court appearance to his wife.

Chapter 21

Nisha ~ Tuesday ~ day 9

Nisha sits on the edge of Claire's bed and rummages through the spotty make-up bag of nail varnishes. She finds a lovely rich plum colour that will look fantastic against her tanned skin. If she'd chosen a different outfit for tonight she could have painted her nails now. On the bed beside her are more make-up bags containing lipsticks, eye shadows, different sized brushes. On the bedside cabinet is Claire's jewellery box. Nisha can't wait to have a nosy in there, see what Claire's bought that she can borrow sometime.

'Find anything you like?' Claire asks, appearing in the doorway dressed in just her underwear. 'There's a nice plum one...oh, you've found it. I knew you would.'

Nisha holds up the tiny bottle. 'Can I...'

'Of course you can borrow it.'

Nisha smiles and slips it into her evening bag.

Claire opens the wardrobe and slides hangers across the rail as she searches for her chosen dress. Hanging on the back of the door is a black sleeveless dress, patterned with pink and purple shapes. It's a very Sixties style, with a short hem and a high neck.

'Is that new?' Nisha asks, leaning over to feel the material. The little shapes are triangles. 'It's nice, really soft. I've got a pair of knee high boots that would look great with that. Not that it'd fit. I'm still a size fourteen and what are you again? Oh, yes, size ten.'

Claire peers around the door and pulls a face. 'It's not my fault I can't put weight on despite the number of cakes and biscuits I eat. I wore that dress to a wedding...I forget whose. I was uncomfortable all day; it kept riding up. I spilt wine on it; Will had to take me home so I could get changed! He swears to this day I did it on purpose.' She smiles wickedly. 'I'm going to put it on eBay if I can be bothered or, failing that, just shove it in a charity bag.'

Nisha remembers Claire's friend William back when she and Claire shared a flat. On cold evenings, he'd stay in his car and beep his horn for Claire to come down, and on warm days he'd run up the four flights and knock the door. He went to prison about a year ago...what was it for? She can't recall the details, but remembers it was something to do with his brother who was in trouble. He was about to get married too, but not to Claire. Nisha could never understand why Claire and Will didn't get it together; they were so close. Wasn't he a fireman or something?

'Ta-da!' Claire announces. Nisha snaps out of her thoughtful trance and looks up at her friend who is posed in the middle of the carpet in bare feet.

'Wow! I love you in red. You look great,' Nisha tells her reaching out her hand to touch the soft material.

Claire grins. The low neckline and short hem are respectable lengths. Enough to cause a man to double-take but for the right reasons.

'I know! You told me to wear red.'

'Did I? I don't remember.'

'Hang on; I've got something for you.' Claire opens her jewellery box, removing an item which she holds out to Nisha. 'Goes with your dress.'

Nisha opens her hand. She loves this bracelet. It's silver with turquoise stones all the way around. It's too big for Claire's slim wrist so she never wears it. When Nisha and Claire used to go out clubbing, Nisha would always borrow it.

'Tell you what. Keep it.'

'I can't!'

'I can't remember the last time I wore it. You have it and remember all our good times whenever you wear it.'

They stand close together; Nisha wrapping her arm around Claire's waist and elevating her mobile phone high in the air, the screen pointing down at them.

'Sausages,' they shout and Nisha's finger presses down on the button.

*

The Azure Hotel, a moderately priced place is situated in the heart of town within staggering distance of the restaurants and bars. Its guests range from those spending a weekend shopping or socialising, to those travelling here from further afield for conferences and meetings. Nisha is familiar with the hotel and its layout having sprung a couple of honey-traps here in the past. It's an oval shaped building, 39 storeys high and made of blue glass. At night, when it's lit up it looks like a huge blue gemstone.

They pause outside the revolving doors and look at each other. Nisha gave Claire a short briefing on the drive over that the target, Mr Snell is socialising with colleagues who are staying at the hotel. Mr Snell and company are dining out but will be returning to the hotel bar for drinks.

'You set, Rachel.'

'I'm not Rachel, remember?' Claire reminds Nisha.

'Oh, yes, of course. Glad you reminded me.'

Nisha tries to drill into her head that tonight Claire is Claire, not Rachel. Although initially Claire had agreed to the name change, later on in the day she texted Nisha to tell her she'd never remember her new name and could they stick to Claire.

'If it was something exotic or pornographic then I might remember, but not Rachel. I'll only end up contradicting myself and we don't want that. It's just until I get back into the swing of things,' Claire had assured her.

They stroll confidently into the bar. Gentle jazz music is playing at an appropriate volume. The atmosphere is pleasant, a little lively with the occasional loud laugh from drinkers. Nisha scans the room. There are a few people waiting at the bar to be served by barmen dressed in black. They work quickly, filling glasses from the large selection of spirits which fill the wide shelf behind them. In the far left corner is the biggest wine rack Nisha has ever seen. It's made completely of glass and must stand at 9 feet high. Its shape is similar to two diamonds standing tip to tip on top of each other and has maybe over 40 slots for bottles. Beyond the bar is a water feature. Gold water runs down a massive wall into a pool. It shimmers like molten gold.

The money they've spent doing this place up, Nisha thinks.

They head for the bar and wait to order their diet cokes. They always start with a soft drink, that way they can lie to anyone who asks that it contains vodka or Bacardi. When an offer is made to buy them a drink then they make it an alcoholic one but only ever one. After that Nisha uses the excuse that she's had enough to drink in the day.

Nisha leans against the edge of the bar and looks nonchalantly around. She's studied the photos Mrs Snell gave them of her husband.

There's a family a few feet away. The parents are sharing a bottle of red and their children both young teenagers are politely drinking cokes and playing games on their mobiles with the volume muted. The father asks his wife in French if she enjoyed the show tonight.

The bar is half full. A trio of smartly dressed women in their seventies is sharing a bottle of Champagne; a man sits in the corner in front of an open laptop; a young couple are sitting beside the fountain sipping cocktails.

Nisha and Claire take the bar stools at the end of the bar where they have the best view of the entrance. There are plenty of tables for the target and his group to sit at when they arrive.

A noise approaches the bar; male laughter and banter. Nisha sits up, crosses one leg over the other knee, her hem rides up her thigh and she wets her lips in anticipation.

A man with a shaven head is walking backwards through the doorway as he continues his conversation. He's short wearing a crumpled grey suit, his tie dangles from his right hand. Three men are following chatting loudly, discussing one final drink for the road.

Nisha looks the other men over as they wait at the bar. The second man is in his fifties and looks Italian: dark hair and eyes, stylish suit. The third man is mid-thirties, blond with the physique of a rugby player. He's laughing loudly, sharing a joke with the fourth man.

Nisha recognises him from the photos his wife gave her. Tall, mid-forties, short dark hair, clean shaven; he carries himself like a manager, confident and commanding.

That's James Snell, Nisha thinks. We're on.

She nods at Claire who smiles her acknowledgement.

They turn to each other and engage in pretend conversation. From the corner of her eye, Nisha watches as the men turn away from the bar, drinks in hands, eyes seeking out a comfortable looking table.

'Let's see where they sit first,' she mutters to Claire who's watching the group reflected in the mirror behind the bar.

The bald guy points to a table by the fountain, but the blond man shakes his head and says something about it being two degrees tonight. The tables are close to the exit and would receive a cruel draught every time someone went out.

Nisha talks to Claire about how many shopping days there are left till Christmas, all the time slyly glancing at the group who can't seem to make up their collective mind where they want to sit.

'How difficult is it to just sit down?' Claire laughs quietly. 'And they say women can't make their minds up.'

Nisha is pleased to see it's Mr Snell who sensibly makes a decision and points to the table that Nisha had her eye on for them. He strides across the room taking the lead, pulling out chairs from around the circular table as he goes around. The men sit; Mr Snell helpfully takes the chair which doesn't have its back to the room.

'He's quite attractive,' Claire mutters. 'I like a man who can make a decision.'

Nisha chuckles. 'Good, because he's yours. Are you ready?'

'Oh, yes.'

Nisha and Claire slide off their bar stools and with their drinks, they stroll over to the nearest table to the target's party. And just so they can't be missed, Nisha whispers to Claire, which results in Claire replying rather loudly: 'You're joking! Oh my God. I don't believe it.'

It has the desired effect. All four men turn and look around to find the source of this delightful laughter. Claire's hand is over her mouth as if to suppress her amusement. Nisha is giggling, holding her drink safely in the air.

'Stop it! You're making me spill my vodka.'

The blond man is grinning; his blue eyes sparkle with interest. Nisha slyly glances at the target. Mr Snell is looking over the rim of his glass at them, but he turns back to the bald man who is speaking. Mr Snell shrugs and pulls a face as if to say I don't know.

'Here will do,' Nisha says, pulling out a chair at the table which is directly in front of the target's. They won't be missed here. They sit opposite each other and cross their legs, their hems riding up to expose a length of slim leg. Nisha sips her drink and lazily gazes around, allowing her eyes to just rest on the target's table. The blond man is smiling at her. Mr Snell is still engaged in conversation with the bald guy.

'I wish I'd had a cocktail,' Claire is saying as she reads the drinks menu. 'I've never heard of some of these.'

'Ooh, show me,' Nisha says, leaning over for the glossy card. Deliberately, she extends a leg straight out across the carpet showing her entire leg and high heel to the target group. Out of the corner of her eye, the blond guy is nudging Mr Snell who leans around the bald guy to see. Both men smile.

'Is the cocktail with the filthiest name the one that gets you the most drunk?' Claire asks.

'Maybe. Bet it's guaranteed to pull the barman though. You try asking for Sex on the Beach!'

Claire turns in her seat to look at the bar staff. 'Ha ha! And get sand in my bikini bottoms? No, thanks! Anyway, they're a bit young for me. I like them more mature, definitely more sophisticated and one who knows how to treat a lady.'

Nisha sips her drink, really wishing it was a cocktail. 'Yeah, good luck with that, Claire!'

Claire leans across the table but doesn't lower her voice. 'Oh, I don't know,' and she nods at the table of men. This time Nisha blatantly looks at them, holding the gaze of the blond man whose smile is positively beaming. Mr Snell is sipping his drink, his dark eyes dancing with amusement.

Suddenly the blond man turns to his colleagues and reminds them of the time, that tomorrow's meeting is at half nine, the flight was long, shouldn't we make a move? The bald guy and the man in his fifties discuss this proposal and nod their approval. They stand up, hands are shaken and the blond guy suggests to the bald guy that he be responsible for making sure Angelo gets to his room safely.

'James and I are going to finish our drinks.' The blond guy slaps the back of the bald guy. 'Don't forget, Rod, that you have a baby at home, I'm sure you want to kiss the little 'un goodnight. See you tomorrow!'

Swiftly packed up and away without it even registering, the bald guy leads the Italian man out of the bar and away.

Nisha smiles at Claire. How helpful can one man be? But then sometimes the target can be the friend especially if that friend is more receptive to flirting.

'Can we join you?' asks the blond man and Nisha smiles up at him. His hand, she's pleased to see, is lightly resting on the back of the chair nearest to her.

'By all means.'

He sits and reaches for the bar menu, presenting it to her, open on the cocktail page. 'Let me buy you both a cocktail.'

'Ohh, how generous,' Claire coos excitedly.

Mr Snell stands at the side of the table, clutching his drink, unsure if he should join them or make excuses too.

'Hi, I'm Julia,' Nisha says to him, easing the chair towards him. 'This is Claire. Please sit down; you're making the place look untidy, and I doubt your friend can handle more than one woman.'

He laughs nervously and sits.

'I'll have you know there isn't a woman in this town that's too hot for me to handle!' the blond man boasts playfully. 'Anyway I'm Rich and this is James. What brings you both to the Azure? Do you live in Lexington?'

'Wow, you move right along to the key questions, don't you?' Nisha teases with a laugh.

'Yes, my mother always said I wasn't backwards in coming forwards!'

'We're just visiting; doing some early Christmas shopping, a couple of nights away lets the mice play. I haven't been to Lexington before and my brother has been nagging me for a while to give the town a try so we booked some time off and drove down yesterday.'

'Oh,' Rich says, 'I get you. Change of scenery and meeting new people can make all the difference. Have you chosen a drink yet?'

She looks at Claire and raises a surprised eyebrow: Claire and James reading the cocktail menu together. Blimey, Nisha thinks, she works quick.

'I'd like one with brandy in it...what's that one there...*Between the Sheets*?' Claire looks at Mr Snell. 'Sounds naughty.'

Mr Snell blushes and nods. 'Yes, it does. It might be a bit embarrassing asking for that one. How about a *Side Car*?'

'It doesn't sound half as sexy!'

'Let the woman have what she wants, James,' laughs Rich. 'And for you, Julia?'

'Always a Margarita for me,' Nisha replies. 'That's very kind of you. Let me give you a hand.' And she pushes back her chair and walks with Rich to the bar, standing where she can see Claire and Mr Snell chatting.

'Looks like my friend likes your friend,' Rich whispers to Nisha, handing the money over to the barman.

Nisha nods. 'Yes, they do seem to have clicked.'

'It'll do him good to chat to an attractive smart woman.' Nisha raises an eyebrow questioningly. 'He has a bit of an unhappy home life. Oh, I'm not spinning you a sob story, really I'm not. This job comes with a fair amount of pressure: sales targets to reach, you know that kind of thing.'

'And what line of work are you both in?' Nisha asks, placing the cocktails on the coasters.

'We're in lingerie,' Mr Snell announces.

'Ha ha! What now?' Nisha laughs.

'Stockings *and* suspenders? Or just a Basque?' giggles Claire.

Mr Snell blushes again and hurries to correct himself. 'I mean we work in lingerie.'

'That sounds worse, mate,' Rich tells him, shaking his head. 'I bet you've both got some picturesque images in your heads now, haven't you?'

Nisha and Claire nod through their laughter.

'You're so funny,' Claire tells Mr Snell, laying a hand on his arm.

He smiles shyly and looks away.

An hour and two cocktails later, Nisha comes up for air from her conversations with Rich about the monotony of work, what they'd do if they won the lottery and who in the world of celebrities they'd each like to spend the night with. She's found him pleasant company too. Normally she gets lumbered with the pompous bore whilst Claire has all the fun.

'Have you ever, I don't mean spent the night with a stranger, but just shared a few kisses with someone you've met in a hotel bar?' Rich asks.

'Not someone from a hotel bar. With a man I met at the theatre...and a man I met in a supermarket. I don't see what's wrong with it at all. Have you? Met someone in a hotel bar and shared a kiss?'

Rich shakes his head. 'No. Not yet.'

'There's a first time for everything,' she teases, glancing at Claire and James whose heads are almost touching as they speak into each other's ears. It's not as if the barman has turned up the volume of the jazz music and they can't hear each other. Claire has turned her entire body around to face James and their knees are touching. Claire deliberately twiddles her earring allowing a lock of blonde hair to fall from behind her ear and tickle her cheek.

Go on, Nisha urges him. Do it. Put it back. Touch her.

She can tell he's contemplating it. Claire continues to chat, blowing out of the corner of her mouth at it to stop it from tickling.

Do it, you idiot. Make a pass at her.

Claire touches her face where the tip of the lock brushes against her skin. Even Claire is indicating at James what needs to be done. Then James raises his hand hesitantly and carefully hooks the offending lock back behind Claire's delicate ear. He smiles gently.

Bingo, Nisha thinks. It's time to wrap this up. She looks at her watch, commenting that it's getting late.

'Actually I could do with a breath of fresh air before bed,' Claire says. 'Come with me?' she asks James.

'Best put your coat on. It's dropped cold,' he says, handing Claire her scarf before holding out her coat for her to slide her arms into the sleeves. It's such a natural gesture; Nisha can see how comfortable they are with each other already. She thinks it unlikely James will turn down a kiss.

Nisha allows Rich to walk her to the foyer. At the lifts, she turns to him. 'I must go; I have to ring home before I go to sleep. It was lovely to meet you, Rich.' She presses the button for the lift and its doors automatically open. As she steps inside and turns to give him a little wave, his hand darts inside and presents her with a business card.

'In case you're in town again.'

She smiles and presses the button for the 27th floor, a random floor high enough in the heavens for him not to run up dozens of flights of stairs after her. She brings her mobile out of her bag and dials Claire's number. Claire answers it straightaway.

'Hi honey. It's your husband. Hope you've been a good girl.'

'Yes, I have,' she replies clearly and then her muffled voice mutters, 'I've got to go. '

Ten minutes later Nisha meets Claire in the hotel car park huddled behind a white transit van where their photographer is also waiting. The driver's window lowers and a familiar face appears. Gerry the agency's photographer and security guy smiles. On the seat beside him is his camera. He was in the bar before Nisha arrived, sitting by the wine rack with a laptop and a Continental lager watching and waiting.

'Well?' Nisha asks them.

Gerry shakes his head regretfully.

'No.' Claire tells her, her expression miserable. 'He said he couldn't do it to his wife.'

Nisha shakes her head with disappointment. 'Unbelievable. He looked like he was really keen. I'd have put money on it.'

'Well, it's a good job you didn't,' Gerry says.

'I tried twice, but he just stepped back and put up his hands in case I jumped on him,' explains Claire.

Gerry nods, confirming Claire's testimony.

Nisha sighs. 'It appears that Mrs Snell has no reason to doubt her husband's fidelity after all. And I'd put money on that really pissing her off.'

Chapter 22

Fiona ~ Wednesday ~ day 10

For the second time in two minutes Claire's phone rings causing Fiona to huff with irritation and slams her clenched hands on the desk. She glares around at her colleagues to see if any of them intend to answer it in Claire's absence. Anne is busy typing along to the recording on her tape machine; the earphones' lead trails across the front of her pink sweater like a length of liquorice. Tara has been on her desk phone for the last ten minutes. Fiona assumes it's a personal call because she's turned her swivel chair to face the window as if her back can prevent her words from being listened to.

The ringing stops.

'Thank God for that,' Fiona mutters, turning back to her work. Her throat is dry and she considers making herself a sly drink. If I take my cup to the kitchenette now, Anne and Tara won't notice me return with a cup of tea. I don't see why I should offer to make a drink for them after what they've done to me, she thinks bitterly.

Fiona is still smarting from the outcome of the meeting with the Department Head. The stern reminder that they're supposed to be professional stings like a slapped cheek. The lecture rightly included the mortuary staff as well as the other secretaries, but it excluded Claire. And Fiona can't believe *she* escaped a telling-off. In her desperation she tried to explain to Prof that Claire had betrayed her confidence and was behind the offensive photo but the pathologist had raised a hand silencing her.

There's nothing else she can do, but promise herself not to have anything to do with any of them again. In fact she spent the evening uploading her CV onto countless job sites. The sooner she gets another job with decent people the better.

Fiona is reaching for her cup, decision made, when the office door opens and Claire waltzes in, glasses on top of her head. She doesn't glance at Fiona as she walks to her desk. And that angers Fiona, to be ignored when she's the one entitled to do the ignoring.

Claire's phone starts ringing again and Fiona sighs loudly, slamming the cup down on the desk. 'Can you answer your phone, please, Claire?' she demands angrily. 'That's the third time in two minutes it's rung. It's interrupting my work.'

If Claire reacts to Fiona's harsh words, she doesn't show it. She picks the phone up and says, 'Hello. Pathology secretary. Claire speaking.'

Fiona stands, cup and teabag in her hand and is about to walk out of the door when she notices the odd tone to Claire's voice.

'Who's here?' she questions. 'Oh. Well, I'm busy, I can't really speak to him...I see. I'm sorry. Yes. Yes, I'll come down to reception now.'

Fiona's ears prick up with interest. He? Who's he? He must be important to drag Claire away from her desk again.

Fiona watches as Claire slams the phone down, gets up and leaves. The door smacks into the hat stand behind threatening to topple coats onto Anne's head.

Fiona waits a few seconds, puts the cup back down and heads for the door. This I've got to see, she thinks, cautiously opening the door. She peers left then right down the corridor. Lab staff in white coats are crossing the corridor from room to room oblivious to her. Claire is almost at the end of the corridor; she opens the door and heads down the stairs.

She's in a hurry, Fiona thinks, heading the same way. I must be quick; I don't want to lose her.

She follows, treading on the balls on her feet. She keeps a safe distance in case Claire spots her or hears hurried footsteps. As Fiona enters the stairwell, she looks over the banister and sees Claire hurrying through the door one floor below.

Haematology reception, Fiona thinks, grabbing the handrail for safety. At the bottom she punches the door release button and steps into a public seating area where people are waiting for their blood screening appointments. The reception desk is in the far corner opposite the double-door entrance. Did he show up here? Fiona looks around, scanning the faces for Claire and this mysterious caller. From behind the support pillar, Claire appears striding past the notice board and outside.

Fiona steps forward but stops when an idea comes to her. She turns around, re-enters the stairwell and uses her swipe card to open a door that people often mistake for the exit. It leads into a room used for the collection of blood and tissue samples from the hospital's smaller sister hospital 20 miles away. From here the samples are whisked upstairs to the labs.

'Hello?' Fiona calls out warily, but there's no response so she enters, ensuring the door closes behind her. The dimly lit room is small containing two wide shelves on either side of the walls; these house the collection bags and trays, little stickers helpfully inform the drivers which sample goes where.

The other door opens outside, but more importantly onto a paved ramp. At the top of the ramp is the pavement where Fiona, if she's lucky, may at least be able to see who this man is even if she can't hear their conversation.

She presses down on the handle, pushes the heavy door open with her shoulder and steps outside. Fallen leaves and litter are cluttered against the bottom of the door. Though the entrance is protected directly from the wind, Fiona's skin quickly feels cold.

Should have popped my coat on, she thinks.

Nevertheless, she concludes it's worth a bit of pain if she can do a bit of ear wigging. And it looks as if her luck is in: Claire is stood less than ten metres away on the pavement; her arms folded against the cold.

Fiona quickly assesses her position. If she can get nearer and keep low, she should be able to hear a treat. There's no reason why Claire should look around. A large metal bin bolted to the iron railings which separate the path from the building offer Fiona some shelter.

Fiona squats and like a crab moves closer to her quarry. She stops where she can still see and hear.

A man is crossing the hospital road, a big smile on his face, a skip in his step.

'Thanks for coming down to speak to me. I'm sorry for bothering you when you're at work, but I didn't know what else-'

'What do you want, Ralph?' Claire demands, her tone unfriendly and rude.

Fiona looks him up and down appreciatively. Though she wouldn't ever admit it to anyone, Fiona has a thing for workmen.

He's slim with a broad chest and toned arms. His wet-look auburn hair reminds her of John Travolta from the film *Grease*. With his worn dark blue jeans, red T-shirt and black workman's boots, Fiona wonders if he is a mechanic, but she bets he isn't here to discuss Claire's car.

He's pleading with her.

'I told you I'd come down here if you didn't ring me. And you didn't so here I am.' He smiles proudly making Fiona wish a man would go to such lengths for her.

'Well, you needn't have bothered because I'm not interested in anything you have to say,' Claire replies angrily.

'Please, sweetheart...'

'Don't call me that!'

He puts his hands up apologetically. 'I'm sorry. Claire,' he sighs. 'You're all I think about.'

'For God's sake.'

'Please,' he pleads. 'Don't be like that. Don't you understand how important you are to me? I love you.'

Claire puts a hand up to her forehead and shakes her head.

Blimey, Fiona thinks, I wish someone declared their love for me like that.

'Ralph,' Claire begins, her voice edgy but firm, 'when I finish flings, or relationships if *you* insist on calling it that, I do it for good. I don't change my mind-'

He lays a hand on her sleeve and Claire shrugs his touch off as if his hand is on fire. 'Let me change your mind; I'll do anything.'

'Why can't you get it into your thick head that I don't want you? If you don't leave me alone then you'll know what I'll...' she threatens but Ralph grins.

Fiona dares to inch further forward; her ankles complain of cramp, but she ignores the pain.

'I don't care if you do it. It'll save me a job,' he laughs. 'I will happily give everything up for you...'

'No!' Claire suddenly shouts and steps away from him.

Fiona ducks her head down. Her heart is thumping; her ankles feel like they're going to snap in two.

'Look, you're freezing. We'll go inside, get a coffee and talk.' He holds up an arm as if to steer her toward the steps. Claire shakes the touch off even before contact is made. She jumps away rounding on him nastily.

'If you come near me again or contact me then I'll ring the police. Do you understand, Ralph?'

His shoulders sink with defeat. 'Claire, I love you.'

'Fucking leave me alone,' she screams, her face twisted with rage. She spins around and stomps back inside.

Fiona looks at Ralph. He looks crushed as if he's lost several inches in height. Her heart goes out to him. She doesn't deserve you, Fiona wants to tell him. If you knew what kind of a bitch she is you wouldn't be declaring your love for her!

He hurries away and Fiona stands up so she can see. Her numb ankles are so painful and she's bloody freezing, but she walks to the top of the ramp. Ralph throws open the driver's door of a red van, which is parked up on the kerb. The nearside rear tyre is missing a hubcap; dried splashes of mud adorn the doors and panels. The van starts with a splutter before pulling away, its tyres bouncing onto the road. She reads the signage painted down the side of the van in white letters. R. Pearson. Alarm Services.

Back at her desk, Fiona logs onto the patient database and types Ralph's name in the appropriate boxes. She estimates his age to be between 35 and 45, and if she can't locate him, she'll extend the age range.

The database has one promising result: Ralph Edward Pearson, age 41. It gives his date of birth, address and patient number. She makes a note of this number on a scrap of paper and opens up a tab regarding patient history. She clicks on the A & E tab and reads that in August this year he attended with a lacerated finger, the year before with a sprained ankle and under the tab entitled 'Admitted' Ralph had an inguinal hernia repair three years ago.

Let's see if he lives with anyone, Fiona says to herself with relish. She memorises the postcode and resets the boxes, typing in the surname and the postcode, and changing the sex to female.

A name appears. Antonia Pearson-Bell, aged 37. Is it a sister or a wife? She must have kept her maiden name, Fiona thinks. If she's recently had a hospital appointment or treatment that would indicate they live together, therefore they aren't separated. But Ralph must be single. Surely Claire wouldn't get involved with a married man.

She enters Antonia's patient number into the database and clicks on the maternity tab. The data is in three separate eras: nine years ago, six years ago and earlier this year. Antonia had three pregnancies resulting in three children with the youngest only being born earlier this spring.

Ralph is a married man with a family.

Fiona stares at the evidence, her upper lip twitching angrily. Claire has been having an affair with a married dad. The dirty fucking home wrecker. And Fiona has sat here every morning pouring her heart out to Claire after Nigel's departure, confiding his dirty tricks and his girlfriend's pregnancy to someone she thought she could trust. She even admitted how it made her feel; the confidence she lost, how depressed and even how suicidal she has felt, and all the while Claire has been guilty of causing similar crap to someone else. Or maybe his wife doesn't know. She continues cooking, cleaning and raising their children blissfully unaware her husband has today been begging his mistress to continue their relationship, declaring his love in a hospital car park.

Somehow it doesn't seem very fair.

Chapter 23

Nisha ~ Wednesday ~ day 10

Nisha regrets not conjuring up an excuse to avoid the second meeting with Mrs Snell, but as a partner of the agency and the operative on the honey trap, she's obliged to attend and explain why it failed to give the desired result. And she's in no doubt that the client will see this as a total failure on her part especially since she recommended Claire, and also because Mrs Snell was so sure her husband would be unfaithful.

'I can only assume that your photographer missed the shot. Whether he was cleaning his lens or had run out of film; the kiss happened and he missed it!'

'I can assure you, Mrs Snell, that our photographers are professionals and they use digital cameras so there's no chance of running out of film,' Mrs Hughes reassures her.

Mrs Snell glares at her. 'Well, with *whichever* type of camera they used, the shot was missed—'

Nisha interrupts. 'He did not miss the shot; it didn't happen. Your husband and my operative went outside and when she leaned in to kiss him, he put his hands up, stepped back and declined her. Well, you can see that from the photos,' and she taps the photo, even holds it up for Mrs Snell to see.

Mrs Snell huffs with annoyance, glances at the picture but doesn't allow her eyes to rest on it.

'Then I blame your operative,' she continues saying the word the way a wife would say prostitute if she discovered her husband had been seeing one. 'She did a poor job of enticing my husband and he only accompanied her outside out of politeness.'

Mrs Hughes looks to Nisha for her reply.

'It wasn't like that,' Nisha insists. 'They really connected, talked for ages and sat so close together you would have needed a crowbar to part them. When it was suggested he accompany her outside for some fresh air, he went willingly and I was confident that we would get a result, but it didn't happen. Our operative attempted to kiss him twice! Here. See,' and she thrusts forward the photo of Claire leaning towards Mr Snell, her lips pouted. 'He pushed her back and told her he couldn't do it to you.' Nisha's voice softens in the hope of reminding Mrs Snell that she should be rejoicing about his fidelity instead of being hugely disappointed.

Mrs Snell shakes her head. 'I know my husband; he can't resist a pretty blonde!'

Her words strike Nisha as being odd. Mrs Snell's reason for setting up her husband was to see if he was looking for someone else because she believed their marriage had gone stale. Is she suggesting that he's been unfaithful before; if he has then why come to an agency and set up a honey trap? Surely she'd have evidence from previous dalliances.

'I'm sure you do know your husband,' Mrs Hughes says diplomatically, 'but we can only report what actually happened and as I told you in our first meeting, at times our information will disappoint, enrage or please our clients. If you truly believe we have failed and your husband has the capacity to be unfaithful, or has in the past, then you must seek out another way to prove this. Maybe your husband is aware of your lack of trust in him and has sensed that you would try to gather proof.'

'If James has cottoned onto my lack of trust then it certainly isn't through my doing. I can only assume he saw the falseness in your operatives.'

'There was no falseness on our part,' Nisha butts in, incensed by this woman's ignorance. 'We did our job professionally and thoroughly. It's hardly our fault if your husband won't fall into the trap.' She wants to add that she's surprised he hasn't strayed before being married to her, but she doesn't. Her heart is thumping as she fights to keep her temper.

Mrs Hughes reaches across the front of the desk drawers to soothe Nisha by tapping her wrist and

Nisha is comforted that her partner is of the same mind.

'It's your fault if you and your operative gave the game away,' Mrs Snell accuses.

'We did no such thing,' Nisha replies vehemently. 'We were assertive and as predatory as possible without appearing obvious and desperate. Claire acted according to your instruction.'

'Claire!' Mrs Snell booms. 'I insisted on Rachel. I told you it was his favourite name and you didn't use it, so what else didn't you do? Was she blonde? Was she even female?'

'Mrs Snell, please,' pleads Mrs Hughes. 'You can clearly see from our photos that the operative is a blonde female. The name was an oversight on our part, but if your husband had been attracted to Claire then I'm sure he would have responded...'

'I paid good money, a lot of money, for a service that I haven't received. I paid for a Rachel and got a Claire. Now why was that?'

Maybe this is what she's after, Nisha thinks, because she hasn't got the desired result she wants a refund.

Nisha remembers that initially Claire had agreed to the new name, but later explained that she'd struggle to remember it since she was out the habit of using other names and didn't want to contradict herself and mess things up. Nisha isn't going to admit this since she'd promised them Claire was brilliant at honey trapping. She's not so brilliant that she can't remember to use an alias. And yet Claire remembered everything else such as the fake job, the pretend reason they were there. Why not the name?

'Mrs Snell, I can only apologise if you feel you've received a poor service, and that the result isn't what you were hoping for. You're welcome to the photographic evidence,' and Mrs Hughes again points to the photos.

'What use are they to me?' Mrs Snell shouts, flicking the edge of the photos with her fingertips so they slide backwards across the desk.

'It proves your husband is faithful,' Mrs Hughes replies.

'*You* might see a faithful husband who has turned down an extra-marital kiss, but all I see is detective agency who has failed to follow my instructions and subsequently wasted my money!' Mrs Snell stands and Nisha jumps up to hand the expensive black coat to her, but Mrs Snell pulls a face and snatches up her red scarf to wind around her throat before slipping her arms into the coat sleeves and tucking the red tassels inside. It reminds Nisha of something. Where has she seen a red scarf before? James helped Claire on with her coat after he'd handed her a red scarf. It was such a natural gesture. And Nisha remembers how Claire put on her coat in the flat: scarf then coat. It could be nothing. It was a lucky guess on James' part that Claire prefers her attire to be handed in that order, and he would guess that because that's how his wife likes it.

When the door closes Nisha looks at Mrs Hughes. 'I'll talk to Claire; see if she has any idea why he didn't kiss her.'

Mrs Hughes nods. 'I doubt she'll know why. But at least we can say we've tried.'

Nisha isn't confident either but something just isn't sitting right.

Chapter 24

Hock ~ Wednesday ~ day 10

Hock gives Claire the choice of venue for the next meeting. He knew she'd pick somewhere close to her home as she doesn't have access to a vehicle, and predictably she suggested a family pub within walking distance of her flat. He's happy with her choice; it's a location he can control, it's on his territory.

The Three Fish pub is situated on a small retail park along with a garden centre, an outdoor store and a shop that sells aquarium products. There's plenty of dark corners and space in which he can execute some gentle persuasion if required.

He lets Claire choose the table and she sensibly picks one near to the entrance. It's too big for three people to sit around. It's for eight people really but Hock allows this. It amuses him that she sits nearest to the door on a chair rather than the bench seat which is out of his grasp. But Hock's hand can reach farther than she can imagine. He also notices that she's wearing trainers, proper running shoes. Leo told him he's seen Claire out running so he anticipates her making a dash for it and with her trainers on she obviously thinks she can out run him.

Leo sits a couple of spaces over, his eyes wandering to the menus propped up in a wooden stand in the middle of the table. Hock doesn't tell him to move them. He can see Claire's worried face just fine.

'What have you got to tell me, then?' he asks, sipping his lager and wiping a line of froth off his upper lip.

Claire swallows and her reply comes out in an automated fashion. She's rehearsed this, he thinks. She must be lying.

'This is the post-mortem report on your mother.' She slides a brown envelope towards him.

His heart starts thumping, a hand pins it to the table and brings it nearer. Good start. 'Give me the gist of it.'

'The pathologist's notes fully back up the cause of death. For example, the heart weighed 600 grams which suggests a heart problem.'

'She was never diagnosed with a heart problem. My mother was a very active woman. Not on any medication for her heart at all.'

Claire swallows again. She's growing nervous. But like her Hock has rehearsed his responses to her lies too. 'That doesn't mean she didn't have a problem. She was an elderly lady. It's normal for someone of that age to have occluded...I mean narrowed arteries...'

'I know what occluded means. I've studied the medical terms.'

'Her arteries were severely narrowed which means enough blood wasn't getting to her heart which is why it was working so hard and became enlarged.'

He nods. 'I see. What did it say about the cancer?'

'It was confined to the caecum. There were no signs of a spread.'

'Very peculiar since she was in constant agony; doubled over most days, bed ridden, vomiting, shitting herself. She even started to go yellow.'

A flash of something crosses Claire's face like someone has quickly opened a door letting a blast of white light in and then it's gone like the door has been slammed shut. Deliberately using the word yellow has struck Claire as he intended. And her reaction confirms that she's lying.

'Yellow means jaundice, doesn't it?' he asks. 'And that means your liver's fucked and we all know when your liver's fucked so are you. So, why don't you stop fucking lying to me and tell me what you really found out? Forget the report! It isn't worth shit. What did it say in her notes? Did you even find them or were they mysteriously lost?' Hock struggles to keep his voice to an acceptable volume.

Claire leans back in the chair, taken aback by the force of his voice like a tree bent under a raging hurricane. A waiter hurries by, focused on delivering the sizzling steaks on his tray. 'I found the notes,' she replies and her voice wobbles with nerves. 'They weren't lost.'

'They might have been doctored. Excuse the pun.' Hock glances at Leo who smiles. He gets the joke. 'Did you bring me a copy of them?' His voice rises at the end of the sentence in a condescending way.

'No. But you can request to see them.'

'Did you question your pathologist, the surgeon?'

She shakes her head vigorously and Hock frowns.

'I'm very disappointed that you're not taking this as seriously as I hoped. There's a reduction to your debt at stake here. You're not exactly earning it. I want some info in return...'

'I have given you information,' Claire insists.

'You've given me bullshit. As far as I can tell you've made this up on your way over here tonight.'

'I have not!'

'Did you question the mortuary technicians?'

'Yes! They said the cancer hadn't spread. It was confined...'

'To the caecum. I know. Is the technician shagging the pathologist?'

'What? No.'

'Are you sure? Can you prove it?'

'What?'

'Can you prove the technician isn't fucking the pathologist?'

'No!'

'Then how can you prove there wasn't anything to see?'

'Because Isla said...'

'Isla,' Hock says slowly. 'Nice name.'

And he can see that she's kicking herself for falling into a well sprung trap.

'Maybe I'll ask Isla.'

'She won't know anything.'

'But she was there. She opened my mum up, so unless she's as blind as a bat I'd expect her to have noticed something like a massive tumour or a fucked liver.' He glares at her.

Claire doesn't back off under his glare this time and rather than finding himself respecting her confidence it narks him. She doesn't give a toss. She hasn't investigated anything to the depth he'd have liked. She probably read the cause of death before leaving her flat tonight and casually enquired about his mother in passing.

'I think for peace of mind you should request to see her notes. You can even ask to see the surgeon. They don't mind answering the family's questions. If you can tell when someone's lying to you, you should be able to tell with him.'

'You don't sound as if you like him,' Hock states gently.

'He has a reputation for arrogance. He even...' Claire hesitates and Hock finds himself holding his breath. Is she going to tell him something? A little taster?

'...is a typical surgeon. Thinks he's God's gift.'

'Aren't they all?' Hock finishes his lager and glances at his watch. 'I don't think there's anything more you can tell me so you can get off if you want. I'll give some thought to your suggestion. I can't let this rest.'

Claire nods. Her right foot is curling around the chair leg getting ready to push it back and get to her feet and leg it.

'Bye Claire,' he says and she's on her feet, walking quickly away.

Before she even reaches halfway across the floor, Hock is on his feet too and exiting through the other door, hurrying down the well-lit path around to the pub's frontage. Claire is heading towards the path home; he keeps close to the building, shrouded by the shadows.

She's breathing heavily and starts jogging. His hand darts out snake quick and grasps her thin wrist, pulling her towards him.

'Get off!' she shouts.

He shushes her. 'It's only me. One more thing...'

'You're hurting me,' she complains, trying to prise her wrist from his tight grip.

'What were you really going to say about the surgeon?' he whispers in her ear. Her hair tickles his nose.

'What?'

'You fucking heard. I know you were going to say something else; I saw something cross your face: a thought, an opinion, something. Something that might help me. You know what he did and you thought the better for telling me so what is it?' He tightens his hold making Claire squeal.

'There isn't any...'

'Spill it and you can have your reduction.'

Claire's tearful eyes meet his; he can feel her trembling.

'He rang the mortuary. He wanted to speak to the pathologist. It could be nothing, it probably isn't...'

'They're covering up.'

'I don't know.'

'Sounds like it.' And violently he throws away her wrist like he's releasing a lasso.

Claire rubs her sore wrist, bites her lip to prevent herself from crying.

'One more thing...'

She looks up as his right hand connects with the side of her head. The blow takes her feet from under her and sends her sprawling across the damp pavement. Hock stands over her and grins. He's wanted to do that since the first time he met her.

'That's for fucking lying to me.' He steps over her like she's dog muck, but before returning to the warm pub he turns and says: 'By the way, Leo sold your debt. You owe me now. I'll see you soon.'

Chapter 25

Claire ~ Wednesday ~ day 10

Claire staggers home, her head pounding. She wipes her tears on the cuff of her fleece; her nose is running and she's terrified Hock will be waiting at the flat. She crosses the road without paying attention. A car horn rebukes her and that makes the tears start again.

She makes it home safely and there doesn't appear to be any sign of Hock. The mobile in her pocket vibrates and she tugs it out of her pocket. It's a text from Ralph.

'Antonia knows about us. She got an anonymous text. Don't ring me'

'Why would I ring you, Ralph?' she mutters and shoves open the communal door.

She quickly locks the front door behind her and jabs at the light switch. The sudden brightness stings her eyes. The pain in her head is radiating in all directions now. She feels lucky that she hasn't lost consciousness. She goes into the bathroom and leans close to the mirrored medicine cabinet to inspect her eye. The outside corner of her eye socket is red and there's a broken blood vessel under the skin. A lilac area of bruising is starting to appear below the bottom eyelid. She fingers it gently but winces under the touch. She doesn't care who's told Antonia about the affair. That's if she does even know and Claire wouldn't put it past Ralph to have told Antonia himself. And now that she's kicking him out, he's looking for a bed for the night and a resurrection of their affair.

'You can bugger off,' she says out loud, sitting down on the toilet.

The silence overwhelms her and she feels utterly alone. She wants a hug from someone who matters, her dad, even Mr Weeks with his strong arms, but most of all she wants Will. If he was here, he'd no doubt tell her how stupid and reckless she'd been but not before fetching a paracetamol, wiping away her tears and giving her a cuddle. But he's not. And that makes her tears return hard and noisy, reverberating off the cold tiles and echoing around her.

'I miss you,' she sobs, the pain crushing her chest. 'Why did you have to go away, Will? I need you. I can't do this without you.'

It's hopeless, she concludes, sniffing hard, her shoulders shudder. It's hopeless. I want to walk out the door and never come back.

Chapter 26

Claire ~ Thursday ~ day 11

Claire hardly sleeps that night. Her mind is too active, replaying the vicious assault, Hock's revelation and Ralph's text, although she's less worried about his message. She urgently needs to talk Leo round, beg him not to sell her debt to that lunatic. She knows she will always end up owing Hock, and money is not how he'll want to be paid. He'll want information. She can't, won't give him that. There'll be little point in scrounging off family and saving madly to pay off her debt. Hock will greedily grab the cash with a grin and crank up the interest.

'Give me Erikson's address and I'll knock this month's interest off,' Hock will say.

She may as well quit her job and go on the dole, declare herself bankrupt, move back in with her mum and Andrew, and spend her days watching daytime telly. Her life would be over. *Unless I do a runner,* she thinks checking her eye in the mirrored glass of the pathology building. Her first attempt at applying foundation turned her skin orange. The second attempt was better. The eye shadow covered the bruised eyelid, but made her look like she was dolled up for a night out. Eventually she settled on her normal amount of foundation, but came up with a plausible excuse instead. Lots of people accidentally hit themselves in the eye. Her mum did it two years ago and so Claire has borrowed her excuse.

She climbs the stairs to the office, keeping her head down, wishing her hair was longer. It would cover that side of her face wonderfully well.

Anne is walking towards her, carrying the kettle. 'Morning, love. How are you?' she cheerily calls out.

Claire thinks about drawing attention to her eye, laughing about the stupid clumsy way in which she injured herself. It'd get it out the way sooner, but Anne has already pushed open the office door and as Claire follows her inside, she sees that everyone is in.

She goes to her desk, silently telling herself to raise her head, look your colleagues in the face, show them your eye, get it out the way, but she can't. Because no one has noticed she's following their lead. She switches on her computer and sorts out her work as Anne makes the morning drinks.

'Here you go, love,' says Anne.

The warming aroma of coffee wafts tantalisingly under Claire's nose and without thinking she raises her head. 'Thanks, Anne.'

'Oh, lovey,' Anne cries. 'What's happened to your eye?' Her hand instinctively reaches out to soothe it and Claire backs away, her fingers flying to cover the bruise.

'It's...it's nothing...an accident...'

'It looks nasty. What happened?'

Tara waddles over, hand on the small of her back, to join the little discussion.

Claire launches into her excuse.

'I was hoovering the flat last night. There was dried mud everywhere from my muddy trainers; the end of the Hoover was stuck on. I was heaving and tugging, and eventually the bloody thing flew off and I punched myself in the eye.'

'Ow!' agrees Anne, pulling an anguished face.

'I don't know my own strength sometimes.'

'They don't come off easily,' agrees Anne. 'My husband puts them on for me and I can't get them off either. He's too strong sometimes.'

Tara pulls a concerned face. 'I bruised my eye a few years ago by walking into an open cupboard door. No one believed me. They all said my boyfriend must have lamped me because the cupboard door excuse is a classic lie!'

'Surely, Claire,' Fiona begins, raising her voice so everyone turns to her, 'your boyfriend's wife hit you, didn't she?' Tara and Anne turn to her quizzically. 'When she found out you were screwing her husband.'

Claire's heart turns to stone and she holds herself perfectly still, feet frozen to the floor, arms tense by her sides. How does Fiona know?

Tara and Anne are waiting for Claire's reply, but she can't speak. If she could, she'd laugh and jokingly ask which boyfriend Fiona is referring to because she has one for every day of the week, but her mind is a void.

Tara breaks the awkward silence. 'Sounds like you have some juicy gossip, Fi. Where have you heard that from? Or have you made it up?'

'I haven't made it up!'

'It sounds spitefully bitter,' Anne remarks.

Tara nods. 'If you have made it up, that's slander.'

Claire uses these seconds to pull herself together. She keeps her voice calm and even.

'I was seeing a married man,' she admits and her colleagues' eyes widen. 'Well, he was separated, and up until last night his wife didn't know. Someone kindly sent her an anonymous text. And sadly that's ruined any chance of reconciliation they had.'

'Wow, Fiona,' says Tara, 'have you been meddling in other people's lives?'

'No!' Fiona shouts. 'I have not. Be very careful about accusing me of something I haven't done.'

'Likewise, Fi. You'd best get back to those reports. I want them typed by the end of the day,' Tara orders. 'They've been sat on your desk since last week and the pathologists are getting hassled for the results.'

Claire smirks to herself as Fiona skulks back to her desk, her face red. She can't prove Fiona text Antonia because how has Fiona even discovered the affair? Unless Ralph said something the day he rang the office, or someone from haematology gossiped to Fiona, telling her an angry man turned up to see Claire or...she...no she couldn't have seen or heard their conversation yesterday. But Fiona must know something or her wild stab in the dark has struck the target perfectly. Either way Fiona has slandered Claire and Claire knows exactly how to deal with that.

*

Claire's smile is smug, and her arms swing confidently by her sides as she marches back to the office, heels clacking noisily on the floor. The meeting had a positive outcome and that boosts her confidence. Now she's off to deliver the bad news.

Claire throws open the door and looks around. Good. There's only *her* here. The office stinks of Fiona's spicy vegetable soup. She's sweeping the fallen breadcrumbs off her desk with the cupped side of her hand and depositing them into the bin.

Claire strides over, keeps her smug smile in place.

'I've been to HR and made a formal complaint about you,' Claire informs her.

Fiona's jaw drops and her hands fall loosely onto the arms of the chair. 'What the hell for? I haven't —'

'You know why. It's called bullying.'

'Bullying!' she cries, her features distorted with anger. 'I've never bullied you. You on the other hand...'

'But I've spoken to HR first. Anything you say now will look like what it is: pointless revenge. The mortuary staff admitted gossiping about you. I had nothing to do with it, but as you've never believed me, you decided to make up vicious lies about me and spread it around the department.'

'You admitted having an affair with a married man,' Fiona points out hurriedly. 'Everybody heard you.'

'That's not a disciplinary offence, unlike using the patient database to find out information about Nigel and his girlfriend. I've informed HR about that too.'

'I have never...'

Claire laughs. 'Come on, Fiona. Considering you're weeks from your Decree Absolute and that you only correspond through your solicitors, you know an awful lot about what's going on in their lives.' Claire counts the incidences off on her fingers. 'You knew he'd moved address, that she was pregnant, Nigel's wisdom tooth extraction, and her fractured ankle. I could never understand how you "conveniently" discovered all this, until the other day, when I saw her patient record open on your computer. Who else are you spying on? Me?'

'No!'

'Well, my life isn't as interesting as Nigel's. I'd be careful if I were you, Fiona. HR knows about you now, and IT has ways of tracking your movements.'

Chapter 27

Ralph – Thursday ~ day 11

The car comes to a stop with a violent thrust forward, its nearside tyres mount the kerb, the front bumper narrowly misses the lamppost; it doesn't stop the occupants from arguing.

'Jesus, Antonia! Calm down, will you? You're going to cause an accident.'

'Piss off, Ralph. Which is hers? Her flat? Which one is it?' Antonia demands.

'Number eight,' he sighs.

She's out the car and marching around the boot towards the communal door before Ralph can even undo his seatbelt. He feels sick to his stomach as he hurries after her. Antonia is so angry she's liable to take a swing at Claire, and Claire...what's she going to tell Antonia? Will she have the sense to deny it? Or will she take great delight in telling all? That'd be a sure way of hammering into his head that their affair is over.

By the time he catches up with her, Antonia is banging on Claire's front door.

'Come out and face me, you bitch. I know you're there. The light is on. GET OUT HERE!'

'Antonia! For fuck's sake, stop that.' He eases her away from the door, but her foot lashes out and her soft toed trainer strikes his shin. 'She's not in.'

'How do you know that? Did she tell you that? Did you tell her I was on my way over?'

'No! She'd come to the door if she was here.'

'She's fucking cowering in her bathroom probably, too afraid to come out here and face me. You've ruined my marriage, you bitch!'

'What the hell is going on?' a voice demands angrily and they look around to see a young man standing in the doorway of the opposite flat. He wears a crumpled football shirt and his hair is tousled. 'I happen to be on nights; I can do without this shit. Shut the fuck up.'

'Piss off back to bed then,' Antonia spits back.

'Is she your wife?' he asks Ralph who sadly nods. 'Then fucking rein her in or I'm calling the police.' He slams the door. Ralph feels defeated already, preferring the police option. She won't leave till she speaks to Claire and it's obvious she's out which is what he hoped but he doesn't want to be here all night staking out her place.

'Antonia, he's going to call the police and if you're arrested for disturbing the peace you won't see the children tonight. She's out. She's left a light on to fool potential burglars, that's all. Let's just go home.'

'I'm not leaving till I speak to her. Get out here!' She pounds the door again.

The communal door squeaks as nosy neighbour Bev appears asking gently if she can help.

'We're after...' he begins.

She smiles. 'So I heard. I'm afraid Claire's out. I spoke to her about an hour ago and she told me she was going out for the evening. She won't be home till very late.'

Ralph wonders if she's exaggerating how long Claire will be out for, so if it's hours then Antonia won't want to wait. They've left their eldest child looking after his siblings, which isn't ideal and Ralph is anxious to get back. He can't help wondering with jealousy if Claire has gone out with the man with the Jag.

'Her light is on,' Antonia insists. She's stopped kicking and banging the door.

'Security, love. There have been a couple of recent break-ins. Although I think you may have alerted our local burglars that her flat is empty now,' Bev jokes.

'I need to speak to her. I wanted to have it out with her now,' Antonia explains unnecessarily and Ralph rolls his eyes, hoping that his wife doesn't tell this nosy bitch about the affair because she knows who Ralph is and she knows exactly what's been going on. She could confirm everything.

Antonia won't need to talk to Claire. It occurs to him that Antonia may ask her if she knows Ralph, has she ever seen him visit Claire's flat. What will she say?

'I must go. I'm missing my show,' the neighbour says. 'Sorry that you've had a wasted journey.'

'Not to worry,' Antonia says. 'If you see her tell her I've called by. And I'll keep calling by until she explains to me how she can have an affair with my husband. I'm devastated, not to mention my three children.'

The only weird thing the kids noticed was their mum's insistence that Ralph take her out straight after tea. And that George was in charge. His face lit up with the responsibility although he wouldn't find much joy in bossing around a baby. Antonia was adamant that the children didn't pick up that anything was wrong.

'If I see her,' the neighbour says. Warn her is a more appropriate word, Ralph thinks and judging by her face that's what she thinks too.

The communal door closes and Ralph looks at Antonia who is staring at the door like she wants to attack it again. 'Let's go home.'

'I will be coming back. I will have it out with her,' she promises and then leans towards the closed door and whispers to it as if the wood will remember her words and replay it for when Claire returns. 'I'm not going away, bitch.'

Chapter 28

Olivia ~ Friday ~ day 12

Olivia digs around in the bottom of her wardrobe for her knee length boots. She'd forgotten about them till she saw a colleague wearing hers and thought how nice they'd be to wear in this cold windy weather. On the carpet behind her, a pile of discarded clothing and shoes is growing.

'Yeah, so Mum's invited us all round for dinner tonight: you, me, Dan and Fergus,' she says, her voice muffled by the confines of the wardrobe. 'But it's too short notice. I've got something on and Dan's out.'

'Fergus is out too; he's got a stag night. It's just me then. Oh joy.' Sally pulls a mocking face of disappointment. She picks up what looks like a thin red rag and unscrews it. It's an asymmetrical top that Liv bought a couple of years ago in a sale.

'I haven't seen that in ages,' Liv says excitedly, grabbing the top from Sally and holding it up. She pulls a face. 'I only wore it once. The strap keeps sliding down.' She screws it back up and chucks it onto a clear patch of carpet. 'I'll use it as a duster.'

'You said you had something to tell me,' Sally reminds her impatiently. 'What is it? Or did you just want a lift to work?'

Liv laughs. 'I did want a lift, yes. It wears me out catching the bus; it's always rammed. Claire was at Mum's last night.' Liv drags a heaving black bin bag out of the wardrobe, unties the knot and looks inside.

'What was she doing there?'

'Apparently Mum invited Claire for dinner, you know as she hasn't seen any of us for ages. At least she hasn't tried to get us all there together. Claire saw it as an opportunity to work on Dad.'

'How do you know? Or are you just guessing?'

Liv sighs and pulls a long box out from underneath a box of photo albums and flings off the lid. 'Ah-ha!' She slips the boots on but doesn't zip them up till she's given Sally what she's waiting for. 'I don't know exactly, I'm just speculating; but after dinner, Claire went upstairs with Dad and they were in his study for ages,' she says dramatically.

Sally sighs. 'So what? If you don't have any evidence, then they could have been talking about next week's snow for all you know.'

'Mum happened to mention the mood Claire was in when she left...happy. Like all her Christmases had come at once, and she thanked Dad over and over.'

Sally smiles. 'I wonder what he did to deserve all that gratitude.'

'I can picture Claire topping up Dad's wineglass, complimenting him on his choice of red to accompany the beef, telling him how great he looks in his mustard coloured trousers.'

Sally laughs.

'By the end of the meal, he was putty in her hands; they went to his study, faced each other across the mahogany desk and haggled over how much Claire was going to sting him for like a couple of carpet merchants.' Liv looks down at her legs squeezed into the boots and walks across the room. 'They pinch a bit but I'll wear them in.'

'We've no way of finding out how much he's given her or how she changed his mind without asking one of them, and I know what they will say,' Sally replies sadly. 'Come on, we'd better get a move on.'

Liv looks at the mess on the carpet. It looks like the remnants of a frantic jumble sale. She hasn't got the time or the inclination to tidy it up now. She steps over it and returns to the lounge, but as soon as her eyes see the mess in here too she wishes Sally had stayed in her car and beeped the horn from outside. Dan and a couple of his layabout friends came round last night to play stupid video games, and they've left the room in a tip. There are beer cans and bottles everywhere: the floor, tucked between the arm of the settee and its cushions, on the windowsill lined up like a row of vases and one even upturned and stuck in Liv's rubber plant pot.

Liv reaches for the bottle stuck in the plant pot in some half-hearted attempt to tidy up, but Dan promised to do it and she'll make sure he does once he returns from fetching his breakfast.

'Do you think we should talk to Dad?' Sally asks. 'We could air our concerns in a daughterly fashion.'

'What would be the point? He'll only shut his office door in our face. We might get more joy if we confront Claire,' Liv suggests. 'There are things I never got a chance to say to her that I'd like to.'

'If we go looking for a row, Claire won't tell us anything.'

The front door opens and slams shut. The smell of bacon wafts down the hall.

'I want answers. I want to know why she's swanning around in expensive jewellery and we're practically living on the breadline. It's not fucking fair,' Liv replies, her voice rising with annoyance.

'Fucking hell,' Dan says as he strolls into the lounge and drops his coat on one chair and his body on another. 'Are you two still going on about her?'

'We think she fleeced more money out of Dad last night,' Liv explains.

'Then have it out with the thieving bitch instead of gossiping behind her back,' he suggests, unwrapping the greasy paper and unleashing the full aroma of the bacon sandwich.

Liv wrinkles her nose. 'Is there egg on that?'

'Damn right.' He opens his mouth as wide as possible and takes a large bite.

Liv watches as runny yolk squirts out between his fingers. The smell turns her stomach and she hurries from the room. She can't stand the smell of egg and lately it's gotten worse. She takes her coat off the back of the bedroom door and her handbag from under the bed where she stored it for security reasons. Dan's mates are okay but she wouldn't trust any of them, which is about as far as she'd trust Dan these days.

She doesn't know if going to see Claire is a good idea, whether they'll learn anything. If she's honest she doesn't want to see Claire again. Those comments she made at her Mum's birthday were nasty lies. But Liv can't deny feeling a strong sense of injustice that their Dad is giving Claire money whilst watching his other daughters struggle miserably.

She returns to the lounge where Dan has finished his breakfast. It hasn't taken him long to eat the sloppy mess; it must barely touch the sides.

'Make sure you do,' he's saying to Sally and winks.

Liv sees a strange look on Sally's paling face and realises with dread that he's made some sort of pass. He promised never to do that, but a lot of alcohol was consumed last night and he's probably still under the influence.

'Make sure you what?' Liv asks, but she's distracted by the greasy wrapper on the arm of the chair. 'Dan! Put it in the bin. I want this place spick and span when I get home. You promised.'

'Yes, your Ladyship.' He yawns and kicks off his grubby battered trainers, leaving them untidily on the floor. 'See ya later.'

Liv ushers her sister out of the flat, humiliated by her boyfriend's appalling behaviour and wondering what on earth she still sees in him. Fancy making a pass at your girlfriend's sister when she's only in the next room. Disgusting pig!

'Sorry if Dan made a pass at you. He had a lot to drink last night.'

'It's alright, Liv. It's always flattering to have a compliment.' Sally pushes open the outside door and they're immediately greeted by a biting blustery wind. Litter and fallen leaves are flying through the air.

'They've forecasted a white Christmas,' Liv tells her as they walk towards Sally's old Astra.

'I hope not. I hate driving in the snow. I hate standing outside in the freezing evening chipping ice off my car. Thank God for garages. Mine will be nice and snug in there.'

Liv thinks about her car which was stolen two weeks after moving into this neighbourhood. Bored kids, the local beat officer had told her unsympathetically as if it were her fault she could afford to run an old Fiesta.

Her thoughts wander again back to Claire and she makes a decision.

'You're right. We need to speak to Claire,' Liv says. 'This speculation is stupid. We're sisters, we should be able to talk to each other, and if Dad isn't lending her money and she can offer a more sensible explanation then maybe it can go some way to mending our relationship.'

Sally smiles and unlocks the car. 'I'll text her, see when she's free over the weekend.'

Chapter 29

Claire ~ Friday ~ day 12

Claire lifts the lid of her wicker laundry basket, which was her childhood hiding place, and places the envelope underneath her dirty clothes. Later, she'll put the wet towel and her sweaty running kit on top. She doubts any burglars will want to search through it, but it's just a precaution. It won't remain in her possession for long because tomorrow she'll be handing the money to Leo, insisting he calls off Hock. From then on she will have to live within her means.

With all that money in her linen basket, Claire has considered the other options. It's too tempting not to. The obvious choice is to go away, but where? Again the answer is obvious: abroad, somewhere hot, escape from this cold weather that's only going to get colder and now snow is due. She shivers. The money wouldn't stretch to making it into a permanent trip. How would she live? What work could she do? Bar work is no good in winter. She's thought about contacting Ryan, inviting herself out there. He'd be over the moon to see her. She smiles at the thought of the sun on her shoulders, burning a hole in her head like a laser, making her sleepy, the warm sea lapping at her feet.

What about Will?

Her heart sinks. She can't walk away from him. He needs her support for when he comes out, and she needs him. She knows she does. She reminds herself that her mission was to find a holiday for both of them. All she's done is fetch some brochures on cruises.

I'm a useless friend, she concludes, too wrapped up in myself. And I ought to get a move on if I want to be back, showered and fed in time for the start of the new murder mystery.

She plonks down on the bed and pulls on her running shoes. Out the corner of her eye she spots her wage slip poking out of her handbag and thinks about work today. It was lovely without Fiona who had phoned in sick, citing a stomach bug, but Claire knew the real reason she wasn't in. She was either taking union advice, was busy looking for alternative employment or panicking herself into a mad frenzy about Claire's grievance. Perhaps she was doing all three.

Serves her right, Claire thinks, getting to her feet and strapping on the sports watch. She won't turn it on till she's outside. The GPS can't locate her position so she'll do some stretches whilst the satellites find her.

She leaves the hall and living room lights on as security, locks the front door, zipping the key inside the back pocket of her running tights. Pushing open the communal door, Bev is limping from her car to her flat.

'Hi Bev,' she calls, switching the watch on. 'I'll call for the car key about nine in the morning if that's ok.'

'Hello lovey. You can have it now if you want. I won't be going anywhere tonight.'

'You never know. You might get an urgent call.' Bev's elderly mother is in hospital and Claire knows that Bev dreads a hospital phone call. 'Tomorrow is fine.'

'Alright, then. I'll be up. Enjoy your run,' and she waves her stick in the air as a goodbye.

'See you later,' Claire calls as the start screen appears on her watch.

'Oh, by the way, Claire,' Bev shouts, turning from the front door, 'you had a visitor whilst you were out last night. She wasn't very happy...'

'Tell me about it tomorrow. Gotta go. Bye!' And Claire sets off, starting the timer.

Chapter 30

Nisha ~ Friday ~ day 12

As she locks the office door and drops her keys into her handbag, Nisha remembers her promise to speak to Claire about the "failed" honey trap. And since Claire's flat is kind of on the way home, Nisha decides to make the slight detour. With any luck, her fiancé will clock the lateness of Nisha's arrival home and order a takeaway. Beef in black bean sauce with egg fried rice would be lovely, she thinks, indicating right at the end of the road and waiting for the approaching car to pass by but it turns left into her junction.

'Thanks for the sign, moron,' she complains, glad it's dark enough that they can't see her mouthing off. 'Why can't people indicate? Is it really too much trouble?'

Her Mini turns right and she flicks on the full beam to light up the poorly lit road ahead. The flats have only one allocated parking space each and since most couples have two cars, it's inevitable the street is used as an overflow car park.

A few yards before Claire's flat, she spies a space on the left and parks up. She tucks her handbag underneath the passenger seat and opens the car door. She's about to put a leg onto the pavement when a noise attracts her attention. The loud squeak of the communal door cuts across the residents' car park and alerts her to another's presence. A man is walking towards his car from the flats. A familiar man.

Quickly, she yanks her leg back inside and carefully closes the door so her face isn't lit up by the courtesy light. The view will be better in the darkness.

She grabs the steering wheel and pulls herself closer to the windscreen to peer at him. It certainly looks like him. Although he is several yards away and the light isn't brilliant, Nisha is very observant and remembers details about people such as their clothes, the way they carry themselves. It's an important part of her job. She remembers him wearing a long dark coat with a stripy scarf, the kind popular with rugby fans, and the confident way he walks, his arms swinging.

She squints. Is it him? What's he doing *here*? Is this why the honey-trap didn't work? When they stood outside in the hotel's garden in near freezing temperatures, did Claire confess it was a trap and that she genuinely felt attracted to him? And if he felt the same, then the last thing he should do is reciprocate her kiss. But if he did like her and fancied meeting up properly then this was her address.

Nisha dismisses the idea. Claire has never fallen for targets before and there have been better looking and wealthier targets than Mr Snell.

Nisha was gobsmacked when she discovered he hadn't kissed Claire. There was definitely something odd about that. What kind of man turns down a sly one-off kiss with a gorgeous girl like Claire because of a saggy necked acid-tongued harridan like Mrs Snell?

Mr Snell did, a voice reminds her. But maybe not for the reason he gave Claire. Perhaps he did like her, but couldn't risk the kiss being caught on film because his wife would take him to the cleaners in the divorce court. Could Mr Snell have followed Claire home? Perhaps he slipped his contact details to Claire and she liked him enough to meet up later, another night, maybe tonight. This could be him leaving.

Mr Snell points at a stylish car parked in the last space on the right. Its indicator lights flash and the doors unlock. Seconds later the reversing lights come on and Mr Snell leaves. Nisha keeps her head low and watches his departure.

'It's him, alright,' she says, noting his personalised plate. 43JLS.

She gets out and approaches Claire's flat, ready to demand that Claire tell her exactly what is going on, but several minutes later Nisha leaves herself, unable to get a response from knocking the door or phoning both Claire's mobile and landline. Despite only the hall light being on, she concludes that Claire must be in the bathroom and can't hear.

Five months later

Chapter 31

Will ~ Tuesday ~ day 1

'Who's she again?' I ask, leaning over the side of the settee for the half empty bottle of Shiraz.

Mum presses the pause button, freezing the picture so she can patiently explain who the character is and that she's pregnant by her stepbrother.

'She's grown up quickly, hasn't she? Last time I saw her she was in nappies.'

Mum laughs. 'You haven't been away that long.' She unfreezes the picture and the characters continue to argue noisily.

It may be an exaggeration, but Mum's soap operas make me feel as if I've been away decades.

I top our glasses up and push hers closer. The wine and the soaps were her idea. She's got a few days off and it doesn't matter what I watch. It's all new to me.

'And what's this called again? Austrian Roll?' I point at the cake in the middle of the coffee table.

'Swiss roll,' she enunciates clearly. 'It's from Switzerland. They were invented before you went away. Don't you remember them?'

'The jam ones, yes, but this lemon curd one is a new concept.'

She laughs again and gently shakes her head at my humour. She's so pleased to have me home: I'm her much needed ally.

'We could go for an Indian tomorrow. I've heard about this new bread they do. It's called a naan and in some restaurants they're massive!' I know she hasn't been for a curry for a long time. It isn't an easy place to take Dad.

'If I say yes, will you let me finish my soap? I've only got one episode after this and I'm up to date. If you're bored you could always pack your stuff away. I take it you're staying?'

'Well, I was going to see how things went. The screws told me I could have my cell back if I missed the slave labour and the ever present threat of buggery in the showers...'

'Will,' she scolds and I spot the flash of worry in her eyes that I was exposed to this threat every day. Lucky for me none of the inmates wanted to fuck a pig.

'Yeah, you're right, I might as well unpack. Leave me a piece of that Swiss....thingy and I'll have it later when *Bullseye*'s on. What? Has that finished as well? It's too much change for me to take.'

Mum extends a hand to pat my arm affectionately as I walk around her chair. I smile and head upstairs to the first door on the right into my old room, which used to be Eddie's room then the spare room and now my room. When Eddie's back, will he have this room if I've moved on? In twelve months, where will I be? Definitely not where I was but that doesn't appeal anyway. The police wouldn't have me back. The nearest role for me now is a security guard's job on the night shift. Isn't that where disgraced coppers end up?

As for the rest of my life, being inside has given me time to think. A cliché but true nonetheless. I've concluded that had the house, the fiancée, the job and the lifestyle been that great then I would never have risked it for the wafer thin chance of assisting Eddie get away with his crime. The one thing Justine struggled to understand was how I could throw it all away when we were weeks from walking down the aisle. I tried to explain but she was naturally too upset and furious to listen. She stayed on at the house, taking on the mortgage herself, no doubt getting financial help from a new boyfriend. Strange how relieved I felt when we were over, like the links of a chain had snapped and the heavy ball rolled away into the gutter. Ironic since I snapped on a ball and chain of a different kind.

Enough self analysing; back to the matter in hand - unpacking.

I put the books on the bedside table and flick through the photos like I'm shuffling a deck of cards. There are none I want to put on display...except...a photo slips from my fingers and gently swoops left to right down to the floor where it lands face up on the carpet.

It would have to be that one: Claire and me. It was taken years ago at a wedding reception. I can't even remember who got married. We were tipsy, our faces are flushed. I peer closer at the picture and pull a face when I see what Claire's wearing. That dress, the one with the pink and purple triangles on it. We had to get a taxi to her flat so she could get changed. She spilt wine on it, probably on purpose to justify a change of outfit.

We were young, happy, full of life and promise. This photo used to make me smile. Now it brings me misery, emptiness and confusion. I know I'm back where I started, and Claire?

She missed the visiting. I phoned her flat and mobile, wrote numerous letters, but there was no response. Eventually Mum rang the wing to tell me Claire had gone missing; it was in the local papers. There was nothing to indicate anyone's involvement.

I could do nothing, just continue to serve my sentence, but every time I saw this photograph, or missed her visits, a bit more of me was scooped out and thrown on the floor to dissolve like melting snow.

According to Mum, the police suggested Claire had run away. She was an adult, life had gotten too tough and she'd taken time out. Yes, she should have explained but often they don't; the longer they don't get in contact the harder it becomes to do so. This is standard police speak. In some cases regarding missing adults it's true. But not in this case.

Claire isn't close to her parents; it would be odd if she had contacted them. But she wouldn't desert me. I'd bet my life on it. I half expected her to have been waiting for me today outside the gates like we'd arranged but she wasn't. And the reason why worries me.

Chapter 32

Wednesday ~ day 2

'Do you remember breakfast in bed?' Mum teases, placing the tray on top of the chest of drawers before opening the curtains.

'Yes, definitely.' I rearrange the pillows behind my back. The wonderful aroma of grilled bacon wafts towards me. 'We often woke up to the smell of warm croissants and freshly ground coffee every Saturday on D wing. We were lucky to have such thoughtful guards.'

'I bet you didn't get crispy bacon sandwiches and English breakfast tea though.'

She parts the curtains with a flourish; warm sunlight bathes the carpet and my duvet.

'No. The guards never stretched beyond a continental breakfast. This looks great, Mum. Thank you,' I say looking down at the food. Mum smiles proudly and sits on the end of the bed.

She's grilled the bacon exactly how I like it with a couple of dollops of tomato ketchup smeared on the underside of the sandwich roof. Bliss. I avoided bacon inside. I couldn't stand the sight of those awful pink slices all stringy with little white blobs of fat pooling on the surface. In fact I'd easily have turned vegetarian if it hadn't have caused unnecessary attention.

'I'll expect this all the time now, you know,' I tease.

'I'll try my best. I'm just thrilled to have you home, Will. It's been a tough year. It'll be nice to have someone easy to look after. Your dad's deteriorating week by week now. These few days of respite have come at the right time. Last week I was ready to walk out for good.'

'Things have been bad then?' I ask, licking ketchup off my thumb.

'It's relentless. Before he used to sit and watch a film whilst I did some ironing or whatever, but now he's so restless: up and down all the time, in and out of the house. It's like having a toddler. I have to keep an eye on him all the time. I could cope with him constantly emptying the drawers onto the bedroom floor, but not with the leaves being dumped in my hall. The Hoover is permanently plugged in now. I don't bother putting it away.'

'Where's he got the leaf obsession from?'

She smiles and nods at me. 'Remember that time you took him for a walk in the woods. You took a photo of him scooping the leaves up and throwing them into the air.'

'He had a great day,' I say with fondness. 'He was like a little boy.'

'He's had a thing about leaves since that day.'

I frown. 'But that was two years ago?'

She nods. 'I know.'

And it reminds me how long I've been away and how a simple gesture like throwing leaves into the air can have a lasting and negative impression on someone.

'Sounds like this is a much needed break then if only from Hoovering. What do you fancy doing today?'

'Let's hit the shops. You may need to modernise your wardrobe, Will. Flares and tank tops are out,' she laughs.

'The thing with clothes, Mum, is they come back into fashion.'

She pulls a doubtful face and lovingly pats my leg. 'I don't think those colours will.'

Once breakfast is finished, I open the wardrobe door and look through my clothes, sliding the hangers across the rail. They don't look too unfashionable; fashion can't have moved on that fast in a year. I don't really need a lot but I would like some new things, just to herald my homecoming. I've certainly had enough of denim and that fleecy stuff sweatshirts are made of.

'I know one thing,' I say aloud though there's no one there to hear, 'this shirt will look like a smock on me.' I hold one of my favourite shirts against my chest and look in the mirror on the inside of the wardrobe door. 'My arms will look like a couple of flag poles in them sleeves.'

Perhaps I should have eaten them bacon sarnies. Ugh.

I never bothered with the gym either, disliking the clientele. All those bull-necked tattooed Neanderthals outdoing each other with their testosterone fuelled challenges of who could lift the most, who could punch the hardest and who could wear the tiniest vest. Opting out meant that my toned limbs and abs soon sagged into balls of lard before melting away. Thankfully, at least my feet haven't shrunk and my beloved Adidas trainers still fit.

After a lovely shower on my lonesome, I get dressed in my most modern clothes, and Mum and I hit the town.

*

She's spoiling me rotten. I feel like an eleven year old boy buying brand new stuff because I'm off to big school; not only needing a uniform but an indoors and outdoors P.E. kit too. Mum buys me new underwear, stylish jeans which are far removed from prison issue ones, a few tops, slippers, nightwear and even a new pair of shoes. She hands Dad's credit card over and over again, and each time I feel a spear of guilt.

'Mum,' I whisper as she presses his PIN number into the machine. 'I'll pay you back. I will...'

'It's your Dad's treat. It's what he said to do...before...when he still could.'

I nod and take the bag from the counter adding it to the ones already looped over my wrists. 'Well, I do have a fiver...I take it they're still in circulation? The coffees are on me.'

We end up in an American Italian coffee shop ordering coffees with syrup in them and tiny cakes with huge price tags. Despite my complaining the caramel Macchiato is very nice, but the Rocky Road slice could do with being three times bigger than it is.

'I forgot to ask. Do you need any toiletries?' Mum asks, slicing her apple doughnut in half with a plastic knife.

'I could do with a new toothbrush and some proper shaving gear. I still get a rash with an electric shaver.'

'*Boots* is over the road. We'll pop there before we go. Remind me though.'

The shrill ringing of a mobile phone rises up from the floor. She looks around and down, realising it's coming from under the small round table. She hunts through the contents of her handbag. When she sees who's calling her face creases into a frown.

'Who is it?' I ask, but she shakes her head and answers it, her voice sounding resigned to fate.

'Hello. Yes, this is Kay Bailey. Is he alright? Has he? Yes, I understand...'

'Is it Dad?' I ask and she nods sadly.

'He does have a lot of energy. I can, yes, but I'm out at the moment...all morning.'

Loud girly laughter enters the cafe; I glance over, distracted by the commotion. Two dark haired women in their twenties are staggering across the tiled floor to join the long queue at the counter as if they're out on the piss. I peer closer. They look familiar.

The thinner girl is wearing a heavy black coat and a furry scarf; her shoes are sky high so it's no wonder she can't walk properly. Her skirt must be mega short because it isn't visible below the hem of the coat. Her legs are clad in dark tights. Her handbag is over-sized, the sort of thing to give a holdall a run for its money. It's her hair and side-on profile that strikes a chord of recognition: her ponytail is shiny like a model in a shampoo advert.

'An hour at least, maybe two,' Mum is saying, still on the phone.

'They look lovely!' a loud voice announces. 'I want one of them.' And the other girl jabs a finger at the glass counter where an assortment of cakes and pastries are laid out.

'I'm not having one, not at these prices,' the thin girl says loud enough for the staff to hear.

'Well, I am. I'm fucking starving!'

The shorter overweight girl straightens up and looks at the drinks menu on the wall behind the counter. She's wearing a long baggy cardigan, the pockets of which are somewhere down by her knees; her hair is longer but tied back and twisted around so it looks like a cinnamon whirl pinned to the back of her head. The family resemblance is strong, but they're nothing like their older sister.

'I'll come as soon as I can. Thank you. Bye.' Mum ends the call and chucks the phone back in the handbag. 'That was the home. Your dad's been very restless, wanting to go out in the rain and when they've tried to stop him he's turned aggressive. They've asked me to pick him up '

'Why?' I ask, my eyes flicking back to the sisters who are moving towards the till to give their order. 'They're supposed to be trained to look after people like Dad; he's on respite. They can't get rid of him because he's playing up.'

'Unfortunately they can. They can't keep him if he wants to leave.'

'Can I get a medium skinny decaf cappuccino to take out,' the thinner girl tells the barista, her tone impolite and demanding.

'Yeah and I'll have a medium hot chocolate,' the tubby sister adds. 'With cream, yeah, and a cherry an' coconut cookie as well. Cheers.'

The barista reaches for two take out mugs and asks for names for each of the drinks. I lean forward to hear; I don't want to miss this.

'Sally,' says the thin girl.

'Liv,' says the other one.

Oh yes. Claire's sisters. This is an opportunity not to be missed. I push back my chair, Mum looks at me and I nod over her shoulder.

'Claire's sisters,' I explain. 'I'm going to pop over and surprise them.'

At the end of the counter, where the drinks are handed out and names are called, is a group of five people including this pair waiting for their orders. Liv is standing at the cabinet where the sachets of sugar, jars of chocolate powder and those long wooden stirrers are housed. She's pulling two serviettes out of their container to blow her nose. Sally is looking at her mobile.

I walk over and position myself so I'm penning them in against the wall. 'Don't tell me you need sugar, Liv, aren't you sweet enough?'

She turns around; her hand is outstretched to drop the soiled serviettes into the hole in the top of the cabinet which is the bin. Her over made-up eyes with their three shades of brown widen so I can see white all the way around her brown irises. Sally's dark eyes flick up and rest on my grinning face.

'Fuck me!' Liv exclaims. 'When did you get out?'

A middle-aged woman wearing a smart suit and carrying an expensive leather laptop case throws a dirty look over her shoulder at Liv and steps nearer to the counter as if to hurry up her drink.

'Yesterday, but it's not official so keep it under your hat,' and I wink to show them I am only joking. 'How are things with you two? Crikey, Sally, what's the matter? You look like you've seen a ghost.'

She's standing still and rigid like she's under a spell, her mouth droops open like a basking shark feeding. Sally's eyes glance at Liv for her answer.

'You can't blame her,' Liv continues. 'You are a convicted criminal.'

'I can't argue with that. Is there any news on Claire? Remember her? Your older sister.' Liv loathed people referring to Claire as her sister, promptly correcting them that she was her *half* sister.

'Her disappearance is in the hands of the police,' Sally replies finding her voice though it's small and quiet.

'Which you used to be but not anymore,' Liv reminds me spitefully.

'Medium latte for Lyn,' the barista calls out.

I hear the businesswoman cheer from here. She grabs the drink and walks through the middle of our little chat.

'True. I just don't want anyone to forget that Claire's missing.'

'No one's forgotten,' Liv stresses haughtily, 'but we've got to get on with our lives. If the police find anything then they'll let us...'

'What if they don't?' I question.

'She's run away,' Sally announces and I look at her. 'She could be anywhere. I don't know why she can't let Mum and Dad know she's okay...'

I interrupt. 'How can she if someone's done something to her?' The police would almost certainly have prepared them for the worst but if they've chosen not to accept it then I feel sorry for them.

Liv strokes Sally's arm reassuringly. 'No one's done anything to her. Ignore him. He's talking bollocks.'

Sally smiles and nods reassured by Liv's kind but senseless words. She looks at me, her eyes hard. 'No one has a reason to hurt Claire. The police spoke to everyone.'

'Not everyone, eh?' And I wink before walking away.

I return to the table; Mum has gathered our belongings. I lead the way out of the coffee shop, turning at the door to look back at the Ugly Sisters: Liv's hand is on the small of Sally's back, speaking words of comfort into her ear, but as if Liv can sense my burning gaze, she looks up and our eyes meet. I smile and raise a hand laden down with shopping bags to wave a pleasant goodbye.

I'm not going away, you antagonistic bitch, I pledge silently.

Chapter 33

Wednesday ~ day 2

I stand in the lounge window, my nervousness increasing when Mum's saloon appears at the end of the drive and indicates right to pull onto the property; as the car turns and mounts the slightly inclined driveway, its white running lights lift upwards into my face. The rain which started as we left the shops has steadily gotten worse as the afternoon has gone on. Now it's absolutely chucking it down. Puddles are forming where there are dips in the ground and the raindrops are dancing on surfaces. The heads of the daffodils under the window of the detached garage are bowing from the weight of the water. The wind has picked up too; the tops of the trees are swaying.

We're in for a storm, I think, peering up at the steel grey sky.

Mum parks in front of the lounge window and I get my first glimpse in a year of my dad sitting in the front passenger seat. He's staring through the windscreen so I smile but he doesn't react. Perhaps he can't see me. I worry Dad won't remember me, that we will stand awkwardly opposite each other in the hall as Mum makes the introductions. If he doesn't accept me, what will happen? I'm worried my presence in the house will confuse him and worsen the situation.

I open the front door. Mum holds her handbag over her head as a makeshift umbrella and shouts at Dad over the bonnet to shut the car door and 'Come on, we're getting soaked!' I can't hear his reply but I can guess it's something about his need to go for a walk.

He walks around the boot though the quicker route is past the bonnet, swinging his holdall as if he has all the time in the world. Mum steps into the hall and shakes her dripping coat over the doormat. Water flicks off in all directions, striking me across the face.

Dad wipes his feet on the bristly mat and drops the holdall on the floor. He looks up at me, his face breaking into a huge smile.

'Hello Will. When did you get home?'

I exhale with relief; he knows who I am. 'Good to see you, Dad. I got back yesterday.'

Mum explained that he needs some reminding where me and Eddie have been but so far this week he's remembered and has been excited about my arrival.

'Eddie not with you?' and he looks around me as if my brother is hiding behind me.

'I'm afraid not. He's got to stay away just a little while longer.' Thirteen months to be exact. 'It's great to be back with you and Mum. I've missed you both.'

'Us too, son,' he says, removing his coat. 'Prison's no place for a policeman. I know you're not allowed to say but I hope the undercover work was a success,' and he winks. His fingers fumble with his coat zip.

'Can I help you with that, Dad?' I offer. 'Pesky zips, eh?'

Mum shuts the front door and turns the key, preventing Dad's escape. I yank the zip down and pull the coat down over his arms.

He looks at the door then at her. 'I was going to go for a quick walk, love. I won't be long.'

'Mike, it's chucking it down and you're soaked to the bone. I told you in the car we'd have a cup of tea first and then *if* it stops raining you can go for a walk.'

 'If you try and stop me from going out later, I'll cut your throat,' Dad warns with a pleasant smile, walking past me into the lounge.

I look at Mum, shocked. I can hardly believe what he's said like it's nothing more than he's threatened to tweak her nose.

'He doesn't mean it, Will. He doesn't really know what he's saying,' Mum explains with a small smile.

'Has he picked up a knife?'

'No, of course not! Can you keep an eye on him whilst I make the tea? Put the telly on or something. We'll talk about it later.'

I wander into the lounge, my ears still ringing from Dad's threat. Does he remember where I've really been all this time or is the undercover work something he now believes? Certainly at the time of the trial he knew what was going on. How is it that a memory can be wiped away so easily like words on a blackboard? How can a personality change so quickly and dramatically, that a horrible threat can be issued so readily? Are they the kind of thoughts haunting my dad now?

I sit on the settee and watch as he flicks through the channels. My dad always had youthful looks; no one believed him when he told them his age. But now his normally healthy tanned skin looks worn and I can see he's lost weight in the face. Must be due to the never-ending walking. His hair which had hardly any grey in it a year ago is showing signs now. It's similar in colour to a badger's coat.

I sigh with sadness. It's a frightening thing when you spot the signs of ageing in your parents; you realise they're not infallible, that they're not going to live forever.

Mum places a tray of tea and biscuits onto the coffee table. Dad grabs two custard creams. 'Thanks for doing the veg, Will,' she says, relaxing on the settee.

'It's alright, Mum. Whoever said prison doesn't teach you new skills doesn't know what they're talking about.'

'I'll have this tea, Kay, then I'm going for a walk. I haven't been out all day,' Dad says, turning from the telly.

'Okay, love,' she replies patiently.

Dad looks at me and smiles. 'How's that girlfriend of yours these days?'

Does he mean my ex-fiancée Justine? 'Do you mean Justine?'

'No! I mean Claire. How's she doing?'

'I don't know, Dad. I haven't seen her for a while.' I hope this satisfies him and he drops the subject. It's far too complicated to explain.

'I liked her a lot. Loved that impression she did of *Kermit the Frog*,' he laughs.

Mum and I look at each other, completely staggered.

*

'It wasn't odd your Dad mentioning Claire, you know,' Mum says after dinner as she and I sit at the dining table sipping the wine Dad insisted on pouring. He's occupied with a war film in the lounge. 'He often does when we talk about you. He always said she was the perfect daughter.'

'He was very fond of her. I think once Claire turned down a party to go to a pub quiz with Dad.' I reach for the glass of water. I'm so unused to drinking.

Mum leans across the table. 'If you don't think she's run off then what's happened to her? Why would anyone want to harm her?'

I think about it. I know how Claire really felt about her mum and step-father, her opinion of her sisters, how she loved her real dad. Ryan and I meant more to her and though I can see her fucking her family off, I can't see her doing the same to us.

'For her to run off there must be a bloody good reason. When I last saw Claire, she gave no indication that anything was seriously wrong.' I pause, thinking how to word the next sentence. 'She told me personal and private stuff about her life. I don't know how that could have turned nasty. Her family don't really know her. They notice a few clothes have gone, her passport is missing, and they assume she's done a runner. It's not difficult is it to remove those items when you're removing a body.' And my mouth snaps shut as I realise with horror what I've just said.

'Will!' Mum gasps. 'Is that what you really think has happened to her? Oh, the poor girl.'

I slide my jaw across and eventually nod. 'That's what we're talking about, isn't it? It's the only other possibility.'

Mum contemplates my suggestion. 'But why would anyone hurt her? It seems nowadays that people kill for no reason at all: a few quid, a driving misdemeanour...'

'She won't have been killed for any of those reasons. They're impulsive, angry crimes; beatings, single but well-aimed stabbings, a simple push. This is different. It has some cool planning, items are missing to give the impression she went of her own accord. I need to know exactly what's been taken. But I doubt her family could itemise a list positively. If her passport can't be found, her family will assume it expired and she shredded it. I know there was five years left on it because it's the same as mine. We got our photos done at the same time.'

'This all says such a lot about her parents,' Mum comments. 'That they don't know her at all.' She finishes her wine and shakes the bottle to see how much is left. It's empty. 'Are you going to talk to the police, tell them what you know?'

'They'd humour me, Mum. And when they discover I'm an ex police officer they'll remind me I'm not in the job anymore. Then when they discover I'm newly released from prison they'll treat me with disgust and contempt. I'm not willing to betray Claire's confidence for that.'

'You'll have to look into matters yourself then,' Mum says. 'You've got the skills...'

'I haven't got the up-to-date information. I'm going to need that. And I can only get that from the family. News of my encounter with the Ugly Sisters will have reached the parents by now. They won't be willing to talk to me.'

'They will if you have information,' Mum points out cutely. 'It's a trade-off.'

I consider her idea. 'I suppose it is.'

I miss Claire. I miss my best friend. This hollow feeling won't be eased or fulfilled until I try to find out what's happened to her. I'm almost certainly going to need help and if that means ingratiating myself to her hostile family then I'd best put on my best smile and my most sincere tone of voice.

Chapter 34

Thursday ~ day 3

I begin my investigation the next morning. Mum hands me the keys to Dad's beloved Mazda MX5, warning me to go easy until she puts me on the insurance. I hit the road: roof down, stereo turned up, speed reasonable. It feels good to be driving; I've finally got my liberty and independence back.

Claire's parents live in a posh little town called Appleton. The residents are snobs. Or *Midsomer Murder* victims as Ryan called them. "They're just begging for a pitchfork in the back or a stone gargoyle on the head," he once said. Even Claire joined in the fun and we often came up with eccentric ways of killing her parents. It was a good job our childish daydreaming was over by the time I got sent down or the prison authority might have got suspicious.

The houses are large; the minimum number of bedrooms is easily four. Claire's parents have five. That's one for them, one for each of their daughters and a spare should a lucky guest be invited to stay over. I never was. Every house has a conservatory; the gardens are landscaped and well maintained; driveways are block paved or gravelled. Their cars ooze money: new or nearly new 4x4s and executive saloons with heated this and electric that.

Two huge white stone pillars mark the turning for Green Orchard Close. I indicate and drive between the pointless sentries. There's no top to the pillars; they don't even look reminiscent of something that once stood here. It's simply a ridiculous way of making their estate stand out from everyone else's. Marion and Andrew's house is second on the left.

I feel unprepared and that makes me nervous; my mouth is dry. I pull up against the low stone wall surrounding their property, take a swig of water from the bottle on the passenger seat and face the house.

Considering how much it's worth – it's nothing special. I've always thought the windows were too small and the driveway is only big enough for three vehicles. Down one side of the house is a pile of bricks on a wooden pallet and one of those massive canvas bags that aggregate is delivered in.

I step closer, the toes of my new trainers just touching the gravel that's escaped from the edges of the drive, nervous about stepping into their territory. There isn't much of a front garden. There's a narrow well tended border on their side of the wall. Around the front door and windows is a selection of plant pots with spring flowers in bloom: daffodils, tulips and irises.

I walk closer, my feet scrunching on the gravel, the soles flicking up chippings. On the front step is an *Avon* magazine in a clear plastic bag.

I lift the brass knocker and confidently knock the door three times and wait. Thankfully there isn't a spy hole because if she could see it's me, she may pretend she's out. Movement at the door, my heart quickens and the door opens.

'Oh. Hello William,' Marion stumbles over the words. 'When did you get out?'

I wonder why she's pretending. Surely the Ugly Sisters would have informed her I'm back.

As usual she's dressed up. Her beige and cream clothes are expensive and stylish; her jewellery is gold and sparkly. For a woman entering her sixties, she knows how to look after herself which is a good idea when you're married to a younger man, and you need to keep younger female competition at bay. But regular gym sessions, facials, dyed hair, expensive clothes will help hide the signs of ageing.

'If I had a pound for every time someone's asked me that question, I'd have two quid now,' I joke but she doesn't smile. Frosty bitch.

'What can I do for you?' she asks.

Incredible. Has she really no idea why I'm here? 'I won't lie and say I was passing. Do you have any news on Claire?'

'I'm afraid not. The police have told us to remain hopeful and at the moment that's all any of us can do.'

I'm prevented from asking my next question by the sound of an engine and the crunching of gravel. She looks over my shoulder and I turn to see a white transit van pull into the driveway. The driver is in his late twenties with collar length brown hair, his attire suggests he's here to work.

'Morning Fergus!' she calls pleasantly, a great deal more warmth in her voice.

He raises an arm and offers an apology for his lateness.

'It was your daughter's fault,' he calls across the drive. 'Her car wouldn't start and I had to drop her off at the office.' This must be Sally's boyfriend. Claire said something about him being a struggling builder.

'She needs a more reliable car,' Marion replies.

'Yes,' Fergus says tightly. Perhaps he's hoping Marion will pay for it. He gets on with removing various items including a flask from the van and carrying them around to the side of the house. Marion turns back to me.

'I am sorry I have no further news for you. It's a case of waiting for Claire to make contact. I don't know what's going on in her brain that she feels she can't tell us she's safe. I can only assume she's having some kind of breakdown...'

'You need to understand, Marion,' I begin a tad condescendingly. 'Claire and I were best friends; we talked to each other about everything.'

'I hope you're not suggesting that you know my daughter better than her family.' Her chin rises in a challenge.

'I am suggesting that. You didn't even know she visited me, twice a month, without fail. She booked her holidays around her visits. So there are lots of things you don't know. You must have considered that something has happened to Claire.'

'Yes...'

'Good. Then you can't ignore the possibility that she's been harmed. Seriously, fatally even.'

'There's no evidence of violence,' Marion argues. 'Her flat was intact. Nothing valuable was missing, just some clothes and personal items. We've left it as it is, for when she comes back.'

'Would you mind if I had a look around her flat? I want to know if anything else is missing...'

She interrupts. 'I couldn't let you do that. It's Claire's home. It's an unacceptable intrusion.'

What a load of bollocks, I think.

The sound of another approaching vehicle and shifting gravel makes me turn. An expensive sleek silver Mercedes with a personalised plate glides onto the drive, pulling up sharply. It's him. Marion's knight in shining armour.

Andrew's clothing hasn't modernised. He still looks like a model taking a break from a photo shoot for a country life magazine. Andrew wears mustard coloured cords, a thick cotton shirt with a pattern like graph paper and a wax jacket. He's missing the half-cocked shotgun over the crook of an elbow and a couple of dead pheasants in the other.

He races to Marion's side, slipping an arm around her waist and pulling her to him so sharply she puts out a hand to catch her balance.

'What are you doing here?' he demands, his dark eyes blazing angrily. 'When did you get out?'

'Three quid,' I mumble. 'Don't worry; I'm not on the run. I wondered if there was any news on Claire.'

'The *police* are dealing with it,' he stresses abruptly.

'Who was the last person to see Claire alive?' I ask and the question takes them by surprise. They look at each other.

'It...it was a neighbour...' Marion replies, frowning at Andrew for the name. 'A lady...'

'Please leave us alone,' Andrew orders. 'We're upset enough as it is and we don't need you undertaking your own investigation because you're bored.'

'I am a bit bored,' I joke. 'I seriously believe harm has come to your daughter, and if you still want to believe in this ludicrous idea that she's gone AWOL for reasons unknown or maybe you simply don't give a shit. That's fine. I do care and despite your obstruction I won't give up till I find out what's happened.' I turn and march off their property, half expecting like it happens in the movies for them to come after me, agreeing to help, but they don't. I get back into the Mazda and drive away. I glance in the rear view mirror but no one is coming after me.

*

I try not to get too annoyed as I make my way across town to Claire's flat, I knew they'd be awkward, but I can't help wonder why they aren't more worried about Claire's whereabouts. Do they really believe one day she'll just swan in through the front door and say, "Cheers for paying my mortgage, Mum." If Claire was the sort of person to take her parents for money, then you could say she'd left on purpose to get her bills paid, and I wouldn't blame her for that. Marion telling Fergus that Sally needs a new car doesn't mean she'll put her hand in her purse and fork out for one. She'd see Sally riding the bus to work first. When Olivia walked out of university, Andrew made her repay the fees. It's no wonder she can only afford to live in the middle of a ghetto.

Is it really solely to do with them being unable to face the awful, life destroying alternative that Claire is dead? Or do they know something they're keeping to themselves?

An angry honking noise reminds me that a green light still means go so I release the handbrake and move off, apologising to the Royal Mail van with a raised hand. The incident interrupts my train of thought and I concentrate on where I'm going instead.

Crompton House Mews is a complex of ground and first floor flats in a backwards C shape with allocated parking spaces in the centre and at the front where the road passes by into a dead-end where disused industrial units stand. Claire's ground floor flat is number 8 and overlooks the road albeit from behind a low stone wall and a small lawn both communally owned. Opposite is a secondary school and when it's letting out time, you can't park down here for coaches and parents' vehicles.

I pull up against the kerb and look towards Claire's flat. My head swims. The lounge curtains are drawn, and still hanging in front of a window, nailed to the underside of the roof is a wind chime, rusted by age and the elements. She liked to listen to the sound of a breeze tinkling the metal hollow tubes together, saying it sounded like exotic holidays. I said it was annoying and when she left the room I'd close the window. Once I sellotaped the tubes together. She made me go outside with the scissors and cut them free.

I approach her flat, my head swimming again with emotion. Christ, this feels weird, like I'm not supposed to be here and could be caught and told off at any second.

I push open the communal door. It's in need of replacing or at least painting. There's a diagonal fracture in the glass pane from corner to corner and the arm of the door has worn a groove in the underside of the door frame. I step into the cold hallway. A bicycle is chained up under the stairs to my left. There are black scuff marks along the middle of the walls and dead leaves litter the hard tiled floor. To my right is Claire's front door, a staircase rises on my left to the first floor. Through the handrail I can see the front door to number 7 and directly in front of me is another communal door that leads from the rear car park.

I face her door, my heart thumps madly and I'm frightened there might be something to see: scratch marks on the wood, a footprint from where someone's kicked the door in but it looks unharmed. I run my fingers over the wood. Nothing. I wonder how the police entered if they didn't batter-ram the door down. Did they have a key? I was a key holder before I went to prison. Who was Claire's key holder after me? She wouldn't have given it to her parents or sisters.

At the time of her disappearance, speculation no doubt would have been rife through the flats; neighbours gossiping with neighbours about the girl in number 8, did any of them remember her, even if I can't strike it lucky by finding the neighbour who last saw her, I'm sure one of them will know.

I knock on number 7, the logical candidate.

Eventually the door unlocks and the occupant blinks tiredly at me: a bloke in his thirties, wearing a crumpled t-shirt.

'You woke me up,' he accuses, tugging his tousled hair. 'I'm on nights. This had better be worth it.'

'It is. It's about your neighbour at number 8: Claire.'

'Was that her name? What about her?'

'She went missing early December. I understand from the police that a neighbour was the last person to see her. Was that you?'

'She's missing? I wondered why I hadn't seen her for a while.'

Is he having a laugh, I think.

'At the time there would have been a few police officers around, making door-to-door enquiries. I know it was five months ago but...'

'It weren't me. I can't remember the last time I saw her. No one's knocked on my door.'

He must have been kipping longer than Sleeping Beauty not to have noticed the commotion and the police presence.

I mutter an insincere thanks and leave via the other communal door. A wheelie bin stands sentry on the side of the path, under Claire's bedroom windows. Thick net hangs in each of them hiding the view from any nosy-parkers. I walk along the meandering path that passes by other front doors and windows all hidden behind net curtains or blinds until I reach the main car park. There's only a couple of vehicles here. Most people are at work. A cluster of wheelie bins, some bursting with tied carrier bags stand at the end of another path waiting to be emptied. Across the car park are the mews houses which form the top part of the C.

It's certainly quiet around here in the daytime. This witness may not even be around till later. I walk around to the front of the building. A yellow Ford Fiesta has appeared in a space opposite the Mazda. A woman with middle-age spread is unloading shopping from the boot. A crutch leans against the rear light. It's Bev: Claire's neighbour and if anyone knows who saw Claire last she will. Hopefully she'll remember me.

'Hello,' I call out pleasantly strolling over. She turns. There's another crutch in her left arm bearing her weight.

She peers at me before suddenly smiling. First pleasant smile I've been greeted with all morning.

'Hello Will! How lovely to see you. Come over here and let me have a look at you. Claire told me you'd not long left of your sentence. How are you? Come to solve the mystery of her disappearance, I hope.'

She gives me a one-armed hug. She smells of older ladies' perfume. A bit like my Nan did. 'Well, I'll try my best. Can I help?' I offer, nodding at the carrier bags.

'You certainly can. If you grab those two bags, I'll open the door and pop the kettle on.'

'That's a fine idea.'

Chapter 35

Thursday ~ day 3

'I miss her so much,' Bev says, offering me the packet of chocolate digestives. 'I miss our little chats about her running, gossip from the hospital and her smile. Such a lovely girl.'

I dip a second biscuit into my tea and bite the wet end off before it drips onto my new jeans. 'Her parents couldn't even tell me how much they missed her.'

'They're an odd pair. Don't you swallow that rubbish about her having run off.' She points a finger at me. 'And I bet you're looking for me,' she adds with a grin. 'Apparently I'm the last person to have seen Claire alive.'

'Then I've come to the right place. For the tea and the information. What happened that evening?'

Bev sighs and reclines in her armchair. 'I'd just parked up and was heading for my front door when Claire appeared, dressed in her running gear. She told me she'd collect my car key first thing in the morning rather than have it...'

I interrupt. 'Why did she want your car key?'

'She was borrowing my car for the day. Having a day out somewhere.'

'Why? What was wrong with hers?' Thinking about it now I don't recall seeing Claire's silver Peugeot outside. My observation skills are obviously rusty.

'It was stolen one evening around Bonfire Night. The police found it smashed up, tyres stolen; it was irreparable. She didn't tell you about this?'

'No. Where was she going?'

'She didn't say, only that she'd be back by teatime and would leave me with a full tank of petrol as a thank you.' Bev replaces the biscuits into a cylindrical tin. 'You look worried.'

'I'm ashamed I didn't know this about her car. I can't think why she never told me. There I am preaching to her parents that no one knew Claire like me, and here you are telling me about a stolen car she neglected to mention. It's not something you tend to forget. I've been very self-righteous.'

'Nonsense. I felt terrible when I produced a key for her flat. The look her parents gave me said it all. "Our daughter gave *you* a key to *her* flat and not *us*." There could have been a perfectly valid reason why Claire didn't tell you about her car. What could you have done? She didn't want you to worry, or bore you with moaning about her problems when you're in prison.'

I lean forward. 'Did you say you had a key?'

'Yes, but her parents took it. The police were about to bust the door down when I produced it.'

I sit back in my seat, defeated. 'Shame you haven't still got it. Don't suppose you...'

'No. I didn't make a copy.' She smiles regretfully.

'Yeah, why would you? I need to get in that flat, but her parents despise me. I won't gain access with their help.'

'Well, you need to convince them it's in their best interests that they let you in. Or use your charm.' She winks at me.

'I was born without charm.'

'Nonsense. You're a nice looking young man. Don't you know the old saying that flattery will get you anywhere?'

I'm not sure anyone could flatter the Ugly Sisters. 'Did you see Claire later when she returned from her run?'

'No, I didn't. I was too busy watching that new murder mystery on the box, but the lights were on in her flat when I looked out of my kitchen window later.'

'What time was that?'

She thinks, mashing her lips together. 'About nine thirty...oh!' she suddenly cries so loud and sharp that I sit up straight. Her eyes are wide and I just know she has something important to say. 'Of course, that woman.' She nods to herself as it comes back to her. 'I can't believe I'd forgotten that. She was there the night before, on the Thursday, kicking Claire's front door and carrying on, making enough noise to wake the dead. Her husband was with her. He was very embarrassed. And no wonder really, a young mother making such a scene and swearing like that.'

Oh, God, I think. Three guesses as to what that was about.

Bev shifts in her chair, wincing with pain. 'I could hear her from the car park...oh this is awful. You must think I'm a right nosy parker, always seeing or hearing something...'

I smile. 'Well, yes, I do, but I don't care. You were a good neighbour to Claire and you're a mine of information.'

'The woman said Claire had had an affair with her husband. She promised to come back and have it out with her.'

So it is a scorned woman.

'Do you know who either of them were? Their names? Had you seen them anywhere before?'

'Not her, but he often came to Claire's flat, two or three times a week in the evening. He parked his van out front.'

I finger my hair, twisting the quiff around whilst I think. This must be Charlton, Claire's nickname for whatever his real name is. The last time I saw her she was unhappy with him, he was getting romantic and worse – serious. Claire couldn't stand it when affairs took a turn in that direction so when I'd advised her to end it I knew she would and quickly. But why had the scorned wife turned up? Had Charlton refused to accept it was over and Claire had resorted to informing his wife? Or maybe he'd admitted the affair? But if the scorned wife had returned when Claire was home and there had been a fight then I was looking at a possible scenario.

'Do you know if the woman returned?' I ask.

Bev shakes her head. 'You could ask Kenny at number 7. He spoke to her too so if she had turned up behaving like that again then I expect he'd have heard something.'

'I met him earlier. He claimed not to have even known Claire's name...'

Bev laughs. 'He's lived here as long as she has! If you woke him up, he'd deny the earth was round to get rid of you. He works nights and struggles to get to sleep till after all the kids arrive at school. The commotion out here sometimes is ridiculous. Oh, look at the time. It's nearly lunchtime.'

'I should go, leave you to get on with your day.' I stand, stretching my legs, my right knee clicks.

'If you're sure. I'll have a think about this man and his van, and let you know.'

We swap phone numbers, but since I don't yet have a mobile, I give her the landline number.

'Did Claire have any other male visitors?'

'Yes, one other. He was older, smartly dressed. Drove a beautiful Jag.'

'Write down what you remember about him...in fact anyone who was here within the last couple of weeks before she went missing.'

'Leave it to me, Will.' Bev beams.

Chapter 36

Thursday ~ day 3

On the way home I stop off at a stationery supplier's and buy an A3 sized pad and a couple of decent pens. I deduce better when I can write things down.

'I'm back!' I call, opening the front door.

'Good. You're here,' Dad snaps, appearing in the doorway of the lounge, trouser legs rolled up, feet stuffed into his shoes so the tongues are folded down inside and the laces trailing over the carpet. 'I don't know who has done this to my shoes, but the laces keep coming undone and they're all knotty. It's driving me mad.'

'Shall I sort it out for you, Dad?' I offer, closing the door and depositing my items on the hall carpet.

'I wish somebody would,' he complains throwing an accusing look at Mum who stands in the kitchen doorway drying her hands on a tea towel.

She shrugs at me. 'It's the laces today. Makes a change from leaves I suppose, and it's less messy.'

'Take them off then,' I tell him and he flicks them off with the toe of the other foot and leaves me to pick them up. I follow him into the lounge and get to work undoing the tight knots and lacing them properly. Dad sits opposite, like a little boy, hands clasped together in his lap, knees touching, trousers still up so it looks like he's wearing school shorts.

'There you go,' I say, handing them back.

'Thanks, son.' He grins and puts them on, tying the laces easily whilst asking if I've managed to find Claire.

'Not yet, but I've got a couple of leads.'

'You should talk to that friend of hers. The one who's a policeman...'

'Who? You mean me? I was the policeman.'

'Were you?' and he says with total surprise. 'I didn't know that. You learn something new every day,' and suddenly he leaps up, feet secured in his shoes. 'See you later, Will. I'm off out for a walk, Kay!' He opens the front door and is gone.

I wander into the kitchen where Mum is grating cheese onto the bread board. "How did you get on? Flick the kettle down, will you? I'm dying for a cup of tea.'

I start making the tea and tell her about my meetings with Claire's parents and Bev.

'Who's this Charlton then?' she asks tearing open a packet of crisps.

'A recent fling. On her last visit she told me it wasn't working out with him; she was bored, he was getting too serious so I told her to finish it. Perhaps he didn't take it well. Charlton's not his real name. She's always referred to boyfriends by nicknames. Bev's going to write me a description and anyone else that has been to the flat recently.'

'Were there other men?'

'It wasn't unusual for Claire to see two men at the same time. The most was five. That was at college though.'

'Wow,' Mum says impressively. 'I was once seeing two but never...'

I lean across the table, my interest piqued. 'With Dad?'

She nods. 'The other man was...Graeme, I think. I couldn't decide who I liked the most so I saw them both. It went on for quite a while too.'

'So you picked Dad.'

'No. I picked Graeme but he dumped me...then I asked your Dad back out. Sometimes I wonder what my life would be like with Graeme. I certainly didn't think it'd end up like this,' she says sadly.

'Not so soon after retiring, no.'

'I could understand a heart attack or lung cancer even. Your Dad smoked too much when he was young; he only stopped when Eddie was born. I never expected him to get Alzheimer's.'

'I know,' I mutter. 'Nor me.'

'Oh, I've got something for you, something you might need.' She rummages through the stuff on the other dining room chair. 'I contacted the insurance company so you're fine for driving the Mazda.' She pulls out a small black box. 'It's my old mobile. Sorry it's not an all singing and dancing smart phone, but it should do you for now.'

'That's great, Mum. At this rate I should be able to set up my own private investigation company.' I open the box and remove the packaging to find a snazzy flip-top phone with a slightly scratched lid nestling inside. I take it upstairs with my stationery and put it on charge so I can add Bev as my first contact. Time to get to work.

I lay the A3 pad on the bed and pick up a pen. I think better when there's something in my hand.

Before Charlton, Claire was seeing a man who she referred to by an unusual Spanish or Italian name…Eri something…it began with an e definitely. Claire's affair with him lasted much longer, about two years. I got the impression he had money and class, and knew how to treat a woman, which often comes with age. From the start he insisted he wouldn't leave his wife; she was ill and he loved her; but they were going through a stressful time. That suited Claire perfectly. She was his escapism. They had nights away, but she always had to meet him there. And they went to some odd places; not places renowned for beautiful coastlines or outstanding walks, but places inland and flat, concrete and wasted.

Perhaps it was something to do with his job.

'Mixing business and pleasure? Wonder why they had to travel separately though.' I had asked Claire but she wouldn't tell me why. Odd that. Maybe his job was a giveaway to who he was. Maybe other people travelled with him, and a woman would have stood out. It's a pity Claire never told me more about Erizo.

'Erizo!' I say aloud and triumphantly. 'Of course! Where did that come from?'

Sounds more Italian but Claire used to call him 'El Erizo' which is Spanish. She said it was his nickname from when he was out there. It's all coming back to me now. Time to stop forcing my brain to work and let it flow.

She never said he worked out in Spain; the phrase was 'when he was out there' which is odd because what else would he be doing in Spain if not working? He might have been in the forces, but a person is more likely to say 'From when he was stationed out there.' Maybe he lived out there as a child and returned to the UK as an adult.

I turn my attention back to Charlton and think back through Claire's prison visits. They were seeing each other in July because for her birthday Charlton had bought her a charm for her bracelet. She loved that bracelet. I don't remember what it was exactly, but it represented his strong feelings for her.

'Probably a heart then,' I suggest out loud.

She also said that he'd asked her to go away for a weekend because his wife was taking the kids to see their grandparents. Claire wasn't keen so made up a plausible excuse. When was that? School holidays? No, it was earlier. What Whit week? Yes. So she was seeing him in May. Her affair with the Spaniard must have ended around the end of April/beginning of May because she met Charlton soon after.

I write all this down. 'Started May? Over late November/early Dec.'

Where did she meet him?

This I know because she met him where she met El Erizo. She called it a swap-shop moment. 'I traded him in for a younger model,' she'd laughed and I laughed too because it was one of my Dad's phrases.

Did Charlton work with the Spaniard? Were their businesses close together? Bev said Charlton drove a van. What kind of business would require that? A window cleaner; tradesmen like builders, plumbers; undertakers; delivery drivers like postmen, couriers; gardeners; the list goes on. Many of them would require the worker to travel distances for work, to people's houses and properties. And with some jobs there would be co-workers.

I need Bev to remember something. There's no point in scouring the Yellow Pages for tradesmen or courier services for a Charlton. Charlton could easily be a nickname. It could be his surname, a middle name, where he's from, anything.

I throw the pen down with exasperation. 'Why did you have to be so bloody cryptic, Claire?'

*

'Does the term El Erizo mean anything to you?' I ask Mum as she winds the cord around the Hoover. Dad returned with yet more leaves and a couple of daffodils which he appeared to have ripped up from someone's garden and deposited them on the hall carpet like a cat bringing home a dead bird.

'Is it Spanish? El means 'the' doesn't it? Like le and la in French.'

'Le and la are French, Kay,' Dad says, wandering in from the lounge and winking at me.

'You know what I mean,' she says, blushing. 'Ask your Dad. He learnt Spanish at night school.'

'Christ, Kay, that was thirty years ago. The only phrase I can remember is dos beers por favor.'

Mum and I laugh.

'You laugh, but that phrase got your mum and I drunk on many a night out in Majorca.'

Mum's eyes mist over as she remembers their beloved holidays and the hotel they stayed in several years running.

'Google it,' she suggests, opening the cupboard under the stairs to park the Hoover. 'What about Ryan, would he know? Claire might have told him the other half of the information.'

'She might have done,' I agree.

'It's worth contacting him.'

It is. Claire always maintained contact with Ryan, even when he was living in far flung places like Ghana and Malaysia. He'd send the occasional present to her like the elephant she told me about in her last visit. They'd swap newsy emails, ring each other on their birthdays and Christmases. Her bond with him was as strong as ours. It's likely that she'd confide in him like she did with me.

It'll be weird ringing Ryan; I haven't heard his voice for a while. What if he doesn't remember me?

What's going to require a bigger dose of confidence and charm is approaching the Ugly

Sisters. I need to get into Claire's flat and I'm only going to get legitimate access if I can persuade one of them to get me the key. But which sister to try first?

Chapter 37

Thursday ~ day 3

After dinner I ring the only mobile number I have for Ryan. God knows if he still has it. There's silence at first whilst it connects then it rings out – a funny ring, not like the ones you get in this country.

The nervous knot in my stomach pulls tauter and I wonder if I should abandon this when the ringing stops and a male voice abruptly says, 'Hola.'

'Ryan? Is that you? It's Will. How you doing?' I'm aware how boisterous and overjoyed I sound, but it's so good to speak to my friend again.

'Who is this?'

'William Bailey,' I explain. 'We were friends with Claire Millward.' For fuck's sake, I think, he doesn't remember me. Has it been that long?

'Elvis!' he roars, using just one of the many nicknames he had for me on account of my hairstyle. 'How's the quiff? Don't tell me you've still got it. Have you?' He doesn't wait for an answer but continues speaking. 'I'm bloody knackered. This bar has me working day and fucking night for a few pesetas. It's killing me.'

Ryan has always liked to refer to a country's previous currencies. It was his specialist subject in any pub quiz. Unfortunately there were rarely any questions on the subject.

'It's alright. It's been a while,' I say awkwardly.

'It certainly has. What you been up to...Oh shit. Of course. You've been in the big house, haven't you? Yeah, Claire said. What was it like?'

'It was good. If I could have added a few more years to my sentence I would have,' I reply sarcastically and he laughs. Was he always this much of a twat? The nicknames, however, are coming back to me. He loved to take the piss out of my hair calling me such original names as Elvis, Tin Tin, and Morrissey. I put it down to the fact that he had rubbish hair and mickey-taking made him feel better. Thinning from his early twenties, his hair is also ginger. He started shaving it off and it made him look like an action hero, a look he approved of.

'What did you do again? Wasn't it something to do with your brother?'

'Yeah, it was. Jees, Ryan, has it been that long? Do you remember anything else about me?'

'Appalling memory these days, mate. Too much drink and sun, I reckon. Me brain's either dried up or pickled.'

'I'm ringing about Claire,' I tell him, cutting straight to the chase.

He stops chuckling. 'Is there any news?'

'Her family still think she's run away and will turn up one day. I think something's happened to her.'

Eventually Ryan says, 'Me too.'

'I don't know who might be involved or why or anything yet, but I want to do a bit of digging around. At some point I'm going to need the Ugly Sisters' help in getting access to Claire's flat, which is going to be interesting. Her neighbour told me about a couple of male visitors Claire had to the flat.'

'Charlton,' Ryan says.

'I'm glad she talked to you about him because finding him isn't going to be easy, and I need to find out who was the bloke she was seeing before.'

'Ahh, the Spanish dude.'

'El Erizo,' I tell him.

'Yeah, that's him. Hang on. I'll ask Elena what that means.' He starts shouting her name. 'What does el Erizo mean? It doesn't matter what for. A what? Really? Gracias, Elena.' He comes back on the line properly. 'It means hedgehog.'

'Hedgehog?' I repeat, incredulous.

'Yeah, not very useful is it? What did she tell you about him?'

I tell him their affair lasted about two years and ended in May last year. I talk about their weekends away, that they weren't to spectacular places and that he got the nickname from when he was out in Spain, whatever that meant.

'Yeah,' Ryan says thoughtfully. 'I asked her where in Spain he'd been; I wondered if it was somewhere I'd been. She said Murcia, which is on the coast not far from Alicante. It's not your usual tourist destination, but a lot of ex-pats live there. He's not Spanish, I'm sure of that. She'd have bragged about it if he was.'

I laugh with agreement. At college, Claire had dated a French exchange student and smiled smugly for the entire fortnight it lasted.

'Why even give the man a nickname?' Ryan wonders intelligently. 'If his name's Dave then I'm not going to know him. There are millions of Daves. Unless he has a unique first name or he's famous.'

'Where would she meet someone famous around here? It's not exactly London or New York.'

'A nightclub,' Ryan suggests. 'She and that friend of hers...were out clubbing every night when they shared a flat. I'm sure Claire reckoned she'd copped off with some soap actor and possibly some lower division football player.'

'Nisha. I remember. Are they in contact still?'

'Don't know, but I can tell you where to find her: she's a private investigator.'

'Really? I wonder if she can get me some work.'

'You never know, mate. I can't remember the name of the firm, but it's local. Local to you that is, not me. You'll have to do some ringing around.'

'It's a good lead. Thanks, mate. Do you remember anything Claire may have said about Charlton?'

'I'll have to think about that one and get back to you. I'll email you. Give me your address and once I've had a think I'll let you know.'

'I need to set up a new one. Give me yours and I'll email you.' I grab a receipt off the work surface and carefully jot down his address, checking the full stops are in the right places.

'There is one other thing, mate,' Ryan says, seriously. I listen. 'The last time I spoke to Claire, which was early November, she asked me if I could lend her some money.'

'Was she desperate?'

'Mate, she must have been. I mean, I earn enough to sleep in rat-free digs and eat hot food. I had a couple of hundred Euros, but that wasn't going to be enough.'

'What was it for?'

'Don't know. She just said, 'Never mind, it's not important' and changed the subject. She laughed when I suggested she ask Tight Arse Andrew. She replied that she was better off asking her dad!'

Philip, of course. Despite the animosity between him and Marion, Claire always maintained a discreet relationship with him, sending birthday, Christmas and of course Father's Day cards. Philip doesn't have much in worldly goods, but once his father pops his clogs, he's due a windfall. Very nice too; it'd be even better if he had the good health to enjoy it. Ravaged by drink, his liver is knackered. I haven't seen him for years, but I know where he lives – in sheltered accommodation, a couple of junctions down the motorway.

'Hey, I'd better let you hang up. Your phone bill's going be through the roof. Don't forget to email and I'll put my thinking cap on,' Ryan says cheerfully.

'Yeah, I will and thanks for your help. Been really great chatting with you, mate.' Apart from the sarcasm and the name calling, I silently add.

'Next time *we'll* catch up, okay?'

'See you later, mate,' I say, ending the call.

I retreat upstairs to write down everything that I've learnt.

So, I think, reclining against the headboard, what have we learned about el Erizo?

It means hedgehog. Is that because he resembles one? Is it a variation on his names? If he worked in Spain, is it something to do with his line of business? Or is it some kind of pet name? Like Mr Snuggles or Pumpkin?

I'm never going to work it out. But once I have a suspect then I'll innocently ask if el Erizo means anything to him.

What about these weekends away? York was one: nice city, lovely cathedral; Bath, again very nice; but Kettering, Grimsby. They're not exactly renowned for hosting a delightful weekend away not when there are more historic, lively pretty places to visit. Claire liked busy, trendy places like Manchester and London with its outdoor bars and cafes and the clubs.

Ryan's right about Nisha being a good source of information. They lived together and we all know how girls like to talk.

I put the writing pad down and close my eyes. I've got such a lot I need to do tomorrow. Find Nisha, contact Philip and approach them awful sisters.

'Don't forget the loan she asked Ryan for.'

My eyes open suddenly. If she was desperate enough to ask Ryan for a loan then who else had she asked? And what did she want it for? About ten years ago, Claire got herself into debt to the tune of ten grand. She overspent on credit cards and ended up transferring the balance from one card to another, managing only the minimum payment and inevitably the interest caught up with her and the bank wanted their money, which she didn't have. Claire had asked her parents for help, but Andrew wouldn't put his hand in his pocket. Hence our jokes about his meanness. Claire asked everybody for help, even me. In the end the money came from Phil's dad. It was given on the condition that this was her inheritance and when the old man popped his clogs, Claire wouldn't get anything.

Surely she wouldn't be so stupid as to get herself into debt again? I'd read her the riot act at the time. I couldn't believe how she'd let her finances get so out of control.

For years, Claire had been solvent. Maybe there was another reason she wanted the money. Had she seen something she wanted but couldn't afford it? Had she wanted it to repair the car? Was it for an emergency, a broken boiler, a knackered washing machine? I know the other question I should be asking, that's staring me in the face. Did she want it to finance her running away? Did she need it for a flight, a hotel stay or hire a car? But all that begs the next two questions – why and where has she gone? And I reply in exactly the same way as I did to Marion – Claire wouldn't have left until I was out. That I'm sure about.

Chapter 38

Friday ~ day 4

'It's ringing,' Mum says and gives a little throat-clearing cough. I smile appreciatively. I'd do it myself but I don't want to risk the receptionist recognising my voice. An hour ago I rolled up to Andrew's business, 'Elephant Wines', to see Sally. And isn't it just typical, you gear yourself up for something, and it falls flat on its face. Sally isn't in the office today. But as I left, an idea formulated in my head.

Mum looks away from me and puts on her professional voice. 'Good morning. I'm calling from the Inland Revenue. Please may I speak to Sally Lancaster? Oh. I do need to speak to her today; it is important. Is she contactable at...she's working from home,' Mum's voice rises pleased to get the information I need. 'That's great...no, thank you. I have a home phone number for her here. Thank you for your help. Goodbye.' She hangs up and grins at me.

'That's great. Mum, you're a star.' I grab the car keys off the work surface and spin on my heels to face the hallway. She stops me, a cautionary hand on the shoulder.

'Be careful, Will. You've just come out of prison and *I* know you've served your sentence, but don't give the Lancasters any excuse to cause trouble for you.'

'I promise to be careful, Mum.' I kiss her cheek. 'See you for lunch.' I jump back into the Mazda and head back onto the road, Sally-ward bound. Mum was so authentic, I think with a smile and why shouldn't she be? She used to work at the Inland Revenue before Dad needed 24 hour care.

*

I turn right by the social club and pass the parade of shops: kebab shop, hairdresser, bookies, fish 'n' chip shop, newsagents, Chinese takeaway and lastly a barber's. That's all it seems to be these days: unhealthy takeaway food and a choice of places to get a new hairstyle.

'There used to be a nice pub down here,' I comment, 'that served real ale.'

I turn to look at what was the Miner's Arms. Half the roof is missing, burnt out by the looks of it. The charred remains of the rafters look like charcoal briquettes; the brickwork is discoloured and singed. The windows are boarded up with shiny steel panels, now covered with misspelt graffiti.

'Such a shame,' I mutter as the Mazda sails past.

I pull up outside Sally's neighbour's house on Queens Road so she can't see my arrival and hide upstairs.

I rap the door knocker, stand back and wait. Movement through the vertical panels of frosted glass. She's home and so my heart responds by thumping away like a bongo drummer. I can do this, I tell myself. I was good at persuading people to talk, or should that be confess. It's been a while since I've interviewed somebody, but I always adopted the appropriate tone of voice whether it needed to be firm or gentle, and if I didn't get anywhere then a colleague could always give it a bash. But now I have to get this right first time; no one's going to come to my aid and I know the odds are against me. But Sally is the reasonable sister, the one to see sense. She's a more preferable target than Olivia.

The door opens releasing the tantalising aroma of freshly brewed coffee. Bet she doesn't offer me one.

Sally's expression is fixed like she's been caught in Medusa's gaze and has turned to stone. Her jaw is clenched, her eyes wide. Then I notice how quickly her chest is rising like someone struggling to breathe.

'Hi Sally. I need to speak to you about Claire.'

'No,' she squeaks. 'You can't. You've accused me and my sister of not giving two hoots about Claire,' and with both hands she tries to fling the door shut and she's almost successful if it wasn't for my size nine wedging it open.

'Please. Just a couple of minutes,' I reason, 'and then I'll go.'

She brings the door closer to her body as if to prevent me from seeing beyond her into the house. 'Mum told me you might call around,' she says haughtily. 'With your nasty accusations.'

I clench my fists, determined not to rise to the bait.

She sticks her nose into the air and continues rather unnecessarily to put me firmly in my place. 'Claire's *their* daughter. She's *only* your friend. They're worried sick, but they're trying to remain positive. And you turn up, stamping all over their feelings, accusing them of not *even* knowing their own daughter. That was cruel. You had no right to say that.'

'I didn't quite say...'

'Yes, you did. Mum told me everything you said.'

'I suggested that Claire might not have run off, that something might have happened...'

'That she's been murdered! Do you have any idea of how upsetting that is?'

'Well, yes, I do. I was a police officer. I've dealt with many bereaved relatives...'

'Claire has not been murdered! There's no evidence at the flat that anything has happened—'

'How do you know that? Have you been to her flat?'

Sally stares. 'No. Why would I have?'

'How do you know there isn't the tiniest blood splatter in the bathroom? What did you know about Claire's relationships?'

Sally frowns. This is news to her. 'That she didn't have any.'

'Hmm. That's where you're wrong,' but I don't dwell on this interesting titbit and carry on talking. 'All I'm suggesting is that your parents don't leave this solely in the hands of the police. They are not actively looking for Claire. As far as they're concerned she's a mentally stable adult who's run off for whatever personal reason.'

'She has,' Sally insists.

I shake my head and breathe deeply, trying to keep my temper intact. 'I just want you to consider the other possibility. It's been several months now that Claire has disappeared. Why hasn't she got in contact? Your mum told me how close all of you were, but not one of you has heard from her. You must find that odd, worrying...' I trail off hoping she might admit how she's feeling.

She doesn't.

This stubbornness and lack of emotion disturbs me. Have I underestimated her? Why can't she and her stupid fucking parents see that I only want to help? I'm beginning to think they have something to hide. 'Sally, I need access to Claire's flat...'

She laughs out loud. 'No way. I'm not defying my parents' wishes.'

'What about your wishes? You loved Claire. You must want to know...'

'I'm not helping you. Leave us alone,' she sniffs, bringing the back of her hand up to her nose. 'Don't come here again.' The door closes. This time I let it.

I walk back down the path to the Mazda, shaking my head at the stupidity of this family. Is it some kind of conspiracy? I can understand Marion's reluctance. She sees me as a dodgy police officer, somebody who lies and provides false alibis. But Sally...she's intelligent, reasonable, and obviously doing as she's told. Maybe it isn't easy to get the key to Claire's flat. It'd be just my luck if Marion wore it on a chain around her neck, in which case I'd need to decapitate her to get it off. Olivia is Plan B, but Sally will be on the phone to her after she's called Marion glamorising how I've behaved so when I do approach Olivia I'll get the grenade as well as both barrels.

I jump back into the Mazda when my pocket vibrates. A text. My first text.

'Hi W. Got some info for you. Kenny has remembered something about the angry wife. Call around anytime. Will have kettle on. Bev.'

Brilliant. A break-through perhaps? Let's go and see. I put the Mazda in first and head over to Bev's.

*

Kenny yawns. Is this bloke ever wide awake? Bev hands him a steaming hot cup of tea. He mumbles a thank you and raises it to his mouth with shaky hands. He smells of warm bed, a kind of yeasty aroma. He sits on the settee in baggy-kneed blue tracksuit bottoms and a crumpled football shirt.

I sip my hot coffee. Kenny's tongue must be made of asbestos. As he puts the cup down on the coaster, I notice a quarter of it has been drunk. 'Bev says you remember something about the woman that was here,' I prompt.

He looks up bleary eyed. 'She was kicking the hell out of Claire's front door and yelling. I went out to tell her to shut the fuck up. Sorry, Bev.'

She smiles.

'Did you know her?' I ask, sitting up in my seat, buoyed up by this good news.

He shakes his head. 'I'm rubbish at faces. But I recognised her top; it's the uniform of the gym I used to go to.'

'Are you still a member of the gym? Can you get me in? You might be able to point her out.'

'I cancelled my membership about a month before. I hardly went, never had the energy. I might recognise her, but these women trainer types all look the same to me. Muscular, no tits, always running or doing star jumps.'

Bev laughs and I slump in the chair, feeling defeated.

'Kenny, love, what's the name of the gym?' Bev offers him another jam sandwich cream.

'It's called *Super Tone*. Nice place, but I was paying nearly fifty quid a month and that was for off-peak, but I was asleep during them hours...'

You're always fucking asleep, a voice inside my head mutters and I smile.

'What about the van?' I ask.

Bev leans over the arm of the chair for a writing pad and flicks through the pages till she finds what she's after. 'Here. I wrote down everything I can remember about the van man and the man with the Jag. Oh, you take a look, Kenny, you might be able to add something.'

He wipes his fingers down the front of his top before handling the pad. He reads quickly. 'Nice Jag,' he mutters and looks up. 'I know my cars. It was an XJ. Private plate. Something short, pricey.' Kenny taps his fingertip on the paper. 'The bloke with a van: he didn't come in a van that day with his wife. It was a people carrier.'

And I have a vision of them loading Claire's body into the back of his van or the people carrier for disposal at another location.

'The van was one of them car vans; you know the front looks like a car. Not a big thing like a transit,' Bev says and I look at Kenny for the make and model, but he shakes his head.

'Jags turn my head. Vans don't.'

'It was red,' Bev says with certainty.

'It was a shed,' he laughs.

He's a lot more awake now we've jogged his brain with caffeine and biscuits, and I'm learning loads. 'Do you remember any other visitors to Claire's flat?' I ask. 'Say in the last two years till Spring last year? Before the van man and Jag man.'

Kenny shakes his head and my smile melts with disappointment.

Bev looks at Kenny. 'You remember the other man. He visited Claire before either of these two came along. You had a set-to with him when he blocked you in on the car park. It was around Christmas and it was snowing.' Kenny looks at her vacantly. 'He spat at you. Luckily it missed...'

And it's like a switch has clicked on inside his head. A memory as bright as dazzling sunlight shines out of his wide eyes. He wags a finger. 'Oh, yes! I remember. Arrogant prick. He drove a Jag too.'

'What do you remember about him or the car?' I ask.

'Full of his own self-importance, sarcastic, unpleasant. It was an old man's Jag. Not modern or sleek. Sorry, mate.'

'No, you've done well to remember. It's been a massive help.'

Bev tears the pages off the pad and hands them to me.

'It's a bit all over the place; I've tried to remember as much as I can about the vehicles, Claire's visitors, snippets of conversation. I hope some of it helps, love.'

'I appreciate the help you've both given me. I know it's not easy to remember stuff from several months ago. Unless it sticks in your head as being weird or even familiar, like the gym shirt, it just disappears without being registered.'

'You're welcome, mate. Now if you don't mind, I'm off to *Bed*fordshire,' Kenny says, getting to his feet and then I notice he's wearing just his socks.

'Thank you, Kenny.'

'Night night, love,' Bev says, and when he's gone she asks me if I've managed to get access to the flat.

'I've struck out with the parents and the little sister. Only the middle sister remains and she's gonna be tough. She despises me. Aside from breaking and entering, I don't know how else to get access to the flat.'

'You're going to have to be extra nice to her,' Bev says.

How do you be nice to a caustic bitch?

Chapter 39

Friday ~ day 4

I return to Andrew's premises at clocking off time and wait at the front of the building away from where I might be seen. He leaves on the dot at 5pm; driving off at speed, cutting in front of another driver who reacts angrily with a blast of the horn. His employees don't start leaving till after ten past five, probably when they're sure the boss isn't going to come back unexpectedly. Liv doesn't appear till twenty past. She waves goodbye to a colleague and heads in the opposite direction away from me.

'Hey Liv!' I call and her head turns. She stops and waits for me to jog over, grinning with amusement.

'I get it! I'm plan B. You're forced to pay me a visit since you've had no success with Sally, but how are you going to play it – good cop or bad? I prefer bad. So go on: give me your opening line.' And she props a hand on her hip and tilts her head to the side.

'Fancy a lift home?' I offer.

'You have a car?' she says doubtfully.

I nod at the lay-by over the road where the Mazda is waiting. 'It'll save you the bus fare, and think what your neighbours will say when they see you roll up in style.'

We cross the road and I open the car door for her, remembering what Bev said about charm.

'I was expecting you,' she says, looking around at the inside of the car and sniffing the air freshener hanging from the rear-view mirror. 'If you hadn't come to see me, I'd have been disappointed.'

I glance across and she smiles, and this close up I see how heavily, but professionally made-up she is. Her eye shadow is made up of three complimentary shades of brown. She puts a stray lock of dark hair behind her ear and I get a whiff of her perfume, which I wonder if she's freshly reapplied before she clocked off and whether it's for my benefit, whether she can deflect my attention off Claire and onto herself.

'Why don't you tell me what you think has happened to Claire? You must have a lead. What is it?'

I brake at the lights, pondering my next sentence. How can I expect her to help me if I don't give her a little something? But first...

'Only if you promise to seriously consider my request to get the key to Claire's flat, with or without your parents' knowledge?'

'I promise,' and she lays a hand on her ample chest.

'What do you know about Claire's relationships?'

'That she hasn't had a boyfriend for years. She never brought anyone to meet us and I was starting to wonder if she liked girls instead.'

'She didn't,' I reassure. 'Claire didn't do relationships. She had dates and flings.'

'What kind of men are we talking about here? Do they belong to a particular category?'

'Yes. They're usually called married.'

Liv's brown eyes are like saucers. Her thickly painted plum lips open stickily. 'Like father like daughter,' she mutters and I reply, 'Suppose so,' so she knows that I'm aware of Phil's fidelity issues.

'The night before she disappeared, an angry wife visited Claire's flat. She wasn't home. Claire hasn't used her bank cards, withdrawn money, kept her appointments; she had one the next day. It doesn't make sense. There's no reason why she'd run away.'

'Avoiding this woman was a good reason.'

I shake my head. 'No. Claire would have dealt with her.'

'Me and her had a row,' Liv blurts out. 'I thought Dad was giving her money.'

I glance across at her, but the traffic starts moving at the island and I have to concentrate.

When she explains, her voice is small, ashamed, but still jealous. 'She wears such nice clothes and jewellery; she has a lovely flat in a nice area and I thought "How can she afford that on a secretary's wage?" We assumed Dad was compensating for not being her real father. That didn't bother me so much, but he's never given me or Sally as much as ten pence for a phone call. Have you seen where I live? Well, you will. I don't go out after dark.'

'Why would they favour Claire?'

'I don't know. I overheard Dad and Claire arguing about money. And I know that when Claire was little, she told Mum about Phil's affair and I got it in my head that Claire was fleecing money from Dad.'

'How, with blackmail?' I don't mention Claire asking Ryan for a loan; it would only lay weight to Liv's theory.

She shrugs. 'What kind of blackmail? Dad wouldn't cheat on Mum, he adores her.' She's scratching a frayed area of her handbag strap with her nail.

'The money is more likely to have come from the men she was seeing,' I explain and her eyes lift sharply up, and I see immediately what conclusion she's drawn from that. 'She wasn't selling herself. I mean in the form of gifts.'

'Oh,' she mouths.

She's fallen silent now, thoughtful and reflective and I think about asking for her help. I see a sign indicating the bus station is left at the junction. It's not nice around here. Already clusters of hooded youths are congregating on street corners as the buses deposit and pick up passengers.

'Pull up anywhere on the left.'

I indicate and pull up alongside the kerb, the wheels splashing in a puddle. I turn the ignition off and face her, smiling sympathetically. Careful now. Word it correctly. 'Liv, help me find out what's happened to Claire.'

Her noisy sigh doesn't sound promising. Maybe she's seen through the lift for what it is – a ploy to get her to help me all for someone else – a sister she's still jealous of, because even though Claire isn't here, her parents are more concerned about her than Liv and that must hurt deeply.

'I don't know where the key is and I can't exactly ask, can I? My parents will go up the wall if I help you.'

'You could offer to go around and check up on the place. An empty flat is an opportunity for squatters.'

'Just because Claire was shagging married men and a wife found out doesn't mean she was murdered,' she replies suddenly angry. 'I still think she's run off and she's too much of a bitch to let us know she's alright.' And with that, Liv flings open the door and almost falls out of the car, desperately gathering her belongings before they tumble into the wet and dirty gutter. She slams the door and hurries down the side of a kebab shop, narrowly avoiding a collision with a man eating from a polystyrene box of food.

'That's strike number three,' I tell myself. 'You're out.' I start up the Mazda and remember. 'There's still Phil.'

*

Phil Millward lives up to my expectation of a lonely single alcoholic: stick-thin, bruised, unkempt, living out of one or two squalid rooms, surviving on a liquid diet which includes soup and canned meals as well as whisky and beer. I wonder if his living conditions have gotten worse since Claire disappeared.

He welcomes me warmly, offers to make a coffee or get me a can. I opt for black coffee; sure he has no liquid milk in the fridge. He apologises for the mess, stating that he's recently sacked his housekeeper and is struggling to cope with the junk mail that comes through the letterbox. He says it so deadpan that I wonder if he's serious.

He struggles to lift the pile of newspapers off the armchair and looks around for somewhere else to put them. He spies a spot – on top of a bucket under the window.

'I've been ill,' he explains, and I wonder if it contains piss or he's started spewing up blood yet. 'As I was saying, Claire was meant to pick me up on Saturday morning; we were going out for the day – bit of shopping, lunch. When she didn't arrive by ten, I rang the flat, but there was no answer. I was still trying into the evening. I thought something must have come up.' He puts a hand up to his mouth and starts coughing. His chest rattles like coins being shaken inside a metal tube and I think of telling him to get to a doctor's. He clears his throat and reaches for a scrunched up tissue to spit into.

'Was Claire visiting you often?'

He nods. 'Couple of times a month.'

I smile. 'How was she the last time you saw or spoke to her?'

'Alright.'

I sip the coffee. Ugh, needs more sugar. 'Did she ask to borrow money?'

'Nah, she knows I haven't got any till my inheritance comes through and I'll probably die first,' laughs Phil.

'What did you two talk about?'

He thinks for a few moments and reaches for a tumbler but it's empty so the hand automatically reaches down by his lower leg for the bottle of Bell's whisky. He fills the glass and takes a big gulp. 'We talked about the weather; snow was due because she was worried I wouldn't be able to get any shopping in. We talked about the football but to be honest I don't follow it anymore. She asked me what would happen to a manager who was caught betting on his own team. Or rather if the manager asked someone else to place the bet for him.'

'Why did she ask that?'

Phil shrugs and sips the whisky. 'She said she just wondered.'

What an odd thing to wonder. But how likely is it that Claire knows a football manager? I store it away for future reference.

Phil finishes his whisky and pours another. 'I'm drinking more now,' he explains sadly. 'I can't believe there'd be anyone who'd want to hurt her, and I don't buy this running away shit that Marion believes. Claire was due to pick me up. We were both looking forward to it and like you, she wouldn't have left me either.'

I smile. 'I'm pleased to hear someone has the same view as me.'

'Let me know how you get on. And before you go, could you open those bottles for me,' and he points to a cardboard wine carrier on the floor between the chairs; each slot filled with a whisky bottle. 'It's murder trying to open them. Not too good for an alkie, eh?'

*

I return home and walk into full-scale pistols drawn and aimed row. In the blue corner, weighing in at...well, I wouldn't like to say, but a size 12, is my Mum, fingers literally tearing her hair out, her face ugly with despair and stress. In the red corner, weighing in at 14 stone and wearing shoes with knotted laces and holding a broom is my Dad, his eyes flashing with angry determination and something more frightening.

I close the door behind me and glance puzzled at the broom. Dried leaves and twigs stick out of the bristles. Has Dad got a new obsession?

Mum speaks first. 'Lock the door, please, Will, and stop your dad from going out. He wants to sweep the streets now like some council worker.'

'There's no point in locking the door. I'll get out if I want to,' Dad states.

'You will not,' she argues. 'What are the neighbours going to say if they see you sweeping the gutter? They already think your behaviour's odd.'

'They don't. Anyway I don't give a fuck what they say,' and I wince at his language. Dad never used to say anything stronger than bloody or bugger. 'They should mind their own business.'

'Well, they certainly do that. They cross the road to avoid you and your stupid questions about which street is this and which is number six. Not to mention the armful of leaves you keep bringing home. You're like a cat bringing home a mouse.'

'I've never bought leaves home,' he shouts. 'What kind of a stupid thing is that to say?'

'You've done it twice today,' she screams. 'Why do you think the Hoover is permanently plugged in?'

'Mum, please. Just calm down,' I say, watching her face getter redder.

She looks at me with such desperation and fear, and I feel awful that whilst Eddie and I have been languishing in jail, she's had Dad and the horror of his illness to deal with. And she's just about at the end of her tether.

'Yes, calm down, Kay, before you have a heart attack,' Dad says callously.

'Dad, please, that's enough,' I say firmly.

'Don't you fucking speak to me like that?' he shouts, stepping forward, broom in hand looking like a Roman centurion. 'Who do you think you are?'

Jesus, I say to myself, straightening up to my full height of six feet one. Dad might be a few inches shorter than me, but judging by his temper I reckon he fancies his chances. Plus he's armed. Who's to say he won't swing that broom at my head?

'Just go out, Mike,' Mum orders, stepping between me and him. 'There's the door, you've got your broom, go and sweep for England. Give me some peace.'

I manage to open the door before Dad charges through it. I look at Mum in silence, not knowing what to say. I want to apologise for what I stupidly did, how I thought it'd help, but now I see how it's horribly backfired. Eddie and I should have been here to help and support her not exclude ourselves from a worsening situation.

'I can't cope anymore,' she says and I bite my lip afraid that I'll start to cry. She doesn't need my tears not when her own heart must be breaking. 'It's relentless. He has no thought for his own safety. It's my job to keep him safe because he can't do it himself...he can't do anything for himself...do you know what he's started doing now?' she demands tearfully and I shake my head.

'He doesn't know how to use the toilet. He pees on the lid. It drips all over the floor. How disgusting...I can't stand it...'

'Come on, let's sit down.' I steer her toward the dining room and pull out a chair. 'Shall I put the kettle on? Or do you want a whiskey?' I'm thinking that I could do with one; it might bring my heart rate back to down to normal.

'Tea's fine.' She frowns. 'Maybe put a drop of Jameson's in it.'

I fill the kettle and gather the cups and teabags. 'How about contacting Derek from the Mental Health team? Surely there's something they can give Dad to keep him calm.' I pour boiling water into the cups and the teabags swell and rise to the surface.

'I'll ring Derek tomorrow. Now, tell me how your investigation has gone today. I need something else to talk about.'

I thrill Mum with my exaggerated questioning of witnesses and sadly how I couldn't persuade the Ugly Sisters to help me.

'I need to get in Claire's flat,' I grumble. 'There are things I need to look at, not that I can do that with either of the sisters there; I have a plan for that. But it would appear that I've struck out three times, which means I'm out of options. I do have another lead,' I say, injecting some enthusiasm into my voice. 'After the weekend I'll go to the hospital to see Nisha's mother, she works there. Hopefully she'll tell me how I can get in contact with Nisha. It'll save me the painstaking job of ringing every private investigation agency in the county.'

'She may offer you a job,' Mum says, brightly.

'She may. I'll certainly need the money.' I start to tell her what information I might be able to learn from Nisha but I'm interrupted by Dad who has returned having forgotten the row only twenty minutes before. Mum takes the opportunity to pin him in front of the TV with a Western.

I decide to write what I've learnt on my pad. As I pick up my cup to take upstairs, the corner of a writing pad catches my eye. The letter opens with: 'Dear Eddie' and there are a few sentences written underneath. I don't want Mum to catch me reading a letter intended for him so I put the paper back and go upstairs.

Chapter 40

Monday ~ day 7

The next day I head off to the hospital to find Nisha's mum who works in the Linen department. Once in possession of the name of the agency Nisha works for, I return to the main corridor, a thought striking me suddenly. If I can locate Pathology then maybe one of Claire's colleagues will tell me about her work life. Was there something going on there?

On the wall in the main corridor is a big board indicating the direction of the wards, but not pathology. A member of staff helpfully points me in the right direction and I head off.

Most of the wards are on the first floor, but that doesn't stop the smell of shit and illness permeating stairwells and escaping into other areas.

Jesus, I think, hope that doesn't burst. A bearded elderly man is shuffling towards me, wearing a hospital gown over a pair of ill-fitting pyjamas which show off his bandy chicken legs; a bulging bag of piss is strapped to the outer side of his thigh, its tube winding back up his leg and in through his flies.

I give him a wide berth and continue on my way turning left even though the sign overhead says

'Haematology Clinic.' I pass empty consulting rooms glimpsing black leather examination tables covered in protective blue paper, metal trolleys house boxes of purple gloves. The corridor opens up into a large waiting room. I wander over to the reception desk and ask if I can speak to one of the pathology secretaries.

Several minutes later, a portly lady in her early fifties with short dyed red hair appears from the back of the clinic and looks around. Her pink jumper has a sequinned cat on the front and around her neck is an ID card on a strap. The receptionist points her in my direction and she comes over, smiling expectantly.

'Hello, I'm Anne. Can I help?'

'Hello. I'm William Bailey; I'm a friend of Claire's.'

'Oh,' she says with surprise. 'Shall we go over there where it's a bit quieter.' Anne leads me to a cushioned bench beside a drinks machine. She sits down, producing a tyre of fat around her middle. I see a trio of stars of different sizes tattooed along the blade of her hand by her little finger. I wonder what they represent.

'We miss Claire such a lot,' she begins sincerely. 'The office isn't the same. I can hardly believe that she just upped sticks and left.'

'I don't think she did,' I say and Anne's eyes widen at my revelation. 'How was Claire at work?'

Her answer is disappointingly bland. 'Things were fine. No real problems.'

I pounce. 'No real problems? So there were, what tiny problems?'

She fumbles over her answer. 'Not really. You know what women in an office are like: gossiping, bitching, having a giggle. Claire was one of the girls,' and she laughs, but it fails to convince me. Claire was not 'one of the girls.' Anne opens her mouth as if to elaborate, but thinks the better of it and snaps her jaw shut. 'I haven't really got anything else to tell you. You could talk to Isla over at the mortuary. They were pals; they had lunch together.'

Claire's never mentioned Isla before, but it's a lead and maybe she's more willing to tell the truth. I say thanks and follow her directions outside.

The outside entrance to the mortuary is situated at the rear of a small car park. Overhead is a metal canopy where deliveries and pick-ups can be made discreetly. A black windowless van is just leaving as I approach. I ring the bell and wait.

Moments later a skinny girl wearing blue scrubs, her hair in a thick ponytail throws open the door and with a big smile and a cheery voice says, 'Hi!'

Her friendliness throws me off guard and I wonder if she knows me. I tell her who I am and why I'm here.

'Claire,' she mutters sadly, shaking her head. 'I miss my chick. I can tell you loads but not right now. We're about to start PMs with Dr Misery Guts.' She pulls a grumpy face and it makes me smile. 'Do you want to meet here later, about five? We can go to the canteen for a cuppa and a biccie. Is that okay?'

'Perfect.'

'Great. See you, later, Will.' And she's gone; her hair as thick as dreadlocks almost whips me across the face.

Nice girl, I think, this could be a fruitful trip. I turn to walk back to my car and spy a tall woman strolling purposefully towards me. She's wearing an orange top and a pink skirt, its pleats as sharp as knife edges. An authoritative hand reaches out and stops me; I'm about to walk around her, but she tells me her name.

You're Fiona, I think. Now you, I've heard of. But she's not at all what I expect. She could be aged anywhere between 30 and 45. Her mismatched and garish clothes make her look frumpy and quirky at the same time. Her mousey hair hangs heavy over her ears, the tips of each just poke through her locks like she's wearing a fake pair of FA Cup ears.

'I should have been asked to speak to you about Claire as we were friends,' she says haughtily. 'I don't know why Anne took it upon herself to be spokesperson for the office. What has she told you?'

'Not much really. She said things were fine in the office for Claire, no real problems at all. That made my ears prick up. Any idea what she might mean?' I ask and watch for her response, and there it is: a twitch like she has a fishing line hooked in her top lip and the fisherman is yanking on it.

'I've absolutely no idea.'

I decide to test just how honest Fiona is. 'Did Claire talk to *you* about her problems, boyfriends?'

'Of course,' Fiona replies. 'There weren't many boyfriends, she was shy around men, but she'd tell me who she liked. Otherwise we'd just talk about girls' stuff.'

'There were no problems in her personal life either, no disgruntled boyfriends?'

Fiona pauses, but thinks the better of it. Instead she shakes her head and pouts exposing the inside of her bottom lip. Both she and Anne are exhibiting the same behaviour I've seen plenty of lying scroats do in police interviews.

'Were you a close friend of Claire's?' Fiona peers at me. 'Claire never mentioned a man friend.' And that seriously contradicts Fiona's idea that Claire confides in her.

'She wouldn't have mentioned me,' I say lowering my voice dramatically. 'I've been away. At Her Majesty's Pleasure.'

The look of horror on her prim face is priceless. I tell her I'm joking, but she doesn't look convinced so I change my story to part-truth, part-bullshit: I'm an ex-police officer and that I've been away travelling. She buys this which is just as well because it occurs to me that I may need her later on and if I've frightened her off then I won't get what I need.

Another black van enters the car park and sweeps around in a big arc before reversing under the canopy. I turn and watch as a dark suited man climbs out and rings the doorbell.

'I'd better get back to my desk before Anne sends out a search party,' Fiona says pleasantly. 'If there's anything else we can help you with then please get in contact.'

'Thanks, Fiona. That's great. Have you got a mobile number?'

'Er, yes, of course,' and I key it straight into my mobile.

I walk back around to my car pondering the whys and lies Fiona and Anne have told me about

Claire. I need someone impartial and hopefully that's where Isla will come in useful.

*

'Ooh, I'm going to have a sticky bun. I need it after five PMs in an afternoon,' laughs Isla as she drops a Chelsea bun onto a plate and licks her fingers, murmuring with childish delight. I smile to myself and slide the tray towards the till.

'I'll get this,' I tell her. 'I appreciate you talking to me when you could have been on your way home.'

'I might not have anything interesting to say,' Isla says, grabbing a handful of sugar packets off the counter.

'I'm sure you've got more to tell me than Fiona and Anne.' I carry the tray over to a table Isla points out at the back of the canteen by a plant.

'Fiona and Anne don't know Claire,' she says, taking the cups and plates off the tray which she props up against a spare chair. 'Claire thought Anne was a boring old biddy who never stopped going on about her grandkids.' Isla fakes a yawn. 'And Fiona is plain odd. She has an old man living with her. She won't say who he is, but he can't be a boyfriend. I mean that's just creepy and sick.'

I tear open a packet of sugar and tip it into my brew which looks as weak as the shit they used to serve up in the prison.

'She must be raking in the carer's allowance *and* she's in his will too.' Isla cuts the bun in half and shoves a chunk into her mouth. She eats noisily and dramatically, rotating her jaw around like a cow chewing the cud. I'm a bit taken aback. It's so unladylike. But whilst the bun has her attention and she's not speaking, I grab the opportunity to steer her onto a subject I want to discuss.

'Was Claire having any problems at work? Her colleagues hinted at something, but they were reluctant to elaborate.'

'Yeah! With Fiona. What happened was this,' and she swallows her mouthful of bun before launching into a tale of a private life being exposed, a prank involving a pornographic picture and lots of wild accusations. And I thought people grew up when they got proper jobs.

'Let me just recap: even though Fiona knew Kev put the offensive picture on her PC, she still blamed Claire for betraying her confidence?'

Isla nods.

'Did Fiona want revenge on Claire? How angry was she?'

'Fiona was seething! Apparently she told the whole office that Claire was seeing a married man! And Claire didn't deny it, but she said he *had* been married, but now he was separated. And apparently Fiona text his wife telling her all about the affair. Tara said that what Fiona had done was slander.' Isla's words grind to an abrupt halt and she breathes hard, but still stuffs the other half of the bun into her mouth.

Unbelievable, I think. And these are adults. Fiona sounds a right vindictive cow, Tara sounds like a shit-stirrer, and Kev sounds like a nasty prankster. Poor Claire. I know exactly how humiliated she would feel at her private life being exposed in front of people she cared little for. She was always so particular at keeping things to herself. Look what she told me about her blokes: nearly bugger all.

'Did Fiona confess to texting this wife? How did she discover who he was?'

Isla shrugs like a clueless teenager: a big lift of the shoulders. 'Maybe Fiona knew him? But no way would Claire get involved with a married man. She'd want her own man.'

It's obvious she doesn't know Claire, but Isla makes a good point. If this is Charlton whose van was seen at Claire's flat, is his home number painted on its bodywork? How had Fiona got that number? Had she seen Claire and him together at the hospital? Fiona is definitely my new lead. She might not have anything to do with Claire's disappearance, she might have her own reason for exposing the affair, but I have to speak to her again. If only to ask her why she's lied that she and Claire were the best of friends when in fact they could have been the worst of enemies.

*

When I return home, my mind buzzing with my discoveries, Mum tells me Liv has rang and she wants to speak to me. I ring her straightaway, hoping for some sensible news.

'It was kindly pointed out to me by Dan,' she begins, her voice loud and dramatic and yet shameful too, 'that "at least Will's looking for your sister 'cause your family don't give a flying fuck". Hurtful, but true, so on that basis, I'll get you the key to Claire's flat...'

YES!!

'...to go with you so Sally will. It'll be short notice so be ready. Go straight to the flat and meet her there.'

'Thank you, Liv. This is great. Your boyfriend's being hard on...'

'No, he isn't,' she argues. 'He's got a point. I've got to do something; we've got to do something. Let me know how it goes. See you.'

'Bye.'

I smile at Mum as she serves up dinner. 'I'm in. Sally's meeting me at the flat with the key.'

She hands me a plate of buttered bread. 'You're going to have to be careful about what you might find. You want to preserve Claire's privacy as much as possible.'

I touch the side of my nose. 'I've got a plan for that.'

Chapter 41

Tuesday ~ day 8

Olivia's text message gives me plenty of time to get to Claire's flat. I reverse the Mazda into a car parking space which gives me a good view of the road so I can be out the car when Sally pulls up.

She's late.

I drum my fingers on the steering wheel, check my phone every thirty seconds for a cancellation text and start to fret that Liv has been caught with her hand in the biscuit barrel by Marion or wherever she keeps the key. Where the fuck is Sally? I thought we were against the clock.

Eventually I spy an old car coughing its way down the road. This must be Sally. She parks up and takes her time getting out. I stand by her car admiring the missing hubcap and the rust which is slowly spreading over the wheel arches and upwards like a rash.

The door creaks as she pushes it open; the edge of the door just touches the Mazda's door. Fucking hell, I think, rolling my eyes. Be careful.

'Morning,' I say pleasantly, but she glares like it's a sarcastic remark about her tardiness.

'Let's just get this over and done with,' she snaps and I'm tempted to ask her why she's bothering, but I don't want to scupper my chance at getting inside.

I jump in front and lead the way, holding the communal door open for her; I'm about to ask permission if I can unlock the front door when she suddenly stops and stares at the brass number 8 in the middle of the wood.

'I don't think I can go in. I'm...I'm...' she mutters shakily.

For fuck's sake. I keep calm; keep my voice quiet and soothing. 'You're not doing this alone, I'm with you. Remember, we're looking for Claire.'

'I d-don't want to go in...' She backs away, the brass key pokes between her fingers and gently I reach out and touch the tip of the metal and pull it free, reassuring her that it's okay, I'll go in first.

I unlock the front door and push it open, dropping the key casually into my pocket. I keep her mind off what horrors she thinks are lurking inside by asking when she was last at the flat. She blinks; her reply is vague and nervous. 'I'm...not sure... the summer...last year... Yes, just after my birthday in July.'

I step forward onto the brown ribbed mat and glance about. To the left is a narrow recess where Claire stored the ironing board and the vacuum cleaner. On the row of wooden coat hooks, Claire's emergency spotty umbrella hangs. I'm aware of the quickening beat of my heart and the adrenalin coursing around my body. I am so fired up like a furnace. I want to get this over with quickly and get shot of this silly bitch. I'm desperate to look in the places where Claire kept things of importance, but I can't do this while Sally sits on my shoulder like a pirate's parrot.

'Keep your eyes peeled for anything that's missing or out of place,' I tell Sally, ushering her inside. My sarcasm is lost on her. As if she'd know if anything is missing.

She nods nervously and I smile, closing the door behind her. There's a strong smell of vanilla air freshener in the hallway, probably Marion's work to hide any musty smells now the windows are all shut up. Claire hated the smell of vanilla. The flat is completely silent, there's not even footsteps on laminate flooring, doors closing, a dog barking, running tap water from the neighbouring flats.

Something large and dark looms over my head and my eyes snap upwards. A dark wooden elephant stares back; its eyes black and penetrating, its sharply pointed tusks and trunk are raised in an aggressive manner. Its imagined silent trumpeting forces me to step back and I realise this must be the Nellie that Ryan sent Claire from Thailand. Wow! It's massive. I'd imagined some tiny thing no bigger than an egg cup, but this is the height of a cereal box.

'Careful,' Sally warns and I flinch. I'd momentarily forgotten about her. 'It's heavy.'

A memory suddenly pings into my head. The last time I saw Claire we discussed the lucky direction elephants are supposed to face. Though I've no idea which way that is.

'The bedroom,' I say, pushing open the door on the left. Let's get on with it before the clock strikes twelve.

Both sets of lilac curtains are closed casting a purple haze over the furniture and walls; the bed is duvet and pillow-less. Only a white base sheet acts as a dust collector. I wonder how much tidying up and cleaning Marion has done, and what's been left in its original place. I grasp the painted knobs of the built-in wardrobe doors and fling them open.

The few items of clothes sway and the empty hangers rattle at the force of my action. On the right hand side of the wardrobe floor is a suitcase sized gap. Claire parked her case here because there was no room under the bed or anywhere else in the flat. There are gaps in the large plastic clear box in which Claire kept her shoes. Some pairs are missing. There's another empty hanger on the left door knob.

I scan the top shelf: keepsake boxes containing photos and other bits and bobs she couldn't bear to chuck away, folded jumpers, empty boxes that once contained electrical items. I always threw them away, but Claire kept them. I close the doors and face the centre of the room. Sally is rooted in the doorway, looking around with furtive eyes as if she's looking for cold fingers poking out from under the bed or that tell-tale blood splash. 'How often does your mum come to the flat to keep things tidy?' I ask.

She jumps at the sound of my noise. 'Every month, I think. She wants to leave things as they are if Claire returns. I'm starting to see how stupid that is now.'

I don't question her change of mind; I have important things to do. I walk around the bed to the chest of drawers and open each drawer. First two drawers contain everyday underwear: vests, tights, socks, comfy pants and bras. Next two contain tops and nightwear. Bottom drawer is the interesting one. I pull it out and sit on the edge of the bed.

Half the drawer is empty. It's been swept clear by two hands. The other half contains neatly placed lingerie, and I say lingerie because this is different from the first two drawers. The bras and knickers are black and red, lacy and very racy. I do a fingertip search, my fingernails snagging awkwardly on the lace.

Sally appears by my side. 'Nice underwear,' she mutters; her tone is anything but complimentary.

Her prudishness annoys me. Just because she may be a Winceyette nightie and bed socks girl, doesn't mean every woman is. 'What's wrong with a bit of sexy dressing up?' I ask, trying to keep my voice light and non-confrontational. 'I wish my ex-fiancée had been a bit more of a black 'n' red gal.'

Maybe she's disgusted that I'm able to touch Claire's personal underwear. But you never know what may be hidden amongst it.

'Expensive stuff.' I recognise the label. It's designer and costs a pretty packet. I know because I was going to buy something similar for Justine, but put it back when I saw the price tag. 'One of them liked it,' I mutter thoughtfully.

'What?'

'One of the men Claire was seeing, but was it the tradesman or the Jag man?'

Sally frowns. 'Claire was seeing *two* men? Liv said Claire liked married men.' She doesn't hide the disgust in her voice. 'Who were they?'

'I'm trying to find out. Go to the wardrobe and take out the plastic box under the one containing shoes.'

Puzzled, she obeys and we strike lucky. The other half of the drawer contains white and lemon coloured underwear: pretty, girly frills.

'That must have been for Charlton,' I mutter. Claire finished with him and disposed of the underwear he liked in the wardrobe, leaving the Jag man's taste of lingerie in the drawer which means he was still current.

'Who's Charlton? Did he hurt Claire? You have to tell the police,' she insists.

I shut the drawer and look at her. 'Tell them what? Claire referred to them by nicknames. I have to decipher them first. Let's have a look in the living room.' I lead the way through the galley kitchen where I pause to open the cupboard above the unplugged kettle. I slide my hand in between the cups and glasses, moving them aside till my fingers touch the metal tea caddy. I take it out and remove the lid. It's empty apart from...

'That rules out a foreign moon-lit flit then.'

Sally takes the passport from my fingers. 'It was in there! We...Mum looked everywhere for it; we assumed Claire had taken it with her. Why did she hide it in there? I mean it's stupid...'

'When you lead a discreet life, you learn to put things away in locations that really are the last place you'd look.'

'But you knew?' she accuses, hurt.

'We were best friends. You can see why I needed to get in the flat now.'

'What else is hidden away? Mum wanted access to Claire's laptop but it's password protected. Do you know what it is?'

'No,' I lie, replacing the passport. 'Why would Claire give it to me?'

'Because you're best friends,' she mocks. 'As you keep reminding us.'

I ignore her and scan the titles on the bookcase. If there's anything then she'd have left it in...here and I pull out a large hard-backed cookery book entitled 'Cooking with tomato ketchup'. I bought it for her a few years ago in the hope I'd make her a culinary expert. I let it fall open to the page marked with an A4 sheet of paper. I read the title 'Grievance statement against Fiona Bashford'.

I knew there was more to her. Sally moves to stand beside me and we read together.

Claire has written about how Fiona was using the hospital's database to spy on her ex husband and his new partner. Is this how she got hold of the mobile number to text the wife about Claire's affair? If Claire had submitted this then Fiona is up to her neck in trouble.

Sally looks at me.

'Fiona has appeared to have leap-frogged el Erizo and Charlton into suspect number one,' I say, but Sally shakes her head confused. 'Fiona is Claire's colleague and they fell out. It's a long story, but it does explain why Fiona was so cagey when I spoke to her.'

'What did she say?'

'Not much, but she might now.'

I replace the statement, deliberately neglecting to remove the other sheets of paper I can see among the pages. I put the book back into its slot and take down the calendar of owls hanging on a picture hook over the bookcase. It's stuck on November. Scrawled untidily in the squares for each day are numbers: '34.45m, 5.31km' is the entry for Thursday 30th November. She's written similar numbers for various days sometimes weekdays, sometimes weekends.

What are they? I ask myself silently.

Well, m usually means minutes or miles; km means kilometres...so m here must mean minutes. Are these times and dates for something? What was she doing? Was she writing down how long it took her to travel these distances? Why?

Sally looks over my shoulder. 'Claire took up running.'

I look at her.

'She had a charity race in January. Mum and Dad sponsored her. I did too.'

I didn't know. Why hadn't she told me she'd resumed her hobby? We used to run years ago till more important things came along. Wait...Bev had told me about the running, she'd seen Claire warming up in her kit on the Friday teatime. It obviously hadn't registered with my brain at the time. I flick back through the calendar. There's numbers going right back to May which must have been when she'd resumed running. She was doing well, running religiously between two and four times a week all through summer, autumn and winter and obtaining respectable times for her 5 k. She was dedicated. But this absence of a time and distance for Friday 1st December bothers me.

'Why hadn't she written the numbers for this day?' I look at Sally.

She's wearing her clueless expression and her limp shrug irritates me so I rehang the calendar. She offers me an excuse though. 'She must have forgotten.'

'She cared enough to do the umpteen times before,' I answer curtly.

It's proved something I've suspected for a while that Claire went missing on the Friday. Either something interrupted her when she returned here or she didn't return at all, but I don't want to go in to this with Sally.

'We should go. I've got to get the key back before Mum returns from her golf lesson.'

'Yeah. Okay,' I say. I ought to protest and beg for a few more minutes, just to make it look good, but I can't be bothered. Besides, there isn't anywhere else to look whilst she's here so we leave the flat and I lock the door, casually dropping the key into my pocket.

'The key, Will,' she says, holding out her hand.

'Sorry, mind was elsewhere,' I say convincingly, returning my hand to my pocket and dropping a key onto her palm.

We head back to our cars, say a quick goodbye; I thank her again. I look up from my phone slyly watching as she disappears down the road. After a couple of minutes of waiting to see if she's going to return, I arch my back and dig out Claire's real front door key from my back pocket.

I throw the warm key into the air and catch it with a smile. Now I can come and go as I please and find out the rest of what's been going on.

Chapter 42

Wednesday ~ day 9

I move the cup out of the way before opening the pristine file in case I accidentally spill latte over it. I read the notes on Claire's last honey trap and ask Nisha about the Friday evening she saw Mr Snell leaving Claire's flat.

'I have no doubt at all that it was him,' Nisha tells me convincingly. 'And I've absolutely no idea what he was doing there. I can't see how they'd arranged it; there was always someone watching Claire: me in the bar and Gerry in the hotel garden with his camera. I don't know if Mr Snell tracked her down somehow, if they swapped numbers. And I'm supposed to be good at this!'

'Is it possible Claire let something slip in conversation, or that there was a blind spot and Gerry missed a passing of an explanatory note?'

Nisha uses the wooden stirrer to scrape froth off the inside of her cup. 'I've been over it, and I just don't see how. Claire was a professional; she's never fallen for a target before. We rehearsed everything especially our new identities and life stories. Claire loved this part. She said having a new name made her feel like a new wo...' Nisha stops, her attractive face marred by a deep ridged frown.

'What?'

'Mrs Snell insisted Claire call herself Rachel, because her husband liked the name. At first Claire agreed, but later she rang and explained she was a bit rusty and was afraid she'd contradict herself so could she stick to Claire. That was the only true thing she told him. Her job, age, background was made up...' Her voice trails off and we both raise our eyebrows as we realise what she's just said. Claire found it difficult to remember her new name, but not her pretend life. Odd. Very odd.

'More importantly, I was the *one* who had to remember her name,' Nisha explains. 'If I'd slipped up, it could have jeopardised the whole operation.' Another important point.

'This may be a bit of a long shot, but do you think it's possible that the Snells discovered Claire and her whereabouts, and one or both of them paid her a visit? Both have a reason to be angry with her.'

'Mr Snell's local so it's possible he may have seen Claire in a shop or at the hospital and smelt a rat, but I don't see how Mrs Snell could know about Claire unless she was there that night spying on us all!'

'She hasn't seen this file?' I tap it with the clean end of my wooden stirrer. 'There's no way she could have got a hold of Claire's personal details?'

Nisha shakes her head as she raises the large cup to her mouth.

'It's a hell of a long shot that one of these two recognised Claire. The honey-trap was on the Tuesday night, and you saw Mr Snell at Claire's flat on the Friday, that means in those 72 hours they were in the same place at the same time, he followed her or she invited him around if she felt there was chemistry worth following up. Claire was already seeing someone. She'd recently finished with another. There was room for another man.'

'It's bad enough having one man let alone two!' Nisha laughs.

'Have you got the photos of the...what do you call it when they don't kiss?'

'A no-kiss? I printed some copies off. They're in the back of the file.'

I grin. 'You've thought of everything. I'd best take a trip out and speak to Mrs Snell.'

'You don't really think either of them have anything to do with Claire's disappearance, do you?' Nisha asks.

'I don't know, but he was at her flat. And that warrants an explanation.'

'It's frightening to think one of them might be involved.' Nisha holds her wrist over the table to show me a silver and turquoise stoned bracelet. 'She gave me this. I wear it all the time now.'

And it makes me wish I had something similar, something that belonged to Claire, an item she cherished that she'd given to me. My inheritance instead is this mystery and I've learnt more than I expected in such a quick time. I only anticipated a disgruntled boyfriend and a scorned wife not two boyfriends and a possible stalkerish admirer, a grievance against a colleague, not to forget requests for loans, questions about football managers making illegal bets, daughterly blackmail, and that's only what I can remember. I've got far more written down on my pad. I need a secretary to file all this information.

'I should go. Thanks for the file, Nisha. I'll let you know how I get on.'

'You're welcome, Will.'

I think about going home, but I'm not in the mood for one of Dad's tantrums so I return to Claire's flat.

*

I stand in Claire's hallway and think. If I was packing a suitcase for myself or for someone else, what would I take? Toiletries, I think, pushing open the bathroom door and reaching for the light switch, but the light stays off. Marion's had the leccie turned off, probably the water too so a drink's out of the question. I return to the Mazda for the torch and get on with it quickly. There might not be much life left in the batteries.

The toothbrush and toothpaste are missing from the holey pot on the basin; there are gaps in the little metal shelving unit suckered to the tiled wall by the shower too suggesting certain items have been removed. I open the doors of the mirrored medicine cabinet and shine the torch inside.

A blister pack of paracetamol with just two tablets remaining, out of date suntan lotion, a box of tampons and a tube of *Deep Heat.* A spotty make-up bag reveals a rainbow selection of eye shadows and lipsticks. There's nothing else untoward in the bathroom so I return to the bedroom and head straight for the lingerie drawer. I search properly amongst the items and find the perfume I hid from Sally's beady eye. I try to say it out loud, but my French is appalling. At the back of the drawer, my nail catches on something and I pull out a small card, the kind that accompanies a bouquet. It's been Sellotaped back together; the hairline fractures reveal that it was once torn up into angry little pieces, but stuck together again out of regret. In a sloping backwards hand it reads: To Darling Claire. You make me wish Monday was every day. Fondly, Mr Weeks.

Oh shit. I'd forgotten about him. Mr Weeks. He ran concurrently with Charlton. How did I manage to forget him?

'Probably because she never complained about him,' I answer myself.

Claire only saw him in the week hence the nickname. At weekends he'd return to his partner, which suited her perfectly. I finger the card, turn it over to its blank back and wonder why it was ripped up and why it was Sellotaped back together. Claire had never mentioned a row with Mr Weeks. He sounded classy and well mannered. She called him gentlemanly. I put it back and close the drawer.

I have a quick glance under the bed and spy her slippers on the other side, close together, waiting for feet to be placed inside. They make such a sad picture. Forever waiting, empty, lonely. I glance behind the curtains, but there's nothing unusual on them aside from her usual knickknacks: a vase of plastic flowers, a lilac and white striped candle, a small wooden owl and a framed photo of me, Ryan and Claire taken at college years ago.

I look around the room for other places I can search. The single drawer to the bedside cabinet reveals a dog-eared paperback with a chick-lit title; a strawberry flavoured lip salve; a bank statement dated from last year and other assorted papers; and a small flimsy box, the sort that contain pills. I read the patient sticker on the side. Claire L. Millward. Cipralex 10mg. Claire's anti-depressants. Holding them in my hand makes my head swim and I urgently sit down on the edge of the bed. We'd talked about her coming off these the last time I'd seen her and she said she wasn't ready. I suggested she consider counselling, but she said that I was the only person she could talk to. I feel like my heart is going to break open. I was her only friend. She was mine.

I tip the pills out. Two strips slide out, each containing 14 tablets: a month's supply. Why hadn't she taken them with her? Would someone reliant on anti-depressants do that? Maybe she had weaned herself off them. Or maybe she hadn't forgotten them. Maybe whoever had packed for her, didn't know she was on them so they didn't take them. Was I the only person who knew she was on them?

I shake my head. This is all wrong. Soap opera actors can pack their belongings in two minutes; with both hands they sweep clothes off the rail, and stuff them and their hangers into an open suitcase. This hasn't happened here. There are gaps in her wardrobe as if a careful choice has been made. Who would take a summer's dress in winter? If Claire hadn't left in a hurry, then why has she forgotten her anti-depressants, her passport in case she wanted to see Ryan, her contraceptive pill? I know if I was packing without a list to tick off then I would walk around the flat thinking carefully, trying to picture my getting ready routine and not just taking what I saw.

It doesn't prove that Claire didn't pack her case, but it suggests that someone else might have. If Claire didn't make it back home that Friday night and I don't think she did, then who packed the case? Both Nisha and Bev saw lights on in the flat late evening. It doesn't mean it was Claire who was home. Was Mr Snell just leaving Claire's flat after a row or had he received no answer to his door knocking either?

If Claire had been prevented from returning home in say a confrontation, then did that someone steal her key, come here and set the scene for Claire's 'running away'? Is that why essential items weren't taken? Was she apprehended whilst on her run? Who knew her route?

I sigh tiredly, my head is fried with all these unanswerable and difficult questions so I replace the pills, but take the paperwork, the laptop and the ketchup recipe book and head home. Tomorrow I need to track down the scorned wife from the gym and read Nisha's file on Mr Snell.

Chapter 43

Thursday ~ day 10

'What's this drug supposed to do?' I ask Mum.

Her voice crackles down the line. 'Hopefully calm your dad down. But if it doesn't work the doctor may have to consider an alternative.'

Opposite the Mazda, a silver Ford Focus pulls into a car parking space. A super skinny girl with an even skinnier blonde ponytail jumps out of the vehicle, swings a sports bag onto her shoulder and marches to the gym's entrance.

Too young, I think.

'What sort of alternative? A different drug?' I ask.

'Yes, but in order to do that he'll have to go into hospital. There's a specialised unit at...'

'What if he doesn't want to go? He couldn't stay in respite for two nights.'

'They'll have to section him.' Mum's voice is small. 'Let's hope it doesn't come to that. Anyway, what you up to?'

'I'm waiting for a woman I have a very vague description of to turn up to work on a day she may not work to a place she may have left. How can you have a McDonalds's next door to a gym? Talk about temptation. I'm sure they pump out the smell of quarter pounders to entice you inside.'

Mum laughs.

My eye is caught by a maroon people carrier racing into the car park. The driver brakes harshly so the front end hooks itself onto the kerb. Appalling parking, I think, but she doesn't straighten up leaving it at an angle.

'I'll leave you to it, love. See you later,' Mum says.

'Bye, Mum.' And I end the call and get out of the Mazda. As I walk nearer, I see a child's sunshade suckered to the rear passenger-side window, which gives me hope that this may be a candidate for my scorned wife. The driver's door flings open and a woman with dark hair, wearing the gym's signature top stumbles out, hauling a gym bag with her. I hurry before she disappears through the staff entrance.

'Excuse me,' I call.

'Yes?' she says impatiently and glances at the gym entrance.

'I'm looking for an employee of this gym who may have known a friend of mine.'

'That sounds like quite a challenge. Can you be a little bit more specific?'

'Yes, my friend is Claire Millward. She disappeared last December and I'm looking for a woman whose husband had an affair with Claire.' I look for a reaction, but there isn't one, just a tiny frown of puzzlement and a step backwards as if I am some kind of unpredictable nutcase.

'I don't know her and I have to go. I'm late for my Bums and Tums class.' She makes a sharp exit and I shrug. Should have known that my good luck and smooth sleuthing would soon come to an end. Like I said to Mum, this could be a ridiculous waste of time not to mention one big pain in the head. This scorned woman with the dark hair may have dyed her hair blonde; lost weight or piled on the pounds; she may be on maternity leave or left the county to make a clean start. But with any luck, this Bums 'n' Tums teacher may mention to a gossiping colleague about the nutcase in the car park, it may spread even further around till the right person hears and if I appear here over the next few mornings then I may get a result.

I look at the Mazda, but my stomach growls. I'll just pop over to Mackie D's for a Royale with cheese, and if there's nothing by ten thirty then I'll make my way over to the Snells' residence.

*

The Snells' sprawling accommodation is set in three quarters of an acre of mature gardens and bouncy green lawns. The view beyond the property is of nothing but fields. Well pruned variegated shrubs and small shaped trees welcome me onto the property; block paved paths weave routes around the buildings and between clipped box hedges to hidden doors; dotted here and there under ground floor windows and little alcoves set back off the path are plant pots of small daffodils, tall orange and black tulips and little purple grape hyacinths. I know my bulbs.

I follow the driveway round to the rear of the house where a block of triple garages reveal themselves. I swing the Mazda in front of them so it faces the way I came in. Just in case I need a hasty exit.

The Limes speak of people with well paid jobs and good taste. I wonder what his wife does all day. Probably much the same as Marion: sod all.

I pull on the handbrake and look up as my ear detects footsteps. A woman stands in the doorway of a conservatory, a puzzled and unfriendly look on her face. She approaches with a raised hand to indicate that there's no point in my getting out of the car. I do anyway.

'This is private property,' she informs me, nose in the air. 'I believe you have the wrong address.'

'Are you Paula Snell?' I ask and her dark blonde eyebrows rise in surprise. 'Then I believe I'm in the right place. I'm William McClelland. I'm the office manager at Hughes, McClelland and King Agency.' I remove a small notebook from my pocket and flick it open. 'I understand you recently instructed us...'

'If you can call four months ago recently then yes I did. What do you want?' she demands.

'Can we go inside?' and I nod towards the door.

'No. I would prefer it if you tell me why you're here.' She folds her arms, flattening her breasts.

'Mrs Hughes asked me to look into your complaint regarding a honey-trap we set for your husband...' I gaze down at the writing in the notebook pretending it contains relevant information of her complaint. '...James which was...'

'Why are you here *now*?' she demands. 'I hope you do a better investigation of my complaint than you did of my husband's infidelity.'

'We take all complaints seriously,' I continue, 'and I apologise for the severe delay in investigating this.' She nods, accepting my apology and my sincerity. 'Did you pick the operative yourself?' I open the notebook and flick through the pages. 'I'm sorry. I can't find the name...' I run my finger down the page and frown in frustration.

Mrs Snell sighs. 'Her name was Claire. I picked her myself.'

So, you remember that, I think triumphantly.

'She was perfect. Exactly James's type in every way except in name.'

'This is why you requested the name Rachel.'

'Precisely! I gave Mrs Hughes details of where James would be and left it in their supposed capable hands.'

'You said you doubted they did a good enough job, why was that? Did you witness their poor performance yourself? Did you...'

She interrupts aggressively. 'Are you implying that I went to the hotel on the night in question and spied on them?'

'I just want to...'

'In order to do that I must have dressed incognito, sat in the corner and watched my husband flirt with another woman? If I had done that, then I wouldn't have needed photographic evidence, would I?'

'No,' I reply, sheepishly. Blimey, I think, no wonder James didn't snog Claire if it meant being in her firing line.

'Mrs Snell, it has been known for partners to spy on operatives. They've even ruined the traps too, albeit accidentally.'

'Well, I assure you that I haven't. I was home.'

'Did you ever seek out Claire yourself?'

She throws her hands up. 'Where would I start? I wouldn't have the first clue on how to find her.'

'You have the photos though?' I say. 'You knew what she looked like...'

'Mr McClelland, I've destroyed the photos in case James finds them. And I have not trawled the town handing out copies to shopkeepers and publicans in the hope that somebody recognises her.'

'Another agency may have been able to find her for you.'

'I don't have either the inclination or the money to employ another agency to find a woman who failed to trap my husband. If I did find her, what would she tell me, do you think? Exactly the same as Mrs Hughes: that I should be relieved James is the faithful type.'

'Do you think James suspected it was a trap?' I ask cautiously.

'It has crossed my mind.' She glances at the door, wondering whether to invite me in or not, and then pulls back the sleeve of her cardigan to check the time on her gold watch and thinks the better of an invite. 'It'd be just like James to spoil my plans,' and she smiles to herself and I wonder again exactly what her reasons for this trap were. If she's unhappy then why not just file for a divorce. Surely that's less painful than the evidence of an affair.

'If he did know it was a trap, would he say anything to you?'

'Yes. He'd be puffed up with glee that he'd foiled my plan.'

'What if he had discovered it was a trap and was angry, would he confront Claire if he could find her?'

'James doesn't have a temper. He works long hours and his job is pressurised, so he's had to learn how to relax, otherwise his blood pressure would be through the roof. Very little infuriates him. Why all the questions? Do you think James knew it was a trap? How, from the agency?'

'I don't know, Mrs Snell. I need to speak to your husband. How can I get in contact with him?'

She raises her hands again. 'You can't talk to him; he can't know I paid an agency to trap him.' Her eyes are wide with fear. 'What do you think that's going to do for my marriage? Surely you can ask this Claire if James has been in contact with her.'

'I afraid I can't. She disappeared a few days after the honey-trap. No one has seen or heard from her since.'

'Good God. Well, that hasn't got anything to do with James...'

'A reliable witness saw your husband leaving the communal entrance to Claire's flat the night before she disappeared.'

She shakes her head. 'It might be a case of mistaken identity. Or he could have been there for another reason and she just happens to live there.'

'I need to ask Mr Snell that.'

Her eyes dart left and right as she considers how her husband could be involved with a disappearance of a girl he met one night, and a girl he didn't even kiss let alone get the phone number off.

'Nisha saw him leaving the flat. That's why she's reliable.'

'Oh my God,' Mrs Snell gasps. 'Is there any way you could ask him what you need to know *discreetly?* I don't want him knowing there was a trap.'

I nod reassuringly but wonder how the hell I'm supposed to do that.

She pops back into the house through the conservatory door, and like Nisha I wonder why she wanted to trap her husband. Maybe the reason will be obvious when I meet James; maybe he's a boring old twat.

A phone rings from inside the house and I hear her answer it brightly with, 'Hi Teddy. I'm okay, a bit...what? Yes, a gin would be fantastic.' The phone is still clamped to her ear when she returns to hand me a white business card. She places her hand over the mouthpiece and asks, 'If that's everything?'

'Yes, thank you.' I open the car door and hear her organising a time to meet Teddy later for dinner.

I leave the Snells' property, deliberately wheel spinning the Mazda. There's something delightful about the sound of crunching gravel under tyres. As I head off back down the road, a text comes through. Fiona has agreed to meet me in a local pub so I can ask her further questions. Oh, well. I can always follow her home. You never know what spin her old man can put on things.

Chapter 44

Thursday/Friday ~ day 10 and 11

Whilst Dad sweeps the patio, Mum and I sit in the comfort of the lounge. The football match is well into the second half, but I'm so out of touch with the game that I've only got one eye on the telly. I return to Claire's laptop and search through her browser history but the only sites she's been viewing are jewellery, clothes and other girly ones; there's nothing interesting like airline websites or how to travel abroad without a passport. Claire isn't on *Facebook* or *Twitter*, preferring to keep her school friends in the past and her love life private. I click on her email account and scan the five month long list of unopened emails but there's nothing of interest. The only read emails are from her mobile phone provider informing her of the bill; there were a few newsy ones from Ryan but no mention of a future visit.

'Dirty swine!' Mum swears and I look up to see one of the players rolling around on the pitch, hands clamped to his knee, his face twisted in pain.

'Sensible decision from Cooksey to substitute Aguilar,' the commentator says and sure enough the substitution appears on the screen with red and green arrows: Aguilar for Martin. The attending physios support the player as he walks tentatively off the pitch. The name on the back of his shirt says Pollo.

Didn't they just call him...

'And Pollo has to be careful. Cooksey will want him fit for the next Champions' League match in two weeks time,' the commentator adds.

Aguilar and Pollo: two names, one person.

I ask Mum why he has two names, is he Spanish?

'He's Mexican. Aguilar is his surname. Pollo is a childhood nickname; he said it brought him luck so he has it on his shirt. It means chicken.' And she giggles.

My mind is racing. Pollo is Spanish for chicken. Erizo is Spanish for hedgehog. Both are nicknames for men who were 'out' in Mexico and Spain. All Claire did was omit the word 'playing' when she explained where el Erizo got the name. Was Claire seeing a footballer?

I've always had the feeling he was older, so was he still playing when he met Claire? Most players retire when they reach their mid to late thirties or they move down the leagues but surely by forty they've finally hung up their boots. What else have I heard about football? I flip through my notes. Here it is: Claire asked what would happen to a manager who either asked someone to place a bet on his own team or had done it himself. Phil's reply was banishment from the game. Is el Erizo a manager? Or a player who suspected his manager of dodgy dealings? Had Claire placed such a bet for him?

I continue flicking through my notes and come across the list Ryan and I had compiled of the places where Claire had had weekends away with the hedgehog. Do they have anything in common?

Suddenly, the lounge door flings open and smacks the windowsill behind. Mum and I jump with fright. I slap a hand on top of the laptop to stop it sliding off my legs.

Dad stands in the doorway, broom in one hand, a wild expression on his face.

'That bloody bloke...he's been in the fucking garden again...I won't have it, Kay!'

'Mike, what are you talking about? Who? Put the broom down!'

But Dad marches across the room until he stands before the large mirror above the fireplace; his hand brandishes the broom by its shaft, its head vertical. He takes aim.

'MIKE!'

'DAD!'

He swings the broom over and down, its bristly head smacking the centre of the mirror. A large white and silver shape appears in the glass with jagged spokes and spikes protruding from its centre, radiating outwards. It looks like a sinister snowflake.

We sit completely still and silent, watching as triangles of glass rain onto Mum's china figurines; they bounce onto the brick hearth and the carpet.

Dad stabs a finger at the pieces left in the wooden frame and issues a determined and frightening warning to his many reflections, 'If I catch you in my garden again, I'll put a bullet in your head.' Then he turns and leaves the room and the house, the backdoor slamming shut.

We look at each other gobsmacked.

'Who's he talking about?' I ask.

Mum sighs. 'A few months ago he swears Don from next door was lifting the fence panels, coming and going at all hours, removing garden tools and digging up plants. Watch where you're walking.' She points at the hazardous carpet. 'I'll get the dustpan.'

I slip my feet into my slippers and look at the state of the mirror. That's seven years bad luck for Dad not that he'll understand what I'm talking about. And in an hour's time *if* we manage to get him to come indoors, he'll take one look at this mess and ask, 'What's happened here then?'

I wonder why I didn't try to stop him. Are my reflexes slower now I'm not in the force? Or was I frightened of the wild look in his eyes or the brandishing of a weapon? He might have aimed that broom at us. No amount of reasoning with him would have convinced him he was mistaken about the neighbour because as far as Dad's concerned the world has gone mad. He genuinely believes that someone has been in the garden.

Mum returns with the dustpan and brush and a newspaper which she lays on the floor. Together we start carefully picking up shards of glass. I dread tonight. I know he won't come inside easily and that we'll have a battle which will result in a sleepless night, and tomorrow I know what will happen. Things will be totally out of our hands.

'I'll ring the doctor tomorrow,' Mum says.

I feel a tingling in my nose and a hot wetness in my eyes. Oh god. I haven't done this in years; I didn't even cry when they sent me down.

'Are you alright, love?' she asks, placing a hand on mine.

I nod unconvincingly. I feel overwhelmed with it all: the guilt, the loss, the sadness, and I'm angry that Claire isn't beside me, holding my hand and lying that everything will be okay. I need her; I want to hear her tell me she'll be with me every step, that she will soften any blow coming my way.

*

The next morning having slept little on account of Dad's activity, I feel alert and raring to go like I've taken speed. I get on with my sleuthing and sit cross-legged on the floor with my large notepad and try to work out what the destinations of Claire's weekends-away have in common.

After ninety minutes of looking at maps and leagues I've learned that geographically these places have nothing in common; north, south, east and west; inland, on the coast, picturesque, historical, concrete and ugly; they are an even mixture of places you'd visit for a weekend and those you wouldn't leave the motorway for unless you were desperate for a piss. However, all these places have a football team. This is where it gets confusing. These teams aren't in the same league. *But* in the season when Claire was seeing el Erizo all these teams were in the same league. Claire had weekends away at these places when Erizo's team played them. That doesn't help me work out who his team is...unless I can get hold of the season's fixtures and recall *when* Claire visited these towns.

I look down the list of last season's teams for the local ones and spot two.

'Hang on.' I hurry down stairs. It takes an age for the PC to whirr into life and load good old Wikipedia. In the search box, I type Kelsall Town and read about their current manager: Noel Bluglass. There's no mention of him playing in Spain. Doesn't sound very promising as a candidate for being unmasked as el Erizo. So I move onto the second suspect – Lilliton F.C. Their manager is Stewart Murray.

A soft knocking at the front door disturbs me, Mum answers it and begins a conversation with the caller; I switch off from the voices as I study the photo of Stewart Murray.

'Will,' Mum says from the doorway, her voice quiet and tense. My head turns to her, but my eyes have difficulty in tearing themselves away from the screen. Stewart Murray was born in Collyhurst, Manchester.

'There's someone here to see you,' she continues.

'Who is it?' Why is she whispering I ask myself. Murray is 47 years old.

'Justine.'

Now my eyes snap off the monitor and look at her. 'Wha-' But the word ends abruptly. I don't really need to ask why she's here. I should have prepared myself for this eventuality. Stands to reason she would find out I was out considering her job and her connections. Justine is a judge's clerk at the Crown court; she works closely with the police.

'I should have told her you were out, but I couldn't think quickly enough,' Mum apologises.

'It's alright,' I say, pushing the chair back. I want to chicken out; what am I supposed to say? She didn't want to listen when I tried to explain my actions, which had the advantage of saving me the job of admitting the real reason behind what I did.

'She's in the lounge,' Mum whispers.

I check my appearance in the hall mirror, not that it matters if there's a spot on my chin or something is caught between my teeth. I don't have to impress her anymore. But a quick glimpse reassures me that I look presentable. The fiery nerves crackling in my stomach and her impromptu visit prevent me from taking a few minutes to compose myself and think of replies to the questions she may have. I'll have to wing it.

Mum backs into the kitchen making the universal gesture for tea, I shake my head. I don't want Justine to get settled with a hot drink. I cross the hall to the lounge and find her bending over the hearth plucking something from the dried flower arrangement. It briefly crosses my mind to jokingly ask if she's doing that thing you do with flowers when you're a kid – he loves me, he loves me not; but that's the most inappropriate thing I could say.

'Hello,' I say and my voice in the quiet room makes her jump like a leaping tiddlywink. She straightens up and turns, eyes focused on the item in her hand as if too afraid to look at me. In her palm, a triangle of broken glass glints.

I walk further into the room till we're only a couple of metres apart. Her hair is significantly different. Two years ago it was a sleek jaw length bob and the colour of Merlot. Her current look is reminiscent of how she looked when we started seeing each other. This is my preferred look for her. Her hair is back to its natural colour: medium brown; it's short and feminine, arranged around her ears and forehead as if to frame her features: blue eyes, pretty nose, red lips. Justine is popular because she's kind and considerate.

'A piece of mirror,' she says, sounding slightly puzzled. That'll be her inquisitive nature.

'My Dad attacked it with a broom last night. He was trying to kill the Candyman.'

My joke amuses her and she chuckles, looking up into my face. I clearly see the hurt in her eyes and I warn myself to be careful here. I shouldn't encourage her in any way, but she was always a good audience.

My hand rises to take the shard from her, but I shouldn't so I tell her to put it on the mantelpiece instead. She sits on the settee; her black skirt skims the top of her knees which are primly together; a big button on her black jacket is buttoned up but I can see the white and pink striped shirt she wears underneath. I remember this top; it was a bugger to iron. Her shoes as usual are black Mary Janes but instead of a strap, they're fastened with black ribbons. These subtle heels add to her height making her a couple of inches shorter than my six foot one. I choose the armchair by the door and smile at her. A glance at her hands tells me there's no ring on her wedding finger; it doesn't mean she isn't engaged, but if she is she'll want me to know.

'How are you settling back into...er...things, you know...'

I struggle to hear; her voice is quiet and nervous.

'Life on the outside? Yeah, fine. There haven't been too many technological or scientific advances so that's a relief. You know the cars haven't all taken to the air and we haven't colonised Mars.'

Her smile widens and she relaxes back into the settee. 'Good. Is there any news on the job front?'

'Well, I've got an interview next week for a security job.'

'Great. Where?'

'Kelsall United. They want stewards.'

She realises I'm pulling her leg and I want to remind her that I'm not her concern, but I won't be able to say it without it sounding harsh.

'How's your job going?' I ask. 'Plenty of criminals keeping the courtroom busy?'

She nods enthusiastically. 'The Judges are rushed off their feet which means we are too! It doesn't help that we're short-staffed at the moment. But where isn't? Mary retired at Christmas and Kerry's on maternity leave. I've got enough banked hours for a fortnight's holiday in St Lucia!'

Kerry was lined up to be one of her three bridesmaids. I bet her pregnancy is painful for Justine. We'd talked about parenthood a couple of years after marriage. St Lucia was our honeymoon destination. Are her answers deliberate or am I inspiring them?

She reaches an arm around her back to rearrange a cushion. She crosses her leg; the skirt slides up her thigh but it still looks respectable.

'I expect your mum's missed you and Eddie.' I give a little nod, a non-encouraging one but it has the opposite effect because it looks like I'm listening and waiting for more and now I can see where she's heading with this.

'It's been difficult for a lot of people...' She swallows nervously. 'Including me. I still can't get my head around how you could do it.'

'I don't want to do this,' I tell her, my tone hard.

'We were three weeks away from getting married, Will,' she continues. 'Everything was organised and paid for: the venue, the rings, the car, the dresses...' She presses her lips together as her emotions finally grip her tightly. 'My dress...was beautiful.' She sniffs; I let her go on, she will anyway. 'We were just waiting for the twelfth to arrive and...you owe me an explanation.'

'I offered you an explanation at the time but you...'

'In a police cell! Great!' She throws her arms up. 'Like I really wanted to hear why you were walking out on me there!'

'I couldn't help my surroundings.'

'Yes, you could,' she argues. 'If you hadn't lied for your irresponsible brother we'd have got married and everything would...I mean how could you put *him* before us? Eddie killed someone!'

'I didn't know that at the...Justine, please. You haven't seen me in over a year; it's too soon to be going over this. We can talk about this some other time when we're less upset.'

'No. I need to know now before you have the opportunity to make up lies and excuses.'

'Lies?' I question. 'I never told you lies.'

'You've never told the truth either. How do I know that it's not my fault? I mean, you were happy to sit back and let me organise everything! You never said if you felt the wedding was too big, there were too many guests, you didn't like the menu or the flowers. Or maybe it was just nerves. What was it, Will?' She stares at me.

But I can't tell her the truth. A couple of months before the big day she was in the bedroom on the phone to her mum or a friend; the door was shut and I'd gone to use the bathroom but heard voices and crept across the landing to listen. If I hadn't then maybe it wouldn't have had the impact it did. I wouldn't have stuck my neck out for Eddie, I'd have been here for Claire and my parents, and Justine wouldn't be devastated.

'Marriage *will* change everything,' Justine insisted. 'I'll be his wife, we'll have children and that will make me important. At last, I'll be more important than Claire.' It was quiet as she listened to the reply. 'No, I'm not. I know I'm not. He talks to her before he'll talk to me. When his Dad was diagnosed with Alzheimer's, he told Claire first... I felt awful. He made me feel worthless.'

The honesty she shared gave me an insight into my own behaviour. I'd never analysed myself before. I had wanted to tell Claire my bad news first. I wanted her to know before I went home with the dreadful news about my dad. Justine was waiting when I returned; we sat in our lounge furnished in three shades of blue and I told her the results of Dad's MRI scan. She said all the right things, hugged me, comforted me, but her sadness was for me and the changes it would bring to my life.

'I'm so sorry, Will,' she said, putting an arm around me.

Claire's response was different. Her first thought was for my dad. 'Your poor dad. How scared he must be. We must do everything we can to help him and your mum.'

Justine had made me feel guilty, dishonest and weak because marriage wouldn't change anything, it wouldn't propel Justine to a higher rank. Claire was my best friend, the first person I would always go to, wife or no wife, and that made me a heartless pathetic bastard who was denying Justine her right to the marriage she wanted. When Eddie needed an alibi, my first thought was to protect my parents from anymore heartache; I thought it would help everyone. But when my lie was exposed I spotted it as a way out of a marriage that wouldn't work for me and was not what Justine deserved. This way I could cut her and myself free.

'You deserved better than me,' I finally answer.

'Oh, for God's sake. You're not going to use that cliché, are you? It doesn't matter what I deserved, it was *you* I wanted...' and she hesitates and for a second I worry that she's going to admit I'm still what she wants, but her head moves to the right to see behind me and I turn. It's Mum, my saviour. I plead for help with my eyes and she speaks, apologising for interrupting but can I help with Dad.

'Yeah, of course.' I turn back to Justine but she's on her feet, perhaps seeing through Mum's request or maybe she sees it as her way out the door. She strides across the floor, saying goodbye to Mum who has retreated into the hall to make Justine's route clear. She opens the front door and steps outside but stops on the doormat. I wait.

She turns back, her expression fighting back the upset and anger. 'You have no idea how much you've hurt me. I do deserve better and hopefully I'll realise that now.' She marches back up the drive to her little red City car which is parked along the kerb.

I shut the door, feel wrung out.

'She looks very upset,' Mum says appearing again. 'You couldn't have said anything that would have made her feel better.'

I nod and return to the PC, wiggling the mouse so the computer wakes up.

The black screen disappears and I start again at the beginning, reading all about Stewart Murray. Well, well, well, how interesting. He started his career around Manchester and moved to Murcia, Spain when he was 21. He was there for a few years before returning to England and signing for several London clubs before retiring and moving into coaching and managing. Murcia, I think. Claire had told Ryan that el Erizo was there when he was out in Spain. His personal life mentions a wife and two sons. Not that I expect it to list his extramarital affairs. It doesn't mention Murray having any nicknames but I can always ask him. His affiliation with Murcia is enough to warrant a visit.

Chapter 45

Friday ~ day 10

I take advantage of the chink of emerald grass I can see through the open gates of the football ground and slither inside. Wow! The ground is massive, not as magnificent as Old Trafford or Anfield but still it's been a long time since I stood on a terrace and my head swims. I'm at the bottom of a terrace which extends down the left hand side to the corner flag. The stand behind the far goal is called the Bill Pascal Stand. Across the well-looked after pitch is an all-seater stand; above that are the boxes and suites. On my right is another stand named after another affiliate with the club. It's a smart looking ground, painted neatly in the club's colours and the pitch looks to be in good nick considering there's only a couple of games left.

Unfortunately there isn't any training going on at the moment so I can't pop down to the sidelines and call Murray over. I'm going to have to sneak in or blag my way into the offices.

'Hello, mate. You alright there?'

The pleasant voice makes me jump, but I quickly compose myself and turn to face the owner of the voice.

The man is in his late sixties wearing scruffy clothes. He has dirty hands and carries a long handled brush with a large head. The kind used to sweep terraces. A lopsided badge tells me his name is John and he's a groundskeeper.

'Yeah, I was hoping to have a word with Mr Murray,' I say cheekily.

He laughs and replies, 'You and every other fan, mate.'

'It's a long queue then?'

'Put it like this: if everybody who wanted a word with him lined up here, the queue would stretch round the ground thirty times or more. Fans have lost faith in him and his decisions. We're in the play-offs, but by the skin of our teeth. Five years we've been waiting for promotion.'

'He's not around then? I didn't see his Jag in the car park...' and I look back out through the gates to emphasise my point.

'He's sold that. He's got some fancy Merc now. More interested in that than the team,' the groundskeeper mutters bitterly.

I didn't see any Mercs in the car park, so I'm out of luck today not that I'd probably be able to see him even if he was here.

'If you did want to say your piece though,' the groundskeeper starts and I raise an eyebrow hopefully. 'There's the meet-the-manager meeting Monday night.' He nods at the wall behind me.

'Is there? That's handy.'

On the back wall is a brown wooden frame with Perspex windows. The lock is broken. Stuck to the left hand side is a poster advertising the meet at 5.30pm at the White Horse pub, which is the nearest boozer to the ground. Five thirty is an interesting time, an unfair and a deliberate time. Few fans will attend as they'll still be arriving home from work or family obligations will keep them indoors. Maybe Murray is hoping if there's a poor turn-out he can call it off without losing too much face.

My eyes wander to the other half of the frame and I'm taken aback when I recognise the faded face staring back at me: Claire. I lean closer and read the red headline across the top of the poster. MISSING. It gives a brief description of her appearance and her last known whereabouts. At the bottom is a hotline for anyone to call with information. Why haven't I seen any anywhere else? And why is there one here in a football ground several miles away that Claire had no known connection to? Is Murray doing his part because it alleviates his guilt?

I turn to the groundskeeper. 'Can I have this poster?'

'Don't see why not. She's been missing for months. Poor lass is probably dead,' he says sadly.

I open the frame and carefully remove the poster. I don't fold it; I don't want to put a crease across Claire's face. I say my thanks to John and leave. Now to find the nearest t-shirt printing shop.

*

I look around the pub. It's your typical out in the countryside pub: low ceilings, uneven floor, black and white photographs on the wall and an obligatory fireplace which isn't lit but does house a large vase of dried lavender in its hearth.

'Six thirty, thanks,' the barmaid says holding out her hand for the money. Bugger me, prices have increased steeply. I pay her and take the glasses over to the table. Fiona smiles and slides two beer mats into place.

'Thanks for meeting me tonight, Fiona.'

'It's my pleasure. I want to help in any way that I can,' she replies sweetly.

'That's good. The thing is I've been talking to a couple of Claire's other colleagues and I just want to clarify what you told me.'

'So, you've been speaking to troublemaking, poisonous Isla. How nice for you.' And she sips her large red wine disdainfully. 'Did she tell you about the cruel prank she played on me and how she relished spreading nasty rumours about me for everyone to laugh at?'

'We touched on it although her version is different. I know who saw what, who stuck what where and honestly, it sounds like a lot of people need to just grow up. They still think they're in a playground.' And I take a mouthful of shandy. She smiles in agreement so arrogant that she believes she's not included. 'On the day of the porn photo incident, Isla says you accused Claire of telling everyone who Stan was. A logical assumption since Claire was the only person you'd told. Did you really believe Claire had betrayed you?'

Fiona blushes. Is that because I know about her companion or is she angry that I'm on the attack with an accusation? Although I am curious as to who he is, it's not important at the moment and I can always find out later.

She's biting her lip, top teeth scratching her bottom lip over and over as her mind races for a plausible explanation, wondering what else I might know and what else could be asked of her. If things get too much all she has to do is get up and leave. But that action will hopefully give me another witness.

'No, I never thought it was Claire,' she lies. 'She wouldn't have done something like that. I assumed they'd found out about Stan because I was seen accompanying him to a hospital appointment. I never accused Claire.'

'It didn't even cross your mind fleetingly?'

'Good grief, no. Claire would never have betrayed me.'

She must think I came down in the last shower. She's under-estimating how credible a liar she is, the information I have from others and the cards up my sleeve. Time to play one.

I sip my beer first. 'Isla says you announced to the office that Claire was seeing a married man. Now, here's the thing,' I pause and lean forward. She waits with bated breath, her interest piqued. 'She was, but she'd recently finished with him.'

'I wouldn't know...'

'You told me the first time we met that Claire talked to you, but that's a lie because the only person Claire talked to was me. So where did you get your information from? What have you seen or heard? I need to know who he is. He didn't take their break-up well and may have had something to do with her disappearance.'

'I didn't know Claire was seeing a married man...'

'Yes, Fiona, you do, because you accused her; you must have got your information from somewhere. What do you know about him?'

'Nothing!' Fiona sits back and looks around as if other drinkers have noticed the pressure I'm putting on her and want to come to her aid. Nobody is even looking our way.

'Please don't lie to me, Fiona. I don't care that you've announced Claire's private life to everyone. I need to know what you know.'

'I made it up!' And she laughs: a short sharp bark that says look how clever I am.

I laugh too. 'Did he ring the office? Did he show up at the hospital? Did you catch his name?' And there she reacts. At the mention of a name Fiona blinks hard and recoils. 'What was it?' I ask gently, but she stays mute. Any answer will be an admittance that she's lied. 'He may have had something to do with her disappearance, Fiona.'

She sighs noisily but begins. 'The week Claire went missing, haematology reception rang to tell her she had a visitor. When she left the office, I followed.' Fiona's gaze drops down to stare into her glass but she continues explaining. 'I exited through a service door so I could see what was going on and who he was. I was intrigued. They were stood several feet away, but I could hear their conversation. He promised to leave his wife, declared his love and the rest of the flannel men come out with, but Claire said she wasn't interested. Did Isla tell you about Claire's black eye?'

I stare. This revelation throws me off guard. No one has mentioned a black eye.

A hint of a smirk appears on her lips; she can see this is news to me.

'No? I'm surprised they didn't tell you. *He* did it. Because she wouldn't listen. I wanted to step in and stop him, but she shoved him away and ran off. He promised not to give up persuading her they belonged together; he got in his van and sped off.'

'Do you know his name?'

She hesitates. 'Ralph.'

'Surname?'

'I don't know.'

'What about the van? What do you remember?'

'It was one of those car-cum-van things. Red, rundown, rusty looking; God knows how old it was. There were ladders on the roof rack. A padlock on the back doors.'

Impressive description considering this incident was months ago.

'Did you notice what business he was in? Were there any signs, phone numbers emblazoned down its side?'

'I don't know. Possibly. I can't recall now.'

Her powers of observation are incredible, but I know what she's doing. She doesn't want to drop herself in it by revealing his contact details and surname because that points the finger at her for being the one who's told Ralph's wife. I mention it anyway.

'Apparently Ralph's wife received an anonymous text informing...'

'It wasn't me! How would I find out who she was?'

This time someone does look over from the bar but Fiona throws them a-mind-your-own-business glare and he looks back at his pint.

By looking him up on the patient database like Claire suggested, I think.

I know how a scene like that would look to a bystander: dangerous, persistent, annoying, stalker. Love makes people crazy. Ralph has to be Charlton who was in a miserable marriage and Claire was his escapism, his hope for a happier future. He's not going to throw that away obligingly or nicely, but that doesn't mean he's harmed her. Fiona is an unreliable witness. She has her own reasons for deflecting attention away from herself. But it does mean he's worth a visit.

I refrain from telling her about Claire's grievance statement; she'd only deny it and I may need it for essential leverage later.

Fiona finishes her drink quickly. She looks tired, spent like a suspect who's gone several rounds with a bad cop.

'Is there anything else you want to ask, demand, or interrogate me over?'

'Only to ask where you were on the Friday night that Claire went missing.'

'I was at home. I'm always at home. I don't have much of a social life.'

Poor you, I think sarcastically. 'Alone?'

'No, but Stan is an elderly man. He wouldn't be able to corroborate my alibi. He can't be left alone.'

I wonder if he suffers from memory problems and that's why he can't back her up. 'I'm sorry, Fiona if I've been harsh with you. I genuinely think someone's harmed Claire and I just needed to know what you knew. I've forgotten how to talk to people nicely. The police service and prison does that to you.'

She nods, but doesn't question me further on how prison has affected me. Perhaps she assumes I've done undercover police work. She reaches for her handbag and stands. 'I have to get back to Stan.'

I murmur that I'll come with her as I raise my half full glass to my mouth but she indicates for me not to rush. 'Let me know how your investigation goes. Despite everything, I cared about Claire. She was a good friend to me.'

I nod and let her go. When the door swings shut behind her, I slam down my glass and head out of the other exit to the Mazda which I've parked around the back by a collection of metal kegs and plastic crates. Her car is just pulling out of the car park when I fire up the engine. Keeping the headlights off till I join the carriageway behind her, I follow, keeping a good distance back.

She lives less than three miles down an unlit winding lane with tall hedgerows on either side; gated driveways and tracks lurk unseen around corners. Her brake lights flash on and I switch the headlights off as her car slows and turns off the road, disappearing into the hedge. I take my foot off the gas and the Mazda's speed decreases; my fingers rest on the stalk ready to turn the lights back on should another vehicle appear. I give her a few moments to park up and enter the house.

Right, that's long enough. I slip the Mazda into first gear and crawl past the entrance. Gravel has worked its way from the confines of the driveway and onto the edge of the road, a rickety wooden gate with a brass number 17 tacked into its middle is wide open; the house is a detached square with a half brick lean-to attached to the left side like a smaller conjoined twin. Ivy has crawled a path up and over the front porch and is making its way up to the first floor windows surrounding the frames and shrinking the amount of light entering the room.

A light is on in a downstairs window. On the windowsill is a row of house plants. The kitchen.

I smile. I've found where Stan lives.

Chapter 46

Saturday ~ day 12

'I've phoned Dr Ahmad,' Mum tells me the next morning. 'He'll be here after lunch to see your dad.'

I want to leave the house; I don't want to be present when they drag my dad away but I can't possibly leave Mum to deal with that on her own. I use the time to distract my thoughts from the inevitable scenario and pick up Claire's paperwork again.

I put her bank statements in chronological order. The first one dates back to when I was in prison. Her spending was small amounts between £30 and £50 in men and women's clothes shops, restaurants, department stores. The total she owed was £300 and some of that was from the previous month. Judging by the following statements, Claire was only paying the minimum amount but the interest just added more to the overall total, and a few months later she owed nearly three grand. But that didn't stop her spending. She spent over hundred quid at a theatre, two hundred at a hotel and eighty at a restaurant. Who was Claire treating to a weekend away with dinner and a show?

I look at the dates to see what point of her life she was in. She'd finished with Stewart. Is Ralph the theatre-going type or is it Mr Weeks? By July that year the balance owing was nearly four grand and she was still only paying the minimum amount. She was never going to catch up at this rate. And yet the spending continued. I turn to the next statement. My eyes scan the column of transactions – none. And in the total box the amount is £0.00. What? She paid it off? How? I double-check the date but it's correct. How the hell did she manage to pay off such a big bill? Had she taken out a loan? I find her latest bank statement and carefully look for any outgoing amounts that read like a loan payment. There's nothing. There was no loan. Had she borrowed money from Phil or Andrew? Phil told me she hadn't asked him for money in the summer. Had one of her men helped her out? Maybe...but...why was Claire desperate for money in the autumn? She was asking Andrew for money a week before she went missing so did she have to pay the loaner back quickly? Had they suddenly demanded a reimbursement? If they had gotten heavy with Claire she would have finished with them. Only when I meet these two will I know what kind of men they are.

If neither of her affairs were demanding their money back, then who else was? It worries me that she was so desperate....and I stop. There's only one other group of people who fit this bill: money-lenders. They don't like to be kept waiting. Had the money from Andrew been to settle *that* debt?

'Oh, shit, no. No, Claire, you stupid girl.'

A soft knock on the bedroom door makes me jump. It opens and Mum sticks her head around. 'Dr Ahmad's talking to Dad. He has a bed for him.'

'Will he go?' I ask, going to the door.

'Sounds like it.' She pauses. 'We are doing the right thing, aren't we?'

I put a reassuring hand on her arm. 'Yes, we are.'

'Mrs Bailey!' a voice calls from the hall and we head downstairs. Dad is putting on his shoes but he's having trouble with his laces. A tall Asian man with fashionable specs and a caring smile stands at the foot of the stairs. Under his arm is a folder with Dad's name on it.

'Mike has agreed to come with me. He understands that it's just till he feels better,' the doctor says, nodding a hello to me.

'Do you want a hand, Dad?' I offer and he looks up with a smile.

'Please, son.' I kneel on the floor and tie his laces.

But my fingers won't work. My nose starts tingling and tears fill my eyes, and suddenly I feel overwhelmed. I want to grab Dad's hand and pull him around the back of me like you do with a frightened child and scream that no one's taking him! He lives here with us; we'll look after him, but I don't. Instead I bite my lip and tell myself that it is just till he feels better; he needs a break like Mum does. They'll take care of him, sort out his medication and send him home.

'I've packed him a bag, if there's anything else I can bring it tomorrow,' Mum says.

I help Dad put his coat on. He manages to zip it up himself. He smiles at me but I look away guiltily.

'Ahh,' Dr Ahmad begins. 'I wouldn't advise you to visit for a few days, Kay. Let Mike settle in first. This card has all the contact details on.'

'Oh, okay,' she mutters, taking the card and looking at me.

'Are you ready, Mike?' Dr Ahmad asks and Dad nods enthusiastically like a kid who can't wait to visit the zoo.

Mum opens the door and kisses Dad goodbye. 'Take care, love. See you later.'

'See you, Kay. Bye Will,' Dad replies breezily and follows the doctor outside and to his car.

Mum nods, lips pressed together; she can't speak, tears start to roll and she pats her pockets for a tissue. I watch as my Dad is taken away without any idea where he's really going. I can't bear to think how scared he will start to feel once he arrives in a strange place with strange smells and odd people. Will he look at the other patients and know there's something different about them? Will he blame us for abandoning him? I blame me already. I encouraged, pleaded with Mum to call someone. Has my presence in the house increased his erratic behaviour? They were coping before I came home; have I brought this about because I'm the one struggling to deal with him?

*

I return to my notes and get back to Claire's papers. If I'm not busy my mind will wander back to that awful image of Dad leaving the house and think nasty thoughts about how this is all my Mum's fault and that she shouldn't have listened to me.

I pull the notepad closer; the recipe book is on top and it falls to the floor, landing on its spine and spewing out its contents. A folded up wad falls out with printed writing on the back. It's two sheets of A4 paper stapled together in the one corner. The title across the top in bold print says Lexington Hospital Trust. There's a coloured sticker in the opposite corner – 712. Under that is a subtitle that says Post-mortem report and in handwriting 'Phyllis Hock.'

'Hock,' I repeat thoughtfully. 'You've got to be kidding me...'

Under headings: Past Medical History, Medications, and Circumstances are paragraphs stating this lady's previous illnesses and operations, what drugs she regularly took and how she came to have died. I read it and conclude that it's not very interesting. It's not a murder or a suicide.

'What are you doing with this, Claire?' I ask aloud.

I turn the page and under yet more headings such as cardiovascular and respiratory, a typical doctor with illegible handwriting has scrawled down the weight of each organ and a brief description of each. For example, the heart has some narrowing of the coronary arteries. On the back of the document, the hand has written her cause of death as 1a – metastatic carcinoma of the liver. 1 b – carcinoma of the caecum. II - ischaemic heart disease, diabetes mellitus

Sounds nice, I think sarcastically.

I know this lady has no connection to Claire other than hers is a post-mortem report Claire was probably supposed to type. That was her job after all. Claire didn't bring work home with her. If she had then she wouldn't have hidden it inside a recipe book. It looks as if she'd stolen this, but why?

I turn to the front and read the name again.

The name of Hock fills me with dread because I know that name; I've had dealings with it professionally. They aren't a family I'd recommend anyone get involved with, least of all Claire and not when I'm in prison and I can't protect her. Isla may be able to tell me if Claire had an interest in this lady's death but she may not know if Claire slyly took this. Shouldn't its absence be noted?

I sigh and put it to one side. There's not much I can do about it now, not on a Saturday afternoon and not when I have an unfortunate task ahead. I've got to ring Eddie and tell him about Dad. Mum's too upset to do it and I can't really refuse. I would prefer another chat with Justine than Eddie. Things were awful the last time I spoke to him. He blamed me for it going wrong, but if he hadn't lied in the first place about the accident then things wouldn't have ended up so shit.

*

I wait for my call to C Wing to be answered; coldness crawls over my skin like a vapour. I thought I was done with all this: phone calls from prison and having to speak to obstructive guards. It seems that even when you're out of prison it still leaves you with a long lasting chill.

'Hello Mum,' Eddie says coming on the line. His voice throws me off guard and I stumble over my reply.

'I-I-It's not Mum. It's me,' I say, my heart suddenly starts thudding. 'Will.'

His disappointment echoes loudly in his silence. Now he's the one off guard. 'Where's Mum? Is she alright?'

'She's okay, just upset. I'm ringing to tell you that Dad's had to go into a psychiatric unit for assessment and unfortunately they've had to section him...'

'Why?'

'It's complicated.'

'They can't cure the Alzheimer's, can they?'

'No. His behaviour recently has got much worse.' I don't know how up to date Eddie is on Dad's current behaviour. I imagine he's been skipping that part of Mum's letters. I'll tell him if he asks. He doesn't.

'I thought with you being at home things would be better,' he says, pointedly. 'You know you could give her a break and look after Dad. Isn't that what you've been doing?'

'Yes, of course I have,' I state forcefully, but I'm lying because I've busied myself with trying to find Claire rather than giving her a break. Did I do that on purpose?

'I hope so because that's what I would have done if I was out.'

Little shit.

'Isn't it a bit late to play the dutiful son?' I bite back before I even realise the words are out and this is what he wants because this is his deliberate ploy to get the topic onto one of his choice.

'I didn't realise *you'd* been playing the role full time. I love how you've hijacked a phone call about Dad to have a go at me. We were talking about our parents but you obviously think 'us' is more important...'

'You steered it this way, Eddie,' I argue.

'No, I didn't. All I said was...'

'I know what you said. You're not going to miss this chance because it's the first one you've had...'

'Don't flatter yourself, Will, that you're all I think...'

'...for twelve months...'

'...about; I've moved on...'

'Where to? C wing?!'

'At least I didn't have to spend three weeks on the nonce wing till the governor knew where to place me!'

'You horrible little shit! If you hadn't buried us in this mess then at least one of us would have been around to help Mum...'

'It was your alibi that fucked things up,' he says viciously.

'What? You're unbelievable. It was your dangerous driving whilst drugs trafficking and your web of lies that got you locked up. I was just naive to think it was an accident.'

'You should have seen the major flaw in your alibi. As a copper I'd have expected you to know that there's CCTV everywhere especially at football grounds!'

'If I hadn't kept my mouth shut about the drugs you'd be looking at ten years.'

'I thought you did it for the bonus...'

'I did it to spare Mum and Dad more shame.'

'Good for you,' he replies sarcastically. 'But I think they were more embarrassed about their corrupt police officer son than their reckless student son.'

'At least I didn't kill anyone,' I say smugly and though I momentarily feel great that I've shut the wanker up, it is harsh.

'I hadn't forgotten that,' he says, his voice small but his self-pitying tone is just as annoying as his sarcasm and viciousness.

'Once we've gone to see Dad, I expect Mum will give you a ring with an update.'

'Okay, thanks.'

'Bye, Eddie.' And I hang up before he's a chance to reply with a bye or some other kind of retort.

I put the phone back in its cradle and stand alone in the kitchen with the hum of the fridge for company. Shit! I could have dealt with that better.

He's got to find prison tough. He was only 22 when he went inside. But maybe he's taken it in his stride, relishing the change of scenery and the opportunities prison might have to offer. Edward is more academically clever than common sense wise, but he's very adaptable, doing whatever is necessary to get along with people and make his life easier. Hence the reason why he started ferrying drugs around – to make money and fund his student life. A large part of me worries that he's taken to life inside exceptionally well, and when he's released he'll have learnt lessons of a different more sinister kind.

Saying that I shouldn't let him wind me up especially since it's been ages that we've had any contact. Claire tried to persuade me to write to him even if I didn't send the letter; she said it was therapeutic. I struggled, unable to find the words to say how I felt. I couldn't get past the anger I felt whenever I thought about what he'd done to us and our parents. The situation feels irreparable. Would several sessions of counselling help us to move on? Eddie holds grudges. As a child he'd always want to get his own back, sometimes waiting days to retaliate. Our plan, all those years ago, didn't work and he blames me. I blame him for involving me. How can that be resolved? And it's a sad shame because he and I are exactly like Claire and her sisters.

<u>Chapter 47</u>

Monday ~ day 14

I study the photos of the honey-trap. Claire's absence is a dull ache in my chest because it's the last photo ever taken of her and she looks like she did the last time I saw her. I run a finger over her mesmerising image. She's wearing a red dress (her favourite colour), hair up and decorated with diamond and pearl slides, her make-up flawless as she leans towards a tall nervous looking man with dark hair. They look a nice couple; rather like something off a Mills & Boon front cover. Still, I think, sliding the photos back into the brown envelope, they're a useful tool to confront Mr Snell with.

He's keeping me waiting in the reception of Bella Maria Lingerie – his workplace. The receptionist is busy juggling phone calls, admin work and dealing with couriers. On the surrounding walls are posters advertising the latest lingerie sets. One of them is quite racy. A black and white skimpy number that I can't take my eyes off. Well, the model does look like a Russian tennis player: blonde, tall, toned thighs.

I turn towards the opening door. A man wearing a stylish black suit and a pale blue tie appears, smiling pleasantly. It's the man himself.

'Hello. I'm James Snell,' and he holds out a hand. I shake it. He has a firm handshake. Good. I can't abide limp ones.

'Is there somewhere we can talk privately?'

He gestures towards a door and I follow him into the room. The strong vinegary smell of new carpet stings my nose. The room houses a pale wooden table in its centre and four chairs. Two large artificial plants adorn the far corners and there are more advertising posters on the walls.

He closes the door and looks at me expectantly.

'I'm investigating the disappearance of a local woman who went missing November last year. Her name is Claire Millward.'

There's a little crease on his forehead but it may be age related or he's pretending to mull the name over. He shakes his head. 'I'm afraid I don't know her.'

'Do you recall entertaining colleagues in the bar of the Azure hotel last November? You got into conversation with two women: Claire and Julia.'

He presses his lips together, gazes down at the carpet as if his phoney reply is scrawled there for him to read. His eyes dart about as if watching an insect scurrying about.

'Let me jog your memory,' I offer impatiently. 'Later in the evening you accompanied Claire into the hotel's garden where she tried to kiss you. You pushed her away, saying that you couldn't cheat on your wife.'

'I don't...'and he steps towards the door as if to leave.

'Let's see if a visual aid will jog your memory.' I hold up the large brown envelope and slide out the photos. The top one shows the two of them in the garden standing close together. It already makes them look as if they're up to something. It's well focused and framed with leaves from a nearby plant. I hold it out to him but he won't take it. His eyes widen at the image of Claire, his mouth curls into the tiniest of smiles.

'Let me show you another.' The next one I hold up shows James holding both his hands up, fingers splayed, a look of horror on his face.

'Why have you got photos?' he asks, his voice wobbly. 'Were you following me? Did you take them?'

'Did you like Claire?' I shake it harder; it flaps against his hair, lifting a lock over his forehead.

He takes the photos, forcing himself to look at it. His eyes soften. 'Yes, she was lovely. A very pleasant woman.'

'Why did you push her away?'

'I can't cheat on my wife even if it is just a kiss,' he answers robotically.

'I've met your wife. She seems...unexciting.' He doesn't ask how I've accomplished this and nor does he defend my criticism of her. I continue. 'No man would understand why you turned Claire down. What was the real reason? Did the evening feel staged? Did it feel like a trap?'

He shakes his head. 'No. I was flattered that an attractive woman would make a pass at me but...I couldn't kiss her.'

'Did you regret turning her down?'

He nods. 'If I wasn't married then I...'

'Is that why you were at Claire's flat three nights later? To pick up where you pushed her off?'

'What?' he gasps, horrified, his eyes wide, darting about madly. 'I wasn't.'

'You were seen by Julia. She recognised you instantly.'

'Then she must be mistaken.'

'She has exceptional observation skills. She clocked your number plate 43JLS and I see the same car parked outside.'

'Oh, God,' James mutters. He grasps the back of the nearest chair, his fingers digging into the plush cushioning. He sways and I continue, sure I'll get an explanation soon.

'Did you follow Claire home that night?'

He shakes his head wildly.

'Had you seen Claire the next day out and about in town, or at the hospital? How do you know where she lived?'

'She passed me a note,' he spits out.

I frown. 'What did it say?'

'Just an address, nothing else. I thought she was going to cause trouble for my marriage even though nothing had happened. It was stupid of me to go, I know, but I was intrigued. There was no answer when I knocked her front door so I left.'

A note, I think. Is that Claire's style? She knew where he worked so why not contact him later at his workplace? If as he claims, he rejected her, why would Claire pursue him? Any note would have to be written beforehand. How would she know if she'd never met him before, that she'd feel attracted to him?

'Do you have any idea how ridiculous this sounds? You considered the idea that she wanted to sabotage your marriage over a kiss that never happened. A less far-fetched explanation would be that you followed her home that night, noted the address and returned a few days later to find out why that evening felt staged.'

'No. She passed me a note.'

'Have you still got it? No, you don't,' I answer for him and he doesn't correct me.

He breathes hard, his chest rising quickly. He loosens his tie as if the room's temperature has gone up. There's something very odd about all this.

'Tell me everything you can remember. What time did you arrive at the flat?'

'It was after nine but before ten. I knocked the door several times because the light was on and I thought that she must be home but there was no answer.'

'Which light?'

'The hall light.'

How does he know the front door opens into a hall? Some flats open directly into the living room.

'Did you hear noises from inside? Did you see anyone else?'

He shakes his head. 'I saw no one, heard nothing. I just went home.' He glances at the clock on the wall. 'I have to return to work; I have a meeting at twelve.'

'Okay, Mr Snell. I may be back in the future with further questions.' I step aside and give him access to the door.

He places a hand on the handle and I realise he's still grasping the photograph. He raises it up for one last look. He looks sad, upset.

'I hope you find her.'

'Oh, I will. I won't stop till I do.'

On the way across the car park, I take out my phone and take a photo of his Jag. A neighbour may have seen his car over the weekend she went missing or if he returned that night.

*

The venue for the meet-the-manager is packed; the air smells of fags, beer and hostility. I arrive early to grab a chair two rows from the stage. I need to be where Mr Murray won't fail to spot me when I remove my jacket and stand to ask him my ready-made question.

'Late, ain't he, mate?' a bloke sitting to my right asks. He has blue scrawl tattooed on his neck.

'Perhaps he wants a round of applause before coming on stage.'

'He can fuck off!'

And on cue a door to the right of the stage opens and everyone turns as one. You can hear all the neck muscles click and bodies swish around on the hard plastic chairs as a figure walks out of the darkness and across the stage to be greeted by a low howling and sarcastic hand clapping. The first guy wears a snazzy suit with no tie. Overhead lights bounce off his shiny bald head. He smiles nervously. The second guy trudges out behind, wearing a tracksuit and battered trainers. I wonder if this is Murray affected by the hostility already. He looks like a mate's dad and not a very cool one either.

The third guy struts onto the stage with an arrogance I've seen before in cocky unremorseful suspects. He gazes out across the heads of the supporters, his expression hard and unforgiving. This is Murray. He's Claire's type: athletic, masculine, vessels full of testosterone and adrenalin. His dark hair is greying and his stubbled face is lined, but he can still turn a lady's head. And he knows it. He has an air of unpleasantness about him...unless that's just because I know he's into illegal betting.

Hands have already been thrust up; some already are being supported by the other hand like five year olds who know the answer.

I unzip my jacket and drape it over the back of my chair and wait for the right time.

The bald MC guy clears his throat with a sharp cough and surveys the supporters. Murray and his assistant start whispering to each other, hands over their mouths should any of us be skilled at lip reading. The MC picks the nearest supporter with his hand up.

'I'd like to ask Mr Murray why he hasn't given Shane Owen a chance yet. He's been sat on the bench for the last 3 games...'

'Shane's injured,' Murray coolly replies. 'What good is he to the team or himself? This titbit of news was announced on the club's website a while ago...'

'According to Twitter, Shane says he's fit,' the man argues.

'Then perhaps you shouldn't believe everything that's said on Twitter.' And Murray glances at the bald guy to say he's finished with this question.

The next question is from an overweight mum wearing a team shirt that's stretched to breaking point over her massive gut. A fat child sits beside her, licking an ice-cream. 'Why have you frozen out Robert Penn? He's rated as one of the best full-backs in our league.'

Murray raises his hands, fingers apart. 'By whom?' His voice light, sing-song. 'Certainly not by me. What's the point of a full-back who gets past his man and boots it behind the goal?'

The fans are in uproar. Fists and half-rising bodies surround and dwarf me, and I feel like I'm going to go under a swamp of trainers and work boots.

'Fucking wanker,' someone shouts in my ear.

On the stage Murray takes no notice. The MC is on his feet weakly calling for order.

'You're out of order, Murray!'

'C-can we have the next question, please?' the MC calls out.

It's my turn. I stand and puff out my chest like a pigeon wooing its mate; it inflates Claire's face and expands the big red letters spelling MISSING. I've borrowed the entire image from the missing poster and had it placed on this t-shirt.

The trio on the stage see me, their heads robotically turn my way, Murray's eyes flicker with interest when he sees Claire's face; it's almost a double-take albeit a composed one. I've got his attention. The crowd quieten.

'I'd like to ask Mr Murray his opinion on the recent betting scandal at Allerdale United. In case he's unfamiliar with it, the manager Kevin Marsh was charged with betting on his own team.'

'Why would I be interested in that?' Murray demands. 'I thought tonight was for questions about...'

'I'm not asking if you're interested,' I butt in firmly, 'just your opinion. Fifteen years ago Kevin Marsh was manager of this team.'

'I remember him,' a bloke in front of me says. 'He was a better manager than you, Murray!'

'If he's been caught betting on his team then he deserves his punishment,' Murray replies succinctly and turns away haughtily for the next question.

'Kevin says he didn't make the bet himself. His girlfriend did, but it amounts to the same thing.'

Murray locks eyes with me and I can't tell if he understands what I'm asking but then his gaze slips down to my chest and he receives a big clue as to why I'm asking this question.

'What's on your t-shirt?' he asks, frowning.

The front rows turn and look at me. I pull down the corners of my top so everyone can see Claire's face. 'This is my best friend Claire and she went missing last November. But you should be familiar with her face.'

His reply is aggressive and nervous. 'Why?'

'Because her missing poster has been hanging on the terraces for several months. I thought if I wore her face on my t-shirt then it'd jog people's memories.'

'Was she a fan?' a concerned woman asks me.

'Maybe...but she definitely had a connection to this club,' and I look straight at Murray. He's swigging from a bottle of water but I know he's soaking all my references up.

'Can we have one more question,' the bald guy says, 'and then Mr Murray has to get back to training.'

Murray gets his one question. A waste of a chance by someone who asks if he regrets releasing any of last season's players.

'No,' snaps Murray. 'I never regret any of my decisions.'

The crowd groan and complain when the MC calls time on the session. Murray scowls at the audience as he exits the stage which causes a wave of noise to rise up including a chorus of name-calling. The door slams but I'm already up and heading across the pub to the other exit to get to Murray's car in good time.

He's parked his snow white Merc away from the minions' cars. I wait by my own snow white Mazda with streaks of dried mud along the sides. There are a few drinkers milling about waiting for lifts or clustered around lampposts having a fag, comparing insulting names for Murray.

Murray slips out of the pub via a hidden door and hurries across to his car. He slows down, almost stops when he sees me by his car, but quickens up when he sees that I've parked so close to the driver's door he can't get in the vehicle.

He huffs loudly. 'Oi! What's your game? I'm late and the meet-the-manager session is over.'

'I don't want to talk about football. Just your affair with Claire Millward.'

He tries to sidestep me. 'Don't know her. Excuse me.'

'I know she had a nickname for you – El Erizo.'

Now he stops; I continue and his guilt seeps from his face like sweat. 'Hedgehog...' I ponder. 'Why that? Is it a childhood thing? Did you have spiky hair when you played for Murcia?'

'You could have gotten that titbit from any website...'

'It's not on any website I've read. I'm not interested in your affair just if she contacted you asking for money. I need to know. Did you give her any money?'

'Move your fucking car; I'm late.'

'Did she threaten to tell your wife about the affair?'

'What? No...'

'Her ace must have shocked you. Something along the lines of, "Do you remember me placing that bet for you on your own team?" A loaded question and you must have panicked. Stewart?'

'Fuck off. I've got nothing to say.'

'And to show you it wasn't a half-hearted threat she must have mentioned the bookie: Mr Desai.'

Murray's face bursts into an expression of anger, wonderment and panic. His eyes widen so much his eyelids look like they're going to split down the middle.

'Mr Desai keeps an accurate ledger on bets made in his establishment. In fact I know he does.' My stab in the dark has hit its target. Desai was a well known crooked bookie when I was a PC, plus he now advertises at Murray's ground. It's right in Stewart's mug every match day. 'If you don't talk to me, Stewart, then I might have to tip my colleagues off about your illegal betting. And so close to the end of the season...'

He looks at me, searching my threat for *how* I might be able to do this.

'Did I forget to mention that I'm ex-police? Sorry about that.' I grin and hold up my hands with mock apology.

Finally, he gives up. He leans against the boot with his arms folded. 'She rang me out of the blue a week or so before she went missing. We chatted and then she explained she was in a sticky situation and needed money to urgently pay off a debt. I couldn't help her without my wife getting suspicious. I felt awful, I really did, and she was disappointed. But then she casually asked if I remembered asking her to place a bet. She recalled the amount, the bookie, how much I won and the share I gave her as a thank-you. I took it as a veiled threat.'

Claire must have been so desperate to approach him.

'A few days later Mr Desai shows up at the ground for a meeting. I saw a correlation between the two and I convinced myself that Claire had contacted the board about my bet.'

'Did you ask Claire if she was behind the meeting?'

'No. If blackmail was her intention, I assumed she'd threaten me first rather than go to the chairman. I decided to play it cool, see what happened.'

'Where were you over the weekend she went missing?' And I tell him the date.

He smiles with relief. 'Away in the north-east. We had a match on the Saturday and travelled up Friday afternoon with the team. Didn't return till Sunday morning. If you want to confirm my whereabouts check our fans' forum. They would have slaughtered me for abandoning the team.'

'Judging by your welcome tonight, I can imagine they'd be exceedingly kind.'

'I've never been popular but when I take the team up to the next league, then they'll *love* me. Till next season. Look, I'm sorry about Claire,' he says sincerely. 'I was upset when I read about her disappearance. We had a good time together; she helped me through some dark times and I thought a lot of her, and if I could've helped her then I would. The fans may think I'm a bastard but I was never that to her.'

He's still an arrogant prat but it must be a difficult job to do. All that criticism and name calling comes with the job and I suppose acting like you don't give a toss helps to deal with it. I can see why Claire fancied him: he's a man's man, full of himself, certainly not the type to exfoliate his skin or coo 'Ahh,' over a baby seal. I can't understand women's desire for blokes like that. Not that I coo over baby marine mammals, but there's nothing wrong with a bit of skin care.

He could conceivably have travelled up north with the team and then driven all the way back here through the night to kill Claire and then travel all the way back up there, but since the match was over 3 hours away that's a long time to be away and he'd be knackered after all that motorway driving. He has an excellent motive though. But opportunity. Could he have hired someone? Three hours away he'd have the perfect alibi. But how am I going to find a supposed assassin? Is there any evidence of one? No. There's no evidence of anything.

'Thanks for talking so frankly with me,' I tell him, taking the car key out of my pocket.

'Were you sleeping with Claire?' he asks with interest.

I look at him. 'Never,' I admit, 'she was my best friend.'

Chapter 48

Tuesday ~ day 15

A sharp rapping on the passenger side window makes me jump. I look around foolishly but being in such a low car I have to open my door and get out. The wind whips around my ears and messes my hair up. I was already having a bad hair day and now it's got a lot worse.

'I understand you're looking for a betrayed wife,' a woman says over the low roof. She's in her early thirties, wearing a black fleece over the gym's uniform. Her long blonde hair is tied back; a plastic red slide securing her fringe out of her eyes. 'My husband had an affair with Claire Millward.'

'Thank you for coming forward. I know it can't be easy.'

She winces. 'I'm getting over it. How can I help you?'

I walk around the boot and briefly explain that Claire was my friend and that a witness puts her at Claire's flat the night before her disappearance.

'I've had nothing to do with her going missing. Granted I went to the flat to confront her, but she wasn't there or she was hiding behind the settee with her fingers in her ears. I intended to go back to her flat the next day, but family life got in the way. A few days later I read she'd disappeared.'

She doesn't walk away, but waits to be questioned further.

'Your version tallies with what a neighbour says.' I smile. 'I believe you...sorry, I don't know your name.'

'Antonia Pearson.'

'I'm William Bailey. I need to speak to your husband. How can I contact him?'

'Ralph lives with his mother now,' she replies bitterly. 'You can find his contact details in the *Yellow Pages* under alarm services. He moved out of our house a month after Claire disappeared. He wasn't "coping".' She makes air quotes with her fingers. 'He went to be by himself.'

'Thanks. How did you find out about Ralph's affair?'

'I received an anonymous text message.' And from her pocket, she removes her mobile phone and swipes her finger across the screen. She holds the screen up to show me and I walk nearer to read it.

'I can't believe you've kept it.'

The text reads: Ralph is fucking a bitch called Claire Millward. Ask him.

I note the date and time it was sent: the week Claire went missing at 7:54 pm; I make a mental note of the mobile number.

'You don't recognise the number?'

Antonia shakes her head. 'I rang it straightaway, but it went to voicemail. There was no message that identified the caller. I've tried it several times since; it's never been answered.'

'Did Ralph recognise the number? Did he have any ideas who sent it? Who else could have known about the affair?'

'Ralph said it wasn't Claire and he has no idea who sent it. Part of me wishes they hadn't done this.' She wiggles the phone. 'Sometimes what you don't know doesn't hurt you.'

'Won't you have him home?' I ask, gently.

'He won't come home. He loves her. I imagine you do too. Are you another of her men?' Her eyes narrow into a dirty look.

'I'm her friend, that's all.'

Antonia nods sadly. 'Why does she do it? Why take someone else's husband?'

'Because when they're not yours, it's easier to give them up.'

*

'Ooh, I can't tell you how excited I am to be part of your investigation,' Liv coos enthusiastically. She flips the sun visor down and applies more plum lipstick to already well painted lips.

She's been in the car for less than a minute and the entire vehicle is filled with the strong scent of her perfume: black cherry and bergamot. I unwind the window and let some fresh air in before I start choking. The roar of the wind drowns out the sound of the radio and Liv's voice as she tells me how naughty she feels for skiving work.

She phoned the night before to remind me what a massive favour she did in getting me access to Claire's flat. I knew where this was heading straightaway and could do little to dissuade her: she wants to help with my investigation. So I agreed to take her along when I speak to Stan.

'Faithful old Fergus is struggling to find work even though he did a plasterer's course to get another string in his cap...'

'Bow,' I correct. 'String in your bow. Feather in your cap.'

'Whatever. It hasn't put any more dosh in his pocket. I told Sally he should get a proper job instead of fucking about with bricks. I mean nobody's buying houses these days. They can't afford them and I know! I can't get out of that shithole I'm in.'

I don't see any logic to her opinion, but agree with her about the shithole flat.

'Anyway, he's a drip. He may look all man but he isn't. I mean he doesn't even do jobs around the house...'

'It's always the way if you live with electricians or plumbers,' I interrupt so she can take a breath. 'They don't fix flying sparks or leaks because they don't get paid hundreds by the hour.' A 4x4 is heading towards us and typically the driver thinks they own the road so I'm forced to put the Mazda into the hedgerow or lose a wing mirror.

With chivalry, Liv winds down her window and sticks her arm out, pumping her fist in a wanker's gesture at the driver.

I raise an eyebrow but say nothing.

She brings her limb back inside the vehicle and continues with her thread on Fergus.

'Well, at least he's filled in that mechanic's pit.'

I look at her with surprise. Who has a mechanic's pit in the garage? A mechanic, I suppose.

Liv frowns with guilt that she's openly criticising her sister's boyfriend with the enemy. 'I almost broke my leg stumbling around there in the dark whilst looking for a hammer to put that Catherine Wheel up...' she laughs heartily.

We pass the pub where Fiona and I met for a drink. Good, not long now. I need a breather and a break from her fragrance and her non-stop chatter. I reverse the Mazda onto Fiona's property, should I need a quick exit.

Liv stares longingly at the property with its gravel drive and land, protected on all sides by tall hedging. A collection of terracotta pots containing daffodils are positioned around the front door. Now I can see behind the hedgerow, it's hard to miss the plastic greenhouse on its concrete base.

'Wish I had a garden,' Liv says dreamily. 'Wish there was somewhere I could sit out and enjoy the sun with a bottle of chardonnay.'

Not keen on hearing yet again how much she despises where she lives, I've pretty much concluded she's too lazy to do something about it, I turn off the ignition and open the car door.

'She's not home then?' Liv stupidly says.

'Your powers of observation astound me. I already checked; she's tucked up at work. Come on before the old guy takes a mid morning nap.'

We approach the front door, our footsteps crunch on the gravel drive. Liv knocks hard on the door causing the pane to rattle noisily in the wooden frame.

'He might be deaf,' she explains when I raise my eyebrow at her. 'You know what old people are like. They have to have the telly turned way up.'

Nevertheless, the old man hears. A shadow appears and shuffles its way to the front door. He fumbles with the lock and opens up, but rather than greet us and ask what we want, he steps outside, turning back to lock the door behind him.

'Hello Stan,' I say, confidently.

He jumps, dropping the key. It falls onto the gravel and Liv quickly retrieves it.

'Oh, hello.' He peers around my shoulder, being too small to look over it. 'You're not from the day centre, are you?'

Stan comes up to my mid-chest; his frame is slightly stooped, his legs bandy as if his framework of bone is collapsing. His bald head with its snowy hair is marked with white scars where he's bumped his head in the past. His dark blue irises are ringed with white halos. A sign of heart disease. Claire told me once that's what it means.

'Morning,' Liv says pleasantly. 'I'm afraid we're not. Are you on your way out?' She drops the key into his arthritic deformed hand.

'I thought you were the bus knocking but you're early.'

'Then we're in luck. Have you got time for a cuppa, Stan?'

His bushy white eyebrows jump in surprise that Liv knows his name.

'I don't know...' he hesitates. 'I don't know who you are...'

'Well, I'm Olivia. Fiona works with my sister Claire; they're both secretaries. And Will here, met Fiona the other night for a drink. So now you know who we are.'

It's like saying "open sesame"' to a cave door and miraculously it opens. Stan is satisfied with the authenticity of Liv's introductions and reopens the front door, saying 'Come in. Let me get the kettle on. I've already had one; the tea at the centre is like piss water.'

I hope he's not this welcoming to bogus callers intent on robbing him. Fiona really needs to speak to him. He leads the way along a stone tiled floor, past a row of coat hooks, the staircase, two closed doors and into the kitchen.

It's a typical farmhouse kitchen: Belfast sink with wooden X-shaped drainer, floral patterned blind in the window, hanging from a rack above the Aga are a collection of copper-bottomed pans, a bunch of dried lavender sticks out of a china pitcher in the middle of the pine table.

Nice, I think, very homely.

We sit him at the kitchen table and I start making tea following Stan's directions as to where everything is. Liv puts him at ease asking about the day centre, what activities they run, does he enjoy it, before moving onto life here with Fiona.

I keep an eye on the clock. At some point this bus is going to turn up. Behind Stan's back, I circle my finger in the air for Liv to move it along.

'Fiona works with my sister Claire,' Liv reminds him when he asks how we know Fi. He's obviously a little forgetful. 'At the hospital. Did Fi ever talk about Claire?'

'No, I don't think so.' He places his clawed hand on hers. 'She never talks about anyone she works with. She's only interested in one person.'

And I expect him to add, 'Fiona.' But he doesn't.

Instead he replies, 'Nigel.'

'Who's he? Boyfriend?'

'Fiona's ex husband. Such pity she didn't show as much interest in him when they were married. It might have saved them.'

'Why is she so interested in him?' Liv asks.

'She doesn't tell me why. She and her mum spend hours talking about what he's doing.'

'Does he live local?'

'Yes by my doctor's surgery. The house with the green door. Fiona pointed it out once. I don't know why she can't leave well alone and find herself a nice man who wants to be with her.'

'If I asked you where Fiona was one night last winter, would you know?' I ask.

'One day's like the next to me, I'm sorry to say. I doubt I'd remember unless Fiona had written an appointment down on the calendar.' He lifts an arthritic finger to point at the calendar on the wall. The current picture for April is of a cartoon little girl picking wildflowers in a meadow. Talk about deliberately inflicting pain on yourself for what could have been. Fiona must be deranged.

A loud beep beep from outside makes us all jump.

'It's the bus,' Stan announces and immediately goes into a flap, looking for his coat which he's still wearing. We help him up. I make sure the kettle is switched off at the wall and place his mug in the sink. I didn't bother making tea for me and Liv.

'Don't forget your mobile,' Liv tells him, snatching it up off the table.

'Thanks, love. It's only for emergencies. Nobody ever rings me on it,' he explains and a thought occurs to me and I grab it from Liv.

'I'll just make sure it's charged up.'

It's a basic mobile with worn numbers and a little antenna – the end of which is chewed. Stan doesn't strike me as the texting type so I bet it's one of Fiona's old mobiles. I press a button and the small screen lights up. At least it's on; I haven't got to bother waiting for it to fire itself up. I dial my own mobile number from Stan's mobile and wait for it to ring from my pocket before ending the call.

'It's fine,' I say, handing it back. I don't bother wiping clean the calls going out; it'll give Fiona something to think about.

We make sure the house is all locked up and deliver Stan safely onto the bus. He waves at us from the window; we smile back. We follow the bus down the lane; I spy a lay-by up ahead and pull in.

Liv stares at me. 'Why have we stopped?'

I ignore her and take out my mobile to study the missed call from Stan's mobile. The number ends with the digits 007, just like on the anonymous text Antonia received.

'What have you found?' Liv asks, grabbing my arm and yanking it towards her so she can see too.

'Careful!' I cry pulling my arm back. 'It appears Stan sent a malicious text.'

'No way,' Liv cries noisily. 'That nice old man. Why? To who?"

I roll my eyes. 'Well, maybe not that nice old man but the spiteful bitch he lives with.'

She thinks about it. 'It's perfect, isn't it? She gives it to him for emergencies, but no one ever rings him on it and he never uses it. She has total control over it.'

'Exactly. We should have asked him which surgery he goes to.' I drum my fingers thoughtfully on my chin.

'Pitchford Road,' Liv answers. 'I asked him while you tidying up. See? I'm not just a pretty face with excellent communication skills.'

I'm taken aback with her self-compliments but do glance out the corner of my eye as I engage first gear. Yeah, she's alright; could do with losing a few pounds if you prefer your girls size 16 or under, fairly pretty...be better if she eased up on the make-up though. She always looks like she's off on a night out on the pull.

The house we're looking for does indeed have a green door, it's number 29, but then so do numbers 34, 67, 68 and we have to apologise to those that answer their doors for interrupting them unnecessarily. Number 29 is a lovely two bedroomed terrace house with a couple of Box plants standing guard either side of the path. The image is ruined by the parking of a pushchair on the slabs underneath the kitchen window. In a house this small I don't suppose there's much room for a bulky three wheeled vehicle. I ring the bell and suddenly the door flings open by a man with tired darkened eyes; a finger pressed to his lips tells me to hush.

'Sorry,' I whisper.

He steps forward and closes the door behind him cutting off my view of the inside of the hall. 'It's alright, mate, finally just got my daughter down to sleep. What can I do for you? You're not selling double glazing are you?'

I laugh. 'No, I'm not. Are you Nigel?'

He nods.

'I'm Will and this is Olivia...'

'Oh, God, Jehovah's...' and he steps backwards.

'No! We want to talk to you about Fiona Bashford.'

His shoulders slump and his head lolls to one side as if he's fallen asleep. He runs a hand through his greying tousled hair, making it stick up at the front. 'I don't have anything to do with her anymore. We're divorced.'

Suddenly the door is pulled away nearly knocking Nigel over.

'Nigel, what's going on?' demands a woman barging past him to square up to us. She's in her mid twenties, slim, blonde hair pulled back into a hasty ponytail.

She is the dominant one of the pair. The one who gave a dithering Nigel an ultimatum: leave your unhappy marriage and have a baby with me or stay with your crazy barren wife. She is also the one who is going to tell me what I want to know.

I explain who we are and what we want. Nigel stays quiet and presses himself against the door as his partner takes centre stage.

'Just come in. I don't want the neighbours and every Tom, Dick and Fiona seeing what's going on. Just stay quiet. Millie is asleep and I'll be furious if she's woken up.' She tutts at Nigel to move out the way, and points at an open door at the end of the hall. We step into the living-cum-dining room. A pine table and four chairs are positioned at the back of the room in front of the French doors which open out into a small garden where I can see a red painted fence and a bird table. The living room half has two settees both covered with fluffy throws. On the coffee table is a baby's plastic rattle, a dummy and a row of remote controls which will be for the enormous TV, the games console and the Blu-ray player.

'Sit down,' she says. 'I'm Deb. Nigel, put the kettle on.'

Liv and I sit side by side on the orange fluffy throw, moving aside the brown and orange striped cushions. I make the introductions; Nigel gets cracking with making the tea.

'He doesn't like talking about *her*, thinks the problem will go away if it's not discussed. But it won't,' Deb begins.

I wonder what the problem is if they're officially divorced. Unless the money side is still pending.

I begin; Liv butts in a couple of times to clarify various points, but I keep my eyes on Deb so she knows I'm the lead on this. She listens with interest, occasionally nodding and murmuring.

'And you think Fiona murdered your sister?'

Liv looks at me, we both nod.

'Jesus Christ. Well, it wouldn't surprise me. She's a crazy bitch. And though I hope she hasn't harmed your sis, I hope she's done something to get herself banged up because that'll get her out of our hair!'

'What do you mean?' I ask. 'Stan, her...'

'I know who he is.'

'...told us that Fiona is only interested in one person.'

'No, three really. Nigel, me and our daughter. She parks outside our house nearly every night, staring at our house, watching and waiting to see if we go out, which light is on, who visits us. It's pathetic. We've already got an injunction out on her. She's not allowed within fifty metres of our house but that doesn't stop her from parking exactly fifty metres up the road! And we can't stop her until she does something. We used to live in a really nice flat but had to move when she discovered our address; she turned up at our next flat so once again we moved, and now she's in the street every night! I don't know how she finds out where we are. She was hanging around the maternity ward when I bought Millie home. Can you believe it? She's a nightmare.'

'She sounds mental,' Liv mutters.

'She's dangerous,' Deb corrects sternly. 'Why else would she be sitting outside my house? Either to snatch my daughter or put a knife in me. Murdering your sister isn't as daft as you might think.' She points a finger at Liv.

'She uses the patient database to keep tabs on you all,' I tell her, disturbed by the depth of Fiona's obsession. Deb's mouth opens with shock. 'Claire found this out and put it in a grievance statement. She would have been severely disciplined, even sacked, had Claire not gone missing.'

The door opens and Nigel appears, carrying a tray of tea and a bowl of sugar. Deb clears a space on the coffee table.

'I've told them about Fiona sitting outside the house. Will says Fiona is accessing the hospital patient database to find our addresses.'

Nigel nods. 'That doesn't surprise me. She knew everything that was going on with our neighbours.

"Mr Jones at number 6 has had a hernia repair" and "Miss Fellows at number 19 is having IVF". It drove me up the wall. We told the police about her camping outside. They've advised us to keep a log of every time she appears and how long she's here for. We need evidence that she's breached...'

'We've got evidence,' Deb exclaims. 'We're keeping a log. He's reluctant to get *her* into trouble.'

'I'm not...I feel sorry for her...I did have an affair...'

Deb shakes her head with disgust. 'Feel sorry for me and our daughter. Not her!'

Nigel looks away, passing the sugar bowl around.

'Do you mind if I have a look at the log?' I ask.

'Yeah, sure. It's here,' he says, pulling open a drawer on the coffee table and handing me a patterned hardback book.

'Thanks.' I turn to the last page and see that Fiona parked outside their house four times in the last six days. She must have no life.

I turn back through the pages till I find the weekend Claire went missing. *Friday 1st December. Arrived 1800 hours; departed 1830 hours. Activity: sat in car, on mobile.* Why only half an hour? Did she have to get back to do Stan's tea? Did she call in on her way home? Did she leave to seek out Claire?

I turn the page and stop...she came back. Fiona returned at 1900 hours and stayed till 2201 hours. For 3 hours, she sat in car, ate Chinese food, walked up and down street both sides, read newspaper, spoke to a neighbour for a few minutes.

It's possible that Fiona went to Claire's flat after 10 o'clock but it seems unlikely. I feel sure Claire disappeared whilst on her run since she failed to write her time on the calendar. Or else she was disturbed seconds after returning to the flat. Running five kilometres was taking Claire around half an hour to complete so she would have arrived back 7pm at the latest. I doubt Fiona sat outside Nigel's house with Claire's body in the tiny boot of her Fiesta.

Fiona, it appears, has an alibi. And ironically it's been given to her by two people who hate her with a passion. Best not to mention any of this to Deb. I close the book and place it on the table. I finish my tea and look at Liv.

'Drink up. Let Nigel and Deb get on. Thanks for the chat and the tea. You've been helpful.' I stand and Liv slurps her tea as she hastily tries to drain the mug.

We walk down the path and I know Liv is dying to know what I've discovered. Her hand tugs at my sleeve like a child who's trying to draw their parent's attention to the confectionary aisle. I keep her waiting till we get back into the Mazda.

'Fiona has an alibi. A well documented one, given to her by her two favourite people.'

'You're joking?' Liv gasps.

I shake my head and explain.

'I don't believe it. Fiona was our prime suspect.'

'Fiona took her revenge on Claire by texting Antonia and telling her about her husband's affair.'

'Who do we investigate now? Who's left?'

'I've got a few more leads,' I reassure her. Tomorrow I've got an appointment with Ralph but I can't tell Liv that since it's at Claire's flat and I'm not supposed to have the key.

Chapter 49

Wednesday ~ day 16

He's not doing a very good job of following me inconspicuously so I know he's not a copper or any other kind of professional. He was waiting in a lay-by on the main road and pulled out as I drove past. He's stayed glued to the Mazda's boot, cutting people up, running red lights, narrowly missing pedestrians.

I know it's a man because he rubs his face the way a man does when he's got a shaving rash. Plus the number plate of his white Range Rover is a giveaway: LEO999.

You never know, I tell myself, he might have some tasty info.

I pull into Tesco's car park and enter the store.

Twelve minutes later, I'm sitting in the cafe which is right by the entrance enjoying a nice mocha when he enters the store and looks around nicely confused and panicked. He's around 45 years; with narrow boyish arms; short, dark non-descriptive hair; wearing a t-shirt with a faded Union Jack on the front and drainpipe black jeans with white battered trainers – red flashes down the side.

He doesn't spend money on clothes, this one, I think, not like he does on his cars... unless his attire is damn expensive designer ware.

He's created a hazard in the middle of the floor. Shoppers with trolleys and young kids in tow struggle to steer around him. Eventually he looks my way but I'm already pushing my chair back and rising to my feet. His face freezes in horror when I wave and beckon him over.

'Get yourself a coffee,' I say, 'and we'll have a chat. Mine's a mocha. Tray there.'

He looks behind at the stack and sighs, defeated. He sits opposite, removing his latte from the tray along with four sachets of sugar.

'Why are you following me?' I ask, taking a sip.

'I thought you were someone else.'

'Still think I'm someone else?' And I turn my face to the right then the left. 'Does that help?'

He doesn't reply, sips his coffee but it's hot and he winces.

'People often mistake me for the lead singer of the *Smiths*.'

His mouth twitches in a brief smile.

'Why are you really following me? I don't owe you money, do I?' I laugh and his dark eyes sharply look up from his glass. Interesting reaction, I think.

'I heard you're looking for Claire Millward,' he mutters.

'I am. You're very concerned though. Are you a neighbour, a colleague, an ex?'

'No.'

I wait but he doesn't elaborate. This bloke is one annoying twat. He followed me so there must be something he wants. Now he has the chance to explain he's backed off.

'You can stop playing hard to get,' I tell him. 'I've got better things to do than sit here with you...'

'I saw you at Lilliton FC the other night,' he admits with a sigh.

'Oh! Then you already know who I am because I announced it to the audience at the meeting. I'm guessing you're a money-lender and Claire owed you. Leo, isn't it?' His mouth opens to ask why. 'Did she have the money to pay?'

'Supposedly, but I never saw it. When I heard on the news she'd gone missing, I assumed she'd taken the money and scarpered. I didn't blame her.'

'Did you know she had a black eye?'

He can't hide his reaction quickly enough but insists it wasn't him. 'People wouldn't borrow from me if I was nasty and violent.'

'You must have seen her to know she had a black eye...'

He shrugs. I suspect he knows who did it, but doesn't want to say. Why? Is he frightened of them? I finish my drink and put the mug back on the tray. He's not telling me anything useful and I'm not playing these stupid games; I'm prepared to walk away.

'You're lying to me, Leo. I'm sure in the course of my search, I'll lift up the rock you live under and we'll meet again in not so cosy surroundings as Tesco's cafe. Since the police are unaware Claire owed you money or about her black eye, I'll pass your details onto them.' I push the chair back and he leaps into action, grabbing my arm.

'No, wait, look. What do you want to know?'

I remember the PM report on the late Mrs Hock. Let's find out what he knows about that. I sit back down. 'When someone who owes money is struggling to pay, there are other things a money-lender can do. Like sell debts on.'

He shakes his head. 'I wouldn't make much profit if I did that. Besides, she had the money. I've told you.'

'Maybe Claire had something else she could give you...'

'Like what, information?'

That surprises me. I assumed he'd think I was hinting at a sexual arrangement. Interesting that he's on my wavelength.

'Claire had access to patient databases. How about that?'

'Don't know,' Leo mutters. But I feel like I'm getting hotter.

'You do know.' I point a finger at him. 'I found information on a Mrs Hock in the flat. Did you ask Claire to get that? Do you know the family?'

'I didn't ask her to get no report on the old lady!'

'Report. That's exactly what I found. How did you know about it?'

Leo starts scratching the back of his neck as if someone's poured itching powder down his collar. Or maybe he can almost feel the hot oppressive breath of the Hock family behind him. 'Claire works in pathology...it's obvious the woman's dead.'

'No. Many of the patients Claire typed reports for are alive. She had access to thousands of patients. I'm more interested in who hit Claire because someone who hits a woman can do worse...steal her money, commit murder.'

'I don't know...' He scratches his neck again.

'Were the Hocks involved? Did they put pressure on Claire to get this information?' I'm leaning over the table, my palms flat on the top, avoiding the collection of coffee cups, staring right into his face which is buried into his chest. Honestly, I've never met such a pathetic suspect. I bet he's wishing he hadn't followed me today.

A member of staff walks past, her eyes glancing sharply at us. We're creating too much of a scene. This is not the place for playing bad cop. I stand.

'Get up, Leo,' and he does and I can see how malleable he is, how almost completely under a more dominant person's control he is. We head outside.

'You're lying to me, Leo,' I say, 'but I understand why because you're scared. The Hock family are not a family anyone with half a brain would want to get involved with so I'm thinking that this was out of your hands. Out of Claire's too. She was a gutsy girl, able to stand up for herself, but not against them. You've told me enough so that I can pursue a line of enquiry I've recently discovered anyway. If you could keep from telling the Hock family about our coffee morning then I'd be grateful. And I won't disclose that you told me about them.'

'I didn't tell you anything!' he shouts.

I pat his back. 'You didn't deny it either. And that's confirmation enough for people like them. If you want to chat some more then feel free to wait at the lay-by again.' I turn and head back to the Mazda. I'm out the car park before he can find first gear.

The Hock family, I think, driving over to Claire's flat for the appointment with Ralph. Fucking cowardly Leo and stupid naive Claire for thinking that one or the pair of them could take on a family like that. The Late Mrs Hock had two sons and two daughters. One of the sons is doing ten years for manslaughter. It was one of those I-don't-like-your-face-so-I'm-going-to-kick-off-in-the-kebab-shop scenarios. And ended with the needless loss of some poor sod's life. The daughters have raised a troop of fatherless hooded chavvy brats. And the youngest son – mummy's little soldier, is now the head of the family. I've only ever had one dealing with him...never again. I don't fancy accusing him of assault and murder. He'll deny it, and I'm not about to show him the PM report till I know exactly why Claire had it. I could contact Isla but I'm not sure it's a good idea. Claire wouldn't have told her colleagues about possessing confidential information which could have got her the sack.

I arrive at Claire's flat and wait inside. I pace the rooms, rubbing my hands together for warmth. It's cold and damp in here like a dungeon. I wonder when Marion will discover her key doesn't fit the lock. That's if she really does keep an eye on the place regularly. My eyes gaze around at the work surfaces, but are suddenly snagged on an item by the unplugged kettle: a jewellery box, the size a man's watch would come in. I didn't notice that before. I open the box and discover Claire's sports watch nestling inside. Its large screen makes the watch look chunky but it's surprisingly lightweight. I press the ON button but the display screen stays dark and quiet. The battery must be dead. I find the charger on a shelf under the drawer of the bedside cabinet. I put everything on the corner of the work surface to take with me when I leave. A knock at the front door startles me and I remember why I'm here. I open the door and give my best homeowner's welcoming smile.

I look Ralph over. He does the same. He's a couple of inches shorter but as lean as I am now that I've lost muscle and weight through a prison lifestyle. His arms are toned and I glimpse a coloured tattoo on his upper arm poking out from the sleeve of his black t-shirt. His dark red hair is styled not unlike mine although longer at the back: more of a fifties style; it reminds me of Travolta in *Grease*. He's an alright looking bloke, more pleasant than Murray anyway.

'Have you moved in?' he asks.

'No. Claire's parents are keeping the flat on in the hope that she comes back. Claire and I were friends and I'm investigating her disappearance...'

He livens up, bouncing on his heels; his smile is one of hope. 'Investigating? What, like the police? Have you found her? Do you know where she is?' he demands excitedly.

'I wish I did,' I admit. 'Please.' And I beckon him inside. Trustingly, he enters the flat and walks straight into the lounge, but all he finds is an empty settee with a dust sheet thrown over it in a cold room. 'I thought...'

I ease a chair out from under Claire's two seater dining table and smile sympathetically. 'Please sit down. You took some tracking down, Ralph.'

'How did you find me? Not that I was lost.'

'A neighbour remembered your wife when she came here to confront Claire. They recognised the gym she worked at. I spoke to Antonia,' I say gently but his reaction isn't angry but nonchalant.

He looks impressed that I've gone to such trouble. 'I haven't seen Antonia for a couple of weeks. I'm sorry I hurt her again. Did she tell you I had a fling before?' I lie and nod. 'She wanted another baby but I didn't. We rowed about it. She deliberately stopped taking the pill without telling me and got pregnant. So I started shagging the local barmaid.' Ralph shakes his head with disgust at his action. 'Antonia threatened if I cheated again our marriage was over. In order to keep me out of the pub, she came up with a clever idea: to take up coaching the local kids so I did and met

Claire. How ironic is that? Are you normally this easy to talk to?' he suddenly asks.

I chuckle. 'Not really, no. I'm an ex copper so people don't usually want to talk to me. Claire said I was a great listener. Maybe you just need someone to talk to.'

'Yeah, maybe. You're not a boyfriend of Claire's?'

'No. I've been away for a while so I only saw Claire occasionally. When I found out she'd gone missing I thought I should do some digging around.'

'I'm glad you have, mate.' He sits back on the settee and balances one foot on the other knee. 'There's been no mention of her in the papers for ages. It's as if no one cares anymore. Apart from you and me that is.'

'You were seeing Claire up until she disappeared?' I ask, testing him.

'No. She finished with me about two weeks before. She complained that I was getting too serious, that it wasn't fun anymore and she wanted out. I promised to leave Antonia; I may have even offered to go home and do it there and then but Claire said no. I tried to persuade her that I'd change, do whatever she wanted but she just wanted me to leave. I really thought she'd ring and tell me she'd changed her mind and could we start up again. But after several days of moping around, I went to the hospital and spoke to her. It wasn't nice.' Ralph shakes his head. 'She told me to go. I text her later that day. Antonia had received an anonymous text telling her about my affair. Did she tell you about that?'

'Yes. Someone witnessed your meeting with Claire at the hospital. They said you got angry with Claire and hit her.'

He gasps. 'No! I was angry; she wasn't listening. I've never hit a woman. At least of all a woman I love. And I did love Claire. Who said I hit her? The same person who text Antonia, I suppose.'

I nod. 'Yes, it was. They're not important. They were just trying to stir up trouble and deflect my attention onto you.'

'Do you think someone's harmed her?' Ralph shudders at the thought. 'Do you suspect me and Antonia? I suppose you must if you tracked us down.'

'A scorned wife has plenty of motive. Claire had twice told you to leave her alone and maybe you got angry and lost control. Maybe you thought Claire had told Antonia after all...'

He interrupts. 'If Claire had blabbed to Antonia then she did me a favour. But the truth is I never saw Claire again after the incident at the hospital...well, it wasn't an incident...it was just a conversation...I know I was wound up...but...'

I hold up a hand. 'Ralph, relax. As suspects go, you're pretty far down the list. Just tell me where you were on the Friday Claire went missing.'

'Things at home were terrible. Antonia had a weekend away and I stayed at home with the kids. They're not old enough to be left alone in case you're wondering. Is that when you think Claire went missing?'

'A neighbour saw her go for a run after work and saw lights on in the flat later that evening. However, Claire had an important appointment the next morning which she didn't make. Two people visited her flat that night and neither got a response from knocking the door. There's a possibility that she didn't make it home from her run.'

'Have you checked out the route Claire ran? Something may have happened...'

'I don't know where she ran.'

'I'll write it down for you. Some of the route goes through Whiting Woods. Have you spoken to the other guy Claire was seeing?'

'I haven't been able to track him down.'

'Ah, his name's Mr Weeks.'

I raise an eyebrow.

'I knew she was seeing someone else; part of me didn't want to know details but I'm nosy. In a drawer, I found one of those little cards that come with flowers. He'd signed it Mr Weeks. I ripped it up.'

'Claire Sellotaped it back together.'

'Did she? I only saw him the once.'

I pounce on his revelation. 'You saw him? What do you remember?'

'The day Claire dumped me, I hung around outside. A while later, this expensive posh Jag turns up and this bloke gets out. I didn't see his face.'

Whilst Ralph's talking, I'm flicking through the photos on my phone to find the one I took recently. It's a long shot but you never know. I thrust the phone at him.

He peers at it and nods. 'Yeah, that's it. It's a distinctive colour.'

Yes, it is, I silently agree and it proves a certain someone to be a liar. Six days before he met Claire, Mr Snell was visiting her flat. If he's Mr Weeks then they've been having an affair for months and that explains a lot.

'Have you spoken to him?' Ralph asks.

'Yes,' I reply, 'but our second conversation is going to be a hell of a lot more interesting.'

Chapter 50

Thursday ~ day 17

'I sincerely hope that this will be the last time you interrupt me at work or anywhere else,' Mr Snell says, irritated. He ushers me into the same office and closes the door with a little slam. 'I don't see what else I can tell you.'

'There's plenty you can tell me, Mr Weeks.'

He tries to rectify himself before I notice the momentary widening of his eyes and the slight opening of his mouth. His fingers start to pick the upholstery on the back of the nearest chair. The noise is irritating. I glance down at his hand and he stops, putting his hand in his pocket instead. The gesture just makes him look guiltier.

'I've got to hand it to you, Mr Weeks; you've done a nearly excellent job of pulling the wool over my eyes.'

'I don't know who you mean...my name is...'

'It makes perfect sense why you were at Claire's flat on the Friday, why Claire refused to be called Rachel on the honey trap; she'd have remembered her pseudonym but you wouldn't. I spoke to Nisha,' I explain, pulling out a chair and sitting down. 'You'll remember her as Julia. She always thought there was something odd about the way you handed Claire her coat and scarf. When I told her I suspected you and Mr Weeks to be the same person, she said it made sense. You would know which item Claire put on first. Tenuous, I admit, but it's enough. Please don't deny it.'

He pulls out a chair and drops heavily onto it. 'I was in on the honey-trap,' he admits. 'I don't particularly want to save my marriage; it is as poor as Paula says it is. She's been gradually excluding me more and more over the years. She concocted this little plan to set me up. Unfortunately, she picked the agency where Claire used to work and by a mad stroke of luck she picked Claire out of a catalogue of operatives. When Claire discovered I was her target, we decided to foil Paula's plan. It was good fun,' he smiles guiltily. 'A strange sort of role play. It was very hard not to kiss Claire in the hotel garden. I had to remind myself we were being watched.'

'Surely this would be good grounds for you to petition your wife for divorce?' I ask.

'Claire said that too. Paula and I are getting divorced now. She has someone new in her life.'

He looks a lot more relaxed now; his hands lie comfortably in his lap, his smile is friendly. 'Tell me what happened the Friday you visited Claire's flat.'

He sits forward. 'You tell me something first. You don't work for a private investigation agency, do you? Eventually it dawned on me where I've seen your face before: on the windowsill in Claire's bedroom. A photo of you and her.'

'We've been best friends for a long time. I'm an ex police officer.' Mr Snell blinks with surprise at my revelation. 'I've been away; I've only seen Claire occasionally.'

'Did you know she was in debt?'

'Yes.'

'It bothered me; I was worried for her. She owed a moneylender; these people are not nice.'

'Did you lend her money?'

'I managed to get a couple of thousand together. On the Wednesday of the week she went missing, I was driving to London for a meeting and decided to drop the money off at her flat. But on the way I saw Claire walking towards the Three Fish. It's a pub...'

'I know it. Was she alone?'

'Yes. I considered beeping my horn and getting her attention, but she was hurrying and it's a busy road. There's nowhere safe to stop so I abandoned my idea and went on my way.'

'Do you know what she may have been doing there? Had the two of you ever been?'

'It's not my sort of place. It's all kids' play areas and two for one meals. I don't recall Claire ever mentioning the place. I suppose she could have been meeting a friend, although she was hardly dressed appropriately!' He chuckles. 'She was wearing running gear.'

'Did you know she had a black eye?'

He frowns with concern. 'No. She didn't have it the last time I saw her. How...or should that be who did that? The moneylender?'

'I'm not sure. Maybe it was whoever she met at the Three Fish. Tell me the rest of your story.'

'I returned from London late Friday evening and still had the money so I text Claire and asked if I could call in; if it wasn't convenient then text me back. There was no reply so I drove to her flat. I knocked several times, dialled her landline, even went to the bedroom window and tapped the glass thinking that she may have been ill or listening to music on the bed. I went home and phoned over the weekend, but there was no response.'

'At her flat, did you get the feeling there was someone home?'

He thinks about my question. 'Well, perhaps, but only because I was expecting Claire to be home and the lights indicated she was in.'

'If there'd been anyone in the flat then your knocking would have silenced them.' I stand and pace the floor, biting my little fingernail thoughtfully. Does this man have motive to kill

Claire? On the face of it – no. He was lending her money to help pay off her debt. And surely his only motive would be if Claire had wanted to tell his wife about the affair. But in all her prison visits, she never expressed any desire to finish with Mr Weeks. Besides, together they had foiled the honey trap; Mrs Snell was proven to have a 'faithful' husband! Success.

'Which hotel did you stay at in London?'

'Bear with me and I'll let you know.' He removes his mobile from his jacket inside pocket and slides his finger over its screen and says, 'The Royal Lambert. I can get you the hotel receipt if you want. It'll have my check-out time. I left at 5.30 pm and immediately hit rush-hour traffic. It took me nearly four hours to get to Claire's.'

'I can believe it for a Friday.'

'Let me call Veronica, my secretary.' I let him do it. It'll close a line of enquiry and enable me to cross him off as a suspect.

'How did Claire seem to you a couple of weeks before her disappearance?'

'At times she looked so sad. If you two were best friends, then I would say she missed you. She never talked about her family or friends; your photo was the only one I ever saw in her flat. Actually,' he says raising a finger. 'She mentioned you once by name. There was a pile of holiday brochures on the table; she said "I'm looking for a holiday for Will when he gets home." She asked me if I'd ever been on a cruise.'

A cruise, I think. Wow! She had a cruise in mind! I smile. It would appeal to Claire: the dressing up for dinner, a different port every day, the cuisine and wine, the sophisticated guests. A cruise would have suited me too.

There's a soft knock at the door and a young woman comes in to hand James a sheet of paper.

'Thanks, Veronica.'

'Don't forget your 3 o'clock appointment,' she says before closing the door. He slides the receipt across the table and I see that he checked out at 5.20 pm on the Friday.

'I should let you get on,' I say, pocketing the receipt and standing. He gets to his feet.

'I cared about Claire,' he announces. 'She was important to me; I would have helped her any way I could.'

'Do you know the route she ran?'

'Vaguely. She liked to talk about her running, she was proud of her times but despite pretending I was a keen athlete at the honey trap, I'm a lazy sod.' He smiles.

I smile back and hold out a hand. 'Thanks for being frank with me, Mr Snell.'

'Please let me know how you get on.'

And it's ironic that both he and Ralph cared more for Claire than her fucking parents have.

*

If we were in my bedroom then I would really feel like a schoolboy with one ear listening out for footsteps on the stairs and one eye permanently on the door. As it is we're in the lounge and Mum is out. Spread out on the floor are my notes, various photos and other documents. On the coffee table are our empty mugs and the biscuit tin, which contains four types of biscuits. All were unopened till Liv got her greedy mitts on them.

'Are you sure your parents didn't mention changing the locks to Claire's flat?' I got a nasty surprise earlier when I tried to gain entry to the flat. The key went in but it wouldn't turn. On closer inspection, I saw that the keyhole was no longer brass coloured. The locks had been changed. Either Marion assumed the lock seized or suspects foul play. She will no doubt find a new hiding place for the key. Probably around her fucking neck. The bitch. It was one of the most embarrassing and infuriating moments of my life.

Liv's hand is poised, a chocolate chip cookie clamped between her black painted fingernails. She shakes her head slowly and deliberately like I'm thick and having trouble understanding her.

'Why would they tell me? I'm only their daughter!' She takes a bite; crumbs scatter over the front of her black top. 'Anyway, who says they have?'

I don't like the way she's eyeing me suspiciously but I have a ready-made answer.

'One of the neighbour's text me. She was concerned there'd been a break-in.'

She looks down at her cleavage, licks a finger and dabs the crumbs up. 'Yeah, right. Sounds like a nosy Parker. Are you sure it's not been changed because maybe you kept the key so you can come and go when you want?'

'I gave Sally the key back. Ask her.'

'All I know is that Sal told me that you left empty handed and here we are with a selection of Claire's documents. I wonder how they've magically appeared!' She makes a gesture similar to a magician casting a spell.

Her astuteness impresses me or maybe I've underestimated her. It's a good job she doesn't know about the laptop and the GPS watch, which I've yet to charge up. 'You can't expect me to solve a crime without seizing evidence.'

'Now that we've excluded these suspects, what are we going to do about the unpleasant Mr Hock? We can guess Claire was meeting him at the Three Fish on the Wednesday. For some reason he wants this...' and she fishes through the rest of the papers for the post mortem report I'd stupidly brought down. 'Why didn't she give it to him?'

'Maybe it was never her intention,' I say thoughtfully. 'If she didn't approve of what he was going to do with it, she did the sensible thing...'

'The sensible thing has probably gotten her killed!'

'If he killed her then why not turn the flat upside down looking for it? It wasn't hard to find. Hock wouldn't be stupid enough to kill someone who had something he wanted. That's not how people like him work.'

'Well, we won't know till we talk to him.'

I shake my head. 'If you visit Hock and make false accusations you'll piss him off and that won't put you in a good position...safety wise. Show him this,' and I nod at the PM report, 'and he'll just snatch it out of your hand quicker than you can say "dear old mom".'

'Know him from your police days, do you?'

'Yes,' I lie. 'He's a vile thug into all sorts: intimidation, violence, theft. You don't want to be noticed by him because once he thinks you have something that's useful he won't leave you alone.'

'I know all that. I've heard you bigging him up for the last hour, but if we don't talk to him then we won't know what he knows.'

'I'll track the moneylender down and talk to him again. See what else I can prise out of him.'

'That's fucking pointless. He sounds like a right weasely git; anything he tells you is bullshit.'

'Do you ever stop swearing?'

'No. He's probably got his side of the story in first with Mr Hock and warned him about your investigation too.'

Christ, I hope not. I don't want Hock knowing I'm snooping around...not for a couple of more weeks.

'We shouldn't leave it any longer; we should go and talk to Hock as soon as we can.'

'We?' I repeat. 'You're not going.'

Liv frowns sternly. 'Oh, pur-lease, don't go all protectively chauvinistic on me. It's safer if we both go...'

'I'm just being sensible, Liv.'

'Oh, I see, like you were when you boxed Stewart Murray's car in, when you blagged your way into Fiona's house to speak to her old man, like all the other men and women you've interviewed, all of which could have turned on you if they'd had anything to hide. I don't know whether you've noticed or not, but you've ruled pretty much everyone out. Mind, you haven't asked me where I was on the night in question and most victims are murdered by a close relative.'

'I already know where you were. Home alone and ill, although I suspect that's a lie. You can't prove your alibi because Dan was out too. He didn't fancy being a nurse for the evening.' I sit back, proud that I've summarised it well.

'Most of it is true,' she says. 'None of us wanted to attend Mum's dinner party; some of us had better excuses. But I can kind of prove where I was.' Her eyes are sad and I wonder with interest what it is. Was she with another bloke? Had she gone around to see Claire that night? Or is she teasing again?

'I had something I needed to do...' she trails off.

She went to see Claire, I think, to clear the air or continue the row.

'I hadn't been feeling well that week: sickness, tiredness, and even though Sally joked about it, I never seriously thought I could be pregnant.'

Shit. Liv was pregnant, is she still pregnant? She doesn't look it; she's overweight but...I suppose with some women it's hard to tell. Maybe she lost it.

'You haven't met Dan, have you?' she asks bringing me out of my thoughts.

'Er, no...' I don't tell her that I know he's a drug pedlar.

'Well, he's not father material. He's a total waste of space. I'm not mother material either, at least not yet. I went to the clinic for an abortion; I had some pills to take. On that Friday I had the second appointment. I couldn't miss it. I had to take more pills, go home and rest. I was in agony. I could hardly stand let alone get on a bus and go to Claire's. Dan didn't know. Still doesn't.'

She rummages in her large handbag, dropping tubes of make-up and sweet wrappers on the floor. She removes a wad of folded up paper and sifts through them.

I put my hand out to stop her. 'I believe you.'

She ignores me and pulls out a creased letter. 'My appointment.' I take it and read. It confirms that on the 1st December last year Liv had an appointment at the Dinthill Clinic at 5 pm.

One of Justine's married friends had an abortion when we were together. A brief fling had resulted in an unwanted pregnancy. Justine had spent the weekend nursing her in a hotel whilst pretending they were away shopping in London. Justine had said her friend had bled something terrible and writhed in agony. She'd come home distraught and tearful herself. Unpleasant, she said, wasn't the word.

I hand it back. I still don't know what to say but it seems that it's probably for the best. Dan isn't just drug dealing scum, he's a loser too. At least Liv knows this.

'I don't regret it, you know,' she says, reaching for tea, but the mug is empty. I offer to make another pot. She follows me into the kitchen and watches as I put the kettle on. 'When Claire slagged him off, it felt like an attack on me. And I used to reply that at least I had a boyfriend, and she'd be like 'Wasn't I the lucky one?' but I'm not. He does nothing for me. He dosses around all day, sponges off me and slags my family off.'

'You could end it, find someone nicer or try the single life for a while.'

'I couldn't afford the rent on my own and I'm definitely not going back to my parents. As shitty as my flat is it's a lot fucking better than being at theirs.'

'Yeah,' I agree quietly. I can't imagine living with them either.

'Right, you make that tea and I'm going to have one last biscuit!'

When I bring the tea in, I notice Liv has kindly tidied up all the papers and stacked them neatly on the table.

Chapter 51

Friday ~ day 18

'It's a very simple question, Leo, but I'll put it another way so you can understand. I spoke to the manager of the Three Fish and showed him a photo of your vehicle; he recognised your highly distinctive personalised reg. Reason why: a patron of the dining room made a complaint to the manager about your haphazard and selfish parking.'

He frowns with puzzlement and dips a finger into the cardboard cup of coffee and wipes the froth off the inside.

'You parked too close to the vehicle in the next bay. Now, stop with the vagueness and the bullshit because I've never met a less convincing liar; tell me what happened on that Wednesday night. It was a meeting wasn't it? You, Claire and Hock.'

He licks his finger clean and grins, taking his selfish parking as a compliment. I congratulate myself on this stroke of genius. With my observation skills still intact and a bit of creativity, I noticed on the day he followed me how he parked up at speed with a lack of consideration for other drivers. I used this information to my advantage and totally made up the incident to which I now accuse him of. It's a sign of his arrogance and contempt for other drivers that he sees this as something to be proud of.

'Tell me about that night.'

'There's nothing to say.' And he steps forward but meets my hand flat against his chest. He scowls at it like it's dirty.

'Oh, but there is. Claire went to the pub to meet someone. I've proved you were there and so was Hock. I could always ask the pub manager if they've documented 7H9CK in the car park.'

Leo's even more stunned that I know Hock's number plate. My information may be over twelve month's old but it looks to be accurate.

Leo deposits his empty cup on the shop's windowsill where it threatens to topple off until he pushes it further back till it touches the glass. 'Okay. It was the second time we'd all met up. You seem to know Hock so you know that he's a bloke you can't say no to. He wanted information from Claire on his mother's death. He blamed the hospital somehow, accused them of neglect, shelving her because she was old.'

'What sort of information?'

'The old lady had a post-mortem. He didn't like the cause of death. Hock reckons the cancer killed her but the doctor said it was her heart.'

I nod. Hock's suspicions tallies with the PM report Claire had tucked away in the ketchup cookery book.

'Hock wanted evidence of a cover up, also personal details about the doctors. He offered her a reduction in what she owed, tried to make it worth her while. She wasn't keen, tried to explain it could cost her her job, but like I said Hock isn't a bloke you can say no to.'

'Did she fulfil her side of things?'

Leo shakes his head and shrugs at the same time. 'Kind of. Claire gave Hock a copy of this report which proved the doctor's cause of death.'

I interrupt. 'She actually gave him the report?'

He nods.

Weird, I think. If she gave him a report stating the cause of death was the old lady's dicky ticker, then why have I got one that clearly states the cancer killed her? Why are there two?

'Claire didn't have the patient notes either, or the doctor's address. Hock was well pissed off.'

'He wouldn't hit her in a pub full of people, would he? He followed her outside,' I say and a raised eyebrow gives me my answer.

'When he came back he was rubbing his knuckles,' Leo admits.

I feel the anger rising in my chest; my ribs rise and heave steadily. I hide my expression by rubbing a hand along my jaw and turning my gaze away.

'It was only when you said Claire had a black eye that I put the two together,' Leo says.

But would you have done anything about it if it had happened in front of you? Would you have leapt in front of Claire, pushed her aside and taken the punch yourself? No, because whilst Hock was laying into Claire, he was leaving you alone. And I know my attitude is harsh, that Leo must be scared of Hock too, but he was there. I wasn't.

'Hock must have been deeply unsatisfied. What did he expect Claire to do now?'

'Get him what he wanted. He bought the debt. He owned her. It didn't matter if she paid up; all he had to do was add on more interest. There was no way she could keep up with the repayments.'

Fucking hell, I think. No one could blame her for doing a runner in those circumstances because even if she gave Hock what he wanted, there'd always be another favour lurking. Information she could get on someone else. Being in Hock's top pocket meant giving him full access to patient databases. Claire was just what Hock needed. He wasn't going to let her go. And she knew that.

But what use would Claire be to him dead? Once inside the flat, did he harm her? He almost certainly would have searched her flat and found this second confusing report in her book. Her lie would have been laid bare.

This meeting has sent my head into a whirl of confusion. The possibility of Claire owing Hock forever could have sent her running for the nearest bus stop out of here. Why didn't she take her passport and other essentials? And why haven't I heard a word from her? Wouldn't it have been more logical, more Claire-like for her to have waited till I was out? We could have tackled Hock together. Whether Hock is responsible is going to require me to visit him at some point soon. But at least I'll have some evidence to accompany me albeit rather crap and shaky.

A uniformed shop worker appears in the doorway of the cafe holding a brush and a black bin bag. She begins sweeping the pavement at our feet, tutting noisily till we move on. I look back to see her pick up Leo's discarded cup as if a person would hold a dirty nappy and drop it into a gaping bin bag.

'Is there anything else?' Leo asks. 'Only I am supposed to be somewhere.'

'Yeah, I'm finished. Say nothing to Hock.'

'Like I don't value my life,' he mutters, striding off.

*

I ring the bell for attention and peer through the veil of thick netting at the long corridor stretching into the distance. The polished floor gleams and I can almost smell the antiseptic. Beside me, Mum twiddles her wedding ring anxiously. I smile reassuringly. On the wall behind her is a blue sign and in white writing the words read: Poplar Ward. The wards are named after trees. I wonder if they have a problem with escapees. Moments later the door is unlocked by an overweight woman in her early forties with short blonde spiky hair, wearing a badge that says 'Sheila. Nurse.'

'Hello. I'm Mrs Bailey,' and Mum pauses to clear her nervous throat. 'This is my son. I made an appointment to see my husband Mike.'

Sheila's smile widens and she holds the door open. 'Come in. I'll show you to the Family Room and bring Mike through.' She locks the door behind us with a key attached to a chain on her waistband and starts walking, the soles of her sensible shoes squeaking on the floor. She points to a doorway on the left. 'Wait in here, please.'

My heart is pounding nervously and my throat is dry. I've never been on a psychiatric ward before. I'm afraid of what I might see, what the patients might be like. Posters Blu-Tacked to the wall give details about the many different types of dementia and their progression. I can't look at them; I won't read and enlighten myself to what's coming for my dad. I don't want to know.

I follow Mum into a sunny room containing high-backed chairs, occasional tables and in the corner is the obligatory toy chest. We sit down and wait. Several minutes later, I hear a voice say, 'That's it, Mike. Just a bit further. Your wife and son have come to see you.'

A figure shuffles into view and I think that they've bought the wrong man but when he steps into the light I see that it is my dad. My strong, upright, tough dad has been reduced to a shuffling, stooping fragile ghost with a lacerated head. We were phoned two days ago to tell us Dad took a tumble out of bed. He never once fell at home, so what were they doing to him? Are they turning him into a zombie? They're supposed to be calming him down so he's easier to live with.

Sheila expertly sits Dad down on the nearest settee and makes him comfortable before offering us a cup of tea and leaving us alone. Mum sits beside Dad and takes his hand.

'Mike, love, are you alright?'

At the sound of her voice, he tries to raise his head and turn but it's as if his head weighs the same as a ball of concrete. The blood encrusted laceration above Dad's right eyebrow is about an inch long; butterfly stitches hold it together. Her shaky hand reaches to touch, to soothe it but she pulls back in case she hurts him. 'Mike, it's me. It's Kay. Love, can you hear me?'

'Dad,' I say, moving to a closer chair. 'It's Will. That's a nasty cut, but you should see the other bloke, right?' I try to laugh, but it sticks in my throat. My eyes fill with tears and I blink them away hastily.

He doesn't react to the joke like he would have last week. Mum chuckles at my attempt to get a smile from Dad. She strokes his hand and chats to him reassuring him that he'll soon be home, that he hasn't missed much, and slowly as if her voice is becoming louder and clearer Dad shakes his grogginess off and turns to the sound, his mouth curling into a smile.

'Hello! Hello Mike, love.' And she squeezes his hand tighter.

'Hello Kay,' he replies croakily.

'Look, Mike,' and she points to me. 'Will's come to see you. Say hello.'

'Hi Dad,' I say brightly, leaning over. I notice a gap in the line of buttons down the front of his shirt. One button hasn't been buttoned up. Above its pocket is a dried yellow stain which looks like egg yolk. His hair is untidy and greasy. And a shave wouldn't go amiss. He looks a mess. Are these nurses caring for him or what?

'Hello son,' Dad replies.

Sheila knocks gently on the door and brings in a tray of tea things. Before she leaves, I ask how Dad's doing.

'He's doing fine,' she replies, brightly. 'It's difficult for the first week with settling in and sleeping in a strange bed.'

'Yeah, he seems very groggy, like he's been doped up. He wasn't like this at home. He never fell over before,' I continue. I'm aware of my pounding heart and how aggressive my voice is but I can't control my emotions. This is my dad, this is not right.

'Unfortunately, the medication your dad is on has side-effects. They can make patients sleepy, confused, and these contribute to unsteadiness. Once the doctor finds the right medication for your dad, he will be much more settled and calm, and we can look to him coming home.'

'Thank you,' Mum says. 'I think this has been a shock.'

Sheila smiles and leaves. Mum looks at me.

'I'm just saying,' I tell her. 'His shirt is dirty, why haven't they changed it? His hair needs washing and look at the beard he's growing.'

'Well, the trouble is they're nurses, not carers. It's not their job to change dirty clothes...'

'Well, it should be,' I snap. Dad is looking at me, aroused by the anger in my voice. 'Sorry Dad.'

Mum makes the tea, which is weak and tasteless. Visiting time is only for 30 minutes so it isn't long before Sheila returns to take Dad away. She stands in the doorway like a jailor, jangling her keys in an impolite way to hurry us up. Mum hugs Dad tightly, whispering in his ear. I take my turn afterwards, Mum still holds onto Dad's hand.

'Get yourself better soon, Dad. We want you home. Love you, Dad.' I lean towards him to kiss his cheek and hear his voice in my ear.

'Love you too, Will.'

It's the worst thing I've ever done: leave my dad here whilst Mum and I walk away. I nearly make it back to the car before I start to cry.

*

Ryan listens as I relay recent events to him. The only sound I hear is the occasional noisy swallow as he eats his chorizo and tomato Panini. I conclude by telling him that I've still got Hock to talk to and lots of questions for Claire's parents.

'Just in case they don't welcome you with open arms, I have something that will at least lever some truth out of Andrew,' he offers.

'You do? How have you come across this information from Spain?'

'Aha! I may be several hundred miles away, but I'm smart enough to save my emails and lucky enough to find the one I wanted. Remember I told you that Claire had written asking for a loan? Well, she claimed to have some dirt on Andrew and wondered how much it was worth.'

'What is it?' A mental image flashes up of Andrew screwing another woman. A younger woman, half his age, big hair, busty, someone Marion couldn't possibly compete against.

'The email from Claire was sent the day after Marion's birthday party, at the end of November. There'd been a scene, or a moment witnessed between Andrew and a neighbour who'd cut her finger whilst pruning a rose. Andrew had to administer First Aid. Possibly it wasn't the only thing he administered that night. Claire had the good fortune to witness this kiss and grope. We know Marion is paranoid about her toy boy. And we know it's Maz's money that's founded his business; what would happen if the Bank of Maz stopped its funding because she discovered her husband's eyes and hands had gone roaming elsewhere?'

'It explains why she spends so much money on beauty therapies, exercise regimes and designer clothes. Nothing turns a woman off pie and chips quicker than the threat of another woman!'

Ryan laughs loudly and I have to move the phone away from my ear.

'Oh, mate, I'd forgotten how funny you can be at times. Pie and chips. Classic.'

'Did Claire say what she was going to do with this information?'

'Use it against Andrew, I presume. She wrote that it was worth a try, it might buy her some money. I don't know how she got on. In her next email there was no mention of it.'

I remain silent whilst I picture Claire standing over Andrew, one hand on her hip, in the other holding his chequebook, issuing him with a threat reminiscent of *The Godfather*.

'You there, Will?'

'Yeah, just thinking. Would he pay up, do you think?'

'Of course he would. The worrying thing is that he knows Claire wouldn't even have to prove this to Marion with photographic evidence or further witness statements. She's been expecting Andrew to cheat since the day they married because he's younger, and men like that eventually realise their wives are receiving a pension whilst they're still being asked their age in bars! Alright, bit of an exaggeration, but you get my point.'

'And Claire grassed Phil up over twenty five years ago. What if Andrew wasn't prepared to be blackmailed? What if...' I trail off, unable to say what I want because it sounds so awful. I hope he knows what I mean.

'You're the detective, mate. Only you can tell.'

I nod in agreement, forgetting that he can't see me so I just murmur, 'Yeah.'

'I need to go in a minute, mate, but first I need a favour. How are you fixed for picking me up from the airport?'

'What? Really? Are you coming home?' And suddenly my hopes soar that my friend may be coming home.

'I am for a bit. I've got a couple of things to do here and then I'll get a flight home next week or so. It'll be good to catch up.'

'Yeah, it will.'

His voice alters, becomes earnest. 'I should have done a better job of keeping in contact when you were in prison. I had things to say but it would have sounded shit in a letter, like I was kicking you in the face whilst you were down.'

'I felt a bit abandoned but then I chose to put myself there. It's not easy to write to someone inside. I could tell that from my mum's letters.'

'Claire managed it okay. I'm sorry, Will. I'm useless. I'll be around for a while so we'll make up for the lack of contact. Oh, by the way, before you got locked out of Claire's flat, did you spy the elephant I sent her?'

'Yes, I saw it. It was on the shelf in the hall, staring down at me.'

'Ugly bugger, isn't he? Heavy too. You wouldn't want to drop it on your foot.'

'Yes,' I agree with a laugh, but my mind stops. I don't remember picking it up and testing its weight. It looked heavy but it could have been hollow. Why am I agreeing when I never took it down from the shelf?

Sally told you it was heavy, a silent voice reminds me.

Yes, she did. I frown. Something occurs to me, something I vaguely remember but need to verify from my notes. I ask Ryan if he remembers when Claire received his present.

'She would have emailed a thank you. These things take time to arrive but I sent it in the October. It was a belated birthday present.'

October, I repeat silently. Then why the lie?

Chapter 52

Saturday ~ day 19

After a restless night, my mind afloat with thoughts of elephants and money, I finally fall asleep about four thirty and wake suddenly at eight o'clock when Mum shuts the front door firmly behind her. The note by the kettle informs me that she's off to meet her sister to book a holiday. Breakfast in bed hasn't lasted long.

I try to make a cup of tea but I'm too impatient to wait for it to brew. My search of the cupboards yields nothing appetising like a croissant or crumpet, but a box of unappetising muesli and a couple of slices of bread, which have the feel of cardboard.

'Sod this,' I say, stomping upstairs like a stroppy youth. I ignore my hunger, promising to feed it something nice soon. I shower, dress and take the Mazda out to the nearest cafe.

*

The warm and welcoming aroma of frying bacon and toast causes a catalytic rumble in my stomach and I instantly decide only a full English will do. There are a few people dotted around the cafe, hastily shovelling down sausages and beans, or lazily sipping tea whilst turning the pages of a newspaper. I take my place at the end of the short queue and glance around at what everyone else is eating. The beans are a nice tomatoey orange, the bacon crispy, the sausages a healthy brown and the fried eggs have a beautiful sunny yolk. That and a couple of rounds of toast will do me a treat and I won't need any lunch.

'Yes, please, love' says the woman serving. She's about my mum's age wearing a flowery tabard over a lilac top. Except she has a nose stud.

She scribbles my order on a small notepad and slides the torn-off sheet through a hatch into the kitchen. I sense the next customer standing a little too close beside me.

'Coffee, please, sweetheart,' butts in the customer. 'On him.'

I turn to complain and my eyes flick upwards from the dark blue puffa jacket to a face I haven't seen in a while. I have to stop myself from swearing, but I might as well say fuck the way I say his name.

'Hock.'

'Hello William. This is a nice surprise.'

And from my point that's exaggerating it considerably. His smile reveals the gaps in the upper row of his teeth. He lunges across the counter and for an awful moment I think he's going to grab the woman. 'To take out.'

'No problem, beaut,' she replies.

That puts me at ease that hopefully he won't be joining me and spoiling my breakfast. I pay and we wait for our drinks at the end of the counter. I look expectantly at him but he smiles back, keeping me holding on.

'I didn't notice you following me,' I say.

'I wasn't. Just dropped my offspring at his karate lesson and spied you as I was passing. I thought, "I could murder a drink", and say a quick hello to my mate Will.I.Am.'

I roll my eyes at his originality. A blue and white striped mug of tea and a polystyrene cup of coffee appear on the end of the counter. The studded woman points us in the direction of the sugar and milk.

'I've got to say, you've lost some weight, William.' I loathe his use of my full name. He sounds so intimidating; the way a thug calls someone he wants a ruck with 'pal'. 'You were a tad on the bulky side before.' He makes me sound like I was a right fat bastard. 'Bet it's the prison diet. It's all tasteless watery gruel inside, eh?'

I glance at the woman to see if she's overheard Hock but she's busy taking another order.

'You know it's actually not too bad,' I reply, weaving my way around the tables to a vacant one in the corner. 'At Christmas, we had a three bird roast.'

Hock wrinkles his nose at the thought of eating a bird within a bird within a bird. He's no doubt a strictly turkey person. He follows me but doesn't sit. 'How you been then? Settling into Civvy Street okay?'

He knows, I think. I can tell by the fake friendly tone and the sarcastic teasing with the undertone of something unpleasant. Leo's been talking to him. Cowardly little weasel.

'I'm taking each day at a time,' I answer, keeping it brief.

'We must have a chat later.'

'You're two weeks early,' I remind him. 'You said one month.'

'Yeah, yeah, it's not about that. Three fifteen, do you? Good. There's a *Costa* over the road. The lattes will be on me. And don't worry. It's nothing that can't be ironed out,' and he slaps my back with his huge rough-skinned hand. I almost headbutt the table. 'Cheers for the coffee, Billy.'

I scowl at his departing back. I hate being called Billy as well.

*

'I don't really have time to chat, Will. I'm at work and I have a meeting to prepare for,' Sally icily informs me. I'm not sure which of the digs in her sentence irritate me the most. The belittling way she says chat like I've popped over to unnecessarily discuss the weather, or the stress she places on the word work which makes me feel virtually unemployable.

We're standing again in a little office off the reception of Andrew's premises. I've been in a few lately and they're useful for little chats.

'I need you to answer one question,' I say, equally abruptly. 'How did you know how heavy the elephant was in Claire's hall?'

Her resulting frown is severe; it creases her forehead in an ugly way and ages her by fifteen years. Her stance changes. Her folded arms fold more tightly and her back straightens like a cold metal rod has been slipped down the back of her blouse. 'What?'

'In October, Ryan sent that elephant to Claire from Thailand. When we were in Claire's hall the other day, I asked when you were last in her flat and you said...' I pause to produce my notes, the page all ready. '"July, after her birthday".' Sally doesn't get it, I point it out. 'If July was the last time you were in Claire's flat and the elephant didn't arrive till November, how did you know how heavy it was? I went to pick it up and you warned me it was heavy. How did you know?'

'I don't know.' Her shrug is slack and irritates me. She doesn't care about this point, sees it as unimportant, but it's the little details that matter. 'Perhaps I just thought it looked heavy. Are you sure Ryan sent it in October? Maybe he's mistaken.'

'No, he isn't. You could only have known how weighty it was because you'd lifted it. When? When were you in Claire's flat?'

She squeezes her lips together till they bulge out and shakes her head. 'I don't know.'

'You had a row with her...'

'No. Liv did. I tried to reconcile the two of them. I text Claire, phoned, emailed, left voicemail messages, and she ignored every single one of them!'

I remain unimpressed 'Did you go to Claire's flat? Try to speak to her face-to-face?'

'What would have been the point?' Sally demands aggressively, her voice rising in volume. 'Liv wasn't bothered, Claire wasn't interested, and so I abandoned the idea. I never saw Claire again and I deeply regret that.'

'When were you last at her flat?'

She sighs tiredly. 'Let me think.' The frown creases her forehead as she tries to recall the date, the day, the month even. 'I remember her showing me the elephant. It could only just have arrived, that day or the day before. She'd placed it on the windowsill, facing inwards, but elephants are supposed to face the door, for good luck, so when she wasn't looking I put it in the hallway.'

I'm not sure I believe her, but at the moment I can't prove otherwise. I turn to leave, deliberately omitting a thank you.

'Things were shit after Claire disappeared,' she adds and I half-turn, my hand on the door handle. 'Mum and Dad still blame themselves. They can't understand why Claire didn't go to them if she was in trouble. She spoke to *you* and Ryan. And where were you both? In prison and fucking Thailand. No wonder she left. I had nothing to do with Claire's disappearance, nor Liv, and nor our parents. I hope that penetrates your thick head and you leave us alone.'

Her words are heartfelt and passionate, but they fall short of their target.

'I can't do that, Sally. I have questions for your parents too.'

'I have to ask: were you in love with my sister?' she questions, her tone sardonic. 'It must have crucified you witnessing her having affairs all over the place whilst you're about to walk into a miserable marriage. Is that why you helped that loser of a brother? It was the only way to dump your fiancée and take up with Claire? If you hadn't been in prison at the time with the perfect alibi, I'd have blamed you for Claire going missing.'

'Thanks for answering my question, Sally.' I open the door.

'You won't find her. She packed her things and left...exactly like you did to her.'

What is it with this fucking family and their weak and easy theories? It's easy for them to say Claire walked out because anything else is harder to grasp. I turn to face her. Instantly she straightens, her chin lifts fearful of my attack.

'Let me make you and your family a promise. It doesn't matter what you say to me, how much you insult me, I won't go away till I find out what happened to Claire. Thanks for your time.' I step back into reception and grin to myself, proud of the conviction in my voice. At least I'm not in any doubt as to how I feel and whether I'll pursue this. I know I will.

*

Hock's early bird arrival makes my prompt turning up feel like I'm over an hour late. Nevertheless, his grin is welcoming, which instantly puts me on guard. We join the queue and I look at the menu of drinks, but naturally my eyes fall to the selection of cakes and pastries under the domed glass shelter.

'Have one if you want, mate. I'm having a chocolate muffin,' Hock says. 'I won't be having my tea till late.'

The queue shuffles forward. There's a spattering of patrons around the cafe, sitting at small round tables or on striped comfy looking armchairs, reading newspapers, tapping away at mobiles, or chatting to friends. The place is a cacophony of noise which makes it ideal for a chat. There's all sorts of hissing and banging of chrome levers and handles coming from the coffee-making machines as the staff froth coffees, steam milk and heat water; upbeat lounge music with foreign lyrics serves as a background sound; somewhere in a far corner is a young child whining to its parent; all of which is accompanied by the general noise of chatter.

A tattooed lad with dyed blue and black hair slaps a tray on the counter and deals with our order.

I carefully pick the tray up and lead the way around the tables to the one in the corner. A mum with a screaming toddler is just strapping him into his pushchair. Hock is smiling at her with empathy, though she doesn't notice him, and I adjust my scowl; I'm pleased they're vacating the premises.

I stir my coffee and wait for Hock to begin, but he's busy slicing his muffin in half. Chocolate sauce oozes onto the plate. He spears the bite-sized pieces with the point of the knife and pops one into his mouth.

'Are you frightened of me, William?'

Not exactly how I anticipated him starting the conversation. 'Only if you're pointing a loaded gun at my head.'

'After our history, the favours we've done for each other, I thought if there was questions you had, you'd come straight to me. I'm a reasonable man, an approachable man, so why did you send a messenger to do your dirty work? I'm a little bit insulted, I don't mind admitting,' and to enforce that heartfelt plea, he places a palm flat on his chest, over his heart, if he had one some might say.

Messenger, I think, puzzled. 'Who are you talking about? I haven't...'

'A woman too. I suppose your thinking was if a woman angered me, I wouldn't react. I'd stay calm, which I did,' and he wags a cube of muffin at me. 'Because I saw that she was acting on your behalf.'

'My behalf?' I repeat and he huffs tired at my supposed pretence.

'Eat your cake,' he says, nodding at it.

I attack it like him, chopping it up into manageable pieces and start spearing them into my mouth. Mm, I think, bloody lovely. Then it comes to me. Who he means.

'Liv,' I mutter.

'Liv,' he confirms with a nod.

'I didn't send her,' I insist. 'She plagued me to confront you, and I explained that I can't accuse you of something when my evidence is based loosely on what people think they've seen. I knew it had fallen on deaf ears but I didn't think she'd go maverick.'

'And what's your evidence?'

This time I keep him waiting. I grasp the oversized cup in my hands and raise it to my mouth to take a few sips, but it's hot. I wipe my mouth on a serviette and screw it up, leaving it on the plate.

'I have reason to believe that you,' I pause to briefly consider which term I can use here that won't upset him: demand, scare, request; I opt for hope. 'Hoped Claire could find evidence of a cover-up at the hospital regarding your mother's death.'

'And I killed her because of that?'

'Because she couldn't or wouldn't help you. You bought her debt thereby having control of her until she got you the information you wanted.'

'And you know this how?'

'Leo.' Hock doesn't react, probably already knows Leo and I have been chatting. Well, I don't owe Leo anything. 'He and I had a chat. He denied most of it, went all tight lipped but in the end, he talked. I found your mother's name in Claire's flat.' I keep his mother's precious PM report to myself and hope that Liv did too. 'I asked him about it and he told me you'd offered Claire a discount if she got you information. I've been interviewing a lot of people who knew Claire, searching for motive and opportunity. Liv was keen to talk to you as we were running out of suspects.'

Hock sits back in his chair, nodding as he digests this revelation. 'And you think I'd kill a young woman over this?'

'People kill for twenty pence these days. But, no, I don't think you'd do that. But of course, later on, we discovered that you'd slapped Claire and given her a black eye.'

Hock looks scandalised. 'Who told you that? Leo?'

Sounds like a confirmation to me.

'He insinuated as much. At your meeting in the Three Fish, you left the table shortly after Claire, and when you returned, you were rubbing your hand...'

Hock chuckles. 'And that's enough to accuse me of murder?'

'For Liv, yes it is. For me, no. But it's enough to warrant questions. I hope Olivia hasn't made the situation worse.'

'No. I admire her bravery. She started off politely; telling me about her sister's disappearance, accusing me of roughing Claire up, of burying her in a flyover like I was one of the Krays. She has quite a mouth on her. Funny the way she made it clear you were running the investigation.'

'She was hiding behind me or my rep as an ex police officer,' I say. 'It's what cowards do when they've realised they've made a mistake.'

But Hock shakes his head. 'She had enough gumption to face me, on my territory, and accuse me of murder.'

I shrug. 'She's a coward deep down, or a shit stirrer.'

'Mm,' Hock says thoughtfully.

'I have to ask you your whereabouts on the Friday in question.'

'No comment,' he replies, spooning the dregs from his cup. 'Want another?'

'Yeah. Here. On me.' And I hand him a tenner.

When he returns with the coffees, I can see there's something on his mind.

'Liv said that Claire found something on my mother.'

For fuck's sake, I think. Rule number one when interviewing a suspect or witness don't play your ace straightaway. 'And what was that?'

Hock sighs tiredly again. 'Come on, Will, you know what: the original PM report containing the correct cause of death. Liv assumed I knew of its existence and after I murdered Claire, I carefully searched her flat, not disturbing or breaking anything but I left empty-handed. And the weird thing was that the report was there all along, hidden in a book.'

'How strange,' I comment trying to keep my voice casual. Please say you haven't really told Hock there is a document, Liv. You stupid stupid girl.

'Apparently you have it now.' He stares straight at me, waiting and searching for the tiniest reaction.

'There is no other report.'

'Why would she tell me there was?'

'You'd have to ask her that.'

'I did. She says you have it. Do you?'

'No. There is no second report.'

'I don't believe you, William. You said there was evidence of my mother in Claire's flat...'

'Her name was scribbled on a post-it note. I don't believe that you didn't slap Claire. But it's about what we can prove.'

'Liv says she's seen the report.'

'If she's seen it then she's missed her chance to steal it and tempt you with it, hasn't she?' Why didn't she take it, I ask myself silently.

'She couldn't very well bring it with her, could she? That would have been really stupid because I would have just taken it from her. Perhaps she thinks it's safer to get my confession whilst tempting me with it from a distance. Or you could say she's revving me up to come after you for it.'

'Believe me she's not that bright.'

He chuckles at my bitchiness but shakes his head. 'Never underestimate a woman, Will. They're devious bitches.'

'Are you going to tell me what happened at the Three Fish that night? You might as well. If I get further evidence, I'm only going to come back and bother you.'

At the nearest table, a skinny lad wearing baggy jeans and a body warmer struggles to pull out a chair, its feet scrape noisily on the floor. He's disturbing us and it's as if he can feel Hock's threat burning into him. Hastily, he thinks twice about sitting so close and moves somewhere else.

Hock turns back to me and smiles. 'Yes, we had a meeting there. Claire picked the venue. She managed to do some digging around: in the notes, questioned the mortuary technician, gave me a copy of the doctored report. There was no evidence of a cover-up, and honestly I would have let the whole thing drop but she said something. I mentioned the liver, and something...a look flickered across her face. She suggested I request a meeting with the surgeon, read the notes, but I wasn't going to find anything in them.'

'What did you do?'

'I went after her. I did,' he admits. 'I had another question and she answered. She gave me the strongest evidence yet there was a cover-up.'

I lean forward with interest, sliding my cup aside so I can rest my elbows on the table.

'The surgeon rang the mortuary during the post-mortem on Mum and wanted to speak to the pathologist. They didn't actually speak till afterwards. And with Liv's revelation that explains why there are two reports: the before and after. So why would I hit Claire?' He holds his hands up like a protesting footballer having just been given a yellow card by the ref. 'She gave me what I wanted.'

'But why didn't she tell you at the table?'

'I don't know. Leo was a witness, perhaps she didn't trust him. He is a bit of a creepy fucker. It doesn't matter. I had what I wanted, she had her debt reduction, we were all happy. I said thank you and she left. With no black eye from me. I swear on my kids.' Again he places the hand on his heart.

I don't show doubt on my face. I smile and nod, show him that I'm pleased to have an explanation as to how the meeting went despite his version not tallying exactly with Leo's. I'm more inclined to believe Leo but I can't prove Hock hit Claire, maybe she did bump into a cupboard door, how can I prove otherwise and does it really matter? Chances are despite his sincerity Hock did hit her, just to remind her who was the boss. Does that mean he killed her? Well, that depends if he knew she had the original report. He said he was surprised by Liv's revelation that there was one in existence. If he had killed Claire, then I doubt he'd be worried about leaving forensic evidence when he turned her flat over looking for it? Why worry about a rap for burglary when you've committed murder?

'Look, I have to go in a minute, but I hope this satisfies you,' Hock says, wiping his mouth on a scrunched up serviette.

'Yes, it does,' I say. 'It fills in a couple of gaps in my investigation.'

'I'm glad. And I hope you find her, one way or the other.' He pushes his chair back. 'See you in a couple of weeks, Will. By the way, another ten k in it for you, if you can produce that report on my mum. Think about it.'

'Yeah. Yeah, I will. Cheers, Hock. See you later.' I watch him walk across the cafe door and leave. I take out my mobile and text Liv. "You've got some serious Qs to answer" I type. "I'll see you later after work."

Chapter 53

Saturday ~ day 19

Liv isn't wrong about her street. It's a shithole. I drive up and down the road, keeping my eye out for a suitable parking space. As luck has it, outside the bookies and the chippie wittily called "For Cod's sake" is a sort of lay-by/car park. Having betted his hard earned wages on the favourite in the 3.45 at Kempton Park, a white van man wearing a hi-vis bib climbs into his transit van and reverses out so I nip into the space and walk the few metres to her flat glancing back several times to make sure no one is taking a sudden interest in my car. I wouldn't want to leave it here overnight.

A creaking metal staircase attached to the side of the bookies leads up to Liv's front door. I carefully climb it, gripping the handrail, but I swear it's moving away from the brickwork; the bolts no doubt as rusty as fuck. The stairs have the surface texture of a cheese grater. A tumble from here would certainly snap a spinal column or fracture a skull. I doubt it would pass Health and Safety regulations.

I knock the door hard, wait, and flip the flap of the letterbox – still nothing. They must be deaf, dead or stoned not to hear me. I raise my fist and pound the door. Surely Liv will be home by now. Is Andrew mean enough to make her work till 5pm on a Saturday?

I take a bird's eye view of her street as I wait. There's a powerful smell of fried food emanating from fast food establishments up and down the road. Unfortunately they're an assembly point for hooded youths, shaven headed little boys on bikes and legging-clad teenage girls.

Litter of various types has accumulated in little piles over drains and in tight corners. The single bin by the bus-stop is overflowing and I bet at night there's a real problem with rats and foxes. Are Andrew and Marion totally unaware their daughter lives here? It says such a lot about them that Liv prefers to live here.

Finally a noise from the flat. The paint-chipped front door opens with a squeak. A young man stares gormlessly at me. You must be Dan, I think.

He is everything I expected: skinny with a hollowed out abdomen suggesting poor eating habits, drainpipe trousers with saggy knees, a T-shirt bearing an offensive slogan; his dark eyes are devoid of any intelligence and his weak features lead me to suspect he's no thug. His turned down mouth makes him look a gobby twat though. He looks away as he yanks his belt taut. The zip to his jeans is undone. Was he on the bog or having a wank?

'You must be Dan. Hello. I'm William Bailey. How you doing? Is Olivia home yet?' I ask, bombarding him with lots of information at once, an old police trick that he fails to analyse through either sleepiness, stupidity or drugs.

'...er, no, mate, not yet.' He reaches into his back pocket for his mobile but comes up empty-handed. 'She's late, I think.' Like so many people nowadays who have stopped wearing watches; they prefer to tell the time via their phones.

I look at my own watch. 'Yes, she is a bit. Can I wait?'

'Who did you say you were?' he asks, a little more aggressively. Perhaps in his stupor he thinks I said debt collector or landlord, and is preparing to defend his hovel.

'William Bailey. I'm a sort of friend of Olivia's. She's helping me find Claire: her older sister.'

The sarcasm is lost on him. 'Yeah, come in.' He walks away from the door. Hospitality isn't his thing. I step into the dark hallway and close the door, cutting off all light, and in the dark I make out various shapes: other closed doors, a heap of shoes on the floor under the radiator which has an item of clothing drying on it. There's an airless fusty smell which reminds me of unoccupied houses or those where cleaning is low down on the list of things-to-do.

I follow Dan straight ahead and he pushes open a door with a springy hinge that I dart quickly through. Wow, I think, surprised by how light and airy the room is. The windows are huge and panoramic, the ceiling's high and the skirting boards are wide. The womanly touches are obvious: the throws on the sinking settees, the modern rug in front of the TV, where I'm guessing Dan spends most of his time playing on the various games consoles that are strewn untidily under the metal and glass TV stand, the trio of canvas pictures on the wall depicting a forest in the early morning fog, and on the coffee table are matching coasters of Hollywood actors and actresses from yesteryear.

'How's your investigation going?' Dan asks, sitting down and balancing one foot on the opposite knee. 'Have you found Claire yet? Hope she's sunning herself on a tropical beach.'

I smile. 'I wish, mate. I want to say thank you for persuading Olivia to help me with this.' He pushes his lips together into a pout and shrugs. Both actions convey the same message: he doesn't know what I'm talking about. 'You told Olivia that I was the only one to give a flying fuck about Claire because her family didn't. Remember?'

He shrugs slackly. 'Nah. I never said that. I've given up telling Liv what she should do about her weird family. You're lucky you're just a friend, mate. It's fucking mental being invited to family parties. I hate it.'

I nod sympathetically, but wonder why he attends. It's no wonder she had an abortion. This guy is dense, lazy and parasitic; he should be sterilised.

A beeping noise from the settee pricks both our ears up and from underneath a cushion, Dan slides out an iPad. He swipes a finger across it and smiles as he reads something on the screen.

'Is that one of them iPads?' I ask and he looks up with an expression that says "D'uh, don't you know anything?" 'They're meant to be really good. Not that I'd know. My mobile isn't even a Smartphone.' I laugh.

He smiles with sympathy. 'You wanna get yourself one of these, mate, they're fucking great. I'll show you.' And even though it means sitting closer, it'll be amusing to give him the upper-hand as I pretend to be intrigued.

Dan begins his lesson and I respond with favourable noises. 'This is Facebook,' he teases. 'You have heard of that?'

'Yeah, but being a copper it wasn't encouraged to join. So I never bothered.' Claire and Ryan never bothered preferring to leave people from the past in the past.

'You can join now,' he says enthusiastically but the thought of going on such a site horrifies me. Honestly, who'd want to be my friend? Dan's finger glides up the screen and the list of names rolls up.

'How many friends do you have?' I ask.

Justine and her friends measured their popularity by how many friends they had. Justine had over 100 and I often joked that she must have sent friends' requests to everyone she encountered in court.

'Seven hundred and sixty five.'

I make a suitably impressed noise. I wonder if he sends requests to his customers. If everything is online, maybe he conducts his dealing via Facebook too.

A familiar name catches my eye and I reach out a hand as if to stop the list myself. 'Is that Sally's bloke?'

'Fergus Campbell. Yeah. He's alright. I'm not friends with Sally. Stuck up bitch.'

You're right there, I silently agree, but then who'd want to be pals with a low-life pusher like you.

Dan loads Fergus's page and passes me the iPad to look at. 'Want a beer?'

'I'm driving. Got a soft drink?'

'I think Liv bought some coke.' He leaves the room and I get to work.

I scan Fergus' timeline. He looks an okay bloke, like a young farmer: healthy, outdoor complexion; dark red hair, wears rugby shirts. I flick through his statuses. His most recent are: "having a few beers with the lads" and in bolder text are the names of the so-called lads. Also: "celebrating our 5th year together. Love you, babe," and in bold text is the name Sally Lancaster. I continue skimming. In January he announced he was undertaking a course in plastering, and in December are a montage of photos of him in a nightclub surrounded by lads, the tables are adorned with empty and full glasses of alcohol: shots, beer, cocktails. Must have been some drinking session.

I continue clicking on the pictures. I can hear Dan on the phone in the kitchen so I work quickly. Lots of similarly dressed lads with red faces, arms clamped tightly around each others' necks, holding drinks at jaunty angles, the background is a blur of blue and silver disco lights. Across the top is the name of the person who posted the photo: Tim Willis and the date: 1st December.

My heart skips. '1st December. The night Claire went missing.'

The photo has several likes and comments: "Soz I can't be there, have to work", "Great stag night", "So f*cking p*ssed. Get the beers in", "Awesome night. Hope Deano makes it to the church in time! Lol", "Wedding isn't for a fortnight", and lastly "Lightweight Deano for not having his stag the night before the wedding! Now there's a challenge!"

I think about what I'm reading. Were these taken the night of Claire's disappearance and were they uploaded straightaway on the Friday night? I reread them and consider the fourth one especially. "Hope he makes it to the church on time" an event which normally takes place on a Saturday. The last comment suggests the groom was a lightweight for not having his stag do the night before. They must have been uploaded on the Friday, I conclude. Then I see it: the date and time the comments were made. The first one was made at 22:14 on 1st December.

Conclusive proof: Fergus was at a stag party the night of Claire's disappearance. And if he was there, then where was Sally?

Dan returns with my can of coke: a cheap supermarket brand which will taste of nothing but sugar. I say thanks and leave it on the floor by my foot. He glances at the iPad as he sits down. 'You're still looking at Fergus?'

'Don't know how to get out of it,' I reply and Dan raises his eyebrows but I'd rather he consider me stupid than having some obsession with Fergus. He takes the iPad and clicks on his own profile. A picture appears in a box big enough for me to identify the two people: him and Olivia, their cheeks touching, their tongues sticking out; I squint. Has he got a tongue piercing? Good grief. I contemplate asking him about it, but the sound of a key in the front door startles us; we look expectantly at the lounge door; there's a lot of noise in the hall: sighing, grunting, things being dropped or slammed. Dan doesn't shout out hello, I stay quiet too.

'I thought I asked you to do the washing up, Dan!' Liv yells. 'It's stinking the kitchen out.'

If you think that's a surprise, I think, just wait till you open this door.

It flings open, the handle striking the wall behind. There's an indentation and a black mark on the paintwork where it's connected many times. Before the door springs back at her, she sticks out a booted foot and wedges it open and she stands there, hand on hip, face distorted with anger and despair, then her eye catches sight of me.

'Oh. Hello Will.' She smiles.

'Hi Liv. Good day at work?' I ask pleasantly.

'No,' she snaps, slouching in the armchair, her stupidly high-heeled boots lie heavily across the stained carpet.

Without a word or an acknowledgement to her, Dan gets to his feet and leaves the room. Moments later the front door slams.

Liv points to the abandoned can of coke on the floor and says, 'Want some vodka in your coke? After a day like I've had, I feel like getting bladdered. People reckon it's cushy working in a family business but it isn't.'

'No thanks. You can have your coke back. I only said yes out of politeness.'

She pulls a face in response to my haughtiness that her cheap coke isn't good enough. She struggles to her feet, using the armchair and the doorframe for support. On her way back from the kitchen, she grabs the can and pours it into a glass containing two fingers of a clear liquid.

'I presume you want to know how my meeting with Mr Hock went: it could have been better. He denied *everything*,' she states, 'and it wound me up. I wanted to punch his stupid grinning face. I'm sorry but he knows about the PM report. I let it slip; I thought he'd react and admit something, but he didn't.'

He's too clever to do that. 'Did you tell him I have it?' I ask.

'No! I'm not stupid. He asked me where it was and I said I wouldn't tell him.' She sighs like a deflating balloon. 'I know you forbid me from going, but I thought being a young woman he'd take pity or feel less threatened, and talk to me. I hope I haven't made it worse.'

'Time will tell if he suddenly abducts me from my bed, takes me to a warehouse and tortures me till I tell him where it is,' I joke. Liv looks horrified.

'It's not funny,' she scolds. 'He's a nasty piece of work.'

She moves to sit beside me on the settee, smiling apologetically. 'I'm sorry, Will.' Her thigh presses against mine, her short black skirt rides up over her purple tights exposing a massive chunk of leg. Her perfume is different than the last one I smelt. This one is like lilies. 'I wouldn't want anything to happen to you. I quite like you. I haven't always but I can see why Claire thought so much of you.'

'Thanks,' I say, swallowing hard. I don't know why I'm behaving like a cowering virgin; her predatory female style is unnerving.

She leans closer and kisses my cheek. 'Thanks for not bollocking me for visiting Hock.'

'Okay,' I reply uncomfortably and change the subject quickly. 'I meant to say, earlier Dan was showing me around Facebook and I noticed on Fergus' page that on the Friday of Claire's disappearance he was on a stag night.'

Liv frowns. 'So?'

'Sally said she was with Fergus. She's not in the photos and anyway why would a woman be on a stag do? I know she wasn't with you because you were ill and I just wondered...' I wonder to myself why I'm telling her this. Perhaps I want to test what she does with the information.

'If she was bludgeoning Claire's head in?' Liv laughs.

'Well, if she had an alibi like you, then she might have told you where she...?'

'Sally was not aborting a foetus at the same time as me.' I wince at her bluntness. 'That would be a sick coincidence. I hope you don't suspect Sally.' She stabs a black painted fingernail into my upper arm. 'Because you're wrong. She loved Claire, more than I did.'

'She said she was with...'

'Maybe she didn't want to admit she was stuck home alone on a Friday whilst everyone else was enjoying themselves. Maybe she was fucking another man.'

I raise an eyebrow at this possibility, but Liv quickly follows it up with: 'I was joking. You'd have to ask her where she was.' But I've already pestered her once today. I decide to make a move. I should go home and see if Mum's booked her holiday yet. I stand.

Liv jumps to her feet. 'Are you actually going? You've accused my sister of murdering my other sister and now you're going?'

I notice she's omitted the word half before sister when referring to Claire. 'I didn't accuse her. I was simply asking a question. I'm entitled to...'

'No, you're not entitled. Why do you love arguing with me?'

'I don't.'

'Well, I do,' and suddenly she launches herself at me with her full body weight. The force almost knocks me sideways so I grab hold of her. She presses her mouth hard on mine and I feel sticky lipstick on my lips. It takes me by such surprise that I stand still for several moments deciding whether to respond, whether I like it or not. My mouth, sick of waiting for a decision from my brain, reacts and returns the kiss. It goes on and on too; it must be the longest kiss I've ever had and not the worst either.

A key in the front door heralds the return of Dan and we step back from each other, my hand automatically rises to wipe my mouth free of plum lipstick, Dan goes into the kitchen; the smell of chips creeping under the lounge door and up to our noses. Liv smiles proudly. I raise an eyebrow at her but I get it. Cheating on him must be a thrill, even more so when there's a chance you could be caught.

Liv follows me into the hall; I call a goodbye to Dan who grunts a reply whilst stuffing a hot chip in his mouth. On the threshold, Liv grabs the front of my top and pulls me close to give me one last kiss. As tempting as it is to just shove her all the way back into the flat till we reach the bedroom, meanwhile kicking Dan out, I unlace her fingers from my clothing and tell her I'll speak to her soon.

'Yes, you will, and remember: Sally loves her family. All she wants to do is protect us.'

Chapter 54

Saturday ~ day 19

'The taxi's picking me up at six thirty in the morning, so although it's an early start we arrive in Majorca with the whole day ahead of us. The hotel looks fabulous,' Mum gushes as she unloads several convenience meals from carrier bags and places them into the freezer or the fridge. Lasagne, cottage pie, chicken tikka masala. At least I won't starve whilst she's sunning herself for two weeks.

She gathers all the carrier bags up and stuffs them into the cupboard under the sink. She unplugs her mobile phone charger from the wall and wraps the cable around the chunky plug, muttering that she'll need this.

'How much longer are you going to leave this here for, Will?'

I look. Plugged into the wall next to the toaster is Claire's sports watch. It must be charged up by now; it's been plugged in for twenty four hours.

'I'd forgotten about it.' I unplug it and examine the watch. It's quite chunky but surprisingly lightweight with a rather large screen and several buttons on its face and sides. God knows how it works; it's probably all singing and dancing with functions that you never knew it had; it might even fetch you an energy drink when you're gasping for breath. At most I might be able to turn it on but that'd be it; I should have picked up the instructions.

A tune starts playing in the kitchen and Mum and I look at each other. My mobile rarely rings so I don't even recognise it as being my phone; I pull it out of my pocket. It's Nisha. I answer it as I walk out of the kitchen, still holding Claire's watch in my other hand.

'Will,' she barks, sounding panicked. 'Do you know where St Jude's hospice shop is? It's on Church Road opposite the Black Eagle.'

'Yeah, I think so. Well, I know where the Black...'

She interrupts. 'Good. Get over here as quick as you can. You have to see this.'

'See what?'

'My eyes may be deceiving me, but I swear Claire's dress is in their shop window.'

I park the Mazda on the pub car park and jog across the road, narrowly missing a cyclist dressed in pink and black Lycra. Nisha paces the pavement outside the hospice shop fidgeting with her handbag strap and looking agitated. She grabs my arm and steers me towards the shop window.

'How sure are you?' I ask.

'I need to inspect it. I saw a dress just like it in Claire's flat the week she went missing.'

The display in the shop window is an explosion of bright pink and red. Paper streamers are strewn across the ceiling from corner to corner like bunting in a church fete. Two faceless mannequins similar to the smaller wooden version that artists use for drawing people stand posed in the centre of the display; oversized handbags of red and pink dangling from the crook of their elbows. One mannequin wears a floor length, strapless red evening gown; a row of diamantes sparkle across the plunging neckline like a constellation. The other mannequin wears a sleeveless above the knee-length black dress with a halter neck. It's patterned with pink and purple triangles of different sizes. It looks like Claire's dress alright; like the one from the photo Mum kept of that wedding incident. I peer closer. If it's Claire's, where has it come from? Why has it appeared now? It definitely wasn't in the flat when I was last there.

I look at Nisha. 'What do you remember the last time you saw it?'

She frowns as she tries to recall the incident. 'It was the night of the honey trap; I was at Claire's waiting for her to get ready.' She chuckles momentarily. 'A dress was hanging on the back of the wardrobe door and I asked if she was wearing it that night. She pulled a face and said she was thinking of selling it on *eBay* or putting it in a charity bag. She'd had it laundered because there was a wine stain on it.'

I nod and smile with agreement. 'She deliberately spilt wine on it so she could go home and get changed. She hated the dress.' I look back at the window and smile. 'Thankfully red wine is a bitch to remove.'

Nisha pushes the door open and a bell rings at the back of the shop. Huge racks of shelving house various items: books on such subjects like gardening, military and nutrition; small kitchen items like egg cups and odd saucers; wicker baskets containing items of costume jewellery. In the centre of the floor are a trio of circular racks containing clothes on hangers. Squares of bright orange card with sizes written on are attached at various points around the rack: 8-10, 12-14, 16-18 etc. We squeeze past a rack to get to the back of the display. The mannequin is out of reach. I don't fancy trying to drag it over; I can see it landing on top of me.

'There must be a shop assistant somewhere,' Nisha says and marches down the shop calling out hello. I lift several pairs of red and pink shoes off the base of the dummy so it'll be easier to drag closer.

'Let me do that for you,' a woman calls, striding out of the gloom. She's in her fifties with ash blonde hair. 'I almost knocked it over last week reaching for the cardigan it was wearing. You need the knack.' She smiles.

Together, we take a firm hold of the wooden circular base and the metal pole which holds all the body parts together and inch by inch, the assistant and I walk the mannequin closer to the edge of the display. The accessories sway with the movement and I can see the handbag slapping me across the cheek.

'Let me swivel it around for you,' the woman helpfully offers.

We turn it anti-clockwise; I duck down as the shiny boxlike handbag swings over my head like a wrecking ball.

'The dress is a size twelve,' she tells us. 'Let me know if you want to try it on. There's a changing room at the back.'

Nisha and I look at each other. That's Claire's size.

'Thanks,' we say.

Nisha takes one side of the dress and I take the other and together we peer closely at the material, trying to spot where even the tiniest corner of one of the shapes is darkened by a possible stain. Luckily each shape is surrounded by a thin line of white. The shapes quickly start to blur and my eyes struggle to focus properly. I look away and blink several times.

Nisha pauses too. She rubs her eyes. 'Didn't you say some of Claire's clothes were missing? If somebody took them to make people think she'd left town, they must have seen this dress on the wardrobe door and took it. Where could it have been till now? Why get rid of it now?'

I remove my glasses to rub the bridge of my nose. 'I must have spooked someone. I wonder if the shop has a record of when they received this.' I look around for the shop assistant and call out. A head appears from behind the till counter.

'Yes, love?'

'Do you know when the dress arrived?'

'Yes, we should have a record of it in the book.' She rummages under the counter and brings a heavy ledger over, flicking through the pages. 'It arrived two weeks ago, on a Friday. We didn't dress the mannequin until we had other items to make it into a bit of a display.'

'Do you know how it was donated?' Nisha asks. 'Did someone bring it into the shop or was it left outside?'

'From what I can remember it was inside a suitcase which was in a black bin liner. My colleague found it outside the shop when she arrived to open up. People often leave their donations as they pass. There were other items along with the dress.'

'What sort of items?' I ask. 'Have you got a record?'

'Yes, certainly.' She licks a finger and starts flicking through the pages. 'A pair of size twelve jeans, a pair of orange wedge shoes size 4, a selection of t-shirts size 12, a pink cardigan size ten, black hooded top size 12, and this dress.'

Nisha is closely examining the dress. The shop assistant is frowning at our behaviour. We should offer an explanation, but then Nisha says, 'Will, look.' She tugs the front of the dress. 'Is that a mark? See where the white is broken by an area of dark.' I look where she's pointing. My eyes follow the white border around a pink obtuse triangle until I see a break in its surrounding. One corner of white is missing. I scrape it with my fingernail should it wipe off but it's ingrained in the material. It looks like a stain alright. I peer closer without my glasses on. Yes, the area of darkness has spread down and across into borders surroundings other pink and purple shapes.

'It is a stain,' I confirm.

'I have to ask what you're doing,' the assistant interrupts.

I slide my glasses back on. I'll be glad when I can start wearing contact lenses again. 'This dress may have belonged to a woman who's missing.'

'It was donated honourably.'

'I don't know about honourably, but I'll buy it.' The assistant raises an eyebrow but she can't turn down a sale, my money's good enough, and then I remember that I don't have any money. I smile hopefully at Nisha.

'What happened to the other items in the suitcase and the case itself?' Nisha enquires as the assistant rings the dress up on the till and pops it into a well used plastic bag.

'The case sold the day after it arrived. It was a bargain: lovely condition, perfect for weekends away. The clothes were clean and tidy, and with summer on its way, they sold very quickly. People picked up some lovely bargains. The dress is all that's left.'

Nisha pays the woman; we thank her and leave to discuss our purchase outside.

'I can't be sure it's Claire's,' I admit. 'If I'd seen the other items then I might be more confident. I can't understand why this has turned up now.'

'I bet if you started waving this dress around someone would react. Because whoever brought this dress here knows something.' I nod in agreement. Nisha continues. 'They could have disposed of this dress at any time in the last four months but they chose now. Now because you're investigating her disappearance and that's worried the person responsible; they know enough about you to know that you'd recognise this dress or her other belongings if you found them in their possession.'

'That's a good point,' I say. 'And you can back me up that this is Claire's. I might have to use it to start rattling a few cages. Thanks, Nisha, for spotting this and paying for the dress. I'll pay you back.'

'Don't worry about that. I'm just glad I can help. I'll walk back with you; I'm parked on the boozer too. Who have you got left to interview?' We start walking down the street.

'The parents,' I groan. 'That's if they open the door to me, but I do have some ammunition.'

'You shouldn't leave valuables on show, Will. Didn't the police teach you anything?' Nisha nods at the passenger door window. Lying on the seat is Claire's watch which I accidentally brought with me when I hurried to the car after her phone call.

'It's Claire's. I keep meaning to have a look at it, but technology isn't my thing.'

'Let me have a look.' I unlock the car and hand the watch over. 'Oh, my sister has one of these. They're amazingly clever.'

'Take it and see what you can find.'

'I might need a password. You can download routes and other data onto an online record.'

'Have you got a pen? I'll write it down for you.'

'You know Claire's password?'

'Yeah, we spent an afternoon devising one that no one could guess.' I scribble it down on the back of a voucher. Nisha frowns at it. 'Morrissey lyrics,' I explain. 'Claire said we had similar hair.'

'She was right. I'll let you know how I get on with this. Good luck with the parents.'

*

My confidence and determination to get an answer from Marion and Andrew disappears when I arrive at their house. My recent unpleasant meeting with Sally will earn me a door in the face and possibly a warning of harassment from the police. But so what? I need to try.

I park the Mazda against their wall, pointing at the exit so I can make a quick getaway. Once again the road is quiet except for a clipping noise coming from nearby. I look around and from behind a neighbouring stone wall, a woman pops up like a meerkat who's on watch and has sensed danger. She's in her late forties and well turned out in designer gardening wear, holding a pair of secateurs in her gloved hand. Her eyebrows are raised with interest.

I don't think I'll make it to their front door without her speaking so I smile pleasantly and go over.

'Hello,' I say. 'I'm William Bailey - friend of Marion's daughter Claire.'

'Ah, poor Claire. What a lovely girl. The last time I saw her,' she explains as if I've asked, 'was the evening of Marion's 63rd birthday.'

I stop myself from laughing out loud at the crafty way she drops Marion's age into the conversation, but more than that my interest is piqued that she attended the soiree. Could she be *that* neighbour?

'Marion's party,' I repeat. 'I'm sorry I missed it, but I was away. Quite a do, I'm told.'

The neighbour huffs. 'It was just drinks and nibbles, nothing spectacular. The wine was lovely if you could wrestle the bottle away from Andrew.' She giggles. It amuses me how she criticises her neighbour feet away from their front door and doesn't lower her voice. 'I'm Harriet Woodbead. Is there any news from Claire? I want to ask Marion and Andrew, but I wouldn't want them to think I was prying.'

'There's no news, I'm afraid. In fact you may be able to help me, Harriet,' I say and she beams, honoured to be of assistance and ready to receive any titbit of information. 'I'm doing a bit of digging around; maybe you could tell me how Claire was that evening.'

Harriet removes her gardening gloves and balances them and the secateurs on the wall. 'I spoke to Claire a couple of times. She was chatty enough, a tad quiet, and distracted; she kept looking at her mobile as if she was waiting for a phone call, but everyone knows a watched phone never rings!'

'True,' I agree with a nod. 'And you saw no animosity between Claire and anyone else?'

Harriet's interest level visibly rises a notch. 'Who do you mean, family?' She answers her own question. 'Well, there's always a bristling between Claire and Olivia. You know what I mean, I'm sure. Sly looks across the dinner table, barbed comments. It's no wonder really. Olivia can be rude and uncouth, and seems to deliberately prod Claire. I'm afraid I left early; I was Skyping my son that night. He's backpacking in Australia.' So Harriet wasn't there to witness the row between the two sisters.

'How was Andrew with Claire?' I ask.

'Fine. Why? Had they fallen out?' But I don't answer her question. 'I didn't see them together much. You know how Andrew likes to take control of the wine choices.'

'I understand he took time out to administer first aid to someone,' I joke.

She blushes but doesn't shy away from the remark. 'Yes, that was for me. It's just as well he was on hand with his kit; I might have got lockjaw or a nasty infection. He has a lovely bedside manner.'

'Yes, I heard about that,' I grin knowingly.

Harriet pretends to be scandalised, but I bet she loves causing trouble. 'No doubt you were told that by Olivia's odious boyfriend.'

Dan; I didn't know he'd witnessed the scene; I thought only Claire had seen it.

'He enjoyed himself thereafter, sniggering and winking at me over the canapés. Horrible, scruffy layabout. I mean, nothing went on.' Harriet extends her hand as if to physically stop any rumours from spreading. 'Andrew simply washed the wound and dressed it. And for that I gave him a small thank you kiss on the cheek. Anyone would think I'd ravished him! You ask Claire what went on. She saw it too.' I nod robotically. 'I admit I find Andrew attractive. My husband has recently taken early retirement and his constant traipsing of golf courses has yet to slim his waist down. Plus he doesn't even give me a second glance these days. A lady likes to be admired.'

'Andrew only has eyes for Marion, doesn't he?'

'Who knows? I enjoyed the close contact with Andrew; perhaps I was testing the water.'

'And how was it?' I ask cheekily.

'It was tepid,' Harriet replies coyly.

Is that what Claire and Dan noticed? If she kissed Andrew, did his arm snake around her waist, did he hold her injured hand longer than was necessary, did he whisper in her ear, and did Claire think "I could use this to my advantage." And I wonder if Marion knew about this moment between Andrew and Harriet, what would she do? Would it be severe enough to remind Andrew what happened to the first husband? Or did she discover Claire's intentions and decide one ruined marriage was enough and had gone to see her daughter?

Suddenly, Harriet raises a hand and waves at someone over my right shoulder. I turn to the Lancaster's house and see that their front door is open and Andrew stands on the threshold. Has he heard us? Judging by Harriet's guilty grin he knows he's the topic of conversation. Let him think that, it might grant me an audience.

'I'll let you get back to your gardening,' I say. 'Thanks for your help in getting Andrew to open the door. I don't think he would have otherwise.'

'My pleasure, William,' she smiles. And I can appreciate why wives might keep a watch on Harriet if she comes around to their house. I walk to his front door and notice how worried he looks; a frown creases his forehead and even his moustache is a tad droopier as if it's concerned too.

'William,' he says curtly by way of hello.

'Hello Andrew. Just been having a nice chat with your neighbour; she's quite a woman. I only said hello and she invited me in for a coffee. She told me about all the parties she attends, who she meets, who she flirts with...' I trail off and raise an eyebrow so he knows she talked about Marion's party.

'She's all talk,' he replies.

'I don't know. I've heard the story about her cut finger from three people now.'

His eyes widen with horror.

'Marion home?' I ask and he shakes his head. 'Think we'd best have that chat now, don't you? I don't want to return later and make things awkward for you.' Andrew nods defeated, and opens the front door further to allow me to step into a light airy hall with expensive looking stone floor tiles. On the wall behind the door is a massive silver gilded mirror; in its reflection is the staircase and Claire's face. I turn quickly, my heart skipping, but it's just a photo, a large professional photo of her taken several years ago. Next to that but higher up is a photo of Olivia, her hair is curly and frames a much thinner face; Sally's face completes the album, her hair is longer and she wears a white Alice band which makes her look like a brunette *Alice in Wonderland.*

'Makes me jump every time I look in the mirror as well,' Andrew confides, nodding at Claire's picture. 'Like she's standing over me.'

'Perhaps she is,' I say.

He leads the way down the hall, through the kitchen and into the conservatory. I've never been so far into the house before. The conservatory is a double affair, shaped like the letter B on its back; one half contains a set of wicker furniture, floral printed cushions and tasteful ornaments on a wicker stand. The other half contains plants: a lemon tree and tropical grasses and flowers. I gaze through the panoramic windows; I can see all aspects of the garden including a water feature which is a leaping fish in the centre of a stone bath spurting water from its pursed lips; the shrubs and trees are well established; the lawn is very tidy and looks combed; in the centre of the grass is a large tree with a metal bench encircling the trunk.

Andrew takes an armchair and I choose the settee. He doesn't offer me a drink even though I could do with one. I glance at the ornaments and yet more photos of their daughters at various stages of their childhood. Expensive nondescript pieces of sculpture dot the low window sills.

'What do you want to ask me?' he begins, crossing his legs and folding his hands neatly in his lap like a psychiatrist with a patient.

'Let's start with Harriet...'

'She's a predatory female and big trouble. There is no shame to her flirting as you saw.'

'She fancies you...'

'I expect she does, but I'm a very happily married man, and Harriet doesn't interest me...'

'Does Marion know Harriet tried it on with you?'

'What do you mean?' he asks, unconvincingly.

'Come on, Andrew. I heard that Harriet tried to seduce you in the conservatory with a cut finger.'

'Rubbish.'

'Andrew,' I warn, 'don't dance with me. You know what I'm talking about. There's no one here; I'm not interested in ruining your marriage.'

Andrew considers how trustworthy I am, probably not very considering I've been in prison; nevertheless he realises I have the full story. He sighs. 'Marion doesn't know about it. Harriet made more of her injury and she forced herself on me and kissed me. If Marion thought for one second I had reciprocated, she'd file for divorce quicker than you can say decree nisi. Unfortunately Philip's affair left its scars.'

'Did Claire threaten to tell her mum what she'd seen that evening?'

Andrew takes his time answering. He must believe that to admit that is to admit that he allowed himself to be blackmailed, and with that comes a feeling of guilt, of wrong doing when the only reason you've agreed to cough up is to protect someone else's feelings. It's not necessarily because you've done anything wrong.

'Yes. Claire was in debt again. I agreed to bail her out, but then at Marion's party she insulted me and

I changed my mind about the money. She was furious, we rowed but I still refused. About a week later, she came to the house for dinner and demanded the money or she'd tell Marion she'd seen me kissing and cuddling Harriet. I was horrified and angry that she could stoop so low as to threaten her mother's happiness. I asked how she was going to prove it, but we both knew she wouldn't have to. Marion would believe her...like she did the last time. I had no choice but to give her money.'

'She would have been desperate,' I tell him. 'I'm not excusing her behaviour just trying to explain it. There was someone leaning on her.'

'When we reported her missing, I looked for the money in the flat but it wasn't there and I concluded that she'd left the country to start a new life. When you turned up, we realised that the two of you had remained in contact. I assumed you were in on Claire's escape and your investigation was a ploy to convince us that Claire had come to harm when all the time she was sunning herself somewhere.'

'We'd made plans on my release from prison. There's no way, if she was safe, that she wouldn't have got word to me by now. Harm has come to her. But pretty much everybody has an alibi. Some could be proven water-tight in court. The problem is I'm not a copper anymore; I don't have their resources to hand. I have to resort to old-fashioned methods. Like *Poirot*, I have to talk to people and use my brain.'

Andrew suddenly turns to the conservatory door and stands, poised like a dog that senses someone at the front door before the bell is rung. 'I think Marion's back.' He steps forward but looks at me, his mouth open. I know what he's going to say.

'I won't say a word,' I promise. He leaves to greet Marion. I lean my head back over the chair and hear her complain: 'Well what does he want?' Minutes later, they appear in the doorway. Marion has had her hair done. It's shorter and darker than the last time I saw her. It hasn't taken years off her, but it looks nicer. Her expression, however, is anything but welcoming.

'Hello Marion,' I say pleasantly, staying seated. I'm going to enjoy this.

She pulls a face and looks demandingly at Andrew. 'Why is he in my house? I have nothing to say to him. He's done nothing but harass us since he left prison...'

'Marion, darling, please,' Andrew pleads, stroking her arm. 'He's looking for our daughter. He cares about her.'

Marion ferociously yanks her arm out of his grasp and glares. 'You've changed your tune. Two weeks ago you were calling him all the names under the sun and *now* you're inviting him into our house.'

'He needed to speak to me regarding the money I lent Claire.'

Lent? So he's lied to Marion that it was a loan rather than a blackmail payment.

'Why? She took it with her, didn't she? It's not in the flat.' Marion swings around to address me; she pokes a finger in my face. 'Andrew lent Claire money to clear a debt but instead she absconded with it. There! That's all there is to tell. Or do you want to check our alibis too?' She sounds out of control so I say, 'Yes, if you don't mind telling me where you both were on the Friday Claire went missing?'

Marion shakes her head and mutters something about being treated like a common criminal. 'We were together all evening. We went for a curry at Jopal's; I tried their new prawn dish. We came home and looked at city breaks to celebrate our silver wedding anniversary.'

'Anyone else verify it?' I ask. After all it's not unusual for murderers to have accomplices. Andrew rolls his eyes. 'Most people I've spoken to are happy to provide me with a witness or receipt, a hotel booking. In Sally's case, for example, she said she was at home with Fergus, but Facebook says he was on a stag do. Olivia was busy. Neither of them can prove their...'

'I hope you're not pointing the finger at my daughters,' Marion says, her voice rising angrily. She has taken my bait beautifully. 'Olivia was out with Dan. And I spoke to Sally that night because Fergus was unwell and I wanted to see how he was. He wasn't at a stag do. Ask her, she'll confirm we were at home. Now you can cross us *all* off your list.'

'Thank you for speaking to me. I appreciate...' My voice trails off as my eye is caught by the stone elephant on the windowsill gazing into the room. Andrew smiles, pleased it's been noticed.

'I bought that back from Cape Town,' he explains. 'It was the inspiration behind the name of the business.'

'I'm going to put the kettle on, Andrew,' Marion interrupts. 'When I return I want *him* gone.' She jabs a finger at me just so Andrew is crystal clear on who she means.

'Yes, darling, of course,' he appeases. We watch her stomp away and hear a door slam somewhere.

'Claire had a wooden elephant from Thailand; Ryan sent it,' I tell him. 'It was in the hall, looking down at the front door.'

Andrew nods. 'All my daughters know to face them that way. Although Olivia takes little notice. Elephants bring prosperity into the house if they face the front door.'

'Yeah,' I mumble thoughtfully. 'Claire said something like that the last time I saw her, but she moved it because she'd had a run of bad luck.'

I bid my farewells and return to my car. Further up the road, a lay-by appears and helpfully a parked up burger van is open for business. I pull over, buy a coffee and work out what else I've heard about the movements of elephants.

Chapter 55

Sunday ~ day 20

My early morning wake-up call is reminiscent of my prison days. There was always an inmate kicking off before day broke; worse than the most irritating of any cockerel, they'd create the kind of noise that drives you to violence – an object was usually repeatedly slammed against the heavy metal cell doors, or they'd start shouting: any noise, obscenities, wailing, or even all of them depending on how much attention they sought.

This morning the culprit is Mum. Wardrobe doors and chest drawers close noisily as she double-checks she's packed everything; the shower and taps gush as she gets ready and fills the kettle. I get out of bed to say goodbye and find there's a cup of tea waiting. I wave her off from the lounge window and she grins with excitement at the first holiday she's had for two years where she doesn't have to worry about Dad. Once the taxi disappears from view, I turn back into the lounge and hear it for the first time in years – total silence, the kind of silence you only hear when you know you're alone in the house for two weeks.

I search the cupboards for something nice for breakfast, and strike gold when I find a packet of large teacakes. I slice one in half and pop it into the toaster. A roast is a possibility for dinner tonight. I'm sure I spotted a large Yorkshire pudding in the freezer containing all the Sunday roast items: chicken, stuffing balls, mini sausages, roast spuds and gravy. It'll save on piles of washing up.

The teacake halves jump up and I grab them with nimble fingers and drop them onto a plate, smearing raspberry jam over them. I take that and my tea into the lounge and press the ON button on the remote. A chef appears on the telly announcing he's going to show us how he can cook a roast for four people in an hour.

'Not as quick as me, mate,' I tell him, lifting a teacake half to my mouth. My mobile beeps. A text. It's from Liv: Hi W. Dan out 2day. Wnt 2 cum round 2 flat? ;-) x

'I'm guessing it's not to discuss the investigation,' I mutter, taking another bite of teacake. I contemplate her offer and wonder where's the harm. She's the one in a relationship not me; Dan and her guilt is her problem. But is a fling with Liv wise? I lick jam off my thumb. I'm investigating her family. If I was a police officer, I'd be in serious trouble for fraternising with suspects. But I'm not anymore so those rules don't apply, and Liv's text isn't suggesting long-term. A one-day fling might be fun; if Dan hadn't come home unexpectedly the other day, wouldn't we have ended up in bed?

I reach for my phone and ask what time; her reply comes before I have a chance to start on the second half of my teacake.

12.30. C u then xx.

*

I arrive at Liv's flat fashionably late. It took me seven minutes to find somewhere safe enough to park the Mazda. Even as I walked away from the Pay & Display car park, I wasn't overly thrilled by the cluster of hooded youths on tiny bikes hanging around. I stroll round to the flat, the nerves fiery in my stomach. It's been well over a year since I had sex. I can't say it feels as nervous as when I lost my virginity because that was a surprise event. I can't even remember her name; I only saw her once after that and she gave me a cold stare and a wide berth. Because this event is planned, Liv will expect me to perform. I know one thing it's easier with someone you love. It doesn't matter if you clunk heads, pull a stomach muscle or collapse with the giggles. I haven't felt this edgy since I got sent down, but unlike then this feels weird, like Claire's shaking her head and muttering for me not to "shag my sister". I can't deny that I do kind of fancy Liv, but then I have been spending more time with her than any other female.

I raise a hand to knock the front door but it opens.

'I thought you weren't coming,' Liv complains, hand on hip, scowl on her face.

'I almost wasn't going to,' I lie, equally unfriendly. 'But then I thought of you all dolled up in your negligee, alone in the flat, longing for a bit of harmless no-strings fun and I thought "There's my good deed for the day".'

'Bastard,' she mutters, stepping away from the door.

It doesn't take a genius to work out she must be high maintenance in the bedroom: demanding and aggressive, something I'm not familiar with, but it might be an experience.

I close the door. She stands in front of the open kitchen door. I glimpse untidy work surfaces, a cooker that's seen better days and an overflowing bin. Oh well, I'm not here to assess how clean her flat is. As long as she is.

I look down at her, trying to be equally as intimidating. She holds her ground. Her makeup is over the top for Sunday lunchtime: heavy eyeliner and dark grey eye shadow with sticky plum lipstick. Her shiny hair is knotted loosely at the back of her neck, held together by a band with a red flower attached. If fingers were to gently tug the band, her hair would fall around her shoulders. Her clingy jeans hug her figure, but will be hard to tug off her shapely arse. Her red top with short sleeves and a scoop neck hint at what's underneath and it'd be so easy to lift up and over her head. She's enough to put any vicar off his Sunday morning sermon.

'Are you eyeing me up?' Liv asks, accusingly.

'Yeah,' I admit, stepping closer till our toes touch.

Her fruity perfume is having one hell of an effect on me, but then perfume always has. It's like a hallucinatory drug making my head sway and feel like it's attached only by a fine thread; she looks so good. I bury my hand in her hair and tug her head back. Her arms snake around my waist and she presses her mouth on mine, crushes my chest against her ample bust. We remain entwined and like some sort of hideous two-headed chimera, we step crab-like down the short hallway to a door on the right. Liv fumbles behind her back for the door handle and kicks it open.

The room is bathed in sunlight. The bed is neatly made: plump pillows, the duvet in its spotty cover is smoothed out, it's so inviting and dying to be messed up.

Slowly, I run my hand from the outside of her thigh, up over her hip, along her side and just where my thumb touches her-

A noise outside the front door stops me. My hand drops and I turn. A dark shadow appears at the frosted glass panel in the front door. A key scratches the inside of the lock. I step away from Liv, panicked. She closes the bedroom and mutters a swear word. Dan unlocks the door and sulkily removes his hat, which he chucks on top of the radiator.

'Fucking match was cancelled. Waterlogged pitch or something,' he moans.

'So, why aren't you in the pub?' Liv demands, walking up to him as if to prevent from going any further.

He yanks at the zip on his coat. 'Don't want to.' He sees me; a grin explodes onto his face and he welcomes me like I'm a best mate. 'Alright, Will! Fancy a can?' and holds up a four pack of Stella. He doesn't wait for my answer, but pushes past and opens the living room door.

Liv glares at me as if I should have stopped Dan coming in like a bouncer on a nightclub door. She marches into the living room and starts on him. 'You're interrupting us.'

He looks her up and down, and when it registers in his tiny brain that she's dressed way over the top for a Sunday morning laze around the flat, his eyebrows lift with curiosity. Has he added one and one together yet and come up with two? Is he wondering what Liv's sexy outfit and my presence total? Or does he not care?

'Whatever you're doing, you can do it with me here,' Dan replies, flicking on the games console and settling down with the control. 'I'll stay out of your way.'

Fucking hell, I think, not on your nelly.

'Just go down the pub, will you, Dan? Your stupid game with its noisy gunfire and screaming zombies are a distraction we don't need.'

'Get away! It won't disturb you. I'll keep the door shut.' He puts a hand on his stomach. 'I'm starving; I might nip out in a bit for something to eat. Actually...' He looks at her, that eyebrow raised again but for a different reason. 'Tell you what, Liv, if *you* fetch me a kebab then I'll piss off for the rest of the afternoon and leave you to your sleuthing. Deal?'

'What? No, fuck off!'

He settles back into the settee and says, 'Fine. Have it your way.'

I think about leaving. I've gone off the boil now; I might do a Dan, get some beer and slob around in front of the TV at home with a couple of Dad's war films. Liv snorts loudly and stomps from the room, but returns moments later wearing a sensible long cardigan. 'I'll be back in ten minutes and by one o'clock, you'd best be gone, Daniel.' He raises a hand and waves bye bye. She glares at me again and leaves.

'Stupid cow,' he mutters, ripping the ring pull off. 'Sit down, mate.' And he nods at the vacant armchair, but I really want to go now that my afternoon of sex has been ruined both by Dan's presence and demands, and Liv's aggressive subservience.

'How's your detecting going?' Dan asks, snapping me out of my thoughts. 'Any suspects yet?'

'There's plenty of suspects but very little evidence. People are talking to me; whether they're telling the truth is another matter.'

'Bet Marion and Andrew are lying through their teeth. Her especially.'

'It's hard to tell.' That reminds me. I sit forward, resting my elbows on my knees. 'I spoke to their flirty neighbour Mrs Woodbead. She told me about Andrew bandaging her finger.'

Dan laughs. 'Yeah, he practically had her bent over the wicker chair, hands all over her arse, kissing her neck. Fucking hell. It was like watching some kind of middle-aged porno! It was a shit evening; I needed some light entertainment. I hate going round to these family get-togethers. Mrs Desperate Housewife, and she'd have to be fucking desperate to make a pass at Andrew, was sitting opposite me looking all prim, lips pursed, scowling at me so I thought I'd wind her up.'

'Don't blame you,' I agree. 'These housewife types never put their knickers where their mouth is. What did you do to her?'

Dan laughs and sits forward. 'It was class! I kept winking at her, stroking my finger – the same one she hurt - and pretending it hurt. Silly bitch. Think she pissed off home early in the end.'

'Did anyone notice you winding her up?'

'Nah. They're too far up their own arses. A few weeks later, I told that stuck up mardy bitch what her old man had been up to with the neighbour. Her face was a fucking picture!'

'Who do you mean? Marion?'

'Nah,' he scoffs. 'I don't speak to her. No, I mean Sally.'

'You told Sally about Andrew and the Desperate Housewife? What did you say?'

'That he made a pass at her. I exaggerated it a bit, but the effect was the same. I tell you if looks could kill...' he trails off as if the rest of the saying escapes him.

'You'd be stone dead?' I ask what her response had been to his revelation.

'She didn't believe me, so I said "Ask Claire then. She saw them an' all". That really pissed her off.' He tips the beer can towards me. 'Are you sure you don't want one?'

I shake my head, deep in thought. Sally was aware that something happened between Andrew and Mrs Woodbead; she may not know what that exactly was because I doubt she believes Dan anymore than I do. But she knew Claire was a witness. Did she wonder what Claire might have done with this information?

A key in the lock interrupts my thoughts; the smell of kebab meat wafts into the lounge and Dan jumps up excitedly to grab the polystyrene box from Olivia without a thank you. We watch as he stabs the white plastic fork into the lengths of pale grey doner meat and stuff them into his wide open mouth, gasping loudly with each forkful. I haven't seen anyone eat like this for a long time. Even my fellow inmates had more refined dining habits. When he's finished, he leaves the box and its screwed up papers on the arm of the chair, ignoring Liv's protests to put it in the bin. He wipes his mouth on his sleeve, burps loudly and stands. Liv tuts and grabs the rubbish to dispose of it herself.

'Right, I'm outta here. Nice to see you again, Will. Watch her.' He jerks a thumb at Liv who has wrapped the cardigan even tighter around her as if that will make him forget how she's dressed. 'Or by three o'clock you won't be able to walk.' And he winks knowingly. I'm horrified. Does he know why I'm really here? I wait till he's left and ask Olivia.

'Dan's a lazy slovenly skint twat but he's not stupid. Course he knows why you're here. It's alright, Will,' she assures me, slipping the cardy off and laying a hand on my arm. Her nail polish is the same colour as her top. 'He doesn't mind, he likes you.'

I ponder this. I'm not sure I like being another notch on the bedpost, but at least this way there's no ties, just a bit of fun.

'Okay,' I say. 'Fair enough.'

'Good,' and she takes me by the hand and leads me back into the hallway. We stand outside the closed bedroom door. 'Now, where were we?'

'About here.' I take her hand and place it on the door handle.

'And yours was here.' She grins wickedly and places my hand on her breast.

*

I can still walk by three o'clock. I appreciate Dan's warning though; Liv is surprisingly energetic and keen in bed, and in conclusion it's a lot more enjoyable than spending the afternoon in front of the TV with Dad's predictable films. I lie back with my head propped up against the pillow and look around the room. I didn't notice the untidy state the rest of it was in. Opened up around the single radiator is a clothes horse. Thongs and industrial strength bras hang over the rungs to dry; the perfumed scent of washing powder rising from the items. It must be difficult to dry clothing in a flat with no garden; Claire had the same trouble. A wardrobe door hangs off at a crooked angle; clothes spew out from its base. Both bedside cabinets are cluttered. I'm on Dan's side of the bed. Two half empty pint glasses of water stand on coasters encrusted with dried water rings; a mobile phone charger is plugged into the wall, the socket switch on; a squeezed and rolled up tube of cream for dry skin lies on top of the clock radio which shows the time an hour ago; obviously sometime in the past Dan has forgotten that the clocks have changed. Opposite the bed is a chair, its back and seat strewn with discarded clothes. This room looks like a cross between a women's changing room and a jumble sale.

She kicks the door open with a bare foot and carries in a tray of tea and biscuits. Very English vicar, I think, flattening an area of the duvet for her to place the tray on. Her tousled hair is tied back with the same band I pulled off; she wears knickers and a long t-shirt, its logo faded.

'I don't know about you,' she says, ripping open the chocolate digestives 'but sex makes me hungry.'

I take my tea and a biscuit. The fact that I never thought I'd be propped up in *her* bed, sipping tea in my briefs having bedded Olivia embarrasses me. I've had sex with my best friend's sister. I despise blokes who do this sort of thing. Sisters and ex-girlfriends of friends should remain out of bounds. To be fair though, I'm surprised Liv was up for this; I thought she despised me as much as I loathed her. I glance at her and she smiles back over the rim of the mug. She doesn't look regretful or ashamed though. That's something at least.

'Where's your mum and dad gone?' Liv asks, taking another biccie out of the plastic tube.

'Majorca, I think. I was only half listening. My dad hasn't gone.'

'Really? You'd never get my mum going away without my dad. No way.'

'My dad's in a psychiatric unit at the moment. He has Alzheimer's. He was sectioned.'

She clamps a hand over her mouth and her words come out muffled. 'Oh, God, Will. I'm so sorry. I didn't know.' She lays the hand comfortingly on my arm.

'It's okay. He's not dangerous or anything; he's a bit of a handful at home. Once the hospital sort out his medication, he should be okay to come home.'

'What a worry though. No wonder your mum needs a holiday.'

'It's not been easy for her for a couple of years.' I've said too much, but Liv waits, head to one side. I debate whether to continue. It's too weird being semi naked eating tea and biccies post coital and discussing my dad. But if I start the ball rolling, she might open up about her family. 'Getting ourselves banged up wasn't the most helpful thing Eddie and I could have done. At the time I thought if I could help Eddie, give him an alibi, things would be alright. I should have realised that our alibi was easy to disprove in court.'

'How did they do that?'

'I told the police that Eddie was with me at a local football match at the time of the accident, but they obtained CCTV footage of me leaving the ground alone. It was awful, so humiliating. Eddie glared at me from the dock. He still hates me.' I can still see the video of the footage playing in court and can remember how it felt when I realised my lie had been so brutally and stupidly exposed. 'But when your brother pleads for your help, you do your best, especially if it's for your parents too, don't you? Wouldn't you?' I ask Liv.

'Yeah, probably,' she says but doesn't sound very positive. 'Family doesn't top my list of priorities. I think it's because I was the middle child and I know this is going to sound 'poor me' but Claire got loads of attention from Dad because he had to win her over to make the relationship work with Mum, and when I was born, he didn't want her to feel left out so still lavished loads on her! I was a difficult toddler and when Sally was born, Dad was more interested in her, he couldn't be bothered with me. I don't think I'd care if my parents split up. I wouldn't lose or gain anything.'

'You might if they...'

Liv shakes her head and dunks a biscuit into her tea and bites into it, dropping crumbs onto her bare legs.

'Surely one of you would care?'

'Sally would,' laughs Liv. I ask her how come, trying to keep my voice flat but she stops and looks down at the duvet as if she doesn't know why or doesn't want to say why.

'We're different. Sally voluntarily visits Mum and Dad nearly every weekend, she calls their house home. I hardly ever go. She wants what they have: marriage, kids, the house. Family is important to her. Making up with Claire was important to her. She can't bear rows and not talking. After the row with Claire, I wasn't bothered about ever speaking to her again. I don't think Claire was too keen on making up either. You knew her; would she care?'

Claire often told me she never had any time for Liv and her drug dealing boyfriend. It wouldn't have been any loss to Claire if she and Liv never spoke again, but for the sake of her mum, Andrew and Sally, she might have made an attempt at reconciliation. Even if it was only to be a bigger person than Liv.

'I didn't think she would,' Liv replies when I don't answer, but she says it with a smile.

'So in conclusion, you wouldn't help your family, but Sally would pretty much do anything?'

Liv laughs. 'Yeah, she's soft like that. Wouldn't think twice about protecting us from the evil that lurks around every corner.'

Exactly the answer I'm hoping for. It's certainly worth visiting Sally again. But first to distract Liv so she doesn't think the only reason I've slept with her is to confirm my suspicions of her sister. I tug the mug of tea from Liv's hand and ask when Dan's due back.

'About an hour,' she says. 'Unless the pub kicks him out before.'

'Better get on with it then, hadn't we?'

She lifts her arms above her head, the t-shirt grasped in her fists.

Chapter 56

Sunday ~ day 20

I flick the door knocker harder the third time. Bet she's peering through an upstairs window. Unlucky for her I've parked the Mazda out of view and she can't see me due to the overhanging porch. I try a smile, but it feels tight on my face like sunburnt skin. Sally won't buy any kind of smile I can forge; I may as well not bother. Oh, a result: footsteps and a key being turned. The door opens, and politely with no hostility I say, 'Hello Sally.'

Her face falls. 'I have nothing to say to you. Please leave me alone.'

'The last time we spoke it was unpleasant but there are things I need to...'

'You frightened me,' she reveals, in a childishly aggressive tone.

I refrain from retaliating. She didn't appear frightened as I remember it. In fact she was quite insulting.

'I'm sorry if I made you feel like that,' I reply, trying to sound sincere. 'I would like to know where you were the Friday night Claire went missing. You said you were with Fergus...'

'I'm not having this conversation on my doorstep,' she responds angrily. 'There are neighbours around.' And she lifts her head to see these neighbours, I look too. Over the road, an overweight man wearing grey trackie bottoms is washing his old Corsa. There are dark patches across his crotch and the baggy knees as if he's pissed himself. A woman wearing a patterned headscarf is walking her dog on a long lead, and sitting on a low stone wall are two teenage girls, their heads are bent over an iPad. I'm sure none of them are interested in Sally's answers, but they may be interested in the contents of her house if she leaves the front door open any longer.

'Can I come in?' Her hand on the door instinctively closes it a few millimetres. 'I'll just stand in the hall,' I offer non-threateningly.

'No, you can't,' she says terrified at the possibility that I might waterboard her into confessing.

'Okay. How about the garage? It looks like it's going to rain and I don't want to get soaked. I'm sure you don't want to talk in my car.'

'We can't talk in the garage, Fergus's gear is in there. It's a mess.'

'I don't mind a mess,' I say, with a smile. 'I'll stand under the door and you stand inside if you feel safer, but honestly I just want to talk.' I head off down the drive towards the garage so she has no choice but to follow me. The builder's van is absent and Sally's little hatchback is parked over to one side; its nearside tyres touching the concrete kerb that separates them from their neighbours. To the right, coloured recycling boxes and bags stand in a regimented line. I make a move to help Sally lift the heavy door up and over, but she barks no and struggles by herself. Just as I step under the canopy of the door, I feel a raindrop on my neck. Sally positions herself well inside the garage. On the left wall, two bikes are chained together. A small kitchen table laden with tool boxes and other assorted junk stands behind the bikes; there's an out of commission aquarium, several paint splattered sets of stepladders lean against the opposite wall; on the floor are a collection of paint pots, buckets, plastic bottles of screen wash and de-icer; in the centre of the floor lies a piece of patterned and stained carpet covering an area of paler concrete. The air smells of oil and paint.

Sally folds her arms defensively and squashes the front of her pink top, pushing the initial letter of the logo up towards her shoulder. Her fluffy yellow bedroom slippers make her thin legs appear even narrower. 'On the Friday night, I was at home. Fergus was with me. He was ill.'

She's chosen to kick-off with a lie. 'He perked up later though, didn't he? He went on a stag do. I saw the photos posted on his Facebook profile, uploaded that night, so I know he wasn't with you.'

She stares and stammers her reply, hastily thought up: 'I m-must've got my nights mixed up. I was on my own then.'

'Did you speak to anyone, did anyone pop around, did you pop out?'

'No,' she sighs tiredly.

'I spoke to your parents,' I say carefully. 'Your dad said he spoke to you that evening. He rang to see how Fergus was.' Her expression lifts ever so slightly, surprised at the lifeline I'm throwing. Will she catch it? Her eyebrows furrow as she pretends to recall the incident.

'Yes, I remember. Dad warned me to be careful that I didn't catch Fergus' bug. I felt awful for lying to them, but I didn't fancy going to theirs for dinner with Fergus being out.'

'That's understandable...although Liv says you're always visiting your parents. More than she does. Any reason you didn't fancy going on your own? Did you have something else to do? Something more important?'

Sally's top lip twitches with annoyance. 'I didn't want to go. I wanted a night alone...'

I interrupt. 'The other thing I wanted to talk to you about was Claire's elephant...'

She rolls her eyes and huffs. 'Not that again. I told you I moved it when I was at Claire's...'

'I spoke to your dad; he explained the whole thing about which way elephants face to bring good luck into the home. I'm sure you know it by heart. Anyway, I was reminded by something. Twelve days before she disappeared, Claire visited me and told me Ryan had sent her an elephant which initially she positioned towards the front door, but following a run of bad luck she faced it the other way - into the room. By your own admission, you didn't see Claire in this roughly two week period. Remember: you, Olivia and Claire had argued and when asked you said you contacted Claire by all means except to go and see her. During Claire's prison visit, she didn't mention you moving the elephant, but there it was the day *we* went to the flat, facing the door. When did you move it?'

'When did I move some stupid elephant? That's what you want to talk to me about. Weird.' She stifles a bored yawn.

'It's a discrepancy,' I point out.

'I moved it when I said I moved it.'

'You couldn't have. Claire told me she had moved it to face *into* the room. That was 12 days before she disappeared. You didn't go to her flat in that period, yet you claim you did and you must have handled the ornament at some point because you warned me it was heavy.'

'Maybe somebody else moved it? One of Claire's many boyfriends.'

'Since the ornament arrived after the break up of two relationships, the two witnesses wouldn't know of its existence, and there was no new man in her life. None remembered moving it, let alone knowing the old wives' tale surrounding which way elephants are supposed to face.'

'I don't know then. I can't tell you anything else...'

'You can tell the truth.'

'I am!'

I open the plastic bag and remove the pink and purple dress. 'Do you recognise this?' I hold it up. Her eyes briefly flicker over it before landing back on my face. Interesting reaction, I think, like she can't bear to look any longer at it. 'It's Claire's. Her friend Nisha remembered it hanging on the back of Claire's wardrobe door the week she went missing. I know this dress very well because there's a story behind it. Claire spilt red wine on it, and if you use a magnifying glass, you can just about see the remnants of that stain. It turned up on a mannequin in a charity shop.' No reply. 'It was donated two weeks ago. Originally it was inside a suitcase with other clothing all Claire's size. Claire didn't want this dress, her intention was to get rid of it, so why would she take it with her if she was leaving town? Other items she would have taken were left behind. Important things, things she needed.'

'I've never seen it before. Perhaps Mum took it when she cleared Claire's clothes out of the flat,' Sally suggests.

'There's an idea. She cleared Claire's clothes out of a flat she's still paying the mortgage on. So if Claire does return, by some miracle, she'll have nothing to wear. But say Marion did clear some clothes out of the flat, she'll remember clearly which charity shop she took the items to. I'll ask...'

'There's no need to do that; you'll just upset her.'

'Are you sure you don't remember this dress, Sally? It was hanging on the back of the wardrobe door. No? You don't remember seeing it on the Friday night you went to Claire's flat?'

'I didn't go to Claire's flat!'

'Wasn't that the real reason you didn't go to your parents for dinner? You went to Claire's flat because of what Dan had told you.'

Sally's mouth opens and her eyes stare, fixed on me. 'I hadn't seen Claire since the row at my mum's party. What's Dan supposed to have told me?' Finally, she tugs the lifeline card out of her pocket and uses it. 'Speak to my Dad; he'll vouch for my whereabouts.'

'Nobody can vouch for you, Sally, certainly not your dad. It was your mum that claims to have spoken to you that night.' Sally stares, her smile slips from her lips. 'But that didn't happen either; she lied too. Perhaps she knows you're involved in Claire's disappearance.'

'I'm not involved. I haven't done anything; I haven't seen Claire...why would I...?'

'There are a couple of possibilities. One: I think deep down you hated Claire.' Sally opens her mouth to protest. 'You do a fairly convincing job with your parents and acquaintances, but you don't fool me. All that crap about being close to Claire, being sisterly. If you'd wanted to make up with Claire *that* badly then you would have got off your arse and driven over to see her and waited and waited until she relented and granted you an audience, but you didn't. You're jealous and angry because you think Andrew was giving Claire money. He wouldn't give you or Olivia a penny, and you must have spent years wondering why Andrew preferred a step-daughter to the real thing? Was there something sinister going on? You were the one visiting every weekend, playing the dutiful daughter, and what did you get? As far as I can see you were getting jack-shit.

'The other reason I learned today courtesy of Dan. I know you can't always believe a drug-pedalling loafer, but what he says is corroborated by other witnesses.' My grin broadens. 'Claire was in serious debt and owed five thousand pound. Her money lender wanted his cash and through desperation, she asked Andrew and at first he agreed, but at Marion's party, during this infamous row, Claire offended him and he withdrew his help. Ryan received an email from Claire saying that she had some dirt on Andrew, but he didn't know what it was. I heard about an incident between Andrew and Mrs Woodbead. I'm sure you know her. Anyway, they both explained it was nothing really, an unreciprocated pass, but it had been witnessed by Claire and Dan. He thought it fun to snigger and wink at the neighbour all evening, but Claire had an idea. What would Andrew give for her silence? Was it worth five grand? Seems he thought so. He coughed up; Claire had her money and went home. But the next day Dan decided to have some more fun. He told you what he'd seen between Andrew and the neighbour. Only you didn't believe him, so he told you Claire had seen it too. I can imagine the shock. Claire had already destroyed one marriage by grassing on her father's infidelity, would she do it again? It appeared so. But to make sure you had to ask Claire. That's why you didn't go to your parents for dinner; you went to see Claire instead.'

'No,' she snaps. 'I was at home all evening...'

'Claire was threatening to shatter your family life. Demanding money for keeping her mouth shut. You could see it going all tits up: your mother wouldn't have been merciful; she'd have kicked Andrew straight out the front door. Marion would file for divorce, his business would have to be sold, you'd lose your job, no more family parties. Total ruination. But you can prevent this: stop

Claire and you'd be rewarded: glory for saving the day, elevation to favourite daughter status!'

'No!' Sally shouts, but I can see I've hit a bundle of nerves. Her head shakes vigorously and her hair falls from the ponytail, her face is red and contorted. She looks like she's going to explode.

'So you went to her flat. Was she in? Did she open the door only to slam it in your face? Or did you spy her heading off on her run and follow her? Either way, you caught up with Claire.' Sally doesn't reply, standing defensively, arms clamped across her chest, shaking her head again. 'You tried to reason with her, explain that she couldn't do this, it was wrong, but I know Claire. And that's where you failed because you don't. Claire wouldn't have discussed her business with you.' My voice is heavy with contempt and disgust. 'She wouldn't have allowed you to jeopardise her opportunity to clear her debt. She'd have told you to mind your own business and continued on her run.'

'No, s-she...' It sounds as if Sally's going to crack and admit it, but suddenly she pulls it back. 'I didn't see her...'

'Her refusal to talk to you, her lack of remorse, that she was willing to risk even wrecking your parents' marriage for her own welfare must have made you furious. Did you pick up the nearest thing to hand: a rock, a fallen branch? Did you throw it at her, or did you go after her, raising it in the air to bring it down on the back of her head?'

'NO!'

Her reply barely registers before I go off again voicing my theory. 'You've messed up now. You have to move fast. You mustn't be seen by another runner or a dog-walker. Did you phone Fergus for help? He has a van. Much easier to move a lifeless body in a van than a...'

'Fergus?' laughs Sally. 'Do you honestly think he'd help me cover up a murder?'

'Yes, if you paid him.'

'With what?' she screams. 'According to you, my dad is Mr Scrooge...'

'With the money Andrew gave Claire to pay off her debt. The loan shark never received it, and Fergus recently did a plasterer's course, didn't he?'

'Oh my God, you've got this all worked out, haven't you? You're crazy.'

'You must have had help. But anyway, you took Claire's key and her running kit back to the flat to make it look as if she'd returned. It must have shit you up when you heard Mr Snell and then Nisha knocking the door. Once the coast was clear you got to work: filling a suitcase with various clothes and stuff. You neglected to take certain items that I know she would have taken. You couldn't find her passport, assuming it to be out of date and not renewed. You didn't know about her appointment the next day with her dad that she would never have cancelled. You didn't know she was on anti-depressants and that she had to take them. You didn't know that Claire hated that dress,' I hold it up again. 'Because you didn't know her.'

Sally shakes her head at my imaginative theory, very little of which I can actually prove. There is only one thing I don't know.

Sally demands, 'And what am I supposed to have done with her body?'

Chapter 57

Sunday ~ day 20

This is something I don't know. Claire might not have ever left the woods. With no help readily available, did Sally leave Claire's body where it fell, cover it with leaves and twigs and come back later with a sober Fergus? Did Fergus have access to a house, somewhere where he was laying a patio or building an extension? It's a hell of a risk to leave a body where it could be discovered by a wandering dog out on its walk.

Or did she manage it drag it back to her car, haul it into her boot and wait at home until Fergus returned? His van would make the job of transporting Claire to her final resting placed a lot easier. I just don't know and I have no proof of anything.

'Oh!' Sally cries smugly, 'you haven't worked that part out yet, have you? That's because it didn't happen! I did not harm Claire. Or are you basing your theory on the statistic that ninety percent of victims are murdered by someone known to them? From what I know about Claire's love life, there are plenty of suspects to choose from: revengeful wives, dumped lovers, unhinged colleagues and violent loan sharks. Or do they all have alibis, which of course you've checked out to be rock solid.' She cocks her head to one side challengingly.

'You've done nothing but lie to me, Sally. Your answers don't add up; you're hostile and unhelpful; your alibi is shit, you have a motive and opportunity, I can prove by your own admission you were in her flat...'

'Go to the police with that and see how far you get. They'll laugh at you.'

Yes, they will; she's right. She looks at her wristwatch. A glimmer of silver flashes at me. My time has run out. Should I have come here and played my hand? What was I hoping for: a confession, some slip up from her, a sliver of last-minute evidence is hardly going to just turn up, is it?

I feel defeated and stupid. My theory sounded so good when I ran through it in the car, but now it sounds lame and laughable. My thoughts are interrupted by a loud ringing from my back pocket. I really ought to change that ring tone; makes me jump every time. It's Nisha. What else has she found in a charity shop? Can I pretend something incriminating has been found?

'Hello Nisha.'

'Hi Will. I've had a look at Claire's GPS watch and downloaded her final route.' I look at Sally, but step a few feet away, maintaining a sentry outside the garage door should she try and leave. 'It starts off pretty predictably. She followed a route she'd been running a lot which is the route of the race. However, a few minutes into this, her location is the woods at the back of the hospital; she pauses for seventy five minutes. Time is still counting. She starts moving again exiting the woods onto Nightingale Drive, which circles the hospital grounds.'

'I know it.'

'This is now *off* the route she's previously run. The weird thing is her speed is quicker than any professional athlete can run, which suggests she's in a vehicle.' I start to feel sick. Does this indicate Claire's lifeless body in a vehicle? 'She travels down a dual carriageway, exits at the interchange, turns left, right, onto various other streets and eventually stops at Queens Road.'

Did I hear correctly? Did she just say- 'Say that address again?'

'Queens Road. Is it somewhere significant?'

Not half, I think. I'm right. I have proof. Claire's watch has told its own story.

'Will? Are you okay?' Nisha asks with concern.

'Yes.'

'She was there for 135 minutes before moving again across town to another address: Clavenhill Road. She was there for less than a minute before ending her journey back at her flat. And of course when I say she, I mean the watch.'

My last minute sliver of indisputable evidence has shown up. I look at my free hand – it's shaking but not from the cold. I wrap my other hand around it for support.

'Thank you, Nisha. I'm at the first address now with Sally.' Inside the garage, Sally's ears prick up and she stops kicking at bits of debris on the floor.

'Claire's sister? Does she live at Queens Road?'

'Yes.' I lower my voice. 'I could do with some help.'

'Right, I'm on to it.'

I end the call and consider my options. If I keep this to myself, Sally will return to her house and I can sit in my car and wait for help. If I tell her what I know, what will she do, laugh, run? I put the mobile away and look at her, but she's standing almost at the entrance to the garage, a hand raised in greeting. I turn. Olivia is striding purposefully up the drive, wearing the same clothes I pulled off in her flat. A minicab drives past at speed. This is why Sally delayed answering the door: she was calling for back-up.

'What's going on?' Liv demands, glaring at me. She's a lot less friendly than she was earlier.

Sally jabs a finger at me. 'He's accused me of murdering Claire. He says I followed her to the woods and hit her. It's all bullshit. He's insane. And this is all apparently due to something Dan told me. *He* only speaks to me because he wants to shag me. Tell him, Liv!'

'Don't be ridiculous, Will,' Liv berates using the same tone I've heard her use on Dan. 'Sally didn't murder Claire. That's the stupidest fucking thing I've ever heard.'

I try to steady my breathing, but my chest is heaving, my heart is hammering away and blood pulsates at my temples. I don't want to stay calm and sensible; I want to slam Sally's head repeatedly against the wall until she tells me where Claire is.

I take a deep breath and clench my hands into fists to hide the shaking. 'You told me yourself how far Sally would go to protect her family. It's not that far-fetched to consider the possibility that she was angry enough to confront Claire about how her actions could tear you all apart. She wanted to protect her family like we all do, but she went too far...'

Sally's eyes are wide and staring. Liv looks away, uncomfortable that she's provided the background to my accusation. 'Alright, I did say that,' she concedes, 'but it's one thing to protect your family, it's another to kill a sister!'

'I have evidence.'

'He doesn't!' Sally shouts.

I look at them standing side by side: one a thinner version of the other. When they were children, people assumed they were twins. They've always been close. Could they...? I'm reminded by the journey of Claire's watch. There was somewhere else. 'Remind me again, Liv, the name of your road.'

She shakes her head at the ridiculousness of my question. 'You know the name of it; you were just there. It's Clavenhill Road.'

I feel like I've been sideswiped by a truck. My feet wobble on their base and my head spins. I breathe suddenly like I've been holding my breath underwater for ages and have only just risen to the surface. I focus on them. Thin Sally with her narrow legs and hard scowl, her abrupt and hostile manner. Overweight Olivia with her low cleavage tops and plum lipstick, her couldn't-care-less attitude and her sexy wit. I never really considered them. I never considered the *both* of them.

From the day I saw them in *Starbucks*, I assumed their attitude to be an imitation of their parents': annoyed that Claire had left without a word, leaving them to bear the brunt of their parents' upset and despair. But it wasn't. It was altogether more sinister. They tried to deter me from looking for Claire; they deliberately made it hard for me. They refused to get me Claire's front door key, refused to talk to me, but in the end one persuaded the other that they could control the situation and alter the outcome if they assisted my investigation.

They got me the key, they accompanied me whilst I interviewed witnesses; they used these statements to persuade me to consider Fiona and Hock as suspects. Hock, I think. Is that why Liv went to see him alone, informing him about the PM report on his mother? Did she want to wind him up and watch him come after me? He would have put an end to my investigation had he and I not had a past. Is that why she slept with me? To keep abreast of information, be in a position that if I got too close to the truth she could stop me from going any further? Like now. Here we are, the three of us. Like we were at the beginning: enemies.

How could they have done this? Sally, who claims she'd do anything for her family, has ripped out one fifth of it, leaving her parents and Claire's dad heartbroken. And Olivia. Loathes her parents so tastelessly, but is willing to come to the aid of her murderess sister. Claire's watch was only a few moments at Olivia's address, what was that long enough for? To pick Liv up so they could stage Claire's running away? Or was Liv helping from the start? Afterwards did they return to Sally's house and stare down at Claire's naked battered body and wonder what on earth were they going to do with it?

I sway on my feet, the thought of Claire like that sickens me, but I have to hold their attention until the cavalry arrives. 'I should have paid more attention to that statistic, Sally.' I smile but she doesn't understand what I mean. 'You two, right?'

I waggle a finger at them. They look at each other faking confusion. 'The phone call was from a friend who is a private detective. She has Claire's GPS watch...the one she wore when she ran. They're very clever things. Nisha downloaded the route the watch took on the Friday night. It went from Claire's flat to the woods, to Queens Road,' I look at Sally who pales, 'and then to Clavenhill Road.' I turn to Liv, who offers no response. 'You should have turned it off after you killed her. Fortunately, these watches still work from inside a travelling car.'

Liv shakes her head. 'I was at home that night. I told you what I was doing.'

'Taking your second dosage of abortion drugs? I don't think so.'

'Have it your own way; we're not listening to this anymore. Sally, go in the house. You, fuck off before I call the police.' She jerks a thumb at the drive.

'What did you do with her?'

'I said—' Liv shouts.

'Tell me where she is!'

'Liv?' Sally whispers, panicked.

I feel every muscle tense. 'Can't you remember? Is that the problem? You can't recall the exact tree; all building sites look the same, was it somewhere out of town or somewhere near?' At the mention of the word near, Sally's eyes widen and automatically, against her desire, glance down to my feet, to the garage floor where a patch of pale concrete meets an area of dark, dusty, greasy concrete. New meets old. Where a hole that once was is now not. Where Liv once told me a mechanic's pit gaped dangerously in the middle of the garage floor, a ready-made grave; a builder boyfriend could easily fill it in.

'Oh, my God,' I say slowly. 'Tell me you haven't. Tell me you haven't buried her under a floor of dirty fucking concrete!' I stamp my foot angrily on the pale concrete the way a bull might before it charges. Sally backs away till her heels touch the back wall. 'You fucking bitch.' I step after her, consumed with a desire to wring her neck.

'It was an accident.'

'Shut up, Sally,' Liv barks.

'I didn't mean to,' Sally announces, her voice loud and clear. 'She wouldn't talk to me, I pleaded with her not to blackmail Dad, not to hurt Mum again, but she told me it was none of my business and carried on running. I had to stop her, make her understand the hurt she'd cause; she pushed me away. I fell onto the ground and landed on my wrist. There was a branch nearby. I... picked it up and went after her again.' Her voice trails off, but suddenly she looks up, her eyes wet. 'I only hit her once. She crumpled to the ground.' Sally's shoulders sag and her chin drops to her chest. She starts crying and puts both hands up to her face, her sleeve rides up and again I see that glimmer of silver at her wrist.

'What's that?' I demand, striding towards her. 'What are you wearing?' She hurriedly tries to pull her sleeve down but I know what it is; I've seen it before but on someone else. I grab her twig-like wrist and yank her sleeve up. She cries out in protest and tries to pull herself free. 'Sorry are you? This doesn't look like sorry!' And I hook a finger through the charm bracelet and pull. It cuts into her flesh and she yelps. Behind me, I hear a grunt of exertion and a whoosh flies through the air. I stop in my tracks as the air in my throat is sucked back in; something hard yet hollow hits the top of my head. The pain is immense; like my skull has shattered in two, split down a suture line, blood leaking through the fracture. I sway, the floor comes up to greet me as I fall to my knees, my kneecaps crack on the cold hard ground, my toes bend awkwardly inside my trainers. My forehead bounces off the concrete and I come to rest on my cheek. Liv's ridiculously high heels appear by my head as something metallic lands loudly on the floor. I can barely open my eyes.

'Sally! Look at me. What did he say to the person on the phone? Sally!'

'I d-don't know. I c-couldn't hear.'

'Is someone coming here?'

Sally sobs. Liv steps over me to tug Claire's bracelet from my curled fingers; she swears and tries to pull the garage door down, but a vehicle arrives, its brakes screeching to a halt. Footsteps running, voices shouting. My head is agony; it's too painful to lift it off the ground and my eyes are heavy so I rest my cheek against the cool ground, eyes focusing on the line where pale grey meets dark grey wondering if Claire really is below me.

Epilogue

Earlier, we heard from the Home Office pathologist that Claire's fractured skull was consistent with a blow from a branch. The prosecuting barrister asked if the blow had been due to, as the defendant had suggested, a push. The pathologist stated in his opinion no, the bruising to Claire's forehead was consistent with her head-butting the leafy ground.

Listening to the details of Claire's death is painful enough, but I know the worst is yet to come. I'm glad I'm not here alone. Nisha sits beside me on the first row of the gallery; our knees pressing into the balcony, our bodies bent at the waist, and our heads craned forwards so we can stare down at the defendants like a vortex of vultures in a tree, waiting for a pair of sickly animals to die.

Sally sits primly in the dock: knees pressed together: the dark blue skirt a bad choice as it keeps riding up. She bites her nails constantly, dropping torn and bloodied fragments of nail and skin onto the floor.

Her co-defendant sits as far away from her as the small dock will allow. Olivia's body is turned away at a 70 degree angle; her legs are crossed, her arms folded tightly. Her make-up is minimal in an attempt to make her appeal to the jury. You can almost hear Liv's anger sizzling in the air like meat on a BBQ.

I turn back to the proceedings and wait for the witness to resume his testimony.

Fergus has admitted his charge and awaits sentencing once this trial is over. He is the prosecution's star witness.

'What did you see when you entered your garage?' Mr Campbell-Rice, prosecuting barrister asks. He's a stocky man with a barrel chest and a head of thick white hair and an all over tan.

We're at the point in the story where Fergus has told the court that Sally phoned whilst he was on the stag do and begged him to come home straightaway. On his return, he found Sally and Olivia waiting in the hallway, and Olivia had said, 'The garage' to him by way of explanation.

'Claire was lying on the garage floor. She wasn't moving.' Fergus swallows nervously and licks his lips. 'I suggested we call an ambulance but Olivia said Claire was dead. I touched Claire but she was cold. Her fingers were stiffening.

'I asked what had happened. Olivia said that Sally had followed Claire to the woods to speak to her but they'd argued. Sally had hit Claire and killed her.'

Mr Campbell-Rice looks at the jury as he asks his next question. 'Did the defendants ask anything of you?'

Fergus' eyes angrily flick to the dock. 'Sally said we had to get rid of Claire's body, make out that Claire had run away. She said they had a plan but needed my skill.'

The barrister nods and as he asks his next question, his eyes linger on the jury, watching for their reaction. 'What was their plan?'

'They wanted to bury her in the mechanic's pit in my garage and they needed me to fill it in with concrete.'

I suck air in sharply. I can't bear the thought of Claire lying encased in concrete like a fossil. If I hadn't undertaken this investigation, no one would ever have found her.

'Did you do as they asked?'

'Yes,' Fergus replies regretfully. 'The next day Sally gave me an envelope containing five grand. It was the money Andrew had given Claire. I'm sorry I took it.' He hides his guilty expression behind the glass of water.

'I want to just return to that night: can you tell the court what the defendants did with Claire's body?'

'Sally and Olivia undressed Claire and wrapped her body in one of our sheets. The next morning I ordered the materials I would need. It took me four days to fill the pit in.'

The court is silent for a few moments as this revelation sinks into everybody's heads. I look at

Marion and Andrew. Andrew sits upright, his back rigid, his muscles must ache with the exertion, but he is determined to show how controlled he is. His blank expression is set in stone. Marion resembles a veiled widow in mourning. She sighs dramatically and mutters to herself.

'Can you please tell the court what you understand happened after the defendants left your house?'

'Sally took Olivia home and then took Claire's running clothes and watch back to her flat. She came back a couple of hours later with a suitcase; it contained some of Claire's clothes and personal items.'

'What happened to this suitcase and its items?'

'It stood in the garage until several months later; Olivia sorted through it and took some of the clothes away.'

'In the beginning, you said Sally was very upset at what had happened. You've told the court how Sally lost her appetite, became withdrawn and unable to sleep; did her behaviour change over the coming weeks?'

'Yes. She relaxed; she trumpeted that we'd got away with it. Her parents were convinced Claire had run off with Andrew's money. It was only when William Bailey came out of prison that Sally was on edge again.'

'Thank you, Fergus,' the Prosecutor says, halting proceedings. 'M'lord, I would like to resume questioning after lunch.'

*

'I haven't smoked for twelve years,' Nisha tells me, flicking ash into the cigarette receptacle. 'I hope I can stop when they deliver their verdict.'

'I sank half a bottle of bourbon at the weekend,' I confess. 'I can't usually stand whiskey, but it's all I could find.'

She smiles and grounds the cigarette out, dropping it into the bin. 'We're a right pair turning to fags and booze for comfort. It's a godsend the painters cocked up with redecorating the office and the opening of the agency is postponed till next week. I'm in no state to help people with their marital disputes smelling like a Friday night boozer!'

I raise an eyebrow at her. 'Where have you been? Smoking's been banned in pubs for years.'

'Has it? Must have been why I quit.' She fishes a compact mirror and a lipstick out of her handbag and applies some to her mouth.

A month after my own head injury, which resulted in concussion and the worst headache I'd ever had, Nisha's boss decided to retire on her own health grounds. Nisha promptly got a business loan and some money from her family to set up her own detective agency. Impressed by my ability to always see a job through to the end and leave no garage floor unearthed in my quest to find justice, she decided to employ me. She must be desperate. I've been on several honey-traps, only ever as the one behind the camera but it's great to be in gainful employment and earning money. Hock coughed up the ten grand he owed me for keeping quiet about Eddie's muling, and I sold him his mother's PM report (I had no use for it). Twenty k is at least a start.

*

As I enter the courtroom and climb the steps to the public gallery, I feel a change. The atmosphere is charged, almost tangible. People are out of their seats, the volume of their chatter is loud and speculating.

But there's only Sally sitting primly on her chair. Where's the other one? Why isn't she here? Is she ill, has she hanged herself in the cell?

There's a scuffling noise and a raised voice. I peer over the banister and see a female guard assisting a struggling and angry Olivia up the stairs to take her place. Sally smiles reassuringly at her. She's attempted to make contact with Olivia every day but has received nothing in return, not even a frosty look. Today, however, she gets a response.

Olivia scowls and hisses, 'I'll never fucking forgive you.'

The gallery gasps, Marion whimpers and the Judge calls order. Court instantly silences. He asks for the jury to be brought in. Once everybody is seated, there still isn't any sign of Fergus.

The sisters' defence barrister, Mr Braithwaite, stands and addresses the Judge. He explains that his clients have rethought matters and wish to change their plea.

The news spreads through the gallery like a Mexican wave. From one end of the row to the other, people ask in lowered voices if they're really going to admit it, why, what's happened. A woman behind me tells her friend that "It's the mother's doing". I look at Marion again. She's sobbing into Andrew's shoulder.

Liv sits side on in the chair, her entire body facing away from Sally who has curled up like a woodlouse: head buried in her chest, feet on tiptoe as her knees support her elbows. Fergus' evidence is too damning; she feels she has no other choice but to plead guilty. Unfortunately for Olivia, it leaves her up shit creek. Did she honestly believe she'd be acquitted?

'My clients wish to plead guilty to all charges,' Mr Braithwaite confirms to the court.

It feels so unreal to hear their admittance. It's as if a black and white sketch of Claire's murder has suddenly been coloured in and given life like a photo. Sally really did it. She killed her own sister and they both covered it up like it was nothing more than an irritating stain on a rug.

The Judge addresses the court and tells us that the trial is over and he has accepted their guilty pleas. 'Sentencing will take place tomorrow.'

*

I ring Phil and tell him the news before spotting the barrister heading towards his chambers. I collar him and enquire what the sentence is likely be.

'Custodial sentences all around,' he replies with glee. 'Twenty, maybe twenty five years for murder, five for perverting the course of justice. It's a sibling murder; they won't get off leniently.' He smiles reassuringly, raises a hand to another similarly dressed barrister and they rush off in the same direction.

Nisha and I loiter in the cool court lobby, reeling from the news. It's all over. They're guilty. We've got justice. Funny that it doesn't feel quite as satisfying as I hoped. But then it rarely does. It won't bring Claire back, it won't heal our hurt. All it means is that it's over and there's no reason now not to get on with our lives.

'Let's have a drink, raise it to Claire,' Nisha suggests. The pubs around the court are decent places. The Crown, a couple of streets away, does really nice lunches. But before we set off, I see her eyes flick to my left shoulder and she moves her head to look past me; I turn too, feeling suddenly threatened and see Marion striding angrily towards us, Andrew hurrying after her like she's an excited child prone to slipping their reins. Chivalrously, Nisha steps forward as if she fears Marion has a knife.

'You,' she mouths, eyes glaring with rage, 'you...should have left alone...it was none of your business...'

'Back off,' Nisha warns, putting a hand up to stop her trespassing into our space any further.

'You gave Sally an alibi,' I clarify. 'But it was bullshit. You rang and rang Sally's house the night Claire was murdered, but there wasn't any answer. Where did you think she was?'

Her eyes widen at the accusation 'Nowhere...I...'

Andrew reaches Marion and grasps her firmly by the upper arm and attempts to pull her away from the scene we're creating here; we're gathering quite a crowd of onlookers. Marion shakes him off.

'You had an idea though, didn't you?' I continue. 'All those questions they asked about Claire's finances and their suspicions about Andrew's donations.'

Marion shakes her head vigorously, her heavily sprayed hair moves as one, her long diamond earrings sway against her jaw. 'No,' she cries, 'I didn't know.'

'William, please,' Andrew implores desperately.

'William, please, what?' I demand pushing past Nisha's outstretched arm which acts as a barrier against Marion's tirade. 'Go easy on her? She's upset?'

'They're my daughters,' Marion declares, placing a hand on her heart. 'I love them all.'

Nisha snorts with disgust, and my lip curls with contempt. I push her arm once more and it drops weakly. I step up to Marion and look down at her; she holds her ground defiantly.

'In twenty years or so you can have them back,' I say, in a sing-song tone. 'And you can do all those things a wealthy mother like you should have done: buy them a flat, give them a job, take them shopping. Because *that* would have extinguished the flames of jealousy they had for Claire which you fanned.

'It's because of *you* that Claire is dead.' I jab a finger in her face and she jerks her head back. 'And I will always blame *you* for taking Claire away from me.'

'Me too,' Nisha growls.

Feeling cornered by the heat of our anger, Marion soaks up my abuse. I wonder how deeply my speech has hit a nerve. Has she regretted her tightfistedness, has she finally seen what a difference it would have made to their lives, to future events? I shake the thoughts from my head. It's not my business anymore. I'm done with the family. My only connection to them is gone, destroyed and now buried in a proper place, somewhere I can visit when I need comfort.

Turning away from her, gathering Nisha up with a look, we walk away across the lobby floor, the audience losing interest now the show's over. I look back over my shoulder before exiting. Andrew's arms are around her and she sobs silently into his chest. Nisha grasps my elbow and tugs me outside; perhaps afraid I'll go back for round two. I can't deny feeling like a hypocrite. I have no right to criticise Marion so publicly when I'm not without blame myself.

Eddie and I committed an act for similar reasons to Sally and Olivia. We believed our actions would protect our parents, save them from further worry and hurt, but exactly like the sisters it backfired horribly. Mum was left to cope with Dad's devastating illness on her own. Week by week, she continues to watch him retreat into his own world, becoming more and more absent from hers. If I hadn't lied for Eddie then I'd have been with her; together we could have grasped Dad's hand and kept him from slipping away. If I hadn't given Eddie the stupidest of alibis I'd have been with Claire. I would have paid off her debt rather than leave her with no choice but to go to a moneylender; I could have even been her excuse on the night of Marion's birthday party so that she was never there to row with her sisters.

But I was none of these things; I had removed myself. And they all suffered. Because while I was absent, those I loved were alone.

Acknowledgements

This book is dedicated to my Grandpa, Thomas Wright, for his encouragement and support in everything I've ever done. You were my inspiration.

I want to thank the following friends for their kind words of encouragement and support: Caroline Coe, Helen Parr, Ian Ratcliffe, and to Deb Fuller for her help with my book description and lots more.

To Emma Cutler for her fantastic support and for proofreading my novel. You did an excellent job!

To Tim Roberts and James Baylis for the fantastic book cover. And again to Tim for all his technical help and support.

Disclaimer

This is a work of fiction. Names, characters, businesses, places, events and incidents are either the products of the author's imagination or used in a fictitious manner. Any resemblance to actual persons, living or dead, or actual events is purely coincidental.